OFF THE PAGES

Alejandro Gonzalez

Printed in the United States of America
ISBN: 978-1-953910-37-0 (paperback)
ISBN: 978-1-953910-38-7 (ebook)

**Canoe Tree
Press**

4697 Main Street
Manchester Center, VT 05255

Canoe Tree Press is a division of DartFrog Books.

This story was serialized on r/RedditSerials,
where you can find other novels shared one chapter at a time!

CHAPTER ONE

A LOUD CRASH ECHOED THROUGH THE WAREHOUSE. Shouts and expletives shot back and forth, accompanied by the din of conversations stirred up by the fervor. The line manager looked at the spilled boxes of cereal, tumbled from the recently assembled store displays and rolled his eyes. "Alright, goddammit," he shouted. "Fred! Dammit, get back before you screw anything else up!" He looked across his area for someone-anyone-that could salvage this debacle. His eyes landed on someone. "Manny!" His shout got the attention of a heavyset worker supervising a team as they placed shampoo bottles in packages of two to be sent off to stores. "Get your ass over here and fix this shit!"

Manny turned away from his team and towards the source of the shouting. "Aight," he agreed. "Be there in a moment." His eyes scanned for the least stoned person there. "Bobby! You make sure these shampoo bottles get put in the store units! We gotta get a hundred and eight more before the shift ends!"

"No prob," the man said, looking up from his place on the line.

The heavyset man rolled his eyes and trundled over. Sure, he was fat, he knew, but damn, having to walk so far over to a new station to fix a problem was putting a strain on his back. Most of the time, he got to stay in one station and keep to the job at hand, and his ability to sleep might be thwarted tonight, thanks to whatever numb nuts managed to cause a spill. He looked at the manager of the cereal shipments station and down at the mess and pulled up a broom and handed a dustpan to someone next to him. "Is this it?" Manny asked.

"Yeah," the other supervisor said, "but I got rotation duty, so you need to fix this!"

"Yeah, gotcha," Manny agreed. He pointed. "Jackie!" The young man's attention switched from whatever la la land he was in, to the dustpan in his hand. "Help me out with that." He swept bits of cereal into the pan. "Rick, can you get me a trash bag?"

The man with the iron cross tattooed on his shoulder approached with a black trash bag and held it open. "Here," he flatly stated.

As Manny moved cereal from floor to trash, he looked at the station. "Keep the store displays going!" he ordered. He set the last of the cereal into the trash and looked at the sheet on the clipboard by the manager's area of the station. "We've got to get a hundred and two more store units put together." He approached the crates. "Open that, and those three, and that should be it. And try not to spill it again!"

"Hey!" A worker protested. "We were told we were leaving at three!"

Manny sighed and put hands on hips. "You think *I'm* happy?" he retorted, shaking his head. "You think I wanted to leave the station where I had everything under control to come over here? I'm not making much more than you! Maybe a dollar or two more at the most! Don't give me shit about this!" The anger disappeared and he was left with blind frustration. His job paid him maybe eleven dollars an hour, and he wasn't going anywhere upwards anytime soon. The economy had left him behind with all the others who weren't lucky. Now he had to hope that the rejects who'd washed out everywhere else could keep their crap together long enough to get him through another shift without having to hold their hands.

"We're about halfway through the orders," Bobby said, indicating the finished store displays of shampoo at the end of the line.

4

"Good," Manny agreed. He looked around, before his brows furrowed. "Where the hell is Doug?" He threw his arms up. "Fine! Whatever. Bill, help me put these store displays in the crates to go on the trucks."

"Comin'," Bill said, brushing the silver hair out of his face. He and his line supervisor started assembling crates full of store displays of shampoo-conditioner two-packs, sealing them when full, and placing the sealed crates on pallets to go on the trucks.

About an hour later, the last of the orders of shampoo and conditioner store displays had been crated, sealed, and placed on trucks. Manny approached his clipboard and checked his watch. "Alright, everyone," he said to his station crew, "we're done, with eighteen minutes to spare, so no penalties." At least five separate hallelujahs went up. He began filling out his paperwork to indicate that, yes, no disaster had occurred, and life could continue as normal. The other station supervisor would have to fill out paperwork indicating that product had been damaged, but thankfully, that was not *his* problem, so he could go home and not have to worry about anything. "Remember, everyone, scan your badges on the way out or you're not getting paid."

As the stoners, criminals, and other various end-of-the-liners exited the building, completing a ten-hour shift with a quick run of their badge across the scanner, Manny stepped into the break room, opened his locker and removed from it his cell phone, wallet, and car keys, and placed them into his pockets. As his knees grumbled and his back nagged away at him, the chairs, hard plastic as they were, looked awfully inviting, though he doubted he'd want to get up if he sat down. *Yes,* he thought to himself as he exited the building, scanned his badge, and headed for the parking lot. *I'm fat. I get it. Don't need a constant reminder.*

He exited the warehouse and stuck his key into the door of the ten-year-old, 2005 Toyota Corolla. It was beige, with a permanent stain on one of the seats, and a dent in the trunk lid, but it still ran well, most of the time. The lock unsealed and he pulled the door open, sitting down with a whump. He closed his eyes. "Oh, Christ, my back," he uttered as a wave of relief washed over him. He'd been standing for ten straight hours and it felt like a desert traveler finding a bottle of cold water just lying there when he sat in his car. The moment lingered. Finally, after almost a whole minute, he put his other leg in, closed the door, and fired up the vehicle. He pressed the eject button and a disc exited the player. He put it in the case in his middle compartment and put in its place a burnt CD of remixes of old Super Nintendo music. Tiredness crashed into him like waves on a beach, but he steeled his mind and put the transmission in reverse gear and backed up, then put it in drive and headed out of the parking lot.

As old-school video game music played, he drove out of the cluster of warehouses in between Wood River and Edwardsville, Illinois, and towards his hometown of Alton. After passing through chunks of disposable capitalism surrounded by trees and past the Roxana oil refinery, he stopped at Wal-Mart and parked in the lot. From the middle compartment he pulled two naproxen sodium out of a generic Aleve bottle and stuffed them in his pocket. Fat-fingering a bunch of change from his ashtray into his other pocket, he headed towards the building. As he ambled towards the building, he stopped at the vending machine. He examined the coins, removed fifty of the eighty-seven cents he'd grabbed, and purchased a generic diet cola. Finally, he reached into his pocket, stuffed the two generic Aleve into his mouth and took a big swig. "Oh, fuck that's good," he whispered, as his dry throat almost sang to him for the drink.

He headed towards the grocery section and snatched a bag of pre-cooked hot wings from the freezer section and a bag of frozen meatballs. He still had spaghetti noodles and sauce from last week that he hadn't cooked, waiting in his closet. Right now, though, he was too tired to cook. After placing a few more essentials in his cart, he grabbed a footlong deli sandwich for tonight. It was Thursday, after all, and he'd completed a forty-hour, four-day work week. He didn't have to be back until Monday. Cooking could happen tomorrow.

After checking out, he popped the trunk and placed the bags in the back. His shopping wasn't complicated, after all, because he didn't have a lot of money. He had more than enough clothes and his supply of pop culture wasn't needing any upgrades right away. His drive back home passed by almost hypnotically, as he found himself pulling into his driveway with little memory of getting there. Throwing the car into park, he blinked several times to get the tired out of his mind enough to get in the house.

He hoisted all three bags of groceries and huffed and puffed his way up the short steps to his front door. An almost juggling act ensued, as he muscled one bag into his other hand so he could plunge his now-free hand into his pocket, fish out his keys, and open the door, all the while, his other hand shouted pain at him. The door came open and after he rested his body against it to keep it open, he shifted the bag back into his other hand. The bags landed on the kitchen table with a thud, as he pulled the frozen stuff out of the bag and stuffed them in his freezer. A hasty examination of his buys told him nothing else had to be refrigerated.

With a sigh of relief, he set his thermostat to sixty-five, turned the air conditioning on, and plopped into bed, wriggling his shoes and pants off. As his body settled in, the pain pills started to kick in and he made several more groans of relief before falling fast asleep.

His body told him he was awake, and he blinked his eyes as he rolled onto his side and then lurched upward into a seated position. After he stretched and shook the sleep out of his eyes, he saw it was six forty-two P.M. He'd been asleep for almost three hours. It honestly surprised him that he'd only slept that long. Ten-hour shifts for him started at five in the morning and he didn't expect to have any energy remaining after. Certainly, in the past, he'd had plenty of days where he slept until his phone alarm woke him up in time to go to work.

His body made it to the kitchen, and he tucked into his sandwich while reading comics on his old laptop. Midway through, he got up to get a soda and stretch his legs. The latest release of *First Breaker*, a comic he'd enjoyed since being a small child, played out on the screen. The action managed to grab him still, even after all this time, and he logged into a forum to discuss the latest issue.

"How is Cyroya still fighting the Dragon God," one poster, username C_Victimizer01 wrote. "Didn't she finish off this idiot in the previous issue?"

Manny rolled his eyes. "This is a different Dragon God," he reminded. "This is the one she met in Pareion, remember? That happened in issue #181."

A few moments later, a person named LastThunderMage08080 responded with, "Wait, that was a long time ago, which place was Pareion?"

"Basically, the Bakeru religion's hell," C_Victimizer01 posted. "Remember, she's the Goddess of Strength, and got sent there for bad deeds? Way back in volume 1."

"Kareth, the God of Mercy and Creation," Manny explained, "had to fight her back in ancient times. He sent her to hell, she had to do that to become a good guy. It was there that she met the original Dragon God. This was a different Dragon God." As much as it bothered him to answer such basic questions, he couldn't let it bother him. After all, having new fans into a series from the late seventies was a good thing, and he didn't want to let the fandom get toxic like some others were.

After that, he checked to see if there were any new comics in the *Furious Thunder* series, finding an issue one of the latest release, volume seven. Unlike *First Breaker*, this comic was a traditional superhero story, although, it had a unique twist. Being one of the earliest comics to feature a female superhero as the protagonist, it came out originally in 1952, and had been a hit. Manny finished his Diet Coke and pitched it into the recycle bin. A few minutes of reading later, and boredom crept in, so he put all his clothes back on and grabbed his car keys.

The first place his friends would likely be if they were free and bored would be the bookstore in Edwardsville, the nearest in the desert of culture that was rural America. After almost twenty minutes of driving, he found his way to the familiar mini mall with the bookstore and a bunch of clothing stores.

A five-minute roam around the interior told him that, sadly, only he had the idea out of his friends to congregate here. Still, having come all this way, he perused the manga section, reading a few volumes of series he hadn't caught up on, then perusing a few volumes of *Spirit Blood*. Not much later, he couldn't justify staying here. Leaving the bookstore, with no desire to buy anything, he got in his car and began driving back home.

Driving past the endless examples of disposable consumerism reminded him of the reason for his boredom. A few times he'd gone north to Chicago for various reasons, and each time he'd found stuff to do beyond just the reason he went. Here, however, society seemed built for the pacification of the worker, he figured. There were endless cheap fast food options, the Targets and Wal-Marts for workers to spend their meager paycheck at, and it bothered him. He hated being a cog in the machine. The industries had abandoned the rural Midwest decades ago, leaving behind a permanent culture of replaceable part-time workers. All of this weighed on his mind as he lamented the fact that he'd gone almost fifteen miles to another town to get to the one bookstore in hopes one of his friends had gone there.

The sounds of classic rock from the local Saint Louis station played over the radio as he navigated traffic. Not much into Wood River, the radio crackled, and the digital time display went erratic. Frustrated, he fingered the seek button, although it only passed over more distorted signals. Flashing lights reflected in his windshield and on his dashboard. With a racing heart, he looked in the rearview mirror.

That's strange, he thought, *it isn't the cops.*

He pulled over and noticed the reflection kept changing. Colors kept switching and he didn't know what to think. Then, he leaned his head out the window and looked up. His jaw fell open. Cars up and down the road began to pull over, with drivers exiting and standing all over the road, just looking up in disbelief. Almost in a trance, he found his hand pushing the door open and wandering out into the street. The whole time, his eyes couldn't be pulled away from the scene above.

From many points across the evening sky, light shot out in every direction. Each light had a different color and a pattern of movement. Some shot straight out, some wriggled as they moved, but each of them moved incredibly fast. No sound came with the dazzling show. Every conceivable color man could see emerged. Somewhere in his mind, Manny's rational self reasserted itself and he stumbled to his car, fumbling for his cell. He began recording the sky.

The hair on his neck stood up-although he could have imagined it-as he watched wriggling and spinning streaks of color pulse and dash across the darkening background of space. Moist night air passed over his tongue as he stared, agape. The feeling caused him to reflexively spit and shook him out of his stupor. When he returned his gaze to the sky, his thoughts fired off in a storm of questions. Was this because of aliens? Was this religious in nature? Why wasn't there any noise? Almost involuntarily, his right hand scratched the back of his head.

At least ten minutes passed, with streaking balls of colored light firing off in different patterns into the distance. Once the last light fired off, it took a while to register that it was over. He almost fell as he struggled against his racing heart and mind to steady his hands. He shoved the phone into his passenger seat and climbed into the car. Sweat beaded on his forehead. As he reached into his glove compartment for a towel, he noticed his breathing came in fast bursts. The displays on his car returned to normal, and his radio began broadcasting its normal music. Thankfully, he found his trip home uneventful. The whole way, he expected something to crash from the sky or emerge from the ground, or for some horror to occur, but his heart returned to normal as he found his way back.

Cars rapidly found their way back to normal traffic. People congregating outside businesses chatted about what had just happened, and he passed by people on the side of the road freaking out. Thankfully, he had the sense of mind to keep some semblance of calm. His body seemed fine, nothing had changed in his mind, and he didn't see any imminent danger. The scientists and the news media would likely reveal in the coming days and weeks what exactly had happened. For all he knew, it was some bizarre new thing tested out at some lab somewhere that had mucked about with the ionosphere or something like that.

Returning home, he fired up his computer and immediately, the social media feeds had been inundated with every type of post about the events that had just occurred. News agencies were talking about it, and scientists hadn't gotten a chance yet to find anything out about it. Some kind of presence tugged away at the back of his mind, but he chalked it up to worry over the strange light show. *Don't worry, Manny,* he assured himself, *this'll all work out.* He didn't know how true or false it was, but he needed to feel safe in order to function, so he told himself everything would turn out fine.

He took a deep breath and let it out, forcing himself calm. After what had just happened, he yawned and stretched and headed in the bathroom. The electric toothbrush worked its twice daily magic, keeping his teeth clean, and he did his best to push the freaky scene in the sky to the back burner. He spat out the toothpaste and rinsed his mouth, flossing and swishing mouthwash after, and stretched yet again. Lifting a plastic cup to his mouth, he swished some water and spat, then ran his fingers through his curly charcoal hair, ignored the dark stubble on his pasty German-Irish skin, and rubbed a wet finger on both eyes before blinking and drying his mouth and eyes in a towel.

The scale read two hundred and seventy-eight pounds. *Hey, lost three pounds*, he noticed. Setting the toothbrush on its charger, he shuffled off to bed, taking an evening puff of his inhaler and popping a generic Benadryl. One last sip of water, and he set the cup on the chest of drawers and slid into bed.

Ten minutes later, but feeling like an eternity, his eyes popped open, as he realized he couldn't sleep right away. Sliding out of bed, he popped a melatonin gummy to chew on while he perused his bookshelf for comics to read to pass the time. His finger landed on a thick volume of volume five of *Furious Thunder*, the one where they rebooted the Capacitor character in two thousand five, right about the time he entered college. The familiar adventures of one Michelle De Lanter began just as he remembered it. Flipping through the pages, he saw her pull her cousin out of his pod in the river.

I think, of all the powerful characters I'd like to be, he thought, *I'd like to have her powers the most.* He felt a twinge in the back of his mind, and he blinked several times. It annoyed him. He got back to reading. Tiredness began to creep over him after he got a third of the way through the book.

Although it hadn't been too terribly distracting, the feeling...or whatever it was, at the back of his mind, wouldn't go away. What was that? It bothered him that he couldn't get it to go away. He focused on it and found his mental image of it lacking. It had no defined form. A chuckle escaped his mouth. This was insane. What it would be like to be a superhero like Capacitor, like the red-haired Michelle De Lanter and her amazing powers, he figured. It would be so amazing not to have to worry about physical or mental ailments. Just for laughs, he pictured walking around as her. The decision was made; that would be preferable to being fat, dumpy Manfred Voren.

He felt something change about the twinge in his mind.

An electric prickling traveled from head to toe and back down again. A great pulling yanked inward at his bulbous gut. All sleepiness evaporated and his eyes shot wide open as he saw flesh retreat. *Oh, shit! Oh Christ!* He mentally shouted. Fear of death blasted through his mind, and he began grabbing away at his abdomen, pinching flesh uselessly within his fingers as if it would accomplish anything. The retreating stopped at a flat stomach. Chest hair vanished in a heartbeat as his saggy man-boobs pulled upward and moderately outward. An 'eep' sound escaped his mouth as he stared in utter shock as his pudgy arms became slender, his mallet-like hands with sausage fingers lengthening out into pianist-worthy digits. Doughy legs became sprinter's calves and weightlifter's thighs and hips, and finally, hair touched his shoulders, the sensation shocking him out of his dumbfounded reverie. A hand went to cover a gasp, only to feel smooth mouth and chin, with his stubble eradicated. "What the fuck!"

His own voice came back, but it wasn't his. It was the register of an adult woman.

In a mad dash to the bathroom, he almost tripped over his pajamas, which fell to the floor. The sight that greeted him in the mirror froze him where he stood. A woman, no older than thirty or younger than twenty stood in the mirror, hands moving where his hands moved. When his mouth dropped open in disbelief, hers did too, and when he closed it, so did she. He blinked one eye, she obeyed him. He ran toned arms over shoulders and torso, and the reflection cooperated exactly.

No, he decided. This was insanity. He'd lost his marbles, gone off his rocker, and all that.

Every possibility had to be explored, the conclusion said in his mind. Sure, the most likely cause was a mental defect, some kind of tumor or disease, as what just transpired violated everything he knew about reality. Still, as a good skeptic, he had to proceed. What were his options, he wondered?

Was he this woman all along?

Nervously, he stumbled to his room and pulled his cellphone off the charger. Hastily, he snapped a selfie from neck up, and texted it to his friend John. "Have you seen her before?" his message asked. He knew what would happen. If, somehow, he'd hallucinated being Manny-and he couldn't comprehend how that could be-the message would indicate something like that. He doubted it, but he had to be sure.

"No," John's reply was, a minute later. "She's hot. She your new girlfriend?"

"No," Manny texted back.

"Hey," John retorted, a few seconds later, "I'd do her. Don't let this chance slip by."

Manny rolled his eyes, thanked his perverted friend, and put the phone back on the charger. *Okay, one piece of evidence*, he decided. What would serve as another? He snapped his fingers. The identity of this woman! He had to know. Was this some generic redhead, or the Capacitor? Sure, he'd skipped multiple steps, but it gave him a chance to work on more than one hypothesis at once.

He bent to nearly one knee in front of his refrigerator. Even with the muscle tone, he realized, there was no way a woman of this build could lift a refrigerator. Wrapping both arms around the huge white rectangular prism, several long breaths came and went as he steeled his nerves. He pushed up, ready for his back and legs to scream at him.

His body reached a full erect position, holding the refrigerator. It startled him to such a degree that he had to at once right himself to avoid three simultaneous problems: first, hitting it on the ceiling, second, hitting the wall, and third, dropping it. The absurdity of it made him laugh a bit. It felt like holding a bag of bread. Gingerly, he knelt, the huge fridge thumping on the ground.

Alright, great, he decided, but what was a test that could prove he wasn't hallucinating?

"Reading!" he thought out loud.

He stood in his hallway and stared. He squinted. After a long minute of nothing happening, he began to see layers of obstacles becoming transparent to his vision. The character's see-through vision was a power she had, and that itself served as another piece of evidence. After peeling away many layers, the bookshelf in his neighbor across the street's house became visible. A few more layers and he saw the first real page of prose in Hemingway's *The Old Man and The Sea*. He blinked and shook his head and his vision returned to normal.

At once he turned to his phone and bought a digital copy of *The Old Man and The Sea*. The first page matched what he saw precisely.

Alright, this still might be a hallucination, he thought, *but damn, that's a good indicator.*

How would he turn back into Manny, the thought crept into his mind? "No, fuck it," he decided, throwing up his arms. He didn't have to be at work tomorrow. Enough had happened. He would sleep on it and worry about that in the morning. He pulled the string to turn the lights off and just about threw himself into bed. This time, there were no interruptions.

CHAPTER TWO

LIKE A LIGHTNING BOLT A FEW FEET from a hapless victim, Manny's eyes shot wide open when he heard his backup alarm clock ringing. An expletive rang out as he almost fell out of bed, shooting awake, tangled in his bedsheets. "What the...?" he yelled.

Recognition dawned on him. *Right*, he realized. Normally, he'd shut off his backup alarm clock on Thursday night so he wouldn't be woken up on Friday morning, because he needed three days of sleeping in so he could recharge from the hectic work week. It was three forty-five in the morning, and he didn't have anywhere to be. Instinctively, he flopped back into the bed.

A good minute later, he realized an absurdity: he was not only wide awake, but refreshed and not the least bit groggy.

"Strange," he uttered.

His eyes went wide.

Well, shit, he thought. Having raced into the bathroom, in the desperate hope the previous night could be chalked up to a vivid, insomnia-induced hallucination, the mirror quickly removed that possibility.

In his mental...space, he guessed it was called...the images of his male self and the Capacitor, which stood side by side, gave him an idea. He focused hard on his normal self. Nothing happened. An agonizing series of experiments played out over the next few minutes, in which a great deal of nothing occurred. It began to frustrate him, and his nervousness started to bang its shoulder against the door of his reason.

Damn it, his mind settled on. It bothered him that he might be stuck in this form. Yet, why would he see his normal self if he couldn't change back? Could he really live the rest of his life as this woman? How would he even begin? There existed no paperwork, so this person effectively didn't exist. The thought of facing an uncertain future as a woman who, powers or no powers, had no way of conducting business of even the most basic nature, began to eat away at him. Did he have the strength to do that? Could he pull the trigger?

His head jerked abruptly.

"Son of a...!"

The involuntary utterance preceded an important realization. It wasn't a 'mysterious twinge' in his mind. Well, he realized, actually, it might be, but whatever it *actually* was, it was a trigger! It served the important function of protecting him from accidentally letting intrusive thoughts interfere with the power! After all, he knew himself to be the kind of person who could imagine spiders crawling on him at the suggestion, and it only made sense that there would be safety precaution to prevent such ideas from wreaking havoc. *Wait,* he thought, *does that mean someone's behind this?* He shook his head. Such were thoughts for later.

He focused. He focused on the...whatever, the *trigger*, and it came into sharp focus in his mental image. It appeared as an orange sphere of pulsating light jostling in its position. Somehow, as he focused his mind's eye on it, it came to him that it was in the modified position. With will, he committed to pushing it into the default position.

His belly bulged out, hair becoming short and curly, his face and bone structure painlessly rearranged, save for a slight electric prickle, and eleven seconds later, he found himself back in normal, male shape. Almost at once, he felt less energized, less charged up, but he'd never been so happy to see his fat, dumpy self in the mirror. He stepped on the scale, and it read his prior weight, and he smiled at the result.

He sat on his bed, examining his fat sausage fingers, and his thighs that rubbed together, causing him irritation on those long workdays, and felt the weight of fear and worry melt away. Then, as if tasered, he shot over to his desk and retrieved his cell phone. Sure enough, the selfie of her remained. Somehow, it hadn't been a hallucination.

So those lights had given him the superpower to transform into the Capacitor, he realized.

"God, this is fucking crazy," he whispered, closing his eyes.

The next thing he tried, was manipulating his mental images. He changed her head to his, and only her head. The internal image responded exactly to his willful command. It struck him as a hilarious image. Then he dared take the risk and pulled the trigger. He felt a mild static travel from his chin to the top of his head.

"So that's a change that..." His sentence cut off in the middle.

A mental agony hit him. The mysterious feeling of...well, he had no better word than just pure suffering...came upon him like an avalanche. He looked down with her eyes at his male body, from the lower neck down, and a sorrow as intense as any he'd ever felt smashed into him, a mental sledgehammer blow. Tears began to form in his eyes. *Tears,* for Christ's sake. The only sensation as immense as the strange sorrow he could not explain, was the utter confusion as to what it was, and where the hell had it come from? At once he pulled the trigger in the opposite direction. His head transformed back into his own, and...

The feeling of misery was gone.

As if stung by a wasp, he shot to a vertical position, the reversal of mood came so abruptly. "What the fuck was that?" he thought out loud.

He changed his mental image to her whole body, and pulled the trigger, and was Capacitor again, intact from head to toe.

The feeling of misery was still gone. It had not returned.

"What the...?" His thoughts once more leaked out through his mouth. What had that been? What could cause such incredible misery? What, just because there was an incompatibility between her head and his body...

"I'm an idiot," he mouthed, hand slapping his forehead. Incompatibility between a female mind and a male body. "I'm a big freaking *idiot!*"

The term was 'gender dysphoria.'

Inadvertently, he'd stumbled upon the feeling that he'd read about being one of the primary causes of suffering among transgender individuals.

A chuckle emerged at the thought of his utter stupidity, and the slow dullness with which he took forever to realize his problem. It almost immediately raised in intensity to a belly laugh, and he spent a good thirty seconds guffawing at the fact that he hadn't thought of such a thing ahead of time. No, big fat stupid Manny had gone off half-cocked and jumped into the deep end of the pool right away, not taking the time to consider the ramifications of any of it.

After the self-deprecating laugh, he swallowed as the magnitude of his realization hit him. He had given himself a newfound appreciation for the 'T' in LGBT. *This* was how they felt *all* the time? Good god, how could they handle it, he pondered?

Alright, so no more incompatibilities, he decided.

After a quick breakfast of an energy bar, he transformed back into her. Among the immediate problems he faced, was that his clothes didn't fit her form, obviously. His mother's clothes, maybe, he wondered? He shook his head. She'd lost a great deal of weight near the end. But wait, the thought that came to him said.

He put a large shirt on and held his pants up as he exited the house and went into his garage. Shutting the door, he took his pants off and hung them on a dusty old shelf. The stacked tubs of his mother's clothes, packed up and in the garage since her death, bore the labels of each category. He pulled them down one by one and rifled through them until he found some that corresponded to earlier, before her illness. *Aha!* He thought.

A pair of old corduroy pants and a turtleneck looked like the least tacky pair of clothes. Her bras were in a nearby tub, and he took his shirt off his female form and set it on the side. Within his mind, he focused his efforts, and sure enough, most of his body fat transferred to his female self, leaving his internal male image skinny.

The external shapeshifted to match the internal, and he found he could fit the bra on, perfectly. Underpants slid on snug, but not too tight. Finally, the turtleneck and pants came on and he stood, nearly fully clothed and ready to go. Sadly, she didn't have any of her old shoes lying around, but he found two pairs of socks made his feet almost the same size as his normal male feet. He slipped his normal shoes on, and with the extra socks, they fit like a glove.

Being a fat woman bothered him in this form, but practicality won in his mind. The first power he wanted to test was speed. Sure, he could get his keys, and drive to a park or a wooded area, but that could lead to people seeing a strange woman driving his car. Until he had a story for that, he wanted to be able to leave and come back without being seen.

More than once, Capacitor's speed had been revealed to work in multiple ways at once. Sure, she could run or fly incredibly fast, but she also could stand perfectly still with everything frozen around her. This meant she had to be manipulating not just velocity, but in some sense, time as well.

"Alright," he thought out loud. Looking over at the work bench his dad had used a long time ago, he saw a loose screw lying in a box of loose nails and other pieces of metal. He fingered the screw between his thumb and index finger, aimed, and flicked it into the air. As it sailed, he sprung forward, running, and...

It fell to the floor.

"Hm," he huffed, picking it up and walking back to where he started.

In his mind, he drew up his knowledge of the comics and movies. Her power came from otherworldly power, various energies coursing through her body. With his eyes closed, he turned his focus inward. Her body coursed with barely explicable waves of power. Latching on to one that looked like a blue wave passing from his legs upward, he manipulated it. With little effort, he could push its intensity upward, so it roiled and bounced, rebounding back and forth across him in endless repetition. As he did, he found his mind expanded in focus like he'd never felt before. With all the mental effort focused on his power, he expected to have trouble keeping tabs on the world around him. Exactly the opposite happened: the more he focused on his power, the more his mind compensated by expanding the possibility of his focus on the world around him.

"My...God..." he uttered.

This is what the comics meant by "superhuman perception."

She didn't just have super hearing, sight, and intelligence; her body perceived reality around her in ways no normal human could compete with. He didn't just feel the air *better*, he felt it more completely. No longer was it a certain temperature, he could get a near flawless idea of how cold or hot it was relative to energies transferring from each object around him. Transfer of energy from one object to another only scratched the surface. The screw in his hand broke him out of his stupor. Solve the problem now, he decided; ponder this other stuff later.

Her enhanced intellect gave him an exact idea of how many steps it was from his current position to anywhere in the room he could imagine moving. Eyes alight with otherworldly vision perceived each object, and he could tell, roughly, how hard it would be to break.

A flick of his finger cast the screw into the air.

Intensely focusing on his internal storm of power, he manipulated the blue power, and reality froze around him. He stepped forward, the air curving around him, and he plucked the screw out of its place, frozen in the air.

One down, he thought.

His internal spectral environment roiled with powers his mind perceived as different colored waves, moving about, and changing arrangement as they bounced around. It occurred to him that it moved about in three dimensions, and he rotated his internal perception, and discovered these powers bounced around in all directions, but also remained connected at various points. One that shifted and bounced parallel to the blue one, a violet power, matched its sibling precisely, but slightly below. With a nervous mental effort, he nudged it. He took five steps forward.

A stream of images flashed through his mind at once. At his destination in less than a heartbeat, he grasped the frame of the garage to steady himself. It hadn't felt like real time or like slow motion, which were the two things he expected. Rather, he'd seen every detail, and he made decisions about what to do, perceiving each step with an impossible rate of data processing.

So, that's how a superhero can run across the country in minutes, he realized, *without it seeming like days.*

He took a breath. Baby steps, the saying went.

Slowly, he strolled over to the end of the garage. He saw a spot on the wall he would put the screw in. He let the breath out and dashed. When the movement ended, he found his finger on the screw, which he had manually screwed into the wood on the wall, exactly where he decided. In his mind, he had seen every action taken. Great, he knew, this meant his speed could be trusted. He looked at the garage's contents and an idea came to him.

A blink of an eye later, and a tidying up he'd put off since the funeral two years earlier stood finished. All the loose clothes got put in the proper receptacle, the donation items set aside for later donation, and loose tools rearranged into various toolkits.

He looked around with his see-through vision and saw no one in a position to watch him. Houses were empty with people going to work, or else they sat in their living rooms, watching television, or in bedrooms playing games or working on the computer.

Leaving the garage and returning to his room, he grabbed his keys and locked the front door on his way out. He activated only the second of his two speed powers and ran. As the world moved on around him, he zoomed past, his power manipulating the air around him so as not to damage anything by accident. No sudden hurricane force winds would blow cars off the road or create a wake that would explode people like balloons. If he passed by someone a hand's width away, they would hear a slight woosh as the air bent around him, but that was it. In less than a second, he stood in the enormous park in Belleville. He made his way to one of the isolated corners of the park, where woods on all sides made easy access difficult for most people.

He focused his mind on flight. After several failed attempts, he found himself hovering an inch above the ground. Moving in a specific direction required multiple inputs. Actual velocity acted like a gas pedal. Choosing to move at all meant hitting the gas and accelerating. Managing to hit a specific speed and stay at it required dedicated effort. It took eight different attempts just to be able to accelerate slowly and stay at a reasonable speed.

On the twentieth attempt, he flew from ground to the top of a tree without either blasting a hole in the ground or taking a whole minute. Grabbing the top of the tree, he pushed in the direction of a different treetop, and managed to turn his body in the proper direction by power alone, instead of having to wriggle in midair to change the way he faced.

Another forty attempts, and he found he could fly. He changed his focus to energy manipulation. Merely focusing on it allowed him to sense the way various forms changed between each other within the area of his influence. With a subtle shift of his internal power field, he found he could stimulate light into a laser beam. Ten minutes later, he projected a beam of laser light from his finger, which shone as a red dot on the log. It took another thirty seconds of manipulating before he could increase the intensity, and it began to burn through the log.

Soon, he could project beams of white-hot light that torched through the log like a knife through aluminum foil. Having accomplished that, senses had to be worked on. Activating super hearing presented a problem. Being limited to a certain range served a purpose. It prevented certain sounds from being heard. One aspect of super hearing was that being able to hear a larger spectrum of sounds made life miserable. Car brakes squealed at a high frequency, and normal humans couldn't hear it. Now, being able to hear it, it became an irritation. Furthermore, on the low end, being able to hear the deep rumble of the Earth blocked certain other low frequencies.

He shut his eyes and closed his hearing to the specific range normal humans could hear. Within this spectrum, he raised his hearing, and everything for miles around became audible. Focusing on conversation proved taxing. It took full concentration just to be able to hear clear words.

He would perfect super hearing later; right now, he needed to perfect his sight. Sure, he could do some of his vision powers well, but this was one power he wanted to excel at. He managed to stand at a fifty-yard distance and see a ladybug in macro lens detail. With more effort, he could see the internal structure of grass cells from five feet away.

On his way out of the thick wooded area, the pants slid down, and he had to adjust the belt on the pants to make it fit. What was this? At first, his mind raced, but realization hit him and he rolled his eyes at his scatter brain.

Superhuman physiology, he remembered from the comics. Her body probably considered his excess fat to be an impurity that had to be burned off, because she always regenerated back to perfect health if not magically impeded. He took off at super speed, making sure this time to use both speed powers so no one would see him, and made it back home in a single tick of the clock.

What would he do next, he wondered? He could try going out and doing superhero stuff, but he wanted to put that off for at least a few more days. Perhaps just take in the sights? There were an awful lot of places he wanted to go that he'd never had the money to visit before, and with his separate speed powers, he could take as much time as he wanted without having to worry about being seen.

An idea came to him, and he grinned wide.

Twenty minutes later, having changed into his women's clothing, he parked his car in the parking lot of a riverboat casino, one of many dotting the Mississippi River boundary between Missouri and Illinois. In his male form, he changed his brain, nervous system, and eyes into hers. He swallowed hard, steeling his will to repress the returning dysphoria and checked out the mirror. Nothing looked different, except his brown eyes were violet, but he doubted anyone would notice. After all, he hadn't been carded at the casino in years.

He ambled down the ramp, and into the casino's front entrance. The guard at the gate recognized him, saw the stubble on his face and decided that carding him would be a waste of time, and let him through.

"Good luck," the guard said.

Manny smiled. "Thank you," he returned.

A quick trip across the floor saw him arrive at the blackjack table. He'd already gotten his chips at the cage, and he sat down.

"Want to play blackjack?" the dealer asked.

"Absolutely," Manny said, putting on a cheerful tone. He used her sight powers and saw he would win this one. He bet fifty.

"Five and a ten," the dealer read out, handing the cards. He dealt his own. "A king, and a three. Thirteen." He looked at Manny.

Manny knew his next card would be a four. "Hit," he said.

"Four," the dealer read out. "Nineteen."

This forced the dealer to hit. "Jack," the dealer read. A Jack was a face card, worth ten, thus bringing the dealer to twenty-three, which was over twenty-one, and thus, a bust. "Player wins. Play again?"

Manny looked ahead. He would win again. "Sure," he said.

The dealer came up two short of Manny. "Player wins," he said, looking at the cards. "Play again?"

"Yes," Manny said. He looked ahead and knew he would lose this one. He bet only twenty-five dollars.

A few moments later, the dealer hit twenty, two points higher than Manny. "Player loses," the dealer said, taking the chip.

Manny pretended to be mildly annoyed. "Well, you know," he said, "can't win 'em all."

This went on for another hour. When he knew he would lose, he bet low, and high when he knew he would win. He decided to stop before he broke a thousand dollars, because first, security might escort him out, and second, over a certain amount, he had to pay taxes. He might decide to do that at another casino, but not the one closest to where he lived. At nine hundred dollars, he called it quits. He cashed in his chips, counted the bills into his wallet, and exited.

In the car, he reverted his mind and eyes back to normal. His breathing returned to calmness and he found a familiar weight off his mind. Pain or not, he looked with glee at the bills in his wallet. This was more than two weeks' pay before taxes, in cold hard cash, just sitting there. Sure, he cheated, but it didn't bother him, because he hadn't cheated a person so much as a soulless corporation.

After about a fifteen-minute drive past endless road construction, he made his way to another casino, this one closer to the Saint Louis side of the river, and activated her powers in his normal form, once more pushing past the mental anguish.

"Good luck, sir," the guard said, as he walked past.

"I appreciate it," he replied.

Approaching the cage, he pulled out his wallet and removed all nine hundred dollars, converting it into chips. Afterward, he made his way to the blackjack table. By repeating his previous strategy, he managed to play for almost an hour and a half before security came. He got up and went to the cage and cashed out his chips. The cashier handed him a tax form and a pen.

"Here you go," he said, handing the completed form to the cashier. She counted out his winnings, a total of eleven thousand dollars and some change, and he placed it in his pocket and walked out the door with security following him to his car to make sure he left.

He shut his eyes and reverted to his fully male self and opened slowly. His breathing slowly returned to normal as he left the lot and drove towards the nearest branch of his bank. Careful not to hit the curb, he pulled into the drive-up window lane.

"Mister Voren," the cashier said via intercom. "How can I help you today?"

"Just had a great day at the casino," he said, making sure to 'explain' the sum of money. "I want to make a cash deposit into my savings account." The tray extended out and he placed his driver's license and the cash into the tray.

"I'll be right back," she said.

Manny couldn't believe the money in his hand. It amounted to a stone's throw away from half his yearly pay. Sure, he cheated, but by playing blackjack, the only thing he cheated was the giant companies that owned the casinos in his area. That was his logic for specifically avoiding poker, where he would have had to play against other people. By playing the house, he took chump change out of the pocket of an enormous business that had no feelings to be hurt and never had to worry about the rent being due, so it didn't bother him.

"Mister Voren?" the cashier asked.

"Hmm?" he replied. His heartbeat quickened; was there a serious problem?

The tray extended and his license and receipt with current balance sat. Taking them, he smiled, and put his identification in his wallet. "Your deposit will become available within one business day," she explained. "Will there be anything else?"

He shook his head. "No, thank you," he replied.

She waved, as the tray retracted. "Have a nice day," she said. "Thank you for banking with us!"

The shifter slid into drive and he moved forward and out of the lane. He'd gotten away with it. Sure, he would have to pay taxes on his winnings, but he'd drastically improved his financial situation. He felt a twinge of worry about his lack of guilt but shook it off as he remembered that his actions amounted to a drop of water in the bucket of a corporation that wouldn't notice.

Once home, he put the receipt in his desk drawer. His body plopped down into the loveseat in his living room, and he turned on the television. When he had been a teen, he'd fantasized about being a superhero, but as an adult, the harsh reality had set in. Now that the option stood wide open to him, the logical side of his brain argued with his child mind, insisting that the issue was not as simple as mere desire. The law, he knew, didn't act like it did in comics. In the comics, there existed systems in place to allow supers to go about saving the world. They could fight crime, and be de facto police, with examples rife from fiction of heroes simply rounding up villains and dropping them off at police stations. This would not fly in the real world.

He needed to know about what the law actually meant.

A decision was made. He clicked off the television and grabbed his house keys once more and shifted into his female form.

"Excuse me," Manny in his female form said to the librarian, "where's your law section?" He'd made his way to his local library, Alton's Hayner Library, and walked in, approached the circulation desk and asked his important question. The fact of the matter was, he wanted to know what he could actually do as a super.

The man regarded the heavy-set redhead in front of him, a twenties-ish young woman dressed like a septuagenarian. It wasn't her weight that struck him as odd, but rather, her traditional fashion sense. Or maybe, he figured, it was because she was sensitive about her weight that caused her to dress that way. In any case, he had to be professional. "What specific categories are you looking for, ma'am?"

"Well," she replied, "I'm doing research for a comic book a friend of mine is writing, so I was wondering if I could read something about civilians being involved in crime fighting."

The librarian pondered for a minute. "Here, let me look that up," he said. He typed away at his computer and his eyes scanned several paragraphs of results. "I think..." He stopped scrolling and landed on a specific result. "Here. Let me see if that's still on the shelf."

He got up and Manny followed him. The section held a solid wall of bland, legal texts, and it became apparent right away that the answer would be hidden and would require a needle in a haystack search. "Is it in this area?" she asked.

The librarian put his hand on a book. "It says the most cases related to civilian involvement in vigilantism are in this book," he explained. "It has cases going all the way back to the early eighteen-hundreds."

Manny smiled. "Great," she said. "Thank you." As the librarian retreated to the front desk, it struck Manny as odd that, in her female form, she started thinking of herself in female terms, and male terms in her standard male form. *This duality of mind thing is really weird,* she thought. Carefully, she plucked a volume off the shelf and sat cross-legged on the floor. With a quick scan by her senses, she felt safe that no cameras or wandering eyes were watching her, and she activated one of her speed powers. If anyone had walked by, they'd have seen a bit of a blur as a woman opened and shut a book. In truth, she'd read the whole thing in under a second of real time, devouring over a thousand pages of legal tripe. The boring academic read did, however, provide her with interesting points.

The main takeaway was simple.

If I'm a super, she realized, *I can't act like they do in the comics.*

If any clue as to her involvement in stopping criminals became apparent, it would mean the prosecution's case would be thrown out at once. That meant it would be safer just to act either when no one could tell she'd gotten involved at all, or to only fight against crimes that fell far outside the realm of what ordinary people could do even if they had weapons.

It gave her a sense of laser-thin focus on what her purpose should be. She should be more of an example, than a crime fighter. Besides, as she pondered it further, it didn't make much sense anyway. Most crime came about because of an imbalance in the system itself.

The average criminal was not a mastermind who sought to perform acts of 'wickedness,' because such would be a childish motivation. No, her focus should be the saving of lives. Just out of curiosity, she devoured several more tomes on the law before the minute hand ticked one over.

While she was here, she might as well read some of those books she'd put off, she decided. A few minutes later, she exited the front door. "Have a nice day," the librarian said.

"You too," she replied, waving absently.

Out the door, she had to adjust her belt again. Back home, she locked the front door and went into the bathroom. Two hundred and fifty-five, read the scale. Her head jerked rapidly in disbelief. "Twenty-three pounds?" she exclaimed. Sure, she knew her regeneration treated his weight as a harmful thing, but this fast? It dawned on her that she would soon have to buy real clothes once the body stopped losing weight. Capacitor's bio in the comics meant she didn't have to eat, so weight loss *would* stop, but given that she still loved to eat, well, she'd have to worry about that later. Right now, she had to see if any emergencies required her immediate intervention.

The television back on, the news returned to the wildfires raging in southern California. "Up until now," the news anchor spoke, "there have been concerns as to whether the shifting winds would bring the fire into the path of a neighborhood of expensive properties. Just this morning, though, the worst happened as the winds shifted the fire away from the upper crust neighborhood and towards an area with campgrounds and various other groups. It has since cut off all exits for the people within who are now surrounded on all sides by fire encroaching in on their position." An image of aerial photography of the affected area popped up in the corner. "Firefighters have been dropping fire-retardant chemicals, attempting to open a pathway, but it appears as if the populace, which could number as high as seventy people, are trapped. The fire chief has sworn..." But she didn't wait around long enough to hear the rest.

Out the door and up into the atmosphere, she barely felt the cold as the chill of the thinning air shifted around her. From the vantage-point, she focused her vision and saw the affected region up close. Like a shot from a railgun, she rocketed towards it.

A team of firefighters sprayed water and chemicals into the blaze. "Damn it!" a commanding voice swore. "We gotta punch through that wall or else these people are goners!"

"Captain!" shouted the one manning the nozzle. "I just...what the hell?" He'd happened to be looking in the direction of a smoke plume for clues as to a change in the wall of flame, before he caught a vague blur that popped into his vision for just long enough to register. Before his captain could answer, a person appeared by them, holding two people by the waist. After setting them down, the person was gone again, disappearing before their very eyes.

The fire captain blinked several times. "What was that?" he asked.

Manny zoomed over the wall of flame, protected by an other-worldly field of power, and activated several senses, becoming aware of the exact count. Fifty-four people stood across an area of some fifteen square miles. She collided with two more victims of the blaze, her power coursing through them as she grabbed them by the waist, allowing them protection from the laws of physics. She deposited them safely outside the danger zone, in the custody of the fire crews. One by one, she repeated this process, until she determined repeatedly, she'd gotten everyone.

"Wait!" the fire captain shouted.

Manny shot him a quick glance, then took off. At home, she stripped and changed back into her male self. After throwing on some guy clothes, he sat on his sofa, heart still racing. The television news had a breaking story.

"Our story of the hour is the California wildfires," the anchor reported. "What was the situation earlier is radically different, and the authorities are not clear as to why." The scene went to a fire chief.

"My captain was on duty," the chief reported, "under orders to do whatever was necessary to make a pathway to secure those trapped campers and other guests. Approximately twenty minutes ago, I get a call that all the victims are safe, and that someone who could disappear kept bringing them back."

The on-site reporter interviewing the chief raised skeptical eyebrows. "What do you think it means?" he asked.

The chief shrugged with his hands. "I wish I knew," he admitted. "It could be some kind of chemical in the air from the flames, but, here's the thing." He leaned in, a spooked look on his face. "Every one of my men says there was no way in hell they were gonna be able to get through to those campers."

It cut back to the main anchor. "Multiple corroborating reports from aerial views as well as FEMA crews have told the same story," they stated. "They say it was utterly impossible for the fire to be penetrated enough to create an opening. So, many expert groups are stumped as to what has transpired to allow..." Manny shut off the television. The feeling of satisfaction that washed over him felt almost transcendent. He had done *something*.

CHAPTER THREE

"YOU SHOULD GET YOUR BROTHER LUTHER something for his birthday!"

In a hotel suite in Manhattan, a thirty-one-year-old rolled his eyes at his mother's voice on the phone. "Mom," he argued, "you know Luther and I don't get along, and quite frankly, I'm not going to get into it with him again."

"Jericho," she countered, "you need to cut this out, and…"

He clicked end call. Jericho Torvalds didn't have the stamina to go down this road again. Wiping the sleep out of his eyes, he got up and walked into the bathroom. He reached into his toiletries bag and pulled out a fresh sponge. With a quick rip he tore open the package and deposited it in the can. The shower felt good on his skin as he rubbed the sensitive skin body wash onto the sponge and washed himself. After that, he reached out through the curtain and pitched it in the garbage. A handful of face cleanser went on and came off. Finally, he scrubbed shampoo into his hair and goatee, and washed it off, before using conditioner and repeating.

He dried himself in a towel, before combing his chin-length sandy brown hair parted in the middle. He regarded his appearance in the mirror. A Newsweek article about him had mentioned that "the young billionaire's skill belies his youthful appearance," and he thought about it as he scratched his goatee, questioningly. He'd been growing it for a week and a half now. Hastily, he reached for his shaving cream and razor. Screw it, he figured. If they could continue to underestimate his performance, he would lean into the "young" aspect of it. Time Magazine bothered to take the effort to describe how his "remarkable, almost supernatural ability to pick stocks," was the main aspect to focus on, not his age or appearance. A towel dabbed the dots of cream and the strands of loose hair stuck to his now-smooth chin and upper lip.

After putting his boxers on, he donned a short sleeve undershirt and opened the wardrobe. He stared at the collection and weighed his options. The Armani or the Gucci, he pondered? Dark blue or black, which color scheme worked best with CNN? Ultimately, he settled on a Clamshell White dress shirt and Evening Sea Blue vest, suit jacket, and slacks, with his custom-made shoes. From the suitcase, he removed a small wooden box and opened it. The Rolex, or the Bulova, it was a difficult choice. After a long moment, he settled on the Bulova. Sure, it was only worth ten thousand, but the tv cameras probably weren't high definition enough to give audiences much of a difference. In the process of testing each watch against his wrist, he noticed the back of his hands had minor pink spot, possibly from sweat from exercising having been poorly washed away, or a minor bug bite. He made a mental note to put makeup over it before the interview.

Right now, though, he had hours to kill and he had to get some food in him. He looked at the clock and saw that it was nine-thirty in the morning. He searched for a familiar name and found it on his phone, dialing. "Yes," Jericho said, when his call went through. "I'd like to place an order. Delivery."

"I'm sorry sir," the man said, "our deliveries are on hold because we had a big order just ten minutes ago and our delivery crew had to go deliver to..."

"Wait," Jericho interrupted, "your *entire* crew? You don't have *one* delivery person free?" A sigh escaped his lips. Who could be so important?"

"Sir," the man argued, "it's just that last night, the King of the African nation of..."

"Never mind," Jericho countered. "I'll be there in person. Can I still place an order so I don't have to wait in line?" This level of service was unacceptable. The idea that such a nation's delegation could swoop in and interrupt service indicated this restaurant needed to plan for such an occurrence.

"Yes, what would you like?"

Jericho paused for just a moment at the man's question. "I'd like," he began, "the Mediterranean apple chicken sandwich with avocado on whole wheat bread, hold the cheese, with Dijon mustard." He paused to receive confirmation. "Yes, lettuce, tomato, and black olives. I'd also like a small bowl of your deluxe lentil soup and a side salad with almonds and Italian dressing." He received the total. "You have my card on file. Jericho W. Torvalds. Security code two-eight-seven."

"Thank you, sir," the man cried, "we'll see you here soon!"

"No problem," Jericho replied, and ended the call. He closed the wardrobe and put on a polo shirt and some loose-fitting khakis and headed out of the hotel towards the bistro. Exiting the front door of the hotel, he moved into the crowd of people. He felt at home in the bustle and the noise of street, as the people moved back and forth, serving as the lifeblood of the city. As people shifted around to avoid running into each other, he saw his destination over a line of heads. The bistro sat at the end of a line of restaurants and he picked them for a reason. They typically had the best light meal food in this section of Manhattan.

The front door of the bistro slid open, and the crowded early morning lobby had a line stretching to the condiment counter. He found a seat and removed his phone, texting a number. His order popped up on a large screen by the entrance. To kill time, he switched over to his news app, and it brought up a strange occurrence. The screen reported a psychedelic sight; in the sky, last night, over much of the world, otherworldly lights, moving in all different kinds of patterns, bathed millions of viewers in a sight unlike any ever seen before. A tap set the video playing without sound. The lights moved outward from singular points dotted across the sky and faded only as they crossed the horizon. It had been less than twenty-four hours since the event and he had missed it because he was researching stocks in his hotel room with the curtains drawn. Now that he thought of it, he'd assumed the lights in the curtain had been police responding to some incident.

Scrolling through related news, it seemed to him that no obvious effects had occurred on telecommunications, so his investments in those fields didn't need to change. It would, however, mean that he would have to watch certain markets because countries with certain mineral resources also had very superstitions populations, and the market was, after all, a representation of perception of reality rather than reality itself. He scratched the back of his head as he felt a twinge somewhere in his mind.

"Mister Torvalds," the waitress said, setting his tray down on the table, "your meal is ready."

He pulled a five out of his pocket and handed it to her. "Thanks," he said. "Your tip."

She gave a fake smile. "You're welcome," she said. She left his table and walked back towards the front. Her foot landed on something and she slid, and in her rush to correct her balance, placed a hand on his neck.

Jericho's eyes went wide.

In a heartbeat, he got torn out of his senses.

The scene in front of his eyesight was that of the waitress, standing in front of her mirror. Every thought she experienced flowed through his consciousness, and every sensation her nervous system had at whatever moment this was at came to him. He realized this was from shortly after the night before, where she'd realized the twinge in her mind not an hour after the lights in the sky. The twinge appeared to her as a trigger mechanism.

He felt her flip the switch in her brain and become aware of the objects in a field of ten feet around her and will her toothbrush holder closer to her. Exactly like she commanded it, the object left the sink and flew outwards and into her waiting right hand. Three more times she tested her newfound power on various objects in her bathroom.

All at once, he felt his mind get thrust back into its proper place. Gasping involuntarily, he jerked his head around to see the familiar sights and smells of the bistro. "Oh, I'm terribly sorry, sir!" the waitress cried.

"Huh?" he exclaimed, looking up. "Oh! Oh. Yes, of course. No problem."

As she pulled away nervously, he held up his cellphone. No time had passed while he was...where had he gone? Was that a vision, of some kind? Had he gone mad? Was there a tumor? In any case, he had to know immediately. He dialed a number. "Yes, Ruth?" he said to his secretary. "Get me a doctor's appointment today and tell him to call me. Also, contact CNN and tell them I'm going to have to cancel. Thank you." Hanging up, he put the phone down.

Out of curiosity, he decided to test this insanity. Superpowers couldn't be real, but he also didn't have an explanation for the lights. He stuck out his hand and focused his inner mind. The gasp couldn't have been louder if he'd done it physically. There sat two separate trigger mechanisms in his mind, and he somehow knew that one belonged to the one the woman who'd just touched him.

As he desired, the fork slid across the table and up to his hand. His eyes went wide. It took him a moment to realize he had to breathe. At once he set about finishing his meal as quickly as possible. He'd never devour food with such reckless abandon, but a desperate urge overcame him. One of two outcomes would emerge, he decided; either he would prove himself insane, or, should this prove true, a wondrous opportunity would emerge. After all, if superpowers were, somehow, impossibly, real, then that meant they would become the new currency. It only stood to reason that if there were people who could do impossible things, and those that couldn't, it would be the new market, so to speak.

After finishing the last of his salad and soup, he stood up, focusing on this power, assuming it was real.

In his mind, he somehow knew the distance and direction of people who, what, had powers? It seemed the only logical conclusion. The nearest one to him was less than fifty yards away, outside. Scrambling, he made his way out the door and pushed his way through the crowd. The man wore a flat cap on his head and a black t-shirt. He walked with hands in pockets and appeared to be looking left and right, nervously. The billionaire made a show of bumping into him from behind, brushing against his hand.

The man, in his living room, stared at the wall. He stood in his living room and focused on the room on the other side of the wall. The switch in his mind flipped, and he disappeared from where he stood and emerged in the room opposite the wall. The man blinked several times and let out a whoop of excitement. It then moved forward ten minutes as he discovered he could teleport from a seated to a standing position, and vice versa.

Jericho landed in his body with a mental thud. "Hey!" the man shouted, addressing the disturbance. "Watch where the hell you're going!"

"Yes," Jericho apologized. "I'm sorry." He stepped away from the man and disappeared away into the crowd. Further up the street, he saw a boy sitting on a step, watching something on his cell phone. Drifting away from the street, as he approached the steps, he pretended to trip and caught himself on the steps with his hands. A hand drifted towards the boy's exposed pant leg.

A young black boy watched the lights in the sky above. It had awoken him. The scene moved forward an hour or so when he should have been asleep. The boy flipped the switch, and an eyelid twitched. The television turned on. A moment later, he reverted it, and the tv went off. He repeated this experiment with the tv un-plugged, and it continued to run until he stopped his power. The next morning, he watched from his seat at the kitchen table as his mother struggled with a jar. He tried his power, and she suddenly jerked the lid, a noticeable pop sound as it came open.

"Hey man!" the boy cried. "Be careful!"

Jericho got up and gestured an apology. He focused on the new power he'd gotten. The man's ability was teleportation, that seemed obvious. The boy had, what, enhancement? Maybe he had empowerment? In any case, it seemed to be able to increase the power of things. Perhaps, Jericho thought, he could use it on his other powers.

Combining it with his normal ability, a mild push on it and he could sense the exact location and what power each person had for miles in every direction. Carefully, he drifted away from the crowd and into a hotel nearby.

The clamorous concert of the outside became a gentle breeze of the quiet interior of the front lobby. He walked into the public restroom perpendicular to the front desk at the end of the lobby and took his place in a stall, shutting the door behind him. Eagerly, he combined his enhancement power with teleportation. External reality seemed to pause as a three-dimensional map, showing twenty miles in every direction, appeared in his mental image. His consciousness could roam free around, looking for a place to teleport, and it would be updated for him in real time as soon as he came to it. Meanwhile, no time passed in the outside world. The mental image showed his hotel room, and he chose it, causing him to immediately disappear from the bathroom and emerge in his room, at once popping back into his normal consciousness.

Wow, that's messed up, he thought, as he came back to his senses. He stood in his room. Everything had been as he saw it.

Bzzz!

"Ah!" he shouted, flinching. As he realized it was his cell phone, by his ringtone a moment later, a laugh escaped his mouth.

"Yes?" he asked, answering.

"Mister Torvalds?" his secretary, Ruth, said. "You have an appointment an hour and a half from now. Is that okay?"

His mind slipped him a moment. "Hmm?" he asked. It hit him. "Oh! Yes, the doctor's appointment. Got it. That's perfect! Thank you very much." He hung up the phone and set it on the table. This was progressing quickly, and he didn't know how to take it other than to simply sit down and ponder. In his mind, the powers and locations came up for him. Combining teleportation with enhancement and his main ability, he could see each person and their power, and location. It made him the ultimate voyeur. Comics hadn't been his thing growing up. Still, even the casual movie-goer would know the obvious powers to start with included strength and durability. Moving through the mental image of the city, he came across a person who had both at once. It was a rather nasty looking individual in a parking garage.

Jericho appeared behind a pillar and looked out from his vantagepoint. The bruiser with the flat-top, who had to be standing at least six and a half feet tall, wore soot-stained jeans and combat boots as well as a wife-beater. At once adrenaline started racing as the billionaire knew he stood somewhere he didn't belong. Still, if he could get those powers, he would.

"Hey, c'mon!" a shorter man next to the huge man whispered aggressively.

They took shelter behind a pickup truck and waited. Jericho looked to their line of sight and traced it to a balding, late fifties man exiting the building and reaching into his pocket for his key fob. A dark blue BMW beeped, and he opened the door and climbed in.

"Hey! Miss us?" the huge man half-spoke, half-growled.

At this the man shrieked and slammed his door shut. Before he could fire the engine up, though, the two approached and a giant fist smashed the window. Two huge hands wrapped around the man's torso and pulled him clear out through the window. "Please! I was going to have the money tomorrow!" the poor businessman shouted.

A laugh escaped the shorter man. "Did ya think Benny was just gonna keep waiting?" he asked, sarcasm dripping.

"I'm gonna take the money you owe Benny outta yer ass!" the ogre-like man shouted.

Jericho returned to hiding. He slammed his eyes shut and forced himself to calm. *Walk away,* he thought, *this isn't your battle. It isn't in your rational self-interest.* He swallowed. Could he return to his hotel room and pretend this didn't happen? The Objectivist in him said he could. Somehow, though, he didn't think he'd be able to.

"Maybe some debts shouldn't be settled out of court," Jericho shouted, appearing thirty feet away from the brute and his criminal companion.

All three turned in his direction at once. A miserable scowl drew itself across the larger goon's face. "Who the fuck are you?" the shorter goon shouted.

Jericho had acted. Now, he had to do his best to stifle his heart's desire to shoot out of his body. Sweat beaded on his forehead. "That doesn't matter," he said.

"You just fucked up!" the huge hulking man shouted, dropping his original target, who scampered to his car.

The shorter goon shouted something and reached for his pistol at his hip. Instinctively, the billionaire activated his telekinesis and turned the enhancement on it up as far as he could. Both men stood frozen in place, held stiff as stone statues. Nervous as a cat, and ready to leap out of there at the slightest irritation, he approached.

His logical side protesting against him, he placed a hand on the brute's chest.

The scene showed a man punching through various substances, such as concrete, steel, and his skin not marred by the sharpest of metal edges. His buddies and he had been up most of the night drinking and partying. Scenes played showing various skulls being bashed in as they'd served some late-night revenge to their boss's less reliable clients. They banished sleep with hard drugs, which only stirred the brute up, no ill effects at all. Knives, pistols, and car impacts didn't injure the man. Finally, a high-powered shotgun to the chest had drawn some slight beads of blood from the surface skin. All in all, a brutal montage of murder and violence played out.

Jericho came back to himself, sputtering. "Oh, Christ," he uttered, almost forgetting to keep up his offensive attacks. "Good God, holy shit..." He blinked as his eyes began to water. When his eyes settled back on the goons, feelings of anger, disgust, and hatred filled his mind. Acting without thinking, he activated his teleportation on the two of them, banishing them miles out into the depths of the ocean.

He collapsed onto the pavement, in a seated position. Squealing tires echoed through the garage as the would-be victim hightailed it. Before anyone else could show up, he returned to his hotel room. At once he collapsed into his bed, weeping into the bedsheets.

How long he lay there, hands covering his face to stifle his tears, he didn't know. At some point, a text message notification broke him from his stupor. Rolling to his left, he twisted position and wound up in a seated position. Somewhere the strength in his hands returned and he pushed himself off the bed, stumbling and shuffling like a zombie towards the bathroom. A handful of cold water splashed into his face, and it smashed his senses back to reality.

He blinked his red eyes as he watched himself in the mirror. The emotional storm hadn't subsided, but he needed to get back to reality. The phone registered again. He returned to the table and unlocked the phone.

"You've got 30 minutes until your appointment," the text from the doctor's office said. "Please check in at 15 minutes before."

He took a deep breath and wiped his face with his hands again.

Ten minutes later, he walked up to the front desk at the doctor's office. "Mister Torvalds!" the receptionist noted. "Please fill this out."

He hastily looked over the form and filled it out, handing it over. "Is there anything else you need?" he asked.

She looked at his record on the computer. "Is your insurance still the same?' she asked. He nodded. "Great! Just have a seat over there and the doctor will be with you soon."

He sat in the hard, wooden seat, with the too-thin cushion and forced his brain to stop pestering him with these ragged emotional outbursts. The fact that horrific violence occurred all over America was something he knew academically, but to actually see it, to actually experience it, overwhelmed him. He might never be able to forget the things he experienced.

"The doctor will see you now," the receptionist said.

He stepped into the office, and the familiar sight of the doctor put his mind relatively at ease. Somewhere in his mind, comfort washed over the tempest, and he felt a sense of normalcy return. "Jericho!" The doctor announced. "I heard you had an emergency! You had to make this appointment in a hurry. What's wrong?"

Jericho opened his mouth to speak. Words didn't come out. A long moment passed, as he sat there, stumped. Finally, he closed his mouth and made a decision.

The doctor's cell phone fell off his desk. He let out a gasp and reached for it.

Jericho pointed. At that instant, it froze in place midair.

The doctor pulled back, sitting up straight in his seat. A suspicious glance traded between him and Jericho. Finally, the phone levitated upward and safely back onto the desk. For almost a minute, no one said anything. "Tell me how you did that," the doctor slowly asked.

"I'm willing to pay extra for all the tests," Jericho said. "I want to know for sure whether or not I'm insane or if I have a huge brain tumor."

"Well," the doctor replied, tilting his head in confusion. "If you're crazy, then *I'm* crazy too, because I just watched you do that."

Over the next two hours, the doctor pulled every string he could, called in several favors, and lied his way into test after test. Enough blood had come out of Jericho to constitute a donation, and he'd been scanned up and down, left and right. While the billionaire waited in the doctor's office, the doctor assembled the results as they came in, scrutinizing each data point, comparing all the numbers and values as best he could. "I gotta tell you, Jericho," the doctor said, pushing the door open, "This is one hell of a result."

The billionaire noted the lack of alarm in his doctor's face. Instead, the expression seemed a mixture of confusion and apprehension. "Well, what's the verdict?" he asked.

The doctor gave a single chuckle. "It's clean," he said. "Everything is normal. Brain scans, MRI, everything comes up negative for any lesions, tumors, damage, drugs. You're basically physically fit as anyone in their early thirties."

Jericho blinked, breathing in and out hard, and leaned back in the chair. "Okay then," he said, surprised. "So, it's either an incredibly vivid hallucination, or superpowers are real."

The doctor pulled his phone out and showed it to his patient. "You ought to see this," he advised. The screen showed CNN reporting on a man in the U.K. who caught fire in the middle of a crowded shopping center, and then returned to normal, unharmed. "Looks like you're not hallucinating."

"So." Jericho's single word held a mountain of weight in his mind. He drummed his fingers on the armrests of the chair. He swallowed. "So, this isn't a dream, or brain damage. We're in a brave new world."

The doctor had no words, so he simply nodded. He sat down and looked around the room in silence for a few moments.

Jericho shrugged and got up. "In that case," he continued, "I have plans to make and research to do."

The doctor got up and extended his hand. "Always glad to help," he said, putting on a cheery voice. "Send your bill to your office, as always?"

"As always, doc," Jericho said, exiting the exam room. Out the door, he opened his phone and dialed his secretary. "Yes? Hi. Get the plane gassed up and ready, as soon as I get some research done, I'm going to need to fly out of here."

"Destination, sir?" Ruth asked.

"Get back to you on that," he ordered. "Just get it ready to go at a moment's notice."

"Yes, sir."

He smiled. "Thank you," he stated, hanging up. Outside the office, he saw no one in the hallway, and no cameras, and vanished, reappearing in his hotel room.

He'd seen only the comic book superheroes in movie form. True, some of them had been passable action films, he didn't have the slightest idea about how their fictional worlds worked. One of the online retailers for digital comics allowed buying of multiple different companies' comics, so he purchased their unlimited package, and started reading. The first place to start, he figured, were the 'guidebooks' that occasionally got published, the 'encyclopedias' of each comic book universe. It startled him the degree to which people categorized and archived each character's powers and unique traits. Comic book fans took these things deadly serious, it occurred to him. Next, he read the origin stories of most of the mainstream supers and the most famous stories about them. None of these tales particularly fascinated him; it was mere research. He had to have a heads' up if he wasn't going to get left behind.

After almost an hour and a half of reading, he closed his laptop, and packed up his bags. Then he made a call to his secretary.

"Mister Torvalds!" the front desk receptionist announced, seeing him step up to the front with all his belongings on a cart. "You were scheduled to have the room until two days' from now. Is everything okay?"

"Plans change in a heartbeat in the world of Wall Street," he said. "I'm checking out."

After the room keycard entered her hands, she checked him out. "Will you be staying with us again, Mister Torvalds?" she inquired.

He put on a smile. "Be delighted," he exclaimed. "By the way, I don't need a vehicle. I'm being picked up."

"The best of wishes!" the receptionist cheered.

He waved. A bellboy pushed the cart outside as he walked. A Mercedes pulled up and the driver opened the trunk. As the bellboy loaded his luggage, Ruth stepped out of the car. "Mister Torvalds," she said, "I've collected the information you asked for."

He sat in the back as she took a seat next to him. "And?" he asked.

She opened a thin laptop and pulled up a series of documents. "There hasn't been much activity so far," she explained, as he read the information. "But by leaning into our connections, I discovered a small bunch of people who, so far, have shown powers and have been lazy or unaware enough not to have concealed it well."

"Great," he announced, pointing to a result. *"That's* one of the ones I want the most."

"That," she explained, "is a woman in one of the towns outside Chicago who got shot during a botched robbery. By the time she arrived at the hospital, the bullet wound to her heart had been perfectly healed. The EMTs reported being startled by the dead woman reviving in front of them." She thought about his words. "So, what are you planning, if I may ask?"

"I've got a power," he explained, "and it's to copy powers. I'm going to copy her ability, and there's one thing everyone needs and that's money."

"Are you sure these people will go for that?" Ruth asked.

He looked at her like she'd asked how to eat a baby. "It's basic Ayn Rand," he explained. "Everyone wants money. I've got a lot of it. She has a power. *Obviously,* these people are going to go for that. Especially the ones who have a power but are living in the impoverished areas."

Ruth did the math in her head. "But sir, even with *your* wealth," she advised, "you won't have enough to get them all."

He laughed. "I don't have to get them all," he reminded. "Just the most useful ones." He decided to take a risk and explain his motivation. "I got ultra-rich by being good at accumulating currency. Superpowers are going to become the new currency. Someone might be poor financially but if their power is incredible, they're set. Set our destination." Ruth dialed the airport.

CHAPTER FOUR

I.

M ANNY WOKE UP AND SHOWERED , then put on some clothes he'd bought. Being skinny for the first time since before high school had forced him to buy a new wardrobe for his male self. The microwave reheated leftovers from the night before and he ate his breakfast in his bedroom. As he pondered the previous days' events, one major problem hit him. The outfit he'd been wearing in his female form didn't fit anymore. Sure, his grandmother had some clothes from when she'd lost weight, but even then, she hadn't gotten quite as thin as the woman he turned into, and furthermore, the height difference hadn't bothered him at first, but it started to as the acts of heroism increased in frequency.

He unlocked his cell phone and dialed his friend.

"Hey, Manny," Ed said, "how's it going? Would you believe I was at Burger King last night, and some lady called me the N-word?"

Manny scoffed. "That's terrible!" he lamented. He collected his thoughts. "Say, do you think you could get Annie to take my friend out to shop for clothes?" His friend and Ed's girlfriend seemed like the obvious choice. The girl had a common, average frame, long, chestnut-colored hair and an above-average face. That combined with her ability to form a stylish look without being rich made the decision.

There was a pause. "You mean that girl that John said you had living with you?" Ed asked.

Manny closed his eyes and silently swore. He *knew* he shouldn't have texted John that picture. "Yes," he said. "She just wants another woman's opinion about clothes, because she's not that fashion-savvy."

A laugh escaped Ed's end of the line. "A woman who doesn't have fashion sense?" Ed said, skeptically. "That's a new one. Anyway, I'll ask. Hey, uh, what's her name?"

It took Manny a brief instant to realize Ed wasn't talking about Annie, whose name he already knew. "Oh, uh," he said. In haste, he fired off a command to his mind to produce a name, posthaste. "Jennifer. Jennifer Black." His eyes slammed shut and his teeth grit. *Damn it,* he thought, *that's a terrible name.*

"Hmm," Ed replied. "Doesn't sound familiar at all. I usually recognize names pretty well."

"She's not from around here," Manny explained. Immediately he regretted his words.

"That's what I figured!" Ed exclaimed, his hypothesis confirmed. He just *knew* a woman that looked like Jennifer couldn't be from southern Illinois. "Where's she from?"

"California," Manny said, stating the first place to pop into his mind. *Please don't ask where in California,* he mentally pleaded.

"Where in California?"

Think of a city, Manny told his brain. "Santa Cruz," he replied to Ed's question.

"Neat!" Ed said, excited at the prospect of meeting someone from the west coast. "I'll get Annie to call you, and then you can put your friend on the line."

"No problem!" Manny said, hanging up. "Well *that* was a disaster." He took a drink of his Diet Coke and waited. About five minutes later, his phone rang. "Yes?"

"Hey, Manny?" Annie said. "You said your friend wanted me to take her out and help her buy clothes?"

"Yeah," he replied. "She wants to expand her wardrobe and she isn't used to buying clothes that often."

"No problem!" Annie cheerily replied. "I'd be glad to help her out. Just put her on the line."

"No problem," Manny said.

A few seconds later, Jennifer held the phone up to her ear. "Hey, this is Jennifer Black," she said. Obviously, this wasn't going to be the only step she'd have to take. In the near future, she would have to get all kinds of official paperwork sorted out so she could do business in her female form, and be official, but she had to remind her self that things worked in steps. Also, this expanded her wardrobe beyond the basics.

"Hey," Annie replied. "So, which place did you want to go to? What is your budget?"

"I don't want to break the bank," she answered, "but at the same time, I don't want to look cheap. Does that make sense?"

Annie laughed. "Yeah, that does," she said. "So I'd recommend a place in Edwardsville. It's about a half mile from the Hardee's and the Fish place."

"You mean the store by what used to be a barbecue place?" Jennifer asked.

Annie paused. "I thought you weren't from around here," she thought out loud. "Well, yeah, anyway, that is the place. So, you know how to get there?"

"Yeah," she said. "I'll meet you there."

"See you there," Annie said. "Bye." The call ended with a beep.

Jennifer got all of Manny's identification and the money in cash since she couldn't use his card in her form. She put on the best fitting of her mother's outfits and headed out. She had to drive carefully because she didn't want to get pulled over and have to change back into Manny and attempt to explain that whole mess that would follow.

After close to a half hour of navigating traffic at the safest of paces, she arrived at the clothing store. Annie exited her car and greeted the woman at the front. "Hey, you must be Jennifer!" she greeted. "Nice to meet you." She stuck out her hand. "Wow, you are tall."

Jennifer stood at six feet tall and she suddenly became acutely aware of it. "Nice to meet you too, Annie," she greeted, putting her calm face back on.

They went inside the store. "First," Annie said, leading her. "Let's get you some pants and skirts." She looked at the woman carefully. "You're built like a gymnast or a body builder, you know that? Let's see what'll fit these tree trunks."

Jennifer noticed something peculiar to her. "None of these pants have pockets more than a couple inches deep," she said.

Annie laughed. "Yeah, that's common," she replied. "I don't get it either."

They examined several racks of pants. There were stylish jeans, both blue and black, and pants of imitation leather and similar fabrics. Annie gave her advice on each one, and after a good forty-five minutes, they had six different pairs of pants for various types of events, both casual and slightly formal.

"What about these?" Jennifer said, holding up a skirt.

Annie looked at it. "Might look a bit odd considering how tall you are," she advised. She searched through the rack. "Ah! Try these instead." She held up a similar design, but a few inches longer.

Jennifer tried it on, and when she stepped out of the fitting room, she got a thumbs up. "What about tops?" she asked.

Annie did a balancing gesture with her hand. "We have to thread a fine line," she explained, "between looking like you're showing off, and wearing a tent."

Jennifer picked out a top. "What about this?" she asked.

Annie looked at it and cringed. "If *I* wore that," she said, "it'd probably be acceptable. If you wear that, you'll definitely be the center of attention."

Jennifer cocked her head in confusion. "Is that bad?"

The shorter girl blinked a moment. "Just try it on," she advised, "and tell me what you think."

Jennifer looked down at her chest a moment. Then she thought about herself wearing it. Then she cringed and her hand shot out to put it back. "Oh wow," she said. "No. No thank you."

Annie gave a chuckle. "Anyway, try..." She sorted through a few different outfits. "...Try these." She presented five different tops.

Jennifer examined each one. She hadn't initially thought they were that stylish, but as she tried each of them on, she realized they looked great on her. The patterns and designs complemented the color scheme of the outfit very well, and it impressed her how Annie could tell just by looking at it. After that, they approached the bra fitting section.

"It looks like your bra doesn't fit quite well," the woman said. "Would you like a professional bra fitting?" The employee led Jennifer to a private area where they sat obscured from the rest of the store. She removed her shirt and the woman regarded the undergarment with a look of sympathy and confusion. "I'm definitely seeing that this needs replacing. It's entirely the wrong size."

Due to her powers, she hadn't felt any pain, because it couldn't hurt her, but once she realized it, she went with it. "Yeah, absolutely," she told the employee. "I can't wear this for very long." It had been just one more thing that she hadn't had a chance to get used to since she'd only been in this form for less than a week. What more would she learn was obvious to women who'd been that way their whole life? She removed her bra.

"Stand still, arms up," the employee advised. She pulled out her tape measure and made a measurement under the breasts. This number made its way onto a notepad. Then, she wrapped the tape around the torso, covering the outermost part of them. This number made its way onto the notepad. A quick bit of math later, and Jennifer had a number and a letter, and she had a vague sense of what they meant but decided not to make an ass out of herself. "There's good news and bad news." She looked at her customer with a frank expression.

"Bad news first," Jennifer implored.

"Alright," the employee said, "very practical. Most bras are not made for women of your bust size. All the cute and expressive ones are largely designed for more petite women. Fuller framed women such as yourself typically find their selection rather bland. Oh! Also, expensive. They're not typically cheap."

Jennifer scoffed. "What's the *good* news?" she asked.

Eyebrows went up and down. "The good news is," the woman replied, "that we carry bras in your size."

Jennifer shot her a skeptical look. "Good news," she lamented. "Right."

As she put her shirt back on, the tall redhead made her way to the section of the brassiere racks where her size could be found. Passing by a selection of wonderfully decorative and artistic bras she might have wanted, but were much too small, she came to a pair of metal racks where some beige and brown brutalist monstrosities that looked like government assigned clothing hung next to a few scant ones that had a halfway decent design to them.

"The good news is," the woman advised, "most of the blander ones are at least built well. These have a reputation for taking a beating."

Jennifer looked at one that certainly would do the job, and her eyes went wide. "Ninety-six dollars!" she mouthed. The woman silently nodded.

"We even have a few sports bras in your size," the woman said. She cocked her head. "I *think*." She pulled up the store's app on her phone. "Ah! We do. Give me a moment. How many do you want?"

"How much are they?" Jennifer asked.

"One hundred twenty," the woman stated.

I can always cheat at the casino again, the super thought. "Three. I think I can do with three." She looked in her purse and saw that she had gotten enough cash out of the bank as Manny for the transaction.

"Very well." The woman nodded politely and headed towards the back room.

Jennifer decided to forgo style and grab a few of the more reliable looking ones, as no one was going to be seeing her bra anytime soon. It amazed her that it was easily the most expensive part of the outfit.

About five minutes later, the woman returned with the sports bras. The super stood in awe of the amount of fabric present in the products in front of her. Nevertheless, she took them and put them in her shopping bag.

Thankfully, she got a reprieve from difficult shopping when it came to shoes. She wasn't wearing heels, period. That was that, she decided. So, Annie helped her pick out several shoes, some for running, some for casual events, and at least one for formal. That only took about fifteen minutes.

"Your total comes to eight hundred and fifty-two dollars and eighty-seven cents," the cashier said.

"Most expensive thing was the bras," Jennifer noted.

"Yeah, that's the crappy part," Annie noted. "Clothing designers aren't making clothes for outliers."

Jennifer paid in cash, counting out the bills. The change stuffed into her purse, she grabbed the bundle of shopping bags and headed outside. She popped the trunk and put the bags in. "Did you want to get something to eat?" Annie asked. She'd been feeling hungry for the last twenty minutes but hadn't wanted to say anything until the shopping was over.

"Yeah, no problem," Jennifer replied. "How about the Italian place down the street from the comic book shop?"

"Sounds great! I'll meet you there." Annie gave an approving hand wave and headed to her car.

When she saw her friend get in her car and leave, the tall hero opened the trunk again. A quick glance around saw that no one was looking in her specific direction, and the cameras for the lot would not be able to see inside the front of her car. She grabbed a top, some pants, and a bra, and set them in her front passenger seat. Her mother's shoes would work for the time being, so she shut the trunk and got back in her car. Everything froze still around her as she changed clothes in the front seat. Her hands teased her hair into the right formation. Convinced she looked more than acceptable, she drove off towards the Italian restaurant.

"This place always has great pasta," Annie noted, as they sat down and waited to order. "I think their chicken dishes are always great."

"The chicken spiedini is to die for," Jennifer agreed.

"What would you ladies like to drink?" The waiter asked.

"Diet Coke," Jennifer replied.

"Sprite," Annie answered.

As the waiter walked away to get their drinks, Annie briefly looked at her phone. She blinked in surprise. "I didn't know how much of this whole 'super powers are real' thing I believed," she admitted, "but if the government is making statements about it, like they are now, then enough people think it's real that, well, it's *real*." She put her phone away.

"It's different, I'll tell you that," Jennifer replied. "You'd think everyone would start causing mayhem, because, hey, isn't that what movies have always told us?"

Annie leaned her elbows on the table. "Yeah, why do you think that hasn't happened?"

Jennifer gestured outward with her hands. "I dunno. Maybe most people are nervous and the few cocky people who think they're all that aren't strong enough not to get taken down by a small army of cops." Her friend seemed to accept this explanation.

The waiter returned and set down the drinks. "What would you like to order?" he asked.

"Chicken spiedini and a large salad with house dressing," Jennifer ordered.

Annie glanced over the menu. "Tutto mare and a small Caesar salad," she requested.

"I'll have these orders right in!" the waiter exclaimed, then left.

"So," Annie asked, "how did you meet Manny?"

"Well, you know." Jennifer used her enhanced intellect to assemble a believable story as hastily as possible. "I had just arrived in town and I needed a place to stay and he was the only person at the local Wal-Mart who said he would help me and didn't want to hit on me. He said he wanted to help me in whatever way he could."

A surprised look washed over Annie. "I have to admit, I didn't think he had it in him, but hey." She lifted her eyebrows a moment and took a drink. "People can surprise you sometimes."

The redhead couldn't hide her mixture of mild disgust and confusion. "What's wrong with Manny?"

Annie scoffed as she took another drink. "Nothing's wrong with him." She took a moment to assemble her thoughts. "Honestly, he's a good enough guy, it's just that I find him to be a bit...drifty." The look of confusion she got told her to continue. "Well, you know,

Manny is kind of unmotivated. He got a job making minimum wage because he needed to, and now it's been a few years and, what, he makes a few dollars more than he did before?"

"I just don't see why he has to have some grand goal in life."

The chestnut-haired girl let out a chuckle. "Oh, believe me," she replied, "I don't actually mind what he does. It's his life. I just think it's kind of a waste because he could do so much more."

"He might surprise you yet," Jennifer shot back.

"Excuse me," a male voice, possibly late fifties, said.

Both women looked up to see an overweight man, gray strands in sandy hair, standing with a look of apprehension and excitement. Jennifer glanced over at his phone and saw an image of when she pulled the semi out of the river in Kansas. There had been some people and she hadn't gotten away in time. "Yes?" she asked.

"Forgive me if I'm wrong," he began, "but you look just like the woman in this picture. If you are, I just want to thank you for helping out in the wildfires and the traffic that went into the river."

Jennifer's eyes glanced over, and she saw that Annie sat dumbstruck. She could play it off now, but it would seem suspicious. After all, she might have superpowers but acting wasn't one of them. So, a wide smile painted itself on her face. "You're welcome," she said. "Someone's got to do something."

The man gasped in amazement. "That's something, all right," he said. "So you just woke up one day and you could do this stuff?"

Jennifer's eyes drifted upward. "I guess it was the Lights," she offered.

"Wow," the man uttered, entranced. Then he blinked, realizing that his presence began to grow awkward, and he nodded. "Well, I'll leave you to your dinner."

He returned to his seat.

And Annie's amazement had turned into mild suspicion. She cocked her head slightly. "Tell me," she stated, "how does a *literal superhero* come to stay at the house of a guy like Manny?"

Jennifer blinked, head moving back a bit, startled. "What?" she replied. Her eyebrows went higher. "Do you think there's something *going on*?"

This seemed to disarm her friend. "No, not at all, I just find it to be odd." Internally, it *did* cross her mind, but the rational part of her mind argued back that, should this person want to take advantage of people, Manfred Voren wasn't exactly the best target. Nonetheless, something nagged at her and she would take this to Edward and see what he thought.

Jennifer knew she would have to get on top of this. "I'm going to be honest with you." Jennifer then let out a sigh and put out the best lie she could come up with. "I don't trust a lot of people. Manny and I talked, and I trust him."

Annie's hand gripped her chin and mouth in a pondering grasp as she contemplated these statements. After a long minute, her relaxed expression told she'd made a decision. "I guess he is the most reliable guy I know," she told. "So that is like him."

A few minutes later, the waiter arrived and brought several plates. Jennifer had a large salad of various greens and vegetables coated in a rich dressing and sprinkled with parmesan cheese, along with perfectly seasoned chicken over a layer of pasta and sauce. Annie got her small salad and a gorgeous seafood pasta in white sauce, and the waiter grabbed their glasses to top them off.

They ate in relative silence for a few minutes before Annie set her fork down. "Look, if I offended you," she said, "I'm sorry, it's just that, there's been a lot of confusion going on lately."

"It's all right," Jennifer replied. "There is a whole lot of weird stuff going on right now, with people getting powers and all that." It gave her a sense of relief that Annie wasn't pushing this any further. Maybe her friend was coming around. What she didn't think of, mostly because she wasn't used to devious thinking, was that her friend wasn't going to let this go. She had just decided not to make it obvious.

Annie finished her meal a few minutes later. The waiter came by with two checks, and Annie handed over her debit card. As Manny's friend handed over the cash, she couldn't help but continue to be suspicious. If this woman didn't have paperwork, how did she earn the cash? Did she charge the people who she saved for saving them? She blinked; no, best to at least give some benefit of the doubt. Maybe they gave her a reward. Still, why was she driving Manny's car if she could fly? As if by command, the rational side of her mind interjected and she figuratively smacked herself; it was because she needed to take the stuff home without damaging it. Clearly, she decided, she alone didn't have the wherewithal to adequately decide if this made sense by herself, so she would tell Edward, and possibly, John as well. Even though her friend was kind of a pervert, he still had his wits about him almost all the time.

"Hey, thanks for helping me pick out some clothes!" Jennifer exclaimed, heading out to the car.

Annie put on a smile as she got to her car. "Hey, anytime," she replied. "I try to help my friends out."

Jennifer got in her car and drove away. Annie sat down and shut the door. She opened the messaging app and put Edward's cell number in the destination box. "I'd like to ask your advice on something," she wrote.

II.

ANNIE GOT OUT OF HER CAR AT THE GLAMOUR STYLES in the mini mall with the bookstore and the craft store that always smelled like old wood. Her eyebrow curled upward a moment as she saw the leggy, curvy redhead with the granny clothes step out of her friend Manny's car. The woman had Italian eyes and a sculpted Greek statue face with amazing cheekbones. It took her by surprise that such a woman would be with her friend, much less driving his car. She hated being the kind of friend who mocked them behind their back, but this woman *had* to be desperate if she was willing to bang someone like Manny. Not that he was a perv, like John, or a noted womanizer like Jake, but still, Manny seemed like the kind of guy who would date an ordinary looking chick, not this gorgeous model. This person struck Annie as a high-dollar woman, someone easily capable of wooing the richest men, or raking in top billing as a supermodel, not the kind of person who would be dating a guy from the Midwest.

She put on her politeness and approached the absolute museum statue of a woman. "Hey!" she greeted, cheery and polite as she could muster. "You must be Jennifer!" A handshake, basic and formal, she offered. "Wow, you are tall." The living pin-up stood a head and shoulders above her.

A brief instant of embarrassment flitted across Jennifer's face, and Annie just barely noticed it, before the polite calm face returned. "Nice to meet you too, Annie," the woman replied.

Somehow, Jennifer had a look on her face of complete hopelessness at the prospect of picking out a decent looking wardrobe, so Annie picked up on the cue and motioned them in the direction of the inside of the store. "First," she began, leading her by hand gesture towards the lower half section of the store, "let's get you some pants and skirts." With a careful eye, she gave her shopping partner a twice over. The ill-fitting senior citizen clothes did her a disservice but having done wardrobes for all her female cousins for weddings, she knew how to identify body structure through the worst fitting attire. Where she couldn't tell, she would pat the clothes against the skin to get a better idea. She let out an impressed whistle. "You are built like a gymnast or a body builder, you know that?" She paid extreme care to the legs. "Let's see what will fit these tree trunks."

She pushed through the rack of jeans, with a glance sorting out the ones that didn't have enough give. This woman was active, and likely what crappy women's sports magazines called 'sporty.' That meant that she couldn't have pants too tight or she might tear them, because somehow, she didn't imagine this person *not* doing something athletic while wearing casual clothes. She would there-fore have to look at jeans that had enough give as not to tear when running. The first of several good candidates popped up and she pulled them from the rack and handed them to her physically gifted shopping buddy. After a small handful of both blue and black jeans, she moved over to the formal pants, both khakis and similar trousers. Some obvious good choices poked out and she handed them over.

"What about these?"

Annie looked up at Jennifer's question, having been snapped clean out of her shopping reverie. It was clearly not designed for tall women. One strong breeze in the right direction and the surprise was out. She tried to avoid betraying her mental image on her face. "Hmm, might look a bit odd considering how tall you are," she advised. The design certainly was appealing, so it made perfect sense that this woman might want it, but the shortness kept it as a no. Her hand found its way to the part of the skirt rack where the one had been. She scanned through them, looking for one that better fit. She came across one that looked like a mirror inverse of the design, but also longer. "Ah! Try these instead." She handed it over.

Jennifer took her pants and entered the fitting room. Annie stood and waited. The first thing she tried on was the skirt. Sure enough, it looked great on her and it also was long enough. She gave a thumbs-up. Her input had certainly paid off; each time the woman stepped out with a different pair of pants on, it suited her frame perfectly.

"What about tops?" Jennifer asked, placing the pants on the cashier's desk to be held.

Annie stepped back a few feet and positioned her hands to assemble a mock picture frame. She closed one eye and then the other and examined each part of Jennifer's torso. "We have to thread a fine line," she explained, "between looking like you're showing off, and looking like you're wearing a tent."

The tall redhead's face betrayed her confusion, until she thought about it a moment, then got it. She scanned the rack for designs she liked and came across one. "What about this?" she asked.

Annie took one look at it and couldn't hide the cringe in time. That was the kind of outfit that required copious amounts of tape to wear out in public. "If I wore that," she stated, "it would probably be acceptable." She paused a moment to let her words sink in. "If *you* wear that, you will *definitely* be the center of attention."

The woman bore a look of not knowing. Annie almost couldn't believe her eyes. Surely this woman knew better. "Is...that bad?" Jennnifer asked.

Annie stood at a loss for words. "Uh, just try it on," she advised, "and tell me what you think."

The woman looked down, then a moment later, jerked back as if tased. A visible cringe came to her face and she shot out an arm to put it back. "Oh wow," she said, almost laughing. "No. No thank you."

A genuine laugh escaped Annie. "Anyway, try," she began. The rack showed a few different styles of various cuts, patterns, designs, and each one presented a different side of the same person. "Try these." The woman took the five Annie presented her and went into the fitting room once again.

Predictably, each one fit Jennifer quite well. They formed a cohesive outfit, with matching color schemes and designs, and Annie could immediately tell a different version of her shopping partner would be presented with each. Then, came one of the least pleasant moments of any woman's shopping effort. They approached the bra section. Honestly, the straight-haired brunette didn't envy her red-headed ally. Unlike her shopping buddy, she wore the kinds of bras that could be both affordable in price and flexible in design. It didn't break her bank account to have to buy bras. Jennifer, by contrast, did not have the kind of frame that allowed bras to be affordable or varied in neat, stylish designs. Plus, she'd heard from some of her friends in the same bra range that there were multitudes of other problems, ranging from minor to infuriating, that had to be dealt with.

While her ally went off to get professionally sized, she shopped around for clothes for herself. Twenty minutes of looking through various tank tops resulted in two that she could use for various informal get togethers. After she'd picked a handful of tops, her shopping partner approached and had a selection of undergarments Annie felt glad she didn't have to buy and set them on the counter. They held the clothes as she helped her friend to the shoe section. Thankfully, this woman had ordinary feet and the selection process proceeded smoothly and effortlessly. They chose a pair for the typical occasions, and took them to the counter, where the cashier totaled everything up and read out the price.

"The most expensive thing was the bras," Jennifer scoffed, opening her purse, and handing out the bills.

"Yeah," Annie said, "that's the crappy part. Clothing designers aren't making clothes for…" her eyes darted to her fellow shopper's upper torso, and she struggled for a word, "…outliers."

She snapped out of it and noticed the woman was paying with cash, and there was almost two grand in cash in the purse, and yet, the woman was staying with Manny. As the clothes got bagged and the two took their purchases to their vehicles, the need for answers, combined with hunger, got the better of Annie. "Did you want to get something to eat?"

"Yeah, no problem!' Jennifer answered. "How about the Italian place down the street from the comic book shop?"

"Sounds great!" Annie replied, waving as she walked towards her own car. "I'll meet you there." A short drive later, and she arrived at the restaurant. She parked and went inside, reserving a table, and waiting for her acquaintance. She noticed the woman was wearing one of the outfits they'd chosen earlier. Had she changed in the car? That struck her as odd, but she didn't worry about it because it wasn't relevant. They got to their seat and began looking over the menu. "This place always has great pasta. I think their chicken dishes are great."

"The chicken spiedini is to die for," Jennifer said.

The fact that this woman was from out of town but familiar with this restaurant bothered Annie, but at that moment, the waiter arrived.

"What would you ladies like to drink?" he asked.

"Diet Coke," Jennifer said.

Annie looked at the beverage list. "Sprite," she answered. A moment later, as the waiter left, Annie's phone dinged, and she opened the news tab. There had been a report on the Lights, as the media had taken to calling the event, and the government had announced the President would be making a formal statement about the people in the world developing superpowers. "I didn't know how much of the 'superpowers are real' thing I believed, but if the government is making statements about it like they are now, then enough people think it's real that, well, it's real." What was the world coming to? She let out a sigh and put her phone away.

Jennifer shook her head a bit. "It's *different*," she replied, "I'll tell you that. You'd think everyone would start causing mayhem because, hey, isn't that what the movies have always told us?"

Annie rested her arms on the table. That was a good point. Perhaps she had harshly prejudged this woman. "Yeah," she asked, "why do you think that hasn't happened?"

The redhead gave a hand shrug. "I dunno." She paused to think. "Maybe most people are nervous and the few cocky people who think they're all that aren't strong enough *not* to get taken down by a small army of cops."

That startled the brunette. It made sense, and yet, it seemed a bit...what was the word she wanted...naïve? No, she decided, not quite. Perhaps a bit...optimistic. Yes, she realized. That was it.

Almost on cue, the waiter returned, setting down the drinks. He widened his fake smile. "What would you like to order?" he asked, looking at Jennifer first.

The woman closed the menu with a snap. "Chicken spiedini and a large salad with house dressing," she ordered.

That's an awful lot of calories, Annie thought. She made a show of glancing across the menu. "Tutto mare and a small Caesar salad," she stated. The waiter made some statement confirming that he would put the orders in. She felt she had to broach the obvious question. "So, how did you meet Manny?"

"Well," Jennifer said, obviously stalling, "you know." The shorter woman prided herself on her ability to read conversation with people and this woman just threw up red flags every which way. Something about her just bugged her and she didn't know exactly what. The woman recovered in record time, however. "I had just arrived in town and I needed a place to stay and he was the only person at the local Wal-Mart who said he would help me and didn't want to hit on me." The next statement seemed, not out of character for her friend, but rather, not the kind of statement he would give to someone he literally just met at Wal-Mart. "He said he wanted to help me in whatever way he could."

Annie felt her face betray her thoughts, and she immediately told her brain to do damage control. "I have to admit," she said, course correcting. "I didn't think he had it in him, but hey." She paused to take a drink to prevent her voice from cracking. "People can surprise you sometimes."

The statuesque woman responded oddly; she looked offended, at least to a minor degree. "What's wrong with Manny?"

Annie scoffed; the turn had caught her off-guard. "Nothing's *wrong* with him," she pointed out. Her ability to predict the direction of the conversation was dwindling fast. One thing she had to do was get a feel for *why* this woman was bothered by it. "Honestly, he's a good enough guy, it's just that I find him a bit..." she struggled for the right word, "drifty." Now this Jennifer gave a clear tell: she showed a look of confusion. The look that indicated she needed more detail. "Well, you know, Manny is kind of unmotivated. He got a job making minimum wage because he needed to, and now it's been a few years and, what, he makes a few dollars more than he did before?"

"I just don't see why he has to have some grand goal in life," Jennifer said.

Now Annie just *knew* this woman was a creep, stalker, or the like. No one could get this attached this quickly. "Oh, believe me," she replied, playing it cool to keep the conversation in control, "I don't actually mind what he does. It's his life. I just think it's kind of a waste because he could do so much more."

"He might surprise you yet," the redhead answered.

Annie felt like she had a good grasp on the freakish attachment this woman had to Manny, but something happened next that set off alarm bells in her mind. A pudgy, older guy came up to the table, looking a mixture of impressed and nervous, and his phone was at table height, displaying an image of...

Annie's eyes snapped to attention as she recognized this woman as the picture on the phone, the story she'd heard about a hero saving people from the wildfires in California and pulling a series of vehicles out of a flood in Kansas. The fact that this woman could kill everyone here in a blink wasn't her first concern. Her first concern was the fate of her friend. What part did Manny play in all this? Was he still alive? She tried to smash her feelings down and return to calmness so as not to reveal her thought process, but all hopes of that dashed to pieces when Jennifer glanced over and saw her. *Fuck!* She thought.

"You're welcome," Jennifer said, glancing intermittently between Annie and the man. "Someone's got to do something."

The man stood in sheer awe. "That's something, all right," he said. "So you just woke up one day and you could do this stuff?"

"I guess it was the lights," she replied.

The man let out a semiconscious "wow" and then blinked, realizing he was making it weird. "Well, I'll leave you to your dinner." After that, he made his leave.

Annie put on her best unaware face. She cocked her head slightly, trying to put on an air of minor suspicion, yet full awestruck. "Tell me," she said, "how does a *literal superhero* come to stay at the house of a guy like Manny?"

Jennifer blinked, clearly taken aback. "What?" The next expression indicated confusion. "Do you think there's something *going on*?"

Thank Christ, she bought it, Annie thought. She pretended to be disarmed by that. "No," she defended, "not at all. I just find it to be odd." It made no sense, her rational mind argued. There were lots of bigger targets she could go for. Was Annie reading the superhero all wrong? Still, she wasn't going to let this go, and Edward would tell her what he thought.

"I'm going to be honest with you," Jennifer answered. She sighed and seemed upset. "I don't trust a lot of people. Manny and I talked, and I trust him."

Annie rested her chin in her hand, a thinker's pose. This seemed the oddest turn of events. At first, she'd been utterly sold on the notion that this woman was a stalker, absolutely bad news in a lot of different ways. However, Annie felt like she was nothing if not good at detecting people being deceptive in conversation, and this woman oozed sincerity. Either that, or she was such a phenomenal actor that she deserved to go after bigger targets than a guy working minimum wage. She gave up on it for now. "I guess he is the most reliable guy I know," she said, "so that is like him." The meals came a few moments later, and they ate their rich pastas and sumptuous salads. No words were said while foods were savored. "Look, if I offended you, I'm sorry, it's just that, there's been a lot of confusion going on lately." That statement was to test the waters.

A smile and laugh came from Jennifer. "It's all right. There is a whole lot of weird stuff going on right now, with people getting powers and all that."

After they ate, the waiter came by with the checks and they paid. A laundry list of questions shot through Annie's mind again, and she thought about each one. One obvious question came to mind. Why was she driving Manny's car if she could fly?

Because she needed to take it home without damaging it.

God, you're an idiot sometimes, Annie, she thought. The answer seemed so obvious.

"Hey," Jennifer exclaimed, as they headed to their cars. "Thanks for helping me pick out some clothes!"

Annie put on a smile. "Hey, anytime," she said. "I try to help my friends out." After she drove away, she pulled up to a gas station a few miles down the road and texted Edward. "I'd like to ask your advice on something," she wrote. Then she explained everything she knew.

CHAPTER FIVE

THE PRESIDENT OF THE UNITED STATES took the podium. The graying hair around the edges of the black statesman's temple combined with his serious expression broadcast a sense of command and sternness befitting a statement in response to a once-in-a-lifetime event. He placed his hands on the lectern and approached the microphone.

"My fellow Americans," the Commander-in-Chief spoke. He glanced from left to right, taking in the silent sea of journalists hanging on to scrutinize every word that came next. "I have been in close communication with the top scientific minds of the United States of America, as well as the leaders of every field of academia the world over. CERN and NASA have been in nearly constant contact with one another and with my top advisors in their respective fields, and no event has gone unreported or unexamined." He paused for effect and to take a breath. "As best as can be determined, effects similar in appearance to those before seen only in fiction have appeared in the real world. We exhausted every imaginable effort to disprove this as a hoax, to locate potential efforts by terrorist or other nefarious organizations to create distrust and confusion through grand-scale misdirection, or to simply prove a mass hallucination."

He let his words hang in the air for several long moments. "Our efforts have concluded that this is not fake, this is not a hoax, this is what is really happening. People are gaining superpowers functionally similar to those seen in comic books, fantasy novels, and cartoons. Some of them are members of our own Federal Government." A paper got shuffled from the top to underneath the stack on the lectern. "There have been those who have reacted nefariously, who have used their newfound abilities to cause harm. Thankfully, these individuals are in the extreme minority. Furthermore, well-armed law enforcement has proven sufficient to tackle most of these cases. Nonetheless, we are operating under the assumption that, just like in fiction, individuals with powers much greater, possibly those that would prove difficult to contain should they turn rogue, will inevitably appear. Do not be alarmed, as we are acting at this very moment to establish a contingency plan, and we are looking for ways to get those with powers to either agree not to harm others, or to actively use their powers for the benefit of all the people." He shuffled another paper. He also stared directly into the camera. "To those of you who are already utilizing these new powers to save lives, I wish to thank you. To those of you who are finding themselves filled with newfound power, and have no idea what to do, I would implore you to actively choose not to harm your fellow Americans."

He took a deep breath and let it out through his nose. "However, I must also insist that you not act as a vigilante. Law enforcement is designed to be answerable to the people, and we will not tolerate extrajudicial actions. You are not the law, so please do not take it upon yourself to fight crime. You are not trained, and your actions will be treated as criminal. Together, we will move forward as a nation and as a people, and this is an opportunity like no other. We will not rest until we have a firmer understanding of the situation. We will not rest until an answer is able to be provided to Americans by the best minds we have. Thank you."

The questions started, but Manny turned off the television. He had showered, eaten, and dressed. He'd found that he could store not just his body but his entire clothed self, while transformed into Jennifer. This gave him greater security. It meant he could transform and blend into a crowd. The next thing he did was take a risk; he called in to the warehouse and quit his job. It could be a mistake, and his heart was pounding the whole time. Nevertheless, being able to turn into Jennifer meant he could get money easily if he could. Hell, if nothing else, there were probably rich people who would be more than happy to receive protection.

He shifted into Jennifer's form. She turned on her phone and started scanning for problems. The news mentioned a breaking story. A major dam had failed in China. A lake had emptied into what was effectively farmland. That, combined with the population density of the area, meant some thousands of people could drown. She set the phone down and headed for the door.

Out the door, she froze where she stood. Ed's car was parked in the driveway, and he sat there with Annie and John.

He had his gun in his jacket pocket.

God dammit, Annie, she thought.

"Hi there, Jennifer," Edward said, a thin veneer of politeness over a nervous fear. "Do you mind letting us talk to Manny?" Ed felt close to soiling himself. He'd seen the scant video footage of the few incidents she'd been confirmed to have been at, but thanks to Annie, he knew who she was. Thankfully, he'd had the sense not to tell anyone, and no one outside this trio knew.

Jennifer stood there, inches away from wanting to scream. Her entire strategy had fallen apart. "In the house," she said, pointing.

As Ed headed towards the house, he kept facing her the whole time, hand in his jacket pocket. They ascended the three steps and entered the house, sitting on the couch.

Jennifer stood in front of them, hands on hips. "Unbelievable," she said. "So much for secrets."

Ed, to his credit, was not the kind of person who would back down in the face of a friend being in danger. It gave Jennifer a sense of pride that she knew he would fight against what he thought was his friend in danger. The fact that the tall black man had driven across town to be here with his gun in the car proved his devotion. In the age of racist cops, one false traffic stop could have been a serious tragedy. It put a smile on her face even as she was worried about him.

"Look, we're just worried about our friend," Ed explained. "It doesn't make logical sense that he would give you his money to spend on clothes." He nervously scratched his short, stubby hair.

"And if it was your money," Annie continued, "why didn't you stay at a hotel?"

"I know you can probably kill us right now," Ed said, swallowing, "but we're not going to…"

Jennifer shifted back into Manny.

No one could speak for several long moments.

"This is why I wanted to keep it a fucking secret," Manny said, gesturing aggressively.

"What the fuck?" Edward said, putting thoughts into words.

"Hold that thought," Manny said. "I've got an actual crisis to deal with." He shifted back into Jennifer and took off. The discussion had to wait. People were drowning. In a heartbeat, she made it up to the stratosphere. A glance gave her a destination and she took off like a rocket.

On an elevated roadway above the flooding plain, emergency crews and military officials watched as makeshift levees failed and a giant wall of churning water smashed through houses and carried away bridges, cars, and other debris. A blurry pulse-like object zoomed down from the sky like a comet and flashed through the villages in the path of the water in an instant. On a higher point several miles behind the roadway, a crowd of people materialized, startled, and bewildered, but otherwise okay. News cameras caught a lone glimpse of a red-haired white woman for just a moment, before she disappeared again.

Jennifer paused for just an instant to scan the massive surge of water with her vision powers and energy sensing, before taking off like a particle beam into the water. Her arms latched around three people at a time, and her otherworldly power flowed into them, protecting them from the laws of physics while she flew them away from the water like a bullet.

The hill on which the road stretched out provided plenty of open space between groups of emergency vehicles to deposit people. Jennifer decided these were the best spots to put people because of the immediate access to medical experts. Plenty of ambulances dotted the road in expectation of the survivors emerging from the water. The otherworldly power that surrounded her body shifted with her mental effort. When she emerged into air, it filtered out solid particulates so she wouldn't fly into insects or other small airborne objects at supersonic velocities. In water, it prevented her body from being harmed by the fluid, rendered objects close to her body hydrophobic, and made her travel through it sleeker, as if moving through the air. It allowed her to rush up to people in the water without crushing them with a sudden current.

The rescue workers on the high ground saw a huge collection of victims materialize out of thin air around them. A bedlam ensued, with initial shock and shouts giving way to rescue workers madly rushing, sprinting back and forth to save the nearest victims. Some of them had already swallowed enough water that they choked to death less than a minute later. A hasty count and she recognized that some nine hundred living people lined the roadway from beginning to end. Rescue workers began moving the dead out of the way to move the survivors closer to help. She shot back into the water and opened her vision and energy sensing powers as far as they would go. Post-human senses scanned for signs of active nervous systems, heat signatures from survivors, and movement from struggling survivors. They stretched out for tens of kilometers. Her energy senses told her most of them were corpses. A few hadn't been dead very long and might yet be saved. She rocketed towards them and scooped them up, three or even four at a time in her arms.

An ambulance crew who had treated a family of five, the survivors seated near an ambulance, looked up to see a figure hovering near them. The redheaded woman set down some people blue in the face and water pouring from the mouth. Their initial confusion gave way to shock as they looked to her left and saw a dozen more in the same condition. A shout she didn't understand drew more medical staff. An angry shout in either Cantonese or Mandarin, from a powerful, elderly voice sounded near her.

"Excuse me!"

A young man's shout in English caught her attention.

She turned her body. A graying officer, wearing an obviously important uniform and hat stood, lines of age and sternness on his face. Arms were folded. Next to him, a younger man with a subordinate uniform and no hat stood, arms clasped together in front of his abdomen. Only apprehension and a desire not to be punished lined his face. "Yes?" Jennifer replied.

The young military man stood, awed by the powerful woman hovering a foot off the ground less than a car's distance from him. Her clothes, two layers of black yoga pants, and an orange, short-sleeved t-shirt, tight against her skin—so as not to catch wind during flight, he guessed—dripped water but looked very dry. Her wet hair, past shoulder length and tomato red, sticking to her skin, dried out as water poured from it and pulled away from her skin to return to normal. She looked the image of divinity to him, her arms not rounded and bulky but still presenting the image of muscularity, and her weightlifter thighs pressing outward against fabric. In between the two, an abdomen thin but not skinny, probably possessing chiseled definition, he thought, though he could not tell through the shirt. He swallowed to dampen his fear. "My commander requests that you leave," he relayed in English.

The woman looked at the old man, and back at him, a look of concerned consternation. "I've been doing nothing but helping!" she pleaded.

The young man relayed this to his commander. The senior officer pointed at her and said something aggressive. He turned to the woman. "He says now that you've saved lives," he explained to her, "You are not likely to save any more lives, so leave before an incident is created."

"This is absurd!" she cried. She saw something out of the corner of her eye, and gestured. "See! Some of the ones I thought were dead are coming to!" A few of the drowned had started coughing up water and breathing again.

The commander said something, and his younger officer turned from one to the other. "It comes from above," he told her. "Higher officials do not like China looking bad. Please leave."

Without a word, she was gone.

Jennifer flew back home, tears streaking across her face and vanishing into the wind. A storm of emotions raced back and forth, the excited pleasure of seeing the happiness on the faces of those realizing they would live, comingling with the horror and sorrow of seeing those too far gone to be saved, even with her great speed.

She pushed through the door and collapsed into a loveseat.

"Oh my god," John said, motioning to the television. "You saved all those..." He paused because he noticed she looked lost. "What's wrong?"

"It's weird, you know?" Jennifer asked, turning her head to face the group and wiping her eye with a thumb. "I'm happy and sad at the same time and," she clenched and released a fist, "really *fucking frustrated* at bureaucracy." She sighed.

"If it makes you feel better," Annie said, "we're all really sorry for jumping to conclusions about you."

Jennifer literally waved it off. "Ah, no problem," she replied. "I'm the idiot who couldn't read a conversation."

"So," John said, broaching the subject, "you're Manny...and Jennifer? At the same time? Or does one go to sleep?" A thought occurred to him. "Wait a second. What are your powers?"

Focusing on something else got her out of her funk, or at least, distracted her from it. It put a veneer over it, she guessed. "Energy manipulation, flight, strength, speed, durability, enhanced intelligence, self-sustenance," she rattled off.

"Red hair," Ed said, the gears turning in his head. "and that power set." His eyes went wide. "You're the Capacitor!"

A confused glance between John and Ed saw them arrive at the same realization. "Wait," Edward cut in, "I thought the character's name was Michelle De Lanter."

John switched his glance from his black friend to Jennifer. "Also, I thought the character's boobs were smaller." Ed smacked him in the arm for this.

A laugh escaped her mouth. "They would be," Jennifer corrected, "if I ate *nothing*." She looked at her friends. "You might find this odd, but when I could transform my body, I could transform *parts* of my body. I gave her most of my body fat..." She realized something. "Oh, I'm going to talk about me in this form as a separate person just so it's easier. Okay?" They nodded. "Anyway, I gave her most of my body fat so my mom's clothes from before would fit." She shrugged. "Then her post-human metabolism burned most of the fat away in a couple days, I guess treating it like some kind of impurity to be removed."

"Right," Annie cut in, "because her body is constantly regenerating away problems." She'd jumped ahead in her train of thought and returned. "Wait, so are you Manny or what? If you can change parts of your body, can you have powers in your male form?"

"No Jekyll and Hyde," Jennifer reiterated. She paused to collect her words. "I'm one consciousness, one person. It's just that when I'm her, she's smarter than me in my male form, and also she has a female gender identity. That means that, yes, I can have powers in my male form, but that would cause dysphoria, so that's a no-no for me."

They seemed to accept this. "Hey," Ed said, "I have a thought."

Jennifer turned to him. "Shoot," she replied.

"If you keep taking off from here, won't that lead people to here?"

His question hit her like a gut punch. "I hadn't thought of that," she said.

"You ought to drive somewhere and go into like, a bathroom or something, and transform," John said, "and that way, you can speed out of there and no one will see you. "

Annie snapped her fingers and pointed for effect. "Yeah!" she agreed. "That way, people will see Manny leaving and coming back, and they won't have any recourse to suspect you!"

"What if the Feds find out?" Ed cut in. "Like, they can dedicate entire teams of people to search through hundreds of hours of parking lot footage."

Jennifer pondered this important point. A thought came to her. "What are the Feds afraid of?" she asked.

Edward and Annie exchanged shifting glances as if this were a trick question on a test. "Uh," Annie finally said, "they're afraid of things they can't control?"

"Right!" Jennifer said. "They're also afraid of secrecy and if they catch me being shifty, their suspicion might lead to bad things." She paused to think about it a moment. "Let's say they see me drive to a parking lot as Manny and leave as Manny. Let's say they somehow prove it was to do exactly what you said. What can I say?

I can say, 'hey, I wasn't trying to be nefarious.' It's better than being all secretive."

"That might be true," John interjected, "but do you think they'll buy it?"

"Hey," Jennifer shot back, "I don't know if they'll buy it, but I know that if I'm going to have a life as Jennifer, I'm going to *need* to *deal* with the federal government at some point."

"Yeah, that's right," Annie agreed.

"Hey," Ed said, "I know it's probably really tacky of me to say this, but..." He shuffled his feet nervously. "Do you think you could show us your powers? Like, in person?"

"Edward!" Annie chastised.

"No, it's alright," Jennifer replied, blinking her eyes dry. "It gives me something else to think about." She paused. "What about that big park in Fairview Heights?"

"Longacre?" John recalled.

"That's the one," Annie said.

"See you there," Jennifer said. "I'll meet you there." A thought came to her. "Oh, and Ed? Leave the gun here in case you get pulled over."

He laughed and pulled it out of his jacket pocket, placing it on the table. "Yeah, that was dumb of me," he said. "You know how cops are about black people this day in age."

"I'll take it to your house later this evening," she said. They filed out of the house and into Ed's car. It would be a half-hour drive to Fairview Heights, Illinois, so Jennifer waited a few minutes, resting and stretching her legs as she reclined. In all the mental turmoil of being responsible for human lives, she'd forgotten that the reason she'd longed to have superpowers was because having powers, ultimately, was *fun*. Sure, she would never forget the faces of those she couldn't save but being even partially human meant that per-fection was an impossible standard. Flying still gave her a rush like no other, and the surge of empowerment she felt when lifting things impossible by her male, normal human self had no peer.

She stood up and turned into Manny. He locked the door and got in his car and drove to the Wood River McDonalds. He parked, and went into the men's bathroom, getting into the stall. He didn't need to lock it, as he shifted into Jennifer, his male self and keys vanishing. Speed powers active, the world froze around her, and she zoomed out of there. Forty-something miles vanished in a blink, her seeing and processing every step at unimaginable rates of brain power. Finally, she took her last step and came to a stop in one of the more wooded corners of the ninety-nine-acre public park.

Her friends' car arrived about ten minutes later. She walked out to greet them arms extended outward.

"Nice to see you waited for us," Annie quipped.

Jennifer looked around with super senses and saw no one looking in her direction. She gestured for them to huddle together, and when they did, she wrapped her arms around the three of them. From their point of view, one instant they huddled together for her to grab them all at once, and the next instant, they arrived at an opposite end of the park.

"Whoa," John said, throwing out his arms to stabilize himself. "I don't think I'm getting used to that."

"Wait," Annie cut in, "I took physics freshman year of college. Our brains aren't connected to our skull. How come you didn't just kill us from whiplash?"

"My power protects you while I or something I'm touching is touching you," Jennifer explained. "Because I want that to happen." She shrugged. "I don't get all the intricacies of it either." She looked for an example. She saw a log roughly ten feet long and two feet thick. "Watch." A short stroll later and she wrapped her right hand around it. As she squeezed, fingers dug into the wood, crunching through bark. Once she had a firm grip, she raised her right arm. The log went up to waist height. "Tell me what's wrong with this picture."

"You're not on concrete," John noticed, "you're standing on grass. That log is huge. Why aren't you sinking?"

Ed's head whirled to his friend. "Right!" He exclaimed. "The log should be pushing down on you!"

Annie placed a hand over her mouth and chin, thinking. A moment passed. "Also," she noted, pointing, "you're putting a lot of force into that little area of the log you're grabbing. How come it doesn't break off?"

"That's the problem comics never address," Jennifer said. "How can Superman pick up a building? It *should* be like lifting a Jell-O mold the size of a beach ball with a safety pin." She reached out with her other hand and poked a finger into the log. Bark cracked and wood crunched as she stuck the finger deeper. She pulled it out, revealing the hole. "Somehow my power responds based on what I want it to do."

"Maybe it's a psychic power," Annie thought out loud, "some form of tactile telekinesis, where you have to be touching it but it's obviously not just strength."

"Could be," Jennifer agreed.

"Didn't Superboy in some of the comics have tactile telekinesis?" John said.

"But he could disassemble things just by touching them," Jennifer stated, "I can't do that."

"Still useful as-is though," Edward thought out loud.

"Yes," Jennifer agreed, nodding. "Very, very useful." She set the log down gently so as not to get dirt on anyone.

"How does the speed work?" Ed asked. "I always thought of it like slow motion, but then everything would take forever."

"No," Jennifer said. "I have two separate speed powers. One is like you said, everything is frozen around me, so maybe it's some kind of time manipulation or something, I don't know, but the other is actual hyper velocity."

"So," Annie cut in, "that's another problem the comics never address. Do you have problems with bugs flying into you? Or breathing at hyper speed?"

"I don't *have* to breathe," Jennifer said, "it's just nice to be able to. Also, my power takes care of that for me, and the running into things at high speed issue too." She shrugged. "I've been focusing on these things and it's still a bit of a mystery."

"So," John said, trying to wrap his mind around it, "your power just...moves them out of the way?"

"There's a field around my body," Jennifer explained, "that changes depending on what environment I'm in. When I'm moving so very fast, it moves the air out of my way so I don't kill people I'm running past, and it makes it so I don't create a sonic boom that breaks everything around me." She vanished and reappeared several yards to the right. "Anyone feel that?" They shook their heads. "Yeah, that's what it does."

"Amazing," Ed said.

"Oh," Jennifer said, realizing she missed a point. "Energy manipulation. I believe my super seeing and hearing is an offshoot of that. I can sense different kinds of energy if I focus hard enough. Electricity, heat, so on, and I can emit different kinds." She held up two fingers in the shape of a 'V' and with a thought, electricity arced between them. She pointed a finger at the log and a bright beam of light shot out, catching the dry wood on fire. As it spread to the size of a dinner plate, she waved her hand and the fire slowly died. "I didn't figure all that out until after the wildfires. This whole thing's a learn-as-you-go experience."

"It's crazy," Annie said. "And to think there are still lots of others out there with powers."

"I'm not looking forward to having to fight lunatics with powers," Jennifer admitted, "but honestly, it's only a matter of time."

"Still," John said, "it's good that so many people are too nervous to go out there and fuck things up for the sake of it."

"Did they say how many people have powers?" Ed asked.

"I heard the news reported that New York City had offered a cash prize to those coming forward," Annie said. "So far, I believe, three thousand people had demonstrated they had actual powers from the Lights."

"Let's say that's about fifty percent less than the actual number," Jennifer said, "just to be safe. There's eight million people in New York City, just to use a nice round number, and four thousand five hundred actual people with powers."

Ed lowered his eyebrows in confusion. "Why?" he asked.

Jennifer shrugged. "Just quick math," she argued. "We might be wrong, but let's just ballpark it." He nodded and accepted this. "Okay, so forty-five hundred actual people in NYC with powers, out of a population of eight million. World population?"

Annie pulled out her phone. "Seven point three seven..." she said, rounding up. "Seven point four billion, roughly."

"So," Jennifer said, "that means that five point six two five times ten to the negative fourth power percent of the population has abilities, roughly speaking. Assuming New York City isn't a special cluster of powered people, that means that out of a world population of seven point four billion people, four million, one hundred sixty-two thousand, five hundred people have powers."

Everyone digested the information. "Roughly estimating, of course," Annie said, qualifying the statement.

Jennifer nodded. "Yes," she agreed. "*very* roughly estimating. And we might be wrong, but I think it's a decent assumption."

"Yeah," John said. "After all, I don't think it'd be this peaceful if a decent-sized chunk of the population had powers."

"I think you're right," Jennifer agreed. "If, let's say, five percent of the population had powers, that'd mean that three hundred seventy million people worldwide would have powers, and I doubt things would be this peaceful almost a week and a half out from the Lights." She looked around. "Fair?"

"Yeah," Annie said, recalling what she heard on the news. "Other than a small women's uprising in Saudi Arabia, there hasn't been much in the way of big stuff."

Jennifer rolled her shoulders, breathing in and out, calming herself from this train of thought. "Well," she said, "that's enough serious implications for one day. Is anyone else hungry?"

CHAPTER SIX

I.

MULTIPLE FILE FOLDERS LAY SCATTERED ACROSS A DESK. In an open air office floor, surrounded by filing cabinets and ten year out of date computers, Davis Wilson sat, analyzing photos and travel reports of multiple persons of interest, and beneath these photos and reports sat extensive bios, assembled out of the best data available to the Federal Bureau of Investigation.

The agent wiped his brow and took a drink from his water bottle. Ever since the President had ordered a special FBI task force on superpowered individuals, the man, weeks away from his thirty-nineth birthday, had sweat his way through sixteen-hour workdays. He'd been running on a cocktail of black coffee and Advil for the better part of two weeks. The gel insoles in his dress shoes had worn out from all the walking he had to do moving between offices and communicating important information to persons of interest higher on the federal food chain than he, because people of certain security clearances didn't talk over the telephone or by computer. He probably knew more about certain individuals he'd been looking into over the past several days than his own mother.

He let out a sigh and brushed his rust-colored hair out of his eyes. Normally, haircuts were a twice a month affair, but he hadn't gotten his hair trimmed in almost a fortnight because he'd get home, his wife would feed him, and then he'd collapse into his bed. More than once he'd had to get up at three in the morning because the office called with urgent information.

"Wilson!"

Davis looked up at the gravel road of a voice he knew too well. Sam Louis, his section chief, and the official commander of the task force on supers, approached and placed a palm on his subordinate's desk. "Sir?" Davis asked, tempering his tired voice with politeness.

"Did you finish gathering intel on the two primary cases?" Sam asked.

"Yeah," Davis said, handing over a manilla folder. "This guy's been the busiest of them all." His supervisor flipped open the pages, revealing a long list. "Jericho Wilhelm Torvalds. President and founder of Firestorm Investments, personal net worth of eight point six billion dollars, four billion of which is in liquid assets, thirty-two years old."

"Christ," Sam scoffed, going over the travel report. "This guy's been on the move."

Davis nodded. "Before the lights," he explained, "fairly ordinary travel pattern. Destinations largely line up with meeting important heads of corporations, financial firms, and other bigwigs of industry. After the lights, he goes globe-hopping." He started counting on his hands. "Georgia. Los Angeles. Chicago. Montana. Mexico City. Orlando, Florida. All in the span of two weeks."

Sam read the report. His eyebrows raised. "He set up investments to pay dividends to people?" he asked. He flipped a page. "What did he ask for in return?"

"That's the weird thing," Davis replied. "We got one of these individuals to contact us and he said all the guy wanted in exchange for the money—which is a decent chunk of change, let me tell you—was to shake his hand." He reached over and pointed to an item on the next page. "He said Jericho Torvalds wanted to copy his power."

Sam looked up from the folder. "So, you can confirm we have power consolidation?"

Davis nodded. "Yup," he admitted. "So far, these people do not appear to be coerced, attacked, threatened, or in any way held under blackmail. It appears to be a case of a guy collecting powers for...well, we don't know."

Sam finished the information packet. "Right," he said. "Johnson is going to be further investigating Torvalds. What can you tell me about the girl?"

Davis leaned back in his seat, his fingers drumming against each other while cupped. Sam was about to say something, when he handed his superior a collection of pictures. "We were lucky in one regard," he explained to Sam, "in that we got some very good clear pictures, which is rare for amateurs." He took a breath, held it a moment, and let it out.

Sam looked at the pictures. Some clear, some exceptional, given they came from cell phone cameras. "So," he inquired, "who is she?"

Davis pressed his lips firmly together and opened, making a pop sound. He gave his superior a dead-serious stare. "No one," he said.

Sam's head jerked in surprise. "*Really.*"

The junior agent blinked. "Fingerprints left behind?" He shook his head. "No record. No blood or tissue sample, because...*obviously*. Oh! We got a hair sample for DNA. Guess what? *Nothing.*" A single gasp of a laugh escaped. "Every avenue of data has been explored. This person did not exist prior to the Lights. They materialized out of thin air."

"That's impossible," Sam stated. "Either way, you don't believe that."

"No, sir," Davis answered, "I don't."

"Does this look like anyone in particular?" Sam said, grasping.

Davis pulled up his phone. He displayed a Wikipedia page for a superhero. "Based solely on the powerset," he said, "I'd say this person is incredibly similar to the Capacitor, from Furious Comics. Anyway, I don't believe in coincidences like this."

The senior agent thought it over. "So, honestly," he said, "what's your analysis?" The lines on Sam's face told the story of years of stress from investigating and pursuing all manner of crimes and suspicious actions. He'd seen decades of the worst people had to offer. His unkempt white hair spoke volumes. "That look says you think something."

Davis leaned back. "I believe this is either a disguise," he thought out loud, "or else someone physically transformed into a fictional character." He headed the next question off at the pass. "The reason why I don't think this is just some redhead given powers is how specific those powers are."

Sam folded his arms. "What do you mean?"

"Well," Davis continued, "during the Kansas floods, this person was seen affecting downed power lines to prevent people from being electrocuted. Furthermore, during the wildfires, some of the firemen said they saw heat and flame draw away from the people while she held them. That's energy manipulation."

"And," Sam said, reading from the phone, "Capacitor's powers are strength, speed, flight, durability, super senses, and energy manipulation."

"Hence," Davis added, "the name. The character is a tall redhead. This person is a tall redhead with the same powers. The odds of it being unrelated must be astronomical."

"So," Sam said, "you're going to be investigating her."

"What's next, boss?" Davis asked.

"The only lead we have," Sam said, putting a new sheet down on his subordinate's desk, "is the southern Illinois area. Her actions take her to places where known disasters were being displayed, including the incident in China where she saved almost a thousand people, but she always seems to be coming back to within a half-hour's drive of Madison County, Illinois."

Davis perked up. "Really?"

Sam nodded. "Eleven sightings," he said. The look on his subordinate's face told him the gears were turning. "You'll fly out to Saint Louis tomorrow and you'll be set up with the local office to investigate. Your orders are to either gather intel on the individual, or, if possible, get them to make contact."

"Alright," he replied. "I'll get on it." He got up from his desk.

"Dave," Sam said.

Davis wiped his brow. "Yes, sir?"

The old man wore a look of genuine concern. "I've dealt with the worst of the mob," he explained. "Thirty-eight years dealing with shit, and this is brand new. You're the one who grew up with comics. What's your take on this whole 'superpowers' thing?"

He leaned on his desk. "Honestly, sir?" he asked. He shrugged. "I don't know. We've had it good. Most people with powers haven't done much. I don't know if it's fear holding them back, and they'll eventually start wanting to show off, or if this is just the calm before the storm and once everyone who has powers knows how to use them, everything goes to hell. I don't have a clue."

Sam pondered this. "Don't most comics have a supervillain?"

"Yeah," Davis replied. "And that's what really scares me."

"Yeah, me too," Sam agreed. "Go get some rest. You've done a hell of a job so far."

The car door and Davis almost collapsed into his driver's seat. He plugged his cell phone in to charge and set the Bluetooth to play anime themes. It allowed him to reminisce to the days of college where he got to party, watch cartoons, read comics, and study for tests. Even at his very adult age he couldn't help feeling over-whelmed by the responsibility sometimes. A tired hand pulled the ID badge off his suit jacket and set it on the passenger seat next to his phone and firearm.

"Hey! You're back before nine p.m.!"

He smiled at his wife Yvonne's open arms and cheerful greeting. "Yeah, it's a miracle," he said. They gripped each other for dear life, and he rested his head next to hers on her shoulders. "God, I love you."

"I love you too," she replied. She pulled back. "So, why did Sam let you go early?"

"I got a project," he explained. "Tomorrow I fly out to Saint Louis."

"Saint Louis?" Yvonne asked.

"Lookup 'Capacitor look-alike' on the internet," Davis told her, stumbling to the kitchen and melting into the seat.

She put a dish in front of him. "It's still hot," she said. "Lasagna. Your favorite."

He poked some of the cheddar-covered broccoli with his fork and ate it. "Great," he mumbled, in between bites. "These mashed potatoes are great too."

"Wow," Yvonne said, reading the articles. "This is like a dead-on."

"That's what I told Sam," Davis replied. He took a bite of the lasa-gna. "Oh god, this is fan-freaking-tastic."

"So," she said, "this person gets superpowers, and decides the first thing they're going to do is save lives?" She chuckled. "What a terrible person."

Davis rolled his eyes. "You know," he said. "Typical government bullshit. She's just the biggest target. I mean, look at what she can do."

"Do you think she's dangerous?"

The agent looked at his wife. "Honestly? No," he admitted. "I may not believe in pure good and evil, but this person could do almost anything, and they didn't." He took a drink of his cola. "But I have the unenviable task of either spying on them or getting them to come in. Neither one is a particularly great prospect."

"I love you," Yvonne said, reaching out and taking his free hand. "I want you to know that again."

"I love you too," he agreed. "Don't worry. Don't jinx it."

After he ate, she took his plate and he went into the living room to read comics on his laptop. He had research to do, and his wife understood. "After this," she said, reading on her Kindle, "can we take a vacation?"

"After this," he said, looking up, "we're going to take one hell of a vacation."

II.

BRIGHT AND EARLY, Davis got on his flight to Saint Louis. He took a nap on the flight and when he touched down, he got off the plane and called the branch office. "Hi," he began. "Yeah, this is Agent Wilson."

"Acknowledged, Agent Wilson," the liaison said. "Agent Jackson will be there to pick you up."

"Got it," Davis said, hanging up. He walked over to the entrance to baggage claim and saw a man in a suit holding up a sign. He waved.

"Agent Theodore Jackson," Jackson said, extending his hand.

"Agent Davis Wilson," Davis replied, shaking.

Jackson gestured towards the carousel and Davis stood nearby and grabbed his bags when they came down. They left the airport and Davis put his luggage in the trunk of the Ford Crown Victoria parked near the front of the lot. "We've been briefed on the situation,"

Jackson explained, "and you're being given free reign to run this how you like. What do you require?"

"I'm honestly not suspecting her of being a killer," Davis explained. "So, I'd like to avoid treating her like a terrorism suspect. Just me, running this out of a motel room." He nodded. "I've done it this way before."

"That's right!" Jackson remembered, getting behind the wheel. "You did figure out where the gang was running the cartel's drugs down in Florida, didn't you?"

Davis shot him a look. "You heard about that?"

Jackson laughed. "We didn't stop hearing about it for months," he replied. "Brass kept wanting to reward you for it."

Davis buckled his safety belt. "Well, don't lose your mind about it," he shot back. "It's not that big a deal."

"I've been reading up on this woman," Jackson said. He shook his head. "It's something else, I tell ya. She's survived extreme heat, flood water, sharp objects moving fast, it's just like the comic books."

"Yeah," Davis agreed. "Except for, you know, she's not wearing a costume."

"Hmm? What do you mean?" Jackson shot him a confused glance.

Davis shrugged with his hands. "You know," he answered, "you can walk into Wal-Mart and get what she's wearing off the discount rack for thirty bucks for the whole outfit. Cheap t-shirts, yoga pants, and rain boots."

Jackson chuckled. "I guess she's cheap," he said.

After twenty-seven minutes of driving, they arrived at a motel in Collinsville, Illinois. They pulled up to the back, and Jackson reached into the glove compartment and handed a room key to Davis. They got out and Davis loaded his luggage into the room. The agency had already outfitted the room with a secure phone line as well as video equipment, and a couple firearms.

"So," Davis chimed in, "who do I call?"

"Me," Jackson replied. He handed a card with a handwritten number on it. "Just gimme a call and I'll give you anything you need."

Davis looked under the entertainment center and saw the room had a mini-fridge. "I'm going to need an extra TV and VCR," he explained, "as well as a vehicle."

"No prob," Jackson said. He pulled out his cell phone and dialed. "Yeah?" he began. "This is Agent Jackson. I'm setting up Agent Wilson at the motel room. He says he needs a car and an extra TV and VCR. Okay, no problem." He hung up. He tossed the keys to Davis. "Take the car. I'll ride back with the agents in the equipment van."

"Thanks," Davis said, sitting down on the bed.

"So," Jackson said, "you've read comics, right? What's your take on this?"

"I honestly think that some major villain's coming soon," Davis explained. "Most people with powers are small fry, but there's always one big bad in these stories."

"Do you think everything will be alright?"

"Honestly?" Davis answered. "I don't know. I think it depends on how much we're able to set aside our crap and work together." He pondered further. "Villains in the comics love to divide heroes against each other."

"That sucks," Jackson shot back. "We're not good at that."

"I don't know," Davis countered. "We're bad at it until suddenly we're really good at it. It all depends."

A short while later, there was a knock at the door. Jackson opened the door and three guys brought in a television stand, a second television, and another VCR. They set it up and brought in spare cables and power adapters. "I'll be one phone call away if you need anything else," Jackson said, walking out the door.

Davis sat in silence for a few minutes before he got into the car and drove to the local Wal-Mart and picked up a footlong three-meat footlong deli sandwich and a twelve pack of iced coffee. Then, after returning to the car, he pulled up his map of the sightings. One of them wasn't too far from where he was, so he pounded an ice coffee and drove on.

"Excuse me, miss," he said, approaching the courtesy counter of a Schnucks. "I need to see your surveillance tapes." He flashed his FBI badge.

The middle-aged woman regarded him with indifference until she saw the ID. "Oh!" she exclaimed. "Right this way, sir!"

They entered a small room with four video monitors and two separate video recorders. "Oh, hello!" A man, early fifties, said, startled. "Can I help you?"

"Stevens?" the woman explained. "This is Agent Davis Wilson. He needs to see the security tapes."

"I'm investigating sightings and appearances of the super-powered woman," Davis stated. "I need to see the tape that includes immediately before and shortly after her arrival."

The man nodded. "Sure thing!" he cheerily explained. He reached into a cabinet and pulled out a tape in a plastic case with the date written in Sharpie on the front. "This is the one."

Davis took it. "Thank you very much," he said. "Were there any other dates?"

The man pondered it. "No," he said, "just the one."

On the way out, he bought a bag of sour cream and onion chips and some spare notebooks and pens. He set them next to the food in his front seat and checked the next nearest destination. He repeated this process, checking out each location, and retrieving the relevant surveillance tapes, until he had all the tapes in his passenger seat, eleven in total. He made his way back to the motel and set everything up in his room.

Alright, assumptions, he thought. *Let's assume she doesn't wait around for an hour; she leaves right away.* This assumption made sense to him because, rationally speaking, if she was someone else in disguise, they had a life of their own and waiting around made it more difficult to plan. He popped the first tape in and fast-forwarded to the part where the camera clearly picked up the would-be Capacitor descending from the sky into the rear left area of the parking lot. A moment after touching down, she vanished. Super speed, no doubt, he figured. He paused.

He grabbed a notebook and pen and began jotting down license plates and make & model information of every vehicle that left the lot. "Okay," he said to himself, "next assumption." He would assume this person drove to the place and alone. It didn't make sense to him that someone who intended to be a hero would involve others in their activities. After thirty minutes of video, he stopped it and put on the next one.

Midway through the next video, he ate his deli sandwich with one hand and wrote information with the other. Five hours passed with him filling up almost a full notebook with vehicle information. He stretched and walked around to ward off weariness. He'd completed half the tapes. The laptop opened Excel and he began typing license plates into it, one column for each video. After setting it to compare the lists, he noticed that, out of the six videos he'd completed so far, there were eight vehicles in common leaving the first two places.

However, there were only two that had left all six.

"I'm almost there," he said to no one in particular. He opened a new notebook and wrote down the two license plates, and the vehicle make and model next to each one. Then, he went back to each video tape he'd looked at. Of the two, one of them had no consistent pattern. That vehicle left at random intervals. The other, however, a beige Toyota Corolla, at least ten or so years old, with a dent in the trunk, he noted had a much more consistent pattern. Within about three to five minutes after the woman touched down and disappeared, a man would emerge from the place of business and enter the vehicle. He checked through the other five tapes. Each time, this man walked to the same vehicle, within a short period of time of the woman's arrival.

"Agent Jackson," he said, after the phone picked up. "This is Davis Wilson."

"Agent Wilson," Jackson acknowledged. "Nice to hear from you. Honestly, there was a bet as to whether or not you'd have some kind of major result in the first day. Guess I lost. What do you need?"

"I need you to email me vehicle information on a Toyota Corolla," he stated, "Illinois license plate number 'alpha-kilo-six-eight-two-Charlie-nine-zeta,' and its owner." He thought about it. "And also, a Honda Civic, Illinois license plate number 'beta-seven-five-x-ray-delta-Romeo-three.'"

"Gotcha," Jackson shot back. "Anything else?"

"Not right now," Davis advised. "Keep you posted."

"Got it." Jackson hung up.

Davis checked his email and saw in his secure inbox two separate detail sheets for his only two main suspects. The second one, he kept around for completeness sake. The first one, however, saw a man whose driver's license photo seemed somewhat different from the surveillance image. *You've lost weight, Manfred Voren,* Davis thought to himself. If this man was in fact capable of transforming into a female superhero, that might explain the sudden loss of more than a hundred pounds of body fat.

"Manfred Edward Voren," Davis read. The sheet read like a straightforward account of poverty and midwestern struggle. The father, a Reichard Voren, son of German immigrants, often struggled to find work based on the extensive work history with the varied work lengths. It struck him as strange. The father was a welder; that seemed like a job often in demand. The mother, Paula, often had to support their family on her nursing income alone. The man didn't have a criminal record, nor did his parents, so the likelihood of evil intent, while not zero, seemed diminished.

The sun had gone down, and Davis decided to call it a day. He looked up local steakhouses and saw a number in the area, and chose one based on its Google review score. As he sat in the parking lot, in the agency vehicle, his cell phone rang.

"Davey," Yvonne said. "You did it again."

He blinked, then closed his eyes tight and let out a sigh. "Aw, shit," he exclaimed. "I forgot to call you when I got off the plane."

"It's alright," his wife answered. "I know you're doing all you can to make our future as bright as can be."

"Still," he countered, "I love you, and I shouldn't have forgotten. I don't want you to think I'm putting you second."

"Ha ha, don't worry," she replied. "I know you get all wrapped up and it means a lot to you to solve these cases. How's this going?"

"All I can say is, it's going good," he said. "I've got a primary target."

"Wow," she joked. "Took you *that* long?"

"Funny," he replied. "Anyway, I'm going to have a steak dinner and turn in for the night."

"They can't possibly make a steak as good as I can," she bragged.

"No," he replied, "but they're going to *try*. Love you."

"Love you," she said. "Bye."

"Bye." He hung up and went inside. As he got to his seat and ordered his meal, he thought to his primary target.

You're making this easy, he thought. Like a static shock, it hit him. What did the average person think of the government? The government, to the average American, must seem to be a monolithic mass of paranoia. After all, that was what Hollywood always portrayed. So, perhaps, this man wasn't interested in hiding after all. He wanted plausibility; he wanted to be able to say, "look, I wasn't hiding this from you." After all, if he *had* wanted to make it difficult, if he actually had been stealthy, it would have been almost impossible. It was to ease their mind. It was to demonstrate a desire to be diplomatic with the authorities.

He wanted to be accepted, maybe not as a part of the government, but as a person operating acceptably within it.

I see what you're after, Manfred Voren, Davis thought.

CHAPTER SEVEN

THE HOT NOON AIR OF OKLAHOMA moved about, a breeze that touched all the churchgoers filing out after morning services. The crowd was all smiles, walking back to their cars. Reverend Jack Hurst stepped out the front door of the congregation his father had built so many years before, his suit pressed and neat, happiness painted on his face as he had finished another sermon, had brought God to his little corner of the world. The Full Revival Baptist Church had brought the faithful together since the mid nineteen-fifties, and the son of its founder had sworn that it would continue to do so long after he was gone.

A boy of about twelve approached his father. "That was great, dad!" he swore, tugging on his father's suit jacket.

"I do try my best, Timothy," Jack said, acknowledging his son. "My dad would sometimes stay up half the night trying to write a Sunday's sermon."

At that moment, a car drove by, stopped, and honked. "Reverend Hurst!" a middle-aged woman cried out. "Love the service! Is your wife going shopping with us later this week?"

"I'd love to, Cathy!" Emily said, approaching and placing a hand on Jack's shoulder. "Been looking forward to it!"

"Hey, Jack!" a man shouted from his pickup truck, a cigarette in the corner of his mouth. "You going to Fred's tomorrow night?"

Jack smiled. "I wouldn't miss it for the world!" he cheered. "Maybe this time, Andy's going to have to short his son on laundry money!"

"Dad," a second young boy said, approaching Jack. "Jim and Chris are going hiking in the woods around the Bleachers' property. Can we go?"

"Don't get ahead of yourself, Eric," Jack replied. "First, we have to go home and have dinner."

"Oh, by the way," Emily cut in, "you did great this time. I think we got enough donations to expand the church."

Jack nodded. "That's great," he agreed. "I think I'd like to stop having to use the back room as storage."

The family headed towards the parking lot, specifically to a boat of a car, a well-kept antique Cadillac. The heavy metal door squeaked as Tim opened it. "Why do we always go to church in this?" he asked.

A laugh escaped from Jack's mouth. "We've gone over this," he chided. "My father bought this brand-new in sixty-nine and drove it to church every Sunday."

"Besides," Emily pointed out, "we use the Chevy most every day. This is for special occasions."

"Your uncle Dave used to tell this joke," Jack said, a laugh in his voice, "in the Caddy, my father would pass everything *except* the gas station."

The rumble of the V-8 engine signaled the stirring of the old beast, and the reverend shifted into gear and pulled out of the lot. He turned the radio to a local jazz station as the miles rolled away. "Now boys," Emily said, "what are the rules about hiking in the woods?"

"Always have the first aid kit," Tim recited.

"Don't put anything in your mouth," Eric added.

"And?" Jack piped in. "no credit for partial answers."

"Be home before dark," the kids said in unison.

"That's right," Emily remarked. "We don't want to have to go looking for you or involve the police."

A few minutes later, the car rumbled into the driveway of the two-story, four-bedroom house. The family exited the Cadillac and headed inside. The boys ran upstairs and Jack went into the den, where he took his suit jacket off and hung it up in the wardrobe, then he folded his tie and placed it on the shelf, and finally, hung up his dress shirt and khakis. He changed into a pair of shorts and a t-shirt and headed into the kitchen. He took a diet soda out of the fridge and sat at the table with a book.

"Dinner will be ready in almost an hour! Get cleaned up, boys!" Emily called up the stairs. She headed over to get the fridge to get the food she'd prepared to cook and noticed her husband reading. "Is that a new one?"

"It's some sci-fi number Craig told me about," Jack replied. "It's pretty good." As he sat reading, a twinge made itself known to him. In the back of his mind, a nagging presence kept pointing itself out to him, bothering him. He pushed it out of his mind. This was the second time in almost two weeks that this had happened. What was it? It defied his ability to explain, and he focused on his reading. A few minutes later, it largely went away. Whether it had gone or simply become less obvious, he didn't know. The next time he had a doctor's appointment, he would get it checked out, whatever *it* was.

Many minutes went by. A smell of cooking roast beef wafted through the air. Jack grinned as he closed his book and set it aside. "Almost," Emily said.

"If it tastes even half as good as it smells," Jack commented.

"I hope so," she replied, putting two serving bowls of corn and mashed potatoes on the table. "Kids! We're almost ready!"

Jack grabbed a remote off the counter and turned on the speaker system above the refrigerator. The sounds of Miles Davis played across the kitchen as Emily took the tray of roast beef out of the oven and set it on potholders on the dinner table. Juice and soda got poured into glasses as the boys got their plates and silverware and set it at their spots. Napkins got passed around. The father got up and helped by setting out the condiments and the serving spoons.

"Alright," Jack invited, "join hands." The family formed a large circle at the dinner table, just as he had done with his father decades earlier. "I like to keep it simple, just like my father did. Everyone, close your eyes and bow your head." They did. "Lord, bless this house, this family, and this food that nourishes us, as we worship you and thank you for the bounty you have provided us. Amen."

"Amen," they all said.

Each family member scooped their portions onto their plates and took their turn getting themselves set up. They ate as the jazz music continued to play. "That reminds me," Eric said. "Next spring, Mister Applebaum says I can be first chair."

Tim gave his brother a disapproving glance. "Jazz is okay, I guess," he said, "but I want to play rock and roll."

"As long as you keep an eye on what you're playing," Jack reminded. "You're good at guitar, but you have to be careful not to accidentally praise *the enemy*." The look he got said he didn't have to explain.

"I'm not writing any lyrics," Tim countered.

"I'm not saying anything against it," Jack said. "I'm just saying, be careful. I listened to Black Sabbath growing up, and your grandpa *hated* it. I'm trusting you to know how to be a good Christian."

"Aw, dad, there's nothing to worry about," the boy said.

"Still," Emily said, pointing with her fork, "you're getting really good. Keep playing."

They ate in silence for a while. After finishing his plate, Jack took a final swig of his soda and slid his chair back. "It's my turn to do the dishes, so I'm just going to relax after that, if you don't mind," he said. The silverware he placed on his plate along with his glass and headed towards the sink.

"I'm going to finish the birthday cards for your nephew Taylor's birthday party, "Emily replied.

"Yeah, no problem," Jack answered. The boys finished their meals and placed their dishes in the left sink and headed upstairs. "Now boys, the sun goes down in about five hours. I want you both in that door before that happens, okay?" He placed the leftover food in plastic containers and set them in the back of the refrigerator, on the second shelf above the vegetables on the bottom and the deli meat in the middle tray.

"Got it," they replied in unison.

"Need any help down here?" Emily asked, placing hers in the sink.

"I've done dishes a thousand times," he answered. "I think I've got this covered."

A capful of dish soap and some hot water later, and the dishes soaked in the left sink. John Coltrane's skillful playing serenaded him as he scrubbed the dishes. After each dish no longer bore grime or food, he rinsed it in the right sink, and set it in the drying rack. Some men had a problem with so-called "women's work," but he knew that dividing the tasks prevented a lot of marital strife, and even besides that, he hadn't married a maid. He'd married a partner. It also gave him time to think and do something stress-free. In less than twenty minutes, he had a drying rack full of clean dishes. Two drying towels later, and each dish had been dried and returned to their respective spots in the cupboards and cabinets.

That was easy, he thought, plopping down on the loveseat in the living room. A tap of the remote and the television blinked to life. News appeared before his eyes, one of the mainstream channels. A harsh breath of consternation escaped his mouth. Eyebrows lowered as he saw the typical bad news of usual killing and strife. Without even thinking about it, he shook his head as he disapproved of what he saw. This was the thing that bothered him the most, it occurred to him. This world that God had given mankind had been squandered by mortal men and women. People had succumbed to mortal temptations of the flesh and weaknesses of hate and violence. The Lord would have to come back, it occurred to him, and soon. All that had been good had been wasted by foolish people and their arrogant belief in their superiority over the Earth and its bounty.

A moment later, he wiped his face with the right palm. *What arrogance*, he realized. He had caught himself thinking of himself as separate from the sinners of the world. Somehow, it had slipped his mind the truth behind the teachings that Christ had given to all men and women of the world: all children of God were frail and fell short of the ideal. That was why God's love and grace were necessary. His upbringing and his religious instruction meant nothing in the face of the evil of the Deceiver. With even the slightest slip of his will, his devotion to the Lord and the Scripture, he would be no different from these people who he denounced. *We need you, oh Lord*. His silent prayer passed through his mind. *I need you.*

A familiar twinge appeared in the back of his consciousness.

His first thought in response was, *not again.*

A moment later, though, a thought flashed through his mind like a spark in a puddle of gasoline.

Perhaps it was the Holy Spirit!

A button press later and the news died with the blanking of the screen. Frantically clasping both hands together in prayer, he closed his eyes and focused on the Holy Spirit in his mind. It appeared not as a physical presence, but as a mental image. In his mental space, it resembled a glowing ball of light alone against a dark backdrop. A silent prayer passed through his mind. He focused on the Lord, the image of Jesus that he'd had ever since he was a little boy and his father had shown him the glory of Christ's teachings. The presence of the Holy Spirit in his mind hovered in place, its glowing orb shining to him, obviously with the grace of God, he thought.

Oh Lord, he prayed.

The orb jumped upward. It flashed to a brighter shade of white.

A brilliant light shot out in front of him. He threw his arms in front of his face. After a moment, he felt the soft loveseat become hard wood. He opened his eyes and saw the pews of his church around him. What had happened? He looked up.

The Lord stood before him.

"I am here, my child," Jesus spoke.

Jack's arms went limp at his sides. His body had to remind him to breathe. The dry sensation on his tongue told him his mouth hung open. With eyes as wide as can be, he stared in disbelief at the sight in front of him.

"My...Lord..." said words escaping from Jack's mouth, involuntarily.

Standing less than three feet in front of him, garbed from head to toe in familiar robes and sandaled feet, was his Lord and savior. Everything from the familiar white skin and long flowing brown hair looked exactly like he had expected.

"My Lord!" Jack shouted. "MY LORD!" He hit his knees. "OH MY LORD! I AM NOT WORTHY!"

"My child," the Lord said, "stand."

Jack took the outstretched hand and stood up, barely able to comprehend. Tears began to pour down his cheeks. "I...I can't believe...it..." he stammered, his face red. "You've come back!"

"Dry your eyes," the Lord replied, draping his arms around Jack. "Much is wrong with the world, and much work we have to do. But for right now, be calm. Do not worry. Be sad no more."

"Sad?" Jack uttered, wiping his eyes on his shirt. "I'm so happy I can't describe it in words! I..."

The Lord gently stroked his servant's cheek. "I am here to make everything better," he answered. "I am here to defeat evil once and for all and to bring about my father's glorious kingdom upon this Earth."

"My Lord," Jack asked, "please forgive your loyal servant's questions, but why has Revelation not happened as written?"

"Do not hesitate to ask of me your questions," The Lord replied. "But as for your question, things are different from what the books written by mortal hands, even those with the Father's guidance, have foretold. That's why I need you."

"Me?" Jack said, gasping. "Who am I to be your servant? Surely I am not worthy!"

"You are of the same mortal flesh as all other men, that is true," the Lord explained, "but I have found you most acceptable as my voice in this mortal plane, I request you to be my agent in this war against evil."

Jack swallowed and bowed his head. He made his decision, then looked up. "My Lord," he spoke, "I am not worthy to receive you. But if your will is that I be your right-hand man in the final war against Satan's evil, then I shall not falter!"

"Good!" The Lord exclaimed. "Let me show you what our goal shall be." He touched his hands to the temples of his servant. Jack's mind filled with the sights of Paradise on Earth. He saw, through his mind's eye, a world free of want. People of all colors and histories lived in harmony with one another. No cruelty was inflicted upon anyone. No one committed crimes against their fellow person. There was no scarcity, no fear, no pain, no misery, no disease, or war. People wore clothes made of holy fabric and never shivered in the cold. People never befell accidents and suffered injury. No one saw their neighbor and desired what their neighbor had. No one felt less than anyone else. It was a world where everyone lived in harmony with each other and with nature. They walked all over the Earth without trampling flowers to death beneath the stain of industry. There was no need for industry, or consumerism, or the rat race it engendered. People received the holy love of the Father, and it filled them with joy and satisfied their every desire. It was a world where happiness had triumphed over all else. Nothing would go wrong again, ever.

He saw a perfect world, where joy was a boot standing on the head of all forms of misery, forever.

In that moment, Jack Hurst felt filled to the brim with joy. Men had gone to the ends of the Earth and the ends of their lives to feel such feelings of pleasure, since the dawn of man. Few had ever come anywhere close to the positivity radiating through his heart that day. Words failed to describe in his mind how he felt at that instant.

The Lord smiled as he held his servant, hands gently caressing the man's head. "Do you see?" He implored.

"Oh...God..." Jack uttered, barely able to see through wet eyes. "I see!" He laughed a joyous laugh. "Oh, my Lord! I SEE! FOR THE FIRST TIME, I SEE!"

"That," He told his servant, "is why I must ask you to be strong." A grim expression graced His face. "It is going to get much worse before it gets better. Your faith and the limits of your physical and mental ability to cope will be stressed to the breaking point." He focused a stern gaze on Jack. "Do you have the strength it takes to see our battle through to the final end?"

Jack nodded, strength of will painting itself on his face. "I do!" he exclaimed. "Merely instruct me, and your will I will see done!"

"Most wonderful!" He shouted. He showed an image to his servant, a three-dimensional image of a man in a suit. "Soon enough, you shall be greeted by our first real enemy. I shall be by your side, but I fear he will not be swayed to our cause."

Jack stared in confusion as he recognized the man. "Why, my Lord," he asked, "would Jericho Torvalds come to me?"

"He has much work he is doing," the Lord explained, "gathering superpowers to better protect himself. He will come to you because he believes you have a superpower, rather than the truth that I have come to you."

Dawning realization came to Jack. "I knew it!" he shouted. "I *knew* this was the Holy Spirit!" He thought about it a moment. "Does that mean these powers are the work of Satan?"

"These powers," He explained, "that people are gaining, are tools. Some, undoubtedly, will be drawn to *our* side. This way, we will defeat the King of Lies with the abilities mortal men and women are getting. For no power of mortal men can defeat my Father's will, and through him, me."

"Then," Jack decided, "when this man arrives, I will give him the offer to renounce his evil ways and serve his God in heaven. Even if he won't, I want to try."

"You are a good man, my servant," He replied.

"Hearing you say that, My Lord," Jack replied, "fills me with great joy. When can I tell my wife and kids about you?"

"In time," The Lord said. "Until then, I shall take my leave." He tapped his servant on the forehead. "If you need me in the meantime, call upon the Holy Spirit." He vanished in a beam of light, and Jack found himself returned to his living room, alone.

I will not fail! Jack thought, clenching his fists. He would see the Kingdom of God brought upon the world and the defeat of sin itself.

CHAPTER EIGHT

JENNIFER ROCKETED AWAY from the Target parking lot, up into atmospheric elevations, and saw the scene. Three gunmen stood inside a place of business in Texas. The news had reported the initial standoff and she'd reacted as quickly as possible. The business catered to black people especially and had a mostly colored staff. Racism never failed to emerge in this modern world, she figured.

Descending, she investigated the building and saw a handful of explosives set across the layout of the seven-story building. Moving so fast, everything stood frozen around her, she crashed through one of the upstairs windows and snatched one of the bombs out from behind the desk, zooming it up high into the sky, where a burst of electricity exploded it harmlessly overhead. Four more met their end far away from where they could hurt anyone, and then she descended into the lobby. Before the attackers saw anything, their guns and all their equipment sat outside behind police lines. She left without anyone having been hurt.

She returned to the Target, and zoomed into the men's restroom, locking the stall door. There, Manny reemerged, and he exited to his car, where he got behind the wheel and fired it up. Another successful run. Things had been going smoothly lately, with not many major incidents. The few incidents initially after the Lights had seen some people immediately use their newfound powers for hedonistic purposes, but most of them had been able to be taken down by ordinary bullets. Their hapless example seemed to have shut most of the would-be renegades down. It seemed people had more common sense than he would have otherwise imagined.

As he drove home, he thought of the lives saved. Sure, he'd saved about fifty or so people in the fires, and a dozen more in the storms in Kansas, and almost a thousand in China, but the fact that he hadn't yet been drawn to an incident of millions showed him the resilience of society. He had never been one of those people to believe that society and its contract were frail and to be thrown away at the drop of a hat. He had seen that, in the absence of society, the first thing people seemed to do was recreate it in some fashion.

There was a strange car in his driveway.

He instinctively changed back into Jennifer. With her enhanced senses, she peered ahead to the car. The identification sat in the glove compartment. "Davis Wilson," she read. "FBI."

Her heart sped up. This had been the eventuality that her friends had warned her about. Options crossed her mind rapidly. Should she simply run? That didn't make sense, she figured, as the first thing that would likely happen was a stronger response. Given her powers, one guy didn't qualify as a response. Then again, the government likely figured that they could judge her reaction by one guy. If she retaliated, she couldn't be trusted, they likely thought. So, she decided she would simply talk to him. If he arrested her, she didn't have anything to worry about, at least it hadn't seemed that way. Common sense and her enhanced intellect told her that, if they *had* superior firepower to threaten her with, they'd have brought that person along. And she didn't sense anything odd about this man. Then again, she wasn't going to take chances. If she had to take off, she would.

"Hi there," Davis Wilson said, leaning up against his cruiser.

After parking the car, Jennifer exited the vehicle, a nervous rapid blink in her eyes. "Hi," she flatly stated.

"I spent about an hour thinking about what might freak you out the most," he explained, "and I have to tell you right off the bat, I don't have powers. As far as I know, the government is trying to get people with powers, but they don't have anyone near your level of power. I'm just here because...well, let's face it, you're the biggest player in the field right now."

She looked around and saw most of her neighbors were either at work, or behind shut doors. "Davis Wilson," she replied, "I have to say, I anticipated this, kinda. It still upsets me that I'm going to be arrested just for helping out."

"I don't know what you expected," he replied, "or, for that matter, what I expected. But I think there's a way out of this for you. I think if you make a great impression, there won't be a problem."

She laughed. "Hah! How can you say that when your superiors are paranoid government freaks?"

"Let me make you a promise," Davis offered. "I can't guarantee my superiors will treat you fairly, but I can assure you I'm not lying to you when I say I think you're trying to do the right thing." He took a ragged breath. "After all, you could have made it really difficult to track. Instead, you made it possible to figure out who you were."

"It was a safety measure," she said. "I was trying to have an ace in the hole in case this happened. I wasn't wanting to actually have to use it."

Davis shifted his leaning posture. "I actually think you're great for the world," he admitted. "I grew up with comics and I must say, I never expected someone to get powers on this scale and not immediately use them for purely selfish reasons. Please, help me get the government to see you the way I see you."

She stared into his eyes and looked at his heartbeat. It hadn't changed radically, and his sweat had remained consistent. "Alright," she said, "but if anything looks even slightly fishy, I'm getting the hell out of there."

"Hey," Davis said, shrugging. "No one will be able to stop you."

Fifteen minutes of driving later, they arrived at a federal complex in Saint Louis. The car parked by the curb, and the agent stepped out of the driver's seat. He opened the rear passenger door, and out stepped Jennifer in her standard outfit. A team of agents exited the building, ready to meet their subject, and saw the amazon-esque figure, standing slightly taller than some of them, garbed in an orange t-shirt and yoga pants, with cheap rain boots. They stared as she walked beside the agent.

"Excuse me, ma'am," one agent said, approaching, a stutter in his voice. "We didn't want to do this outside, in case the press was watching, but..."

Jennifer rolled her eyes. "You want me to put some damn handcuffs on," she guessed.

"I apologize," he said. "It's just that..."

"Protocol?"

He nodded. "Yes ma'am."

She stuck out her hands. "Dammit," she swore. "Fine." He clinked the metal around her wrists, and they guided her to one of the free interrogation rooms.

As Davis took his spot in the room opposite her, with several agents watching behind the one-way glass, an important figure walked into the room. The agent looked up and did a double take. "Boss!" he said.

Sam Louis nodded. "As you were," he ordered. He took a seat. "You're a fascinating one, Miss Black."

She gave a skeptical look. "So, you're the big cheese?" she asked.

"I've been put in charge of the task force for investigating super-powered beings," Sam explained. "And that means that you're my priority one target right now, because no one else is demonstrating the kind of power that you are."

"And that makes me a target."

Sam laughed at her flippant statement. "You act as if we're not supposed to freak out at the level of firepower you have!" He exclaimed, setting out pictures of her actions. "You're a living weapon, you know that? You've got nuclear-level capability, or even higher, at your disposal, should you turn against this country. That's not exactly something we can just ignore."

"I know that," she replied. "I just think it's a bit much that I'm being arrested."

"Don't jump the gun," Sam shot back. "That's what we're here to determine."

"Well, how about removing these?" Jennifer replied. "I'd prefer not to accidentally break these and get charged for destruction of property."

Sam nodded and Davis reached across the table and unfastened them. "Let's get the big deal out of the way first," the elder agent said. "You don't exist. You don't have paperwork. How were you going to solve that problem?"

A sheepish look crept onto her face. "I was hoping to be a hero," she explained, "and worry about that later."

Both agents looked skeptically. "You do know how hard the process is," Davis cut in. "It isn't easy, even for people who are applying properly from a home country. You're effectively stateless."

She sighed. "I know," she admitted.

"You do realize you can't do anything official as who you are now," Sam pointed out. "If you're counting on your other self, because that *is* the most likely option, given what we know, that might cause problems for people your other self considers close relations."

"I *know that*," she protested. "I'm actually really concerned about it because I want to spend most of my time as this self, my *useful* self. I've just been more worried about helping people than that."

"I ain't read many comics," Sam stated. "But one thing I know is that the heroes fight crime. Why haven't you?"

"I *have*," she corrected. "Take their weapons away and leave. No one sees me."

"Interesting," Sam cut in, "but that's not what I meant. Why not fight crime?"

"You mean," she asked, "why don't I help arrest criminals?" Sam nodded. "Because I'm not a cop. I'm not stupid. It's not my job. My job is to save lives. I'm not law enforcement."

Sam nodded. "Interesting," he replied. "Eighty years of superhero stories and you decide not to do the one thing all the characters do."

"When I first got these powers," she said, "I went around saving lives, but also having fun. There's no excitement like flying or explor-ing the bottom of the ocean. But for me, being able to do something directly instead of just being a passive observer was a godsend. I don't need to be a cop. I'm more than happy doing what I'm doing. But I also need a life of my own."

The elder agent had seen many a liar in his time. As a senior agent, he'd worked in the field busting many a hardened gangster and criminal. This woman had an honesty about her that he found to be a rare gem. Either that, or she was a fantastic actor, which he doubted very much. He'd seen those types too; she struck him as too naïve to be faking it.

"Tell me," Davis interjected. A question came to him. His career had involved life and death enough times to know a great way to judge character. "What was it like the first time you stared down a gun?"

Jennifer clamped her lips tighter and released a nasal sigh.

Then she told the story.

A man named Jason Nehrmann had burst through the door of the nightclub. Gunshots and screams exploded over the sound of the music, and the DJ stopped playing almost immediately. The multicolored extravaganza overhead died, and all the normal lights went up, bathing the scene in white fluorescence. Bouncers leapt into action to take him out, and a burst from a shotgun opened his chest and then the assailant spun around and caught another in the face. People hit the deck and a few unlucky victims caught rounds to the back as they tried to flee. A woman who attempted to dial 911 on the phone behind the bar caught a slug from a waist-drawn pistol, clutched her neck, then collapsed. He replaced the pistol and returned both hands to his twelve gauge.

"Where THE FUCK IS NADINE?" he shouted. He stepped around a corpse and levied the gun at a waitress who had emerged from the kitchen to see the ruckus. "You! Where the fuck is Nadine?"

She threw up her hands and started blubbering. "I...I don't..." she stammered.

"ANSWER ME!" he shouted.

"She's..." the woman struggled for words. "off today!"

"Bullshit!" he cried, stepping closer, gun levied.

Jennifer had seen and heard all of this as she had left the scene of a meth lab explosion in a small town in south Florida. She crashed through the window and stood between the gunman and the waitress.

Jason cocked his head. "Who are..." Realization dawned on him. "I know you. You're in those pictures!"

"You're not going to win this!" Jennifer shouted.

"I'm not leaving without Nadine!" he screamed, bringing the gun back up to chest level.

119

Her heart pounded. As sweat began to bead on her forehead, and her irrational mind shouted so loud it overwhelmed her focus, she tried to fight back. *I've survived deadlier things,* she thought, trying to reason her way out. The image of the shotgun and the pistols at his hips caused her more primitive fight-or-flight response to work overtime. She swallowed. This was insane. How could she clam up like this?

"Fine then!" Jason shouted. "Fuck you too!"

He pulled the trigger.

Thoughts muddied together. Time slowed down as she instinctively kicked one speed power on. She could see the pellets as they escaped the barrel in their tight cluster. This...this was the real thing. People died from stuff like this. With her arms beading with sweat and palms jittery, she stuck out a hand and scooped the pellets in her grasp and crushed them. A breath caught in her throat as she expected burning and shooting pain.

It never came.

She let out a deep breath, both physically and mentally.

He gasped and pulled the trigger again. The woman's arm blurred for an instant and nothing appeared different. "WHAT IS HAPPENING?" he screeched. He pulled the trigger once more, just as she disappeared from where she stood and appeared with hand over the barrel. A muzzle flash shot out against her skin and pellets fell harmlessly to the floor. A hand reached for the hip, only to find air. His pistols sat halfway across the floor. He made a mad dash for it, only to be tackled by a crowd of people outside the club.

She collapsed onto a barstool and blinked wide eyes. Her lungs took in huge gasps of air as she placed hands on the bar and held herself there. She lowered her head and closed her eyes a moment. This hadn't been a hallucination; she'd stared down a gun. She had taken *actual bullets* to her skin. She stared at her hand. Soot formed a strange spread pattern where she'd palmed the shotgun barrel. A wet napkin under a drink later, and her skin looked unblemished.

"Thank you!" a woman yelled, sitting next to her.

"Ah!" Jennifer yelped and jerked back, closing her eyes, and forcing her racing heart to slow down. "Oh, geez, I'm sorry. You startled me."

The woman wiped her eyes. "You saved us!"

"I did…" Jennifer realized. Her heartrate returned to normal. "Sorry. It's just…guns. You know." Her vision blurred and she wiped her eyes clear. "I'll be alright. I'm just…new to the whole 'guns' thing."

Davis and his boss sat listening to the story. She got to the last thing she said and then Sam got up. "Be right back," he told his subordinate. "I have something to deal with. You and she can have a conversation."

After he shut the door, Davis looked at her. "Well, yeah," he said. "You never forget the first time you stare down a gun."

She laughed. "Yeah," she agreed, "it's kind of funny, thinking about it. I'd already dealt with incredible heat from wildfires and sharp objects. And yet, I'm suddenly scared shitless of guns." She shrugged. "Even though she's seen deflecting bullets countless times."

"Proves you're still human," he said. "Honestly."

"So," she said, "what do you think he's going to do?"

"I don't know," Davis answered. "But really, I don't think he's the scary government guy you make him out to be. I've worked under him for over a decade now, and he's the most reasonable boss I've ever had." He let out a sigh. "If a bit of a pain in the ass sometimes."

"You get why I'm worried, though," she replied.

"Hey," he said, smiling. "I get it. We're the big, scary government. We can make your life a living hell."

"There is that," she agreed.

"Did you know," he asked, "that the year Columbine happened, it was a record low in school shootings?"

She blinked. "I…" she replied. Where the hell had that come from? "I hadn't heard that, but it kinda makes sense."

"You know why?"

"Yeah," she replied. "I guess it's because most of the school shootings used to take place in inner city schools."

"Right," Davis explained. "Columbine was such a big deal because it was everything a school shooting wasn't. Before, school shootings happened all the time, it's just none of them got national news because, well, racism." He gestured. "As you may figure. Columbine, by contrast, was," he began counting on his hands, "an upper-middle class white community, with a low crime rate, and to a white majority affluent area." He leaned forward. "And what really might blow your mind, the boys weren't bullied loners. They were known for being bullies."

"I didn't know that last part," she admitted.

"Yeah," he said. "My point is, I got to where I'm at in the agency by being good at nuance."

Earlier, she'd been jittery. Hands shackled couldn't stop touching each other. With handcuffs removed, she rubbed her wrists. Her left hand scratched the back of her head. She adjusted her shoulders at least three times. Blinking had reached excessive levels. Each sign pointed to her fear and desire to take off as soon as possible. Now, he saw her breathing relaxed, even if just slightly, and her body language had become more passive. This was what he wanted. He wanted her trust, or if not that, her feeling at ease.

"I just don't want to end up a soldier or an attack dog of the U.S. military," she admitted.

"A noble ambition," he agreed. "You just want to save lives without having the feds breathing down your neck."

"I won't kill anyone for the government," she flatly stated.

"I don't want you to be reduced to that, either," he said. "The thing is, there are men above us that we're going to have to massage their ego because they speak imperialistic language and don't blink."

"Hah," she said, letting out a laugh. "That's not something I expect a government agent to say."

"What can I say?" he said. "I'm not a gung-ho type. I just figure stuff out for a living."

"When do I get to go home?" she asked. "I just want to save lives and enjoy having superpowers."

"Gimme a minute," he said, getting up.

He exited the room and headed towards the break room. There, Sam had just hung up his cell phone and sipped on some reheated coffee. "So," he said, leaning against the counter. "What does our princess want?"

"She wants to be able to save lives," Davis explained, "which is obvious, but she doesn't want to be a part of the government and doesn't want to be an extension of the military."

"Oh, is *that* all?" Sam scoffed. "You mind telling me how I'm supposed to tell the brass that? These people are going to know that our answer to the American people is, 'hey, we think we can trust her, just trust us?' Is that going to work?"

"Look at it this way," Davis said, "you can tell them that she could have taken anything she wanted and the first thing she did was save lives." He folded his arms. "Plus, you can point out to them that if *they* think they can stop her, that's something *we* don't want any part of. I think that'll get the point across. We did our job and got them the intel they wanted." He thought about it. "Also, you can tell them she'll save them a fortune in emergency funding."

Sam sipped his coffee. Davis was his most trusted subordinate. The man never broke protocol and he had a real knack for seeing the details. "What's your take on this?" he asked. "I'm only trusting her if you trust her."

"Sir," Davis replied, "I've seen all kinds of people. She looks like she's really *into* this whole being a hero thing. I know what it looks like when seeing violence up close makes someone a ticking time bomb. She saw people drown that she couldn't save, and based on what I'm seeing, she's experiencing a real human reaction, but is also coping *exceptionally* well. It bothers her, so she's not a socio-path, but she's also not constantly broken up by it."

"She's a rare one, then," Sam noted, based on the analysis.

"Very rare," Davis added. "We're really lucky. I say we shouldn't screw this up."

Sam hashed it out. "Ah, screw it," he finally said. "You go tell her she's free to go and take her home." He pointed. "But if this goes haywire, it's *your* ass."

"What excuse should I use?"

Sam waved it off. "She asked for a lawyer and we didn't charge her with anything because we couldn't," he explained. "Or not. If you can come up with something, you fill the paperwork out."

Davis pushed the door open. "C'mon," he said. "You asked for a lawyer, and we released you. I'm taking you home."

As they got in the car and left the complex, Jennifer smiled. "Thank you for believing in me," she said.

"It's not just that," Davis admitted. "I really am glad to have some-one like you around. Especially since, we both know the villains are going to show up at some point."

A dour expression appeared on her face. "Uh, yeah," she admit-ted. "I was worrying about that too."

"Have to take the good with the bad," he said. "Also, they might still make the connection, but I tried to obfuscate the fact that you're Manfred Voren."

"Thank you very much," she said.

"You want to be safe, so you want to stay in your powered female form," he noted, "and you want to have paperwork to do that. I get it. However, for now, you might want to go out every so often and be seen doing something as Manny just to make things seem normal. Buy groceries with a debit card or something."

"Gotcha," she agreed.

As the car arrived at the driveway in Alton, he paused to gather his words. "One last thing," he said. "If you are met by Jericho Torvalds, please let us know."

She cocked her head. "You mean the billionaire Fox Business guy?"

"That's the one," he agreed. "He's collecting powers and offering money, and we need to keep track of it."

She blinked. "That's...mildly terrifying," she said. "Well, I'll keep that in mind."

"Thanks," Davis said.

"Bye," she said, stepping out and shutting the door.

"We'll meet again," he said, shutting the door and driving away. She sped into the house to limit sight of her and shut the door.

What a strange ride it's been, she thought.

CHAPTER NINE

JERICHO TORVALDS AWOKE FROM A NAP as the pilot got on the intercom and told of their arrival. He stretched and unbuckled his safety belt. Lately, the journey across the nation had seen him collect well over a hundred of the best superpowers. At first, he'd only suspected that certain types of abilities would be useful, but as he enhanced his own mind, he began to see outside his usual perspective. Radical changes had been made to his stock portfolio in the past few days to ensure he had plenty of liquidity for immediate offers. While it was true that it only took a few million to set up the kinds of arrangements he offered, as he began to perceive more, he would likely be collecting more abilities. If there was one truth in the world, it was that rich people hated to spend more money than they had to.

"Miss," he said to the woman greeting him at the bottom of the staircase off the plane, "is my vehicle ready?"

"Right this way, sir," she cheerily said, leading him over to the parked car. "Although, I must say, I'm a bit surprised. A Ford Taurus, as requested."

"I'd normally request a higher-end car," he admitted, "but to where I'm going, I don't want to look like I'm showing off."

"Yes," she agreed. "Of course."

They approached the parked car, and she handed him the keys. As he slid inside the driver's seat, he looked up at her. "Keep the jet gassed up," he instructed. "I never know when I might need to take off."

After starting, he connected his phone to the Bluetooth and set his classical music playlist on random. Then he loaded the next addresses into the GPS and drove off. Saint Louis had a ridiculous amount of road construction, and it took him almost twenty minutes longer than he otherwise would have taken. He'd seen it before, but seeing it again always bewildered him. Outside of the major cities, he saw an endless sea of part time existentialist hell. There did not seem to be a museum in sight, scarcely a local music hall, and maybe only one local little theater. Culture ceased to exist outside of the urban centers. Rural and suburban parts of the country seemed to exist only to serve the cycle of, get born, go to school, work to buy trinkets and food, then die. Real jobs seemed almost non-existent, and those that existed held entire towns up by the weight of a single industry, and when those left, towns rotted from the inside out.

The visible decay of East Saint Louis, Illinois was visible from afar. As he drove into the town, he saw buildings left to literally rot and crumble, and piles of bricks left abandoned where homes used to be. Businesses that once were stood boarded up and with broken windows with signs left faded in the sunlight from the early nineteen fifties. As history showed, he knew, white people had fled these cities shortly after World War II, and when they left, they took industry and job opportunity with them. Racists blamed towns like this on the color of the skin of their majority inhabitants; even Jericho, hated by the far left and pilloried by centrist liberals alike, knew better. There was no gene for tendency to commit crime, it was as simple as ABC. People who had more jobs and more money did fewer crimes. People could criticize his Libertarianism, and he would be glad to have those discussions, but he would not argue the racial issues with racists.

After five minutes of driving and taking in the endless examples of human suffering on display thanks to a devastated local economy and endless inescapable poverty, he arrived at an apartment building. He parked his car in the lot and got out. He knew the expensive suit he wore drew attention, and he knew he had painted a target on himself. It all fit into his plan. The language of the legal system and government was plausible deniability. If they saw where he went, and he always had eyes on him, they couldn't accuse him of sneaking around.

"Excuse me," he said, to an elderly black man sitting in a chair at the building's entrance. Jericho looked around and saw the usual graffiti and broken windows, but it looked better maintained than a lot of the places in a town some folks would call a "ghetto."

The old man looked up and stroked the white stubble on his chin. "What you want?" The man asked. This fool was liable to get shot, waltzing in with a get up like that. In all his years, he'd seldom seen people who didn't seem to know better like this kid.

"I was wondering if a Demarcus Edwardson is in," Jericho inquired. "I have business with him."

"What kinda business?" the old man asked.

"If you're worried about violence," Jericho reassured, "I can tell you that isn't it."

"Heh!" The old man's scoff of a laugh came out ragged. "Scrawny white boy like you ain't never fired a gun or stuck someone with a knife in his life." A half-sneer drew itself on his face. "They're on the second floor, eighth from the stairs."

"Thank you," Jericho said, pulling a twenty from his pocket and handing it to the man as he walked past. He'd accomplished one more goal: his arrival being known to at least one person on the premises other than his targets. Up the stairs, where the scent seemed a mixture between marijuana and disease, he saw the cracks in the concrete of the wall and turned, walking down the hall until two of his powers showed him his targets.

He knocked on the door.

"Who's there?" a harsh female voice cried out.

"My name is Jericho Torvalds," Jericho replied. "I'm here to offer your son a business transaction."

"Ha, that's a good one," the woman replied. "Some wall street billionaire I see on TV badmouthing the working man is standing opposite my door. Right."

"I assure you," Jericho retorted, "that I'm the real deal. I mean, the amount of money I'm prepared to offer your son is something I know you won't be able to ignore, given your current financial situation." He paused a moment. "And I also I'm unarmed, whereas you have a gun."

He heard a pistol cock. "Alright," she said, "you can come in. You don't make no false moves! Okay?"

"Yes, ma'am," he replied. The door creaked open. She stood well outside his reach and backed up with each step he took. He saw the lines on her face, aged by the years of struggle just to survive and the hopelessness of poverty drawn around her cheeks and eyes.

Aged or not, her eyes wore an expression of fight-or-flight. She held the gun at chest height, pointed at the center of his torso, finger less than an inch from the trigger. She sat down next to her son, a twenty-something black youth, a scar on his neck. "You got three minutes, you hear?" she commanded.

"I won't need three whole minutes," he said. "I believe in making it simple. You, Mister Edwardson, have a power. I want to copy it and give you a lot of money. Your power isn't affected at all. You don't have to lose it, it's not weakened, nothing. Literally all that happens is, I shake your hand, you get paid, the end."

The woman did not take her eyes or the gun off Jericho. Demarcus thought about the offer. "Tell me, rich man," he said. "Why do this for us? Why do us a favor?"

Jericho gave a grin. "I'm not doing you a favor," he admitted. "I'm an objectivist, I don't *believe* in favors. You have a power I want, I have money, which you want, what's there to say?"

"How much?"

"The important question," Jericho replied. He pulled from his suit jacket a manilla envelope with several pages in it. "I will set up a series of investments in your name that will net you roughly one hundred thousand dollars a year for the rest of your life. All you have to do is leave it alone and collect a check. In exchange, I shake your hand, and copy your power."

"Alright," Demarcus said. "But how can I trust you?"

Jericho nodded. "A legitimate concern," he admitted. He placed a business card on the table. "Nothing will be done until you come to this attorney's office and sign the contract. That way, we both are bound. Your terms are done as soon as I shake your hand, but this way, I am bound, and you can force my position if I back out."

Demarcus picked up the card. "Okay, makes sense," he said.

"One more thing," Jericho said. He reached into his pocket and pulled out his wallet. From there, he placed two thousand dollars in cash on the desk. "That will take care of your rent for this month, as well as your car repairs. Consider this a down payment."

They stared in disbelief at the money.

Jericho made his exit. He felt good; at this point, only two had refused after the contract pitch. As soon as he got in touch with his lawyer, who had written up all of these contracts—and told him he was out of his mind—and set up the date, he would have the power.

"Wait!"

Jericho turned around and saw the woman and her son standing in the doorway. "Hmm?" he asked.

"Let's do this right now," Demarcus replied. "I can get my work buddies who live upstairs to be witnesses. Verbal agreement. Right now."

Jericho pretended to mull this over, to leave them hanging. Internally, he was grinning. He would hold up his end of the bargain; that was a no-brainer. It was chump change compared to the wealth of powers he continued to accumulate. The new order of wealth in the world could make him so much more traditional money than even the stock market, he realized. All his cash wealth wouldn't amount to a stack of beans compared to the *real* power he now wielded. "I accept," he said.

Ten minutes later, five more young black men stood in the apartment, eyeing the white boy and his expensive get-up. "I agree," Demarcus explained, deliberately, and thoroughly, "to shake the hand of Jericho Torvalds."

"I agree," Jericho Torvalds said, not breaking eye contact, "to set up a series of investments in the name of one Demarcus Edwardson, total valuation approximately ten million dollars, to net a yearly payment of approximately one hundred thousand dollars, until the death of said recipient."

They shook, with everyone watching. The billionaire effortlessly added the ability to his collection. It was some variety of memory power. He'd analyze it closer later. Being able to investigate memories had appeared on his radar as something he might want to get. All the physical powers in the world wouldn't matter if he didn't have enough mental ones.

"So," Demarcus said, "is that it?"

"You get all the investment info in a few days," Jericho explained. "If not, you can call my accountant. I always keep my word." He nodded. "Good day."

He left the apartment complex and got into his rental car, firing up the engine and setting his phone GPS to the next major target. The next power his radar had warned him about, had been the redheaded woman who had flown across much of the world performing acts of heroism. To most, this woman must have seemed like a godsend, a hero manifested out of Greek myth. To him, however, she was someone else. His power radar, amplified with several overlapping enhancement powers, located the woman, and identified that she was, in fact, the alter ego of one Manfred Voren.

A good half hour of driving through the endless cultureless wastes of Wal-Mart-land saw him locate the subdivision where his target resided. Pulling into the subdivision, he drove past bends and twists until he came to the house. He parked the car in the driveway and combed his hair. The cellphone on vibrate, he got out and inspected the grounds with several of his sensory powers. No threats came to mind, and he saw a very ordinary living space with no unique aspects. Clearly, this person didn't have some nefarious dungeon or hidden passageway, or a secret cave of some kind. That put him at ease as he stepped up the short stairs and knocked on the front door.

The man that greeted him had modest curly hair, a Western European complexion and face structure, and a chin that indicated he'd recently lost a great deal of weight. What concerned him, however, was the fact that the expression of surprise immediately preceded a look of expectation. "Hello there," he introduced, "I'm..."

"Jericho Torvalds," Manny replied, "CEO of Firestorm Investments." He nodded. "I've seen you on Fox Business, yeah."

The billionaire cocked his head slightly. "I get the feeling you knew I was coming," he replied. "Who told you?"

Manny shrugged. "I've got a power," he said, "you have a reputation of going to people that have powers. It's on the news, you know."

"Oh well," Jericho answered. "I guess you know why I'm here then."

"You're here to what," Manny offered, "steal my power so you have all the powers?"

"Nothing so nefarious, ha ha," Jericho said, amused. "I'm here to offer you a lot of money and copy your ability if you agree. I'm just wanting to add to my collection."

Manny's eyebrows went up and down. "Straight to the point," he said. "I guess that makes sense." He turned around and waved. "C'mon in."

They walked into what Jericho saw as an example of a bland working-class living room. The light brown wall paint combined with the yellowish carpet told of a design choice from the late nineteen-seventies that had never been replaced. He sat in a loveseat opposite Manny, with a small oval table between them.

Manny leaned back, cupping his hands behind his head. "Give me your offer, rich man."

Jericho cleared his throat for effect. "Well," he explained, "you hit the nail on the head earlier with what you said. You have a super-power. Obviously. We both know this." He pulled a folder out of his suit jacket. "Based on the information I have about you, which was all publicly available information, just so you know, you are in need of money. I'm willing to set up a long-term investment that will net you roughly a hundred thousand a year for life. All you have to do is shake my hand and let me copy your power. You don't even have to lose your power or have it negatively impacted in any way."

Manny blinked. That was true, he couldn't ignore an amount of money that big. Plus, it would give him plenty of leeway to be Jennifer full time. "I have to admit," he said, "I can't ignore such a large amount of money." He rested his hands on his thighs. "But here's the problem. What bothers me is the fact that you're collecting all the powers, because you have all this wealth and power already to throw around, and all you want it for is to have more." He paused to breathe. "If you wanted to, with what you're capable of, and what you have at your disposal, you could almost single-handedly save the world. Instead, you're just thinking about you."

Jericho's eyes lowered briefly, as he'd heard such moralizing statements before. "Honestly, Mister Voren," he admitted, "people have laid this tired bit of holier-than-thou dialogue on me already. As a follower of Rand, I..." He noticed a quiet chuckle escape the man. "What?"

Manny wiped his face. "Oh, it's nothing," he said. "It's just that I find Ayn Rand's work to be either hilariously bad or outright nefarious."

The billionaire leaned forward. "Really?" he asked. "Tell me what you find disagreeable."

Manny's eyes widened. "Ooh boy," he exclaimed. "Where do I begin? Maybe with the fact that all her heroes are either Mary Sue perfect or hilariously Disney Villain in their behavior? What about the fact that anyone we're supposed to be against is a blatant strawman? Maybe how her books contain hilarious mistakes?"

"Hmm," Jericho countered, "I didn't get that from the reading of Atlas Shrugged or Anthem at all." It was certainly a familiar counter he heard, that was for sure, but what got him was the man seemed to have more than the usual specific examples.

"We're told that main character Dagny Taggart is descended from railroad tycoon Nat Taggart," Manny began. "And that he didn't use government loans or eminent domain because he was just that good at building railroads."

A long pause ensued. It began to grate on Jericho. "And?" he asked.

"In the real world," Manny explained, "railroads only happened because of widespread eminent domain and lots of government money. Are you expecting me to believe that Nat Taggart got all these people to sell him their land with private money? Also, where did he get that kind of money back then, if not from the government?"

It struck him as a decent point. "Okay," he said, "I'll grant you that. However, that doesn't strike me as a knock against the idea itself. Is that your only example?" He waited.

"No," Manny replied. "Let's take her favorite character: John Galt. This is, without question, the biggest Mary Sue character I've ever seen." The billionaire sat waiting; he took that as his cue to continue. "He straight-up invents a *free energy* machine. You know, the thing the laws of thermodynamics say is impossible? But no, let's go on. Again, that might be a nitpick." He coughed. "His big plan is to whisk all these uber-brilliant heads of business and industry off to a hideaway in the woods and wait for society to collapse." He shrugged in disbelief. "How does that work? How do these companies work *with them* if no one can replicate their ideas? It's absurd!"

"Is it really, though?" Jericho replied. He crossed his legs. "Look at what Henry Ford created. He revolutionized industry forever with his creation of the assembly line."

Manny opened his mouth to say something, but it just hung there a long moment. Finally, he shot back, "You're really telling me you believe *no one* would have been able to come up with that in his absence?"

"Maybe, in time," Jericho responded, "someone might have been able to come up with that, in time." He had a thought and decided to change gears. "But ultimately, the core idea of Objectivism is that governments shouldn't have the power to take from someone who earns, and give to someone who doesn't, and people should not act in their rational self-interest."

"So," Manny said, "everyone helping others should be optional? No one should be required to give back?"

Jericho smiled and nodded. "Exactly," he said. "See, you're getting it."

"Absolutely incredible," Manny said, shaking his head. "That's one of the serious problems with this world. People think selfishness is a virtue. Eighty-six people have wealth equivalent to the bottom three billion people combined."

Jericho's eyebrows lowered. "What's wrong with that?"

"Ah ha!" Manny let out a bellowing laugh, his head leaning back.

"What's so funny?" Jericho asked, sincerely confused.

This only caused the man opposite the billionaire to bellow harder in amusement. "Ah, oh, I needed that," Manny finally said, wiping his eyes. "You seriously don't see what's wrong with that."

"No," Jericho argued, "I do mean it. They earned their money."

"Oh, *please*," Manny snapped back. "Do you honestly believe that? Can you actually, really be that naïve?"

"Okay, I'm not dumb enough to believe that *every* rich man earned every dime of his money," the billionaire explained, "but somebody had to earn that money. Isn't it the right of a parent to bequeath wealth to their children?"

"Holy crap!" Manny exclaimed. "You can't be serious! They didn't earn that money! They stole it by exploiting the workers who they underpaid and overworked!"

"The workers agreed to be exploited," Jericho countered. "Nobody put a gun to their head."

"Unbelievable." Manny blinked hard several times. "The average CEO makes three hundred times what his average worker makes. Do you honestly think he works three hundred times as hard?"

"A successful rich person should have the right to create a dynasty of wealth," Jericho countered.

"Not if it results in generation after generation who doesn't have to do anything except grow a giant pot of money that *never benefits anyone else*," Manny snapped back.

"Well, if it makes you feel better," the billionaire replied, "I can absolutely understand why you feel the way you do. And to answer your earlier question, the CEO doesn't work three hundred times as hard as the average worker, but his job is three hundred times as important."

Manny let out a chuckle. "Even if that were true," he answered, "which I doubt, why does that mean it's okay for him to pay them less than they're worth? Why does he get to fail to share the profits with them? After all, he's not doing them a favor; he needs workers to get his job done. Doesn't that give them the right to share in his wealth?"

Jericho's eyebrows went up in surprise. He hadn't expected such an erudite statement from this common-seeming man. He dismissed the point at once, of course, but it impressed him, none-theless. "They agreed to it," he simply stated.

"That's particularly shitty," Manny argued.

"That's the way it is," Jericho proclaimed. "People are too de-pendent on government assistance." He reached into his pocket and produced a card. "It was interesting having this discussion with you. To finalize our offer, go here." He stood up and turned to go.

"Hold on," Manny said, "aren't I allowed to counteroffer?"

Jericho turned, awestruck and dumbfounded. "Okay," he ut-tered, scarcely able to comprehend. This had never occurred. No one had dared attempt a counteroffer. "What's your terms?"

"Do you have a power in that collection of yours," Manny asked, "that lets you experience someone else's point of view?"

"Yes," Jericho revealed. "Why?" Despite his curiosity, he believed he had a good idea anyway.

"You can cut the money in half," Manny revealed, "if you use that power to see my point of view."

A half-grin appeared on the billionaire's face. "I must admit, Mister Voren," he admitted, "that is not a wise financial decision. I have a huge incentive to take you up on that offer, and not much disincentive. Meanwhile, you stand to lose quite a bit of money." A playful mood came about him, one that he hadn't felt in a long time of gambling in the stock market. It was the first financial gamble in a long time that set his nerves firing. This could be interesting. "Say, I'll give you an offer: tell me about a strong disincentive that I haven't considered, and I'll take you up on it, no discount needed."

Manny didn't hesitate, smiling. "You might end up changing your mind," he stated.

"Not likely," Jericho argued. "Although, I'm certain my arguments will be strengthened."

"That which can be destroyed by the truth should be."

"You know what," Jericho said, "tell me who actually said that, and I'll take you up on it." The popular myth was that astronomer Carl Sagan had been the origin of the saying. It was not true.

Manny paused just a moment. "P.C. Hodgell in 'Seeker's Mask.' Everyone thinks it's Carl Sagan, but there's no evidence he said it," he explained.

The billionaire gave a surprised expression then stuck out his hand. Manny shook it. The rich man's eyes seemed to go dull for a moment. An instant later, confusion and alarm washed over his face. At once he worked to compose himself. "Thank...thank you," he stammered. "You'll hear from my accountant soon."

"Nice doing business with you," Manny said, modestly concerned. "Is everything okay?"

"Nothing's wrong," Jericho lied, waving it off. "Thank you very much."

Jericho sat in his rental car, the only sound being the mild whine of the engine and the gentle hiss of the air conditioner. He hadn't known what to expect, but what he got was Manny's entire life story up to that moment.

These memories were reconstructed not by frail human psyches that changed them every time they recalled them, but by a super-power that acted flawlessly.

CHAPTER TEN

AN EARLY MARCH DAY IN NINETEEN EIGHTY-FIVE, Manfred Voren was born to an Irish mother and a German father. Both parents had immigrant parents. His early life had been on the move, from Millstadt, Illinois to Granite City, and finally, to Alton. Robert Voren had gone to technical school and become a welder, and the family had traveled from city to city because the industry had shifted over the years. Anna, his wife, had gotten her practical nursing license and had supplemented their meager existence.

One Christmas, there hadn't been any presents.

"Aw, Manny," Anna said, clutching her crying son, "we wanted so bad to get it for you, but dad's had to take jobs where he could get them and all the bills had to come first." Her son's tears soaked into her corduroy pants, as his stubby fingers gripped her tight.

"Next Christmas," Robert swore, "we'll get you an awesome present."

"It's not fair!" The seven-year old boy shouted, his words slurring through his storm of emotions. "I didn't do nothing wrong!"

"I know, sweetie," the mother said. "You deserve a present. But we can't afford it right now." The boy wiped his eyes and walked to his room, the sounds of his wailing still audible. "The nursing home isn't giving me anything but part-time hours."

Robert nodded. "Yeah, it's a bitch," he uttered. He sat in the loveseat and rubbed his chin. A man of modest height and build, his curly hair and clean-shaven face gave a deceptive feel to those who didn't know him. Given the chance, he enjoyed proving people's expectations wrong. Lately, however, reality had kicked him in the nuts. "If the copper plant wouldn't have gone kaput, I wouldn't have to go from place to place doing gig welding."

She sat on the couch next to his loveseat. "That's what I don't understand," Anna inquired. "How is it that the company kept some of its welders around for the plant change, but not you?"

"I think there's funny business afoot," Robert admitted. "Who knows." He did some breathing exercises to clear his mind. "I heard they're doing renovations on the water park in Grafton, starting in February, so they can open on time in May. If that's the case, I can get two months and maybe some change in full-time work."

She nodded. "I'm going to bitch at my supervisors to get more time," she told him. "It's insane that I can't get more hours."

Manny hung out in the hallway and heard all of this. He retreated to his room drying his eyes. It upset him, not getting a thing, but at the same time, he couldn't blame his parents for trying. The mystery that is a child's mind raged on. At once he desperately wanted a gift, and also, didn't. The childish part of him argued that he needed it. However, the maturity that only poverty instilled in children this young, shouted back that he should try to stick it out and not think only of what he wanted. One thing that separated him from his peers was his understanding. His friends would not be given gifts for one reason or another, and they would accuse their parents of not wanting to give them. Manny knew better.

Robert had quit drinking. He hadn't been an alcoholic, but even still, a five-dollar case of beer every week was an expense he could give up. Anna hadn't bought wine in almost a year. Their son had noticed. At some point, they had stopped warning him not to drink this or that. It had stopped being a part of their lives, and he paid attention to that much, at least. So, he decided to stick it out and hide his sorrow; if they could sacrifice, so could he.

A few days later, Manny went to school, wearing the worn-out shoes and old jeans that often got him picked on. "Hey dipshit!" one boy cried, walking past him into the building. "Did ya get those pants off a homeless man?"

The chubby boy ignored his schoolmates. He carried his backpack into the school and sat down at his first period class. It was history. The teacher gave a lecture on the lead-up to the election of Abraham Lincoln as the sixteenth president. He listened moderately well, but ultimately his thoughts wandered. History didn't excite him at this point in his life. The thing he really loved was fantasy and science fiction stories. English class bored him with its constant barrage of 'proper literature,' which couldn't have been less interesting. At least they could have given him some different material.

"Miss Jasperson?" the classroom intercom announced.

Miss Jasperson got up and pressed the talk button on the wall. "Yes?"

"Manfred Voren is to report to the office," the voice commanded. "His mother is here."

"Manny?" the teacher announced to the classroom. "Go on."

"Uh, ok," he said, surprised. What was this? His mother never showed up at school. Still, he did as instructed.

Inside the office, his mother finished sighing a document. "Yes, just for today," she said. "No problem."

"Mom?" Manny asked. "What's going on?"

"Let's go," she said. "I'll tell you in the car."

They walked to the car in silence. Once he sat in the back seat, placing his pack next to him, and fastening his safety belt, his mother turned around before starting the car. "Now sweetie," she told him, "we're going to get you some new shoes and pants, and then, if we have enough left over, you'll get to pick out a present."

Manny's mind lit up with a half a million questions at once, all of them related to money. "Wow!" he shouted, not able to contain himself. "Really?"

"My aunt Georgia sent us some money," she said. "I figured, it's Christmas time, so what the hell. Okay?"

A thought came to Manny, and he became suspicious. "I thought daddy didn't want to ask people for help," he reminded.

"He wasn't going to keep a full-time job after the plant closed," she explained, "and so, we needed to get through this winter with no trouble. He couldn't complain after I told him we needed the bills paid for two months until the welding jobs started opening up." She started the car. "So, what we're going to do is pay the bills, and with the leftovers, get you your present."

That hadn't been the last time that his parents and he had to accept help from others. At the age of sixteen, he'd wanted to get a job, and the local Wal-Mart was hiring, but his mother had insisted he take a different job instead.

"I know you want to work around here," Anna told her son, "but Shawn's offering you five dollars an hour more to work and you'll only have to be on a bus for a half hour a day."

"Mom!" Manny protested. "That's going to cost me so much time during the week!"

"I know honey," she explained, 'but this way you won't have to deal with customers."

"This is crazy!" he protested. "You just want me to have more money in case you need it!"

She gasped. "Manny! You don't know what you're talking about!" She shook her head. "Right now, your father and I are both working more often. We're lucky, because so many people we know don't have jobs. The fact that someone we know is willing to give you a job paying this while so many of your friends are flipping burgers for minimum wage? That's something you need to appreciate."

He folded his arms. "Alright, fine," he said. "But the moment I turn eighteen, I'm quitting."

"By then?" she replied. "I hope things are better."

Three times a week after school, and on some weekends, he would get on the bus and ride it up to just south of Jerseyville, where he would help load things onto trucks and out of them for a few hours before returning home. It was hard work. What really bothered him was his lack of free time. Wal-Mart had a lot of horror stories; most of them came from his friends who worked there. Nonetheless, it wasn't as far away, and he could've gotten rides home.

Each day, he came home in the evening, and his parents made a deliberate show of avoiding asking him if he spent his money. He didn't because he didn't want to get yelled at when they inevitably asked him for some. It bothered him on multiple fronts; he was trying to save his money for a car, but at the same time he knew he had a duty to support his family. It didn't make sense to him, any time he thought about it. His mother was a nurse. Sure, she didn't have the fancy RN degree, but it bewildered him how she stayed at the place that kept giving her part time work.

Sure enough, one morning, his mother came to him. "Manny, after school today, you need to stop by the Schnuck's and pay this month's electric bill," she said.

"Fine," he said.

"You know this is as hard on your dad as it is on you," she said.

He shot her a look. "I know," he said. The "I didn't say anything" was implied. He didn't want to have to say it out loud, because if he did, that might be misconstrued.

"Your dad's trying to get a gig at the construction site in Wood River," she explained. "If all goes well, he should be able to work for a good two months."

"Right," he said, heading out to the bus stop. He hadn't asked about being paid back, and she hadn't offered. He knew better than that.

The day at school had been relatively uneventful. That day hadn't been a workday, so after school, he got off at the grocery chain. Inside, he stopped at the ATM and checked his balance. Three hundred and ten dollars he'd saved up. The electric bill was a hundred and sixty dollars. He sighed as he went into the store and paid it at the courtesy counter.

The front door of the house creaked open. It hadn't been far to walk from the store. The receipt and bill plopped on the dining table. "You paid it," Robert acknowledged.

"Yeah," Manny replied, setting his backpack on his bed, removing his dusty jacket and his shoes and socks. He put on his house slippers and returned to the dining table.

"I didn't get the job at the construction site," Robert replied, "but the guys there sent me over to a chemical company in Belleville that'll be completely redoing several huge storage tanks, so I'll be working there for about three months."

Manny nodded. "Great," he said, pouring himself a glass from the generic diet cola in the center of the table. "I'm glad for ya."

"You know we don't like having to ask you for money," Anna said, grasping his hand.

"I know," he told his mother. Honestly, he was okay with not having a new game system since the Super Nintendo he got when he was seven. What bothered him was the idea that his parents kept getting the shaft and by extension, so did he.

"If things go well, you should be able to save up some money," Robert said.

"No problem," Manny said. He hated these discussions. Sure, he understood that sacrifice was needed, but that had been the non-stop unspoken rule since he'd been a small child. A storm of conflicting emotions played out in his head.

His mother saw a hint of his inner thoughts on his face. "Don't hide your feelings now," she chided.

He blinked long so she couldn't see him roll his eyes. "Alright," he began. "Why do you stay at that nursing home, when they keep giving you part-time?"

A disbelieving laugh escaped her. "I thought we've covered this," she remarked. "I'm this close to being the senior LPN on duty." It bothered her that she had to point this out again. Sure, he hadn't asked in almost two years, but loyalty was something that mattered. It was a lesson she wanted him to learn. "I'm making almost eighteen dollars an hour. One more person retires, and I'll be bumped up to senior LPN, and I'll be making twenty-two dollars an hour."

"How does that help if you're only working twenty hours a week?"

Robert's fist met the table. "Manfred!" he shouted. "You do not question your mother's work ethic!"

"I'm not...!"

Another bang on the table. "Excuse me," Robert interrupted, "did I give you permission to talk back?"

"No," Manny said, leaning back in his chair.

"Alright," the father continued. "That's what I thought. Now then, you're upset that they're only giving her twenty hours a week. Why are *you* only working twenty hours a week?"

Manny started forward like he'd been tasered. "Why?" he scoffed. "I'm going to school!"

Robert folded his arms. "And that gives you permission to do it," he asked, "but not her?"

Manny shot a look at the two of them. He had a rebuttal, but he let it die. "No," he said.

147

"Just for that," the father said, "you're doing dishes tonight." The family finished their meal in peace and returned their plates to the sink. As the teen began washing dishes, Anna approached.

"Look, I know it bothers you how we keep coming up short financially," she said, "but you have to understand that it's much worse for us. You're not a parent. You not suffering like we are."

"I know," Manny said, holding his harsher thoughts inside.

"It's a lot worse for us," she continued, "to know we've tried a thousand different things and we keep not getting ahead. It's a lot worse for us because, your father and I, our jobs *matter*."

Manny clenched his teeth inside closed lips. He swallowed his angry retort as he scrubbed dishes. This idea always pissed him off. It upset him that he didn't count because his job didn't 'count' or that his age disqualified him from complaining about being screwed over. One day he would finish growing up, and then, no one would be allowed to tell him he didn't have a job that mattered or that he was too young to complain.

A week later, Manny was heading on the bus up to his job. The engine rumbled on as he read a comic book he'd picked up from the Hayner Library. The minutes drifted away until he arrived at his stop, pulling the cord and waiting. Once the vehicle rolled to a stop, he grabbed his bag and got off. The large building loomed ahead, and he strolled up to the employee entrance.

"Alright, guys," the supervisor announced, "we've got five hundred bags of feed we have to get loaded. There are a lot of farms in the area that are in desperate need. We got to get this loaded quickly. Got it?"

"Got it," Manny said, along with about five other guys. All three large delivery trucks sat, backs open, so he went in the building with the rest of them and began loading bags. It took teams of two to carry the seventy-pound bags into each truck. Hours rolled by as the stack of sacks dwindled very slowly.

"Is Manny here?"

He turned his head at the sound of his name. "I'm here," he said, "what's going on?" Instinctively, he felt cold inside; hearing his name called seldom meant anything positive, especially at work.

It was his mom's friend Jenny from the nursing home. "There's been an accident," she half-shrieked. Tears were rolling down her face. "There was an explosion at the chemical plant your dad was welding at!"

The air seemed to stand still. Manny's heart leapt just about out of him. Before he knew it, he had jumped clear off the loading platform and was racing towards Jenny's car. He hadn't even hesitated to talk to his boss. Damn the consequences, this would have to take precedence. The cold chill continued to race throughout him. She fired up the engine and peeled out of the lot with him struggling to clamp on his safety belt. "What the fuck happened?" he asked, voice cracking.

"I don't know," she said, pushing the pedal to the floor. "All I know is your mom called me and told me to get you."

About five minutes of ninety mile per hour driving later, and several cops dodged, Manny raced into the hospital. "Excuse me!" he cried, almost crashing into the front desk. "My dad, Robert Voren..."

"I'll buzz you in," the receptionist said. She pointed. "Through that door."

The door slid open and he pushed it faster, running past it at top speed. He saw his mother, standing by a window, her face beet red, soaking wet, and painted with a mixture of sheer horror and disbelief. "Manny!" she cried, clasping onto him for dear life. Her son arrived at the window.

Eyes saw the scene for the first time.

"..."

Manny's mouth fell open; words failed him.

The man lying in the bed surrounded by a plethora of medical equipment scarcely resembled a man so much as a horror movie prop. Half of Robert Voren's face looked like the father Manny had grown up with. The other half came seemingly out of a war documentary. Crimson meat covered in blood sat in between large sections of charcoal black crust. The terrifying reality hit Manny that those black sections used to be skin. A mess of tubes protruded from his still good left arm, and a complex breathing apparatus covered his face.

For Manny, the dam seemed to burst.

"Oh god! Dad! DAD!"

His knees seemed to give, and he leaned against the glass, his mother holding him in a death grip. As he began to cry, tears streaming, his open-mouthed wailing echoed down the hall. The man that had once been Robert Voren lay near motionless on the bed, two doctors and a nurse clustered around him. They moved back and forth in a controlled chaos of motion, administering whatever support they could.

The dying man saw his son, and tears began to flow from the single remaining eye. The left side of the mouth moved. "love...y..." Manny managed to translate the mouth movements from across the pane.

An instant later, life vanished.

"NO! DAD! DAAAAD!"

Two burly security guards had to wrestle Manny away from the door, the teen screaming at the top of his lungs. "Manny!" Anna shouted, which got lost in the cacophony.

"LET GO OF ME!" Manny shouted, pulling. "DAAAAD!"

A cart careened past and into the room, several more nurses and a new doctor attached. They administered a series of drugs, struggled furiously in vain for ten more minutes, then stopped. As he saw the finality of the situation, the time of death being recorded, he collapsed to his knees. Anna sat next to her son on the floor, holding his head against her shoulder.

A blur of days later, a new widow and a grieving son sat in an attorney's office. The man held a printout in front of him. "Miss Voren," the lawyer said, drumming the papers on his desk. "My name is Alfred Donovan. You were recommended to me by my partner at your local office."

Anna nodded. "Mister Donovan," she said, wiping her eyes. "I just buried my husband a few days ago. I hope you have good news for me."

He slid the report over. "I have *great* news," he said, then immediately course corrected. "All things considered that is." He pointed. "The U.S. Chemical Safety Board discovered that the company had scheduled a replacement of the tank status mechanism about six months prior, but the parent corporation had cancelled it because they thought it wasn't needed."

Manny blinked tears away. "So," he chimed in, "you're saying we've got a case."

Alfred Donovan nodded. "We have quite a good case," he said. "We have a good chance of nailing them for negligence and that means you should get a substantial payout."

The grieving son didn't pay attention. His mother had the responsibility of being the head of household now. At some point he became aware that he was sitting on his bed in his room, staring at the blank screen of the aging television. Time blurred into oblivion as his raging torrent of sorrow had left him numb. Somewhere in a cold numb void he hovered, barely able to wrap his mind around the fact that his father was gone. Anna had always tried to teach him about God and religion. So, at the very least, she had the luxury of believing her husband had gone somewhere. Manny had no such privilege. The man he occasionally fought, the man who had often fought for him, the man who had taught him much of what he knew of the world, was gone. He cried until he fell asleep.

The company agreed to settle out of court, and the amount Manny and his mother took home paid off their house and their car and allowed them to buy a second. There had even been enough left over to allow the young man to complete an associate degree at the community college in Godfrey. Just like that he barely noticed that four and a half years had gone by since his father died.

"It's just insane," Manny said, talking to one of the free therapists provided by a local charity.

"I agree with you," the woman said. "They shouldn't have been so careless."

Manny gave a single chuckle and shook his head. "That's not what I mean," he clarified. "I mean, yeah, the company should have replaced a few thousands of dollars part that killed five people, rather than pay out to five different families." He took a sip from the glass of water in front of him. "No, what's insane is that my father was a hard-working, intelligent man." He blinked and opened his eyes wider a moment. "He did *everything* right, and yet, he was always getting screwed over, people picking people they knew were worse over him, but had connections, and not paying him enough." He sighed. "What's insane is that while he was here, we could never get ahead, and that killed him. Then, a company *actually kills* him, and *that* gets us ahead."

"I'm impressed with how you're getting on," she replied. "I wonder, you just got your associate's degree, and you're still working at the warehouses."

He shrugged. "Ah, well," he said, "The rest of them get assigned one spot or another. I got a specific task to do, and I'm close to getting promoted. It's not much, but hell, it's stable."

She wrote something down. "Aren't you worried about the future?" she asked. "What about marriage?"

"Ha!" Manny scoffed. "Look at me. I mean, *look at me*." He gestured to his considerable weight. "I'm not getting married. What do I have to offer?"

"So," she fought back, "you aren't worried about your situation? What about aspirations?"

"Aspirations get people killed," Manny said. "Dreams get people caught in a loop of disappointment." He crossed his legs. "We're born to be wage slaves. Why do they celebrate the success stories? Because those people fly in out of nowhere, they win the lottery, so to speak, and they zoom away, to leave us stranded here, desperately reaching out to them, knowing we're going to stumble and fall and spend the rest of our lives behind a Wal-Mart cash register pissed off that we got left behind. We drink ourselves to death crying over the fact that we never got to show the world that amazing idea that would've made us a billion dollars."

"That's a pretty fatalistic way of looking at it," she said. "So, what about those that *do* get to do what they love?"

"More power to 'em," Manny argued. "I'm just saying, there'd be more of them if we didn't live in a world where most people get thrown away." He stretched. "My future is somewhat ok. I've got a paid-off house that I'll inherit when my mother dies, I've got a car that's paid off, and I've got a job that'll end up paying me enough to coast on the money until I fucking just die." He laughed and shook his head. "I'm going to get life insurance money when my mother dies. Why am I so well-off?" He reconsidered. "Well, not well-off, but maybe…I dunno, 'okay-off?' Yeah, that's it." He coughed. "Why am I okay-off? Because my father, who tried his hardest, I mean *really tried*, got killed and we got lawsuit money and life insurance money."

153

"I don't want to belittle you," she told him, "but it seems to me like you're afraid to try because you don't want to risk failure. And you're boiling life down too simplistically."

A half-shrug later, and he replied, "Yeah, maybe. I just don't think I was born one of the lucky ones." He let out a nasal breath. "And there *absolutely* are people born lucky. I just wasn't one of them."

She wrote something down. "I'm going to hit you with a question," she said. "I'm not trying to be offensive, but I think your answer will tell me something." She centered herself in her seat. "Why get a two-year degree if you're not going to use it?"

"If I ever get lucky," he argued, "I might need it." He looked around. "Maybe I wanted to prove I wasn't just some fat idiot. Who knows? My mother said I should. What excuse should I pick?"

She gave him a stern look. "I understand your concern," she explained, "and your worry. Growing up poor has done a number on you, and you don't want to take risks. I'm just worried you're going to reach the age of fifty and you'll wonder why you didn't take a chance when you were younger."

He switched crossed legs. "I'll be feeling that feeling from inside a paid-off house," he said. "Kids from moderately-up-the-chain parents get to have dreams. Kids who barely ended up making ends meet like me? We get to go to work and answer 'yes sir' until we die."

"Well, I'm sorry to hear you say that, Manny," she said. "See you next week?"

He sighed. "Hope so," he said.

On the way home, he picked up some sandwiches from Subway and some diet soda. His mother had been pressuring him to try and lose weight, and he'd tried. In the last six months, he'd dropped twenty pounds to two-eighty. She'd been losing weight as well, and it honestly impressed him. She attributed it to finally making full-time at the nursing home and getting good benefits and being on her feet more, and he didn't know one way from another.

"I'm back, mom," Manny said, walking in the door. "I got the sandwich you wanted."

They sat in the dining room and he handed her the sandwich. They ate in silence for a few minutes before she set the half she'd been eating down. "I just wanted to apologize," she said.

His head jerked up. "What?"

She looked down a moment. "I used to tell you that you didn't suffer like I did," she replied to his question. "I was wrong. It was wrong of me to say."

"No," he countered. "It's okay. It's not a contest."

She reached out and grabbed his free hand. "Manny," she said, eyes locking with his, deadly seriousness present. "I saw it when you showed up at the hospital." A single tear came down. "I lost my husband, I lost the man I loved, but you, I saw you lose the only father you ever knew."

"Mom," he uttered. "I..." He had a response, but it died mid-sentence. They simply drew away from their seats and embraced each other.

A handful of weeks later, he got a call he would never forget.

His mother had cancer.

The first time he took her to her chemotherapy appointment he had to excuse himself to the bathroom to cry. Months dragged on, with the condition not seeming to budge. His mother had good enough insurance that paid for the treatment. In that sense, they lucked out yet again. Unfortunately, it meant he had to watch as she deteriorated. It ate him up inside.

"Some of the tumors have responded," the doctor said, examining the MRI displayed on the computer screen. "Unfortunately, it seems to have metastasized faster than we expected."

Anna squeezed her son's hand as he sat next to her. "So, how much longer do I have?" she asked.

"Mom," he argued. Why would she jinx it by asking?

She held a hand up. "No," she countered, "I want to hear this."

The doctor looked at the MRI once again and looked at her, the frown telling everything. "I'm afraid I doubt it'll be six months."

She lowered her head. "Doctor," she said, "do you think you could give my son and I some alone time?"

He nodded and walked out. "Certainly," he said.

"Mom," Manny argued, "I don't want to..."

"We need to talk about this," she stated. "Because this is the only time we're going to get to talk about it before I get a lot worse."

A hand wiped his eyes. "A...alright," he said.

"I'm going to die."

There it was. She'd said out loud what he didn't want to hear.

He nodded, accepting. "I know," he said. It was a moment of finality he had been desperate to avoid.

"What I want you to do," she said, "is not to have some big funeral *thing*, where everyone sits around and talks. I think it should be just you and me, *there*. Get the basic funeral, spend as little of the insurance money as possible. Okay?"

He nodded. "Okay." Again, the acceptance creeping out of his mouth caused rivulets of tears from his eyes.

"You're going to go somewhere you never got to go as a kid," she said. "I don't want you to just sit in that house and wallow in pity."

"I got it," he said. "Don't you think we can still beat this?"

"We're going to fight," she argued. "But we both know how this is going to end."

So, for weeks, they fought on. The doctors worked whatever magic they thought they could, and she never let it beat her down, despite everything. One day, however, the dreaded day arrived.

"We both know this is it," she said from her hospital bed.

Almost a year had gone by and he saw her become skeletal and emaciated. It pained him just to see how her body had shrunk. "I..." he stammered. His hand covered his mouth. "I can't," he finally said.

"You can," she said, gravel in her voice. "You're going to make it. You're going to live on."

"I know," he uttered, wiping his eyes on his shirt. "But I don't know what to do."

"You'll be okay," she groaned. "This is why I got more life insurance, remember?"

His eyes slammed shut, and he pounded his fist on his leg. "Damn the money!" he shouted. "I don't want to leave you!"

To this, she merely smiled. "Manny," she said, "think of all the times we had together. We went hiking, we went fishing, your dad taught you how to cook over a campfire, remember? All those memories are with you. You've got plenty of me to go around."

"Mom, no..."

She gripped his hand tighter. "Manny."

He opened wet eyes to look deep into her eyes. "Mom?"

She swallowed, which appeared to require a tremendous effort. "Did I do alright?"

Her question very nearly broke him. "You did great," he said.

She gave a nod with a smile.

And having done that, she died.

He honored her wish and decided not to have a wake, just a private affair where he was the only one who saw. As the woman who gave birth to him got lowered into the ground, he found himself unable to watch the dirt go in. He simply drove home, sat in his parents' room, and cried until he found himself woken up by the morning sun coming through the window.

That first morning without his parents, he crawled out of their bed and stumbled to the kitchen. He ran the tap until the water sent clouds of steam into the air and stuck his hand into the stream. The water burned his hand and he pulled it out and recoiled from the pain. *Nope,* he thought, turning the hot off and the cold on full blast to rinse his hand. *Still real, still really happening.*

The next part seemed even less pleasant then he expected. Days passed by, meeting with lawyers and officials of all kinds. After funeral expenses, he had a check for forty thousand dollars to deposit in his account. He sat and looked at the receipt for the deposit.

Forty-eight thousand dollars was the number.

Forty-eight thousand dollars was what his mother's life was worth, according to society.

Sitting alone, in an empty house, he couldn't help but laugh in between the tears. His parents had bought him a stable future by dying.

Something about it struck him as obscene.

CHAPTER ELEVEN

JERICHO SAT IN HIS RENTAL CAR, still reeling from having relived Manny's memories. *How...* His thoughts jittered around from one idea to another frantically as he struggled to comprehend how different his views were from real experiences. *His parents weren't lazy or stupid; how could they fail?* The slight hiss of the air conditioner and the faint rumble of the engine were the only sounds. For a solid minute, he had to just sit and process what he'd just learned. These weren't the type of people who should've come up short, according to Ayn Rand. These were hard working people who worked in fields continuously in demand in modern America. Yet, despite their sincere—and based on what he'd just seen, they were exceptionally dedicated—efforts to get ahead, they'd consistently been dumped upon. Situations kept arising outside of their sphere of influence. All his life, he'd been taught that people were poor because they failed to make good decisions, that it was a 'you problem' rather than a societal problem. Yet, he found virtually no areas where they could have made better decisions. They did almost everything right.

What did he believe? He didn't know. He would have to explore this further. In the meantime, he had a power to explore. He flipped the switch.

Nothing changed at all.

What the hell? He thought.

Once more he tried, and nothing happened. "Alright, I don't…" He exclaimed, getting up and out. He was going to go back in that house and demand to know what was going on. No sooner than his palm grasped the frame of the car to right himself, than did he figure several things out at once.

First, Manfred Voren wouldn't know anything more than he did at the moment. Second, there was a far better explanation at play.

"Goddammit," Jericho whispered. "You're a fucking idiot sometimes, Jericho."

He couldn't imagine himself—sincerely, genuinely imagine himself—as anyone other than himself.

Goddammit, he realized. *They always said you were a narcissist.* He slumped into the driver's seat, laughing. It was a tragedy. He'd bought a power he couldn't use. Oh well, he'd already made an agreement. It would be a violation of his principles to break it now. Manny had held up his end of the bargain, after all. What would he do next?

He had more powers to collect, because he hadn't come close to the amount of money he was willing to spend, and also, he wanted to explore more of people's memories. Eagerly driving away, he headed for a hotel in Saint Louis, calling ahead and reserving a room. Thirty minutes later, he sat in his hotel room suite, at his computer desk. With a technopathic ability, he interacted with the stock trading applications on the internet to conduct his business at hyper speed. His accounts were looking good, and his financial picture seemed rosy, despite the various uproars in the world.

About ten minutes passed with him alone, accompanied only by his inner thoughts. A handful of water he splashed on his face, as he made his decision. The suit went into his closet and, of his clothes the bellboy had brought up, he selected a casual shirt, black jeans, and walking shoes. If the problem were his having lived a sheltered life, he would take it to the streets, so to speak.

The late afternoon crowd densely cluttered the streets, as those walking home from work mingled with those going to evening shifts. Who would he go into the memories of? Several promising candidates immediately came into view. The arc of his glance of the crowd landed on her. She immediately seemed the best target. She looked reasonably attractive to him, having stepped out of an apartment building. The evening dress under the expensive pea coat, combined with the slight mascara run from one eye's tears, told him a story. With some effort, he pushed through the crowd until he found an empty patch around her of a couple feet. Several powers combined at once as he deliberately bumped into her, brushing hands. "Oh, geez!" he apologized, "I'm so sorry!"

"Be careful!" she cried, wiping one eye.

He ducked into a building and headed for the public restroom.

Oh, good grief, he thought, wiping his face with a paper towel. A litany of different ideas came to him immediately.

The experiment had been a success. By combining heightened intellect with enhanced perception, as well as general enhancement, the instant had felt like days instead of real time, as Manny's had been. This meant he'd gotten all the same information, the same level of detail, with much less stress.

The next thought had been, *wow, I've been so wrong about women for so long*!

His sexual history had become a matter of public record, what with his financial status. No less than eight times had he been seriously involved with women only to find them leaving him, blaming him each time. Before he'd been convinced of his innocence. Now, though, he learned just how ignorant he was of what life was like for women. Specifically, he saw, through her memories, how her boyfriend of eight months had hurt her emotionally and didn't even see it. If only the man could see how he upset her.

Jericho cocked his head.

Wait.

"Son of a bitch," he silently mouthed.

In his mind, a handful of powers activated. He saw the location of the boyfriend in question, in the woman's apartment, seated at the couch, watching tv, utterly unaware of his guilt in the fight they just had. A heartbeat later, he stood behind the man, invisible. A single palm stretched out in the direction of the man. *Hope this works*, the billionaire thought.

He willed the man to experience her memories.

"WHAT IN THE FUCK!" the man shouted, jerking in his seat as if stung by a wasp.

Jericho backed up, still invisible, but outside the range of accidentally being touched if the man flailed about. The man sat up straight, hands clenching the seat cushion. Tears began to fall from the man's eyes. "Oh...my god..." he quietly uttered. A hand came up to wipe eyes. "Oh my god!" His words became not just louder, but more urgent. He scrambled for the lamp table by the couch, where his phone sat. "Oh god, I'm such a fucking moron! Please pick up!"

Jericho teleported back to his hotel room.

The soft bed cushioned his head as he collapsed onto it. A rapid heartbeat came rising within him. Breathing came quick and in bursts. This emotion, it was joy? It confused him a moment. This act, this 'good deed' he had done, it meant nothing in the grand scheme of things. So, a couple would reconcile and better understand each other, so what? Yet, a feeling of exuberance filled him from head to toe, the likes of which he hadn't felt since being a child. A moment later, a worry tempered his good feeling. He'd invaded privacy on a level never before seen. He would have to work on that, hopefully find a way to block out certain kinds of private information. A mental note was made.

The cell phone on his nightstand dialed a number that had not called his in years. "Yeah, Luther?" Jericho announced into the voicemail. "I'd like to sit and talk to you." He rolled his eyes. "I know I've been an asshole, but you're my brother, and I think I need a new perspective. Call me back." He hung up.

What other perspectives could he get?

In for a penny, he figured, as the saying went.

"Hey," he called up one of his employees in New York. "Do you remember when Sharon Francis left her phone number with me?"

An awkward pause came and went. "Sir," the woman replied, "she was challenging you to a debate."

He nodded. "Yeah," he said, "I know."

Another awkward pause came and went. "Pardon me for being so frank, sir," she continued, "but I didn't think after the spat you two had on CNN, that you would want to talk to her again. Especially given the way she reacted to what you said." She paused. "But, if you want, I can call her."

Jericho thought about it. "You know what? It'll probably mean more if I call her myself," he admitted. "Just give me the number and I'll call her." He took a deep breath and let it out. "Yes, really." She read him the number. "Great. Thank you." He hung up. He dialed.

"This is Sharon Francis," the woman well-known for her outspoken support of the civil rights movement and Black Lives Matter, said.

"Jericho Torvalds here," he said.

"Oh, *really*?" she stated, getting ahead. "After the shit you said on TV about black people? You actually want to talk to me?"

"First of all," he replied, trying to be graceful, "I was wrong." He gave her a moment to digest his words. "Second, I'm calling because you wanted to talk to me about it, and I want to expand my horizons. I've been sheltered and living in an echo chamber, just like you said. Who better than you to show me a different viewpoint on the subject?"

163

An audible gasp of a laugh escaped her. "Tell you what," she said. "In three days, Anderson Cooper is interviewing me for the opening of a youth center in New York. I'll be in New York tomorrow, and we can talk about it there, IF, that is, you're willing to be recorded, so you can't walk back anything you say. Give me a location."

He cleared his throat. "Tell you what," he argued. "The Waldorf-Astoria at two P.M., and you can even film the fucking thing if you want."

This time she laughed for a solid five seconds. "Okay, you know what?" she challenged. "You're on. Be prepared to be hit with some serious hardball."

"No problem," he said. "Goodbye." He hung up. Next, he called the hotel in question and requested a meeting room with audio-visual equipment and catering service and flexed his financial muscle to get it done. No doubt the media would get wind of this, and he expected to have his mind changed somewhat. He hadn't been converted into far leftism; in fact, he didn't know what his current political beliefs were. What he did know, however, was that it couldn't possibly hurt to get too much empathy with others.

"I need a distraction," he whispered, realizing he wasn't going to get to sleep right away. The last few weeks had been a whirlwind of rushing around to gather powers, making business deals with people, and spending money to add an air of legitimacy. He had explored some of the powers, specifically the ones with obvious uses. He'd made sure to learn all the abilities with offensive and defensive capabilities. There had been, however, some abilities he'd skimped on using.

In the suitcase, he had a bag of clothes he'd bought specifically for an experiment. The shirt and pants were baggy. In the bathroom, he fully undressed and sat on the toilet lid. In his inner mental collection of triggers, he located two specifically. The first, he collected from a young man of almost four hundred pounds, who had lost a tremendous amount of body fat and gained huge muscularity since the lights, without changing anything. The second, a woman got run over by a delivery truck and stood up afterward unharmed.

Sure, his physique had the hallmarks of regular exercise, but the lean arms and flat torso displayed a lack of calories rather than an abundance of muscle. The belt size thirty and the medium shirt showed his lack of dedicated strength training.

"Here goes nothing," he uttered, activating both regeneration and optimization together. In his mind, by combining the two, the regeneration would speed up the process. Nothing seemed to be happening, however. Hmm, he wondered. Maybe his calculations had been wrong. Maybe the regeneration treated his body as it was now as the thing to return to, and the optimization was nullified by...

"ERGH! FUCK!"

His shout came after a bolt of pain shot outward from the center of his chest to every corner of his body. The pain burned outward, as his flesh began to redden from the heat of tissue expansion. It did not spare him the pain, and it prolonged his suffering. Tissue damaged from heat instantly recovered as it grew, and it took all his strength to stumble to his feet, slump over the edge of the tub, and turn the cold water on. "Ah! Ah!" The sharp sting of ice-cold water on his skin rattled his brain as he let out more shouts of pain. As the water began to fill the tub, heat steamed off the wet skin as droplets evaporated. His body heat began to warm the water. A lift of his head allowed the water to drain, and fresh cold water rushed against his reddening skin.

"Oh, fuck, this hurts!" he blurted.

The pain suddenly shut off.

"Ah!"

A sharp breath escaped his lungs as a shout. A trembling hand reached up and shut off the water. A leg stretched over the tub and stood on the shower mat, followed by the other. At once he stuck

165

his arms out to stabilize himself. Stumbling forward, he planted both hands on the counter, and caught his breath. A few seconds later, he looked up.

He legitimately did a double take.

The image that greeted him possessed a bodybuilder's physique, with all of the sculpted bulging muscle. He no longer had a pencil neck, and his chest had pecs and his abs were visible, and it had none of the gross exaggerated looks that a lot of professional body-builders had. Optimization, indeed, he figured. After drying himself off, he dug around in his suitcase and found his new clothes. The underwear fit fine, but the shirt and pants, he'd expected them to still be slightly baggy. Instead, they fit very snugly. Indeed, he would have to have a whole new wardrobe. Could he get a new suit by tomorrow's appointment? He didn't know, but if not, he would just have to show up wearing gym clothes. Hey, why not? They would just shake their heads and call him weird. Poor people were crazy, after all, while rich people were 'eccentric.'

CHAPTER TWELVE

AT A SUBURBAN HOME OUTSIDE CHICAGO, a man stepped through the front door and set his suitcase and guitar cases down beside the front entrance, and after locking the door, slid into the loveseat and closed his eyes. Luther Torvalds had just done a tour with his band, Blood Fury, and the struggles of the road had weighed on his mind, leaving him exhausted. Gentle dreams of wind over the ocean passed through his mind, until he awoke after dark.

A quick glance at his cell phone told him it was seven thirty. He was hungry; he hadn't eaten since he'd gotten off the bus. As he got in his car and headed for the local burger joint, he flipped through the news channels on the radio. A chuckle escaped his mouth as he heard, once more, about his brother journeying about the world. The news media had finally revealed what he'd suspected all along. His brother, Jericho, had long since proven his love of all things Ayn Rand, and had made himself into a billionaire off the privilege brought to him by his family history, although he'd never admit it. The fact that he'd gotten the power to collect abilities had been precisely what Luther thought the man would get after powers became a thing. He himself had gotten an empathic power, although he doubted he would be the only one. Each time his band went to a new city, he found opportunities to use it to spread acceptance by forcing people to experience the histories of others.

It ate away at him that his brother had become the type of person Luther despised the most: the worshippers of wealth. Sure, he'd made the big time with his band, but at least it required him to actually possess some real skill and talent at playing the guitar, singing, and writing songs. His bandmates and he had sweat, bled, and clawed their way to the thirty million albums sold so far and counting. They'd fought off greedy corporate executives that hated their leftist lean and political songwriting. Still, they'd gambled on a deliberately anti-fascist sound and had rode the controversy all the way to the bank. The drive through woke him from his reverie.

"Yeah," he replied, "I'll have a double cheeseburger combo, large, and a Doctor Pepper, no ice."

After paying, and getting his order, he drove home, and sat in his living room, eating. He got a phone call.

"Luther," his mother, Suzanne, said, "have you heard from your brother?"

Luther rolled his eyes. "Mom, you know I don't talk to him anymore unless it's an emergency," he said. "Why? Did something happen?"

"No," the mother said, "it's just that, I feel like something's going to happen. I mean, I knew he was on the news already, what with his stock tips and all that, but now he's on the news for this...well, whatever the hell this is he's doing. It bothers me."

"You know what it is," Luther remarked. "Powers are the new thing he has to collect. Before it was just money."

"Yes," she replied, "I'm just not sure about all this. I just wish grand-father hadn't gotten his hooks into him."

"Tell me about it," Luther said. "He used to be fun. Now he's just so drab. And this culture of wealth, I just can't handle it. I mean, I'm rich, and I'm not worth a hundredth of what he's worth. I couldn't imagine what I'd do with so much."

"Oh well," she replied. "As long as you're okay. How was the tour?"

168

He half-grinned. "Good," he replied. "We sold out all the dates and we don't have to turn in our next album for eight months. I'm looking forward to taking some vacation time."

"That's great to hear," she told him. "Now that the semester's over, your father and I are taking some time off from the university to go on a little vacation of our own."

That piqued his interest. "You're not worried about this whole 'powers are real' thing?"

"Not really," she replied. "I feel like if things were to have gone awry, they'd have done so already. Besides, you're the one who can feel other people's emotions. You tell me."

He pondered the situation. Over the weeks, he'd gotten inside the heads of quite a lot of people with powers. "They typically are afraid to rock the boat," he revealed. "I mean, they are mostly people who, until the Lights, were just average people. There are a few psychos out there who got powers, but the vast majority of them just want to live their life."

"Makes sense," she agreed. A news story she'd heard came back to her. "Did you hear about the preacher in Oklahoma?"

He lowered his eyebrows. "No," he admitted. "I want to hear about that one."

"Well, nobody's saying anything." She paused to recollect. "But basically, he somehow got a meeting with that televangelist, oh, what's his name..." She stopped and thought harder. "Uh, Masterfield?"

"Hiram Masterfield?" Luther remembered. "You mean that disgusting megachurch guy in Oklahoma City who fleeces old people out of their money?"

"That's the one," Suzanne agreed. "I wonder if he used some kind of power on him."

"Hmm, maybe," Luther said. "Maybe. I don't know. I just want you to be safe."

"Thanks," she replied. "I love you, son, if you hear from your brother, get him to call me."

"Love you too, mom," he said. "And I will. Bye."

"Bye."

He hung up. Throwing the wrappers in the garbage, he grabbed a soda from the fridge and headed upstairs. He'd loved playing music since he was fourteen, but the tours and the concerts took their toll on him. Right now, he wanted to unwind from the constant grind, the endless hours of riding in a bus, and the risk of putting himself on the line to use his powers. Sure, it made him feel great, but it ached him to have to experience the worst feelings and memories of people, and to share them with others. Bringing different communities together took a lot of empathy, and that tired him out, mentally rather than physically.

On his computer, he booted up a Sega Genesis emulator and played Sonic 2. The bright colors and simple electronic music made him happy. Controller in hand, he finished the game in a couple hours. After that, he pulled out his Kindle and read until his eyes began to droop low.

He set it on his desk, and stripped down, crawling into bed in just his briefs.

The light streamed through his curtains and woke him up. He wiped his eyes and climbed out of bed. According to his cell phone, it was ten thirty. He had five texts, three of which were from the record label, and he answered them right away. He also had two missed calls from his brother. No voicemails were left. Ah well, he figured. If Jericho wasn't going to tell him why he should return the call, he wasn't going to bother. He sure as hell wasn't going to endure another debate about politics or the economy.

After getting dressed and having a quick protein shake for breakfast, he drove to the gym with his duffel bag. Stepping through the door, he swiped his card at the counter and strolled towards the locker rooms. "Hey, Luther," Andy, who often worked there, said. "I heard your new album. I think it's better than your first one."

He smiled. "I should hope so," he bragged. "The guys have gotten better at playing."

The weight room took a few hours. The road didn't give him much time to work out, so he had a full body exercise to do. By the time his arms and legs burned, and his torso cramped up, it was past lunch time. It wasn't over, though; next he headed over to the cardio room. He put his earbuds in and jogged on the treadmill while listening to podcasts. An hour later, he switched to the stationary bike. By three-thirty, his body gave him warning bells and stood up, blinked sweat out of his eyes, and headed towards the locker room.

Plopping onto the locker room bench, he replaced his earbuds in their case and opened his locker. The shorts and undershirt went in the plastic wash bag, and he pulled his casual clothes out from behind them, along with a bottle of body wash.

"Oh, fuck," he uttered, as the hot water hit his body, sticking his long black hair to his neck and upper back. He let out a soft gasp as he let the water soothe him. After lathering, rinsing, and repeating just once, he shut off the water and reached for his towel.

After having dried off and dressed in his outside clothes, he turned to his phone.

Then he found himself staring in disbelief at the news story presented before him.

"Billionaire investor Jericho W. Torvalds shocked the world today," the CNN anchor began, "when he announced, after meeting with civil rights activist and Black Voices of America spokesperson Sharon Francis, that he had been wrong about race."

The focus then shifted to Luther's older brother. "You see," Jericho said, wiping an eye, "the last time Miss Francis and I spoke was eight months prior on Fox News, and at the time, I said several things that were either misinformed, or based entirely on ignorance." He looked solemnly into the camera. "I had been operating under a complete lack of black perspectives in my views, and I've corrected that to some extent over my journeys across the nation. I will be donating a large sum of money to black causes and activists. I do not believe this makes up for what I have said, but I hope to begin the process of making amends."

The anchor returned. "Sharon Francis met with Jericho Torvalds earlier today," he explained, "and had agreed to film the encounter. However, she has now stated that she prefers not to release the interview, as it was a very personal conversation, and said merely that, it was, 'an eye-opening back and forth.' The billionaire says he will put more effort into taking other perspectives into account in the future."

Luther clicked off the video. He knew the look he saw in his brother's eyes. It was the same look lots of people had when he'd given them the memories and feelings of others to show how wrong they were. He dialed his brother's number. The voicemail greeting greeted him. "Jericho?" he yelled. "It's Luther. Call me. I know something's up, I know that look, you call me, you hear?" He sent the message.

"Luther," a text message reply said. "Call you back later. Much to talk about, I assure you! Business right now."

After lacing his shoes, he stuffed his phone into his hip holster and grabbed his bag. There would be quite a lot to talk about, and he wanted to see if Jericho was honest or if he had simply decided to sell himself at a different angle.

The thought came to him that he'd avoided.

He could use his powers to read his brother's feelings.

"Dammit," he whispered, getting into his car. The idea of privacy was one thing, but what really bothered him was the disappointment. He typically avoided experiencing his brother's memories because they were so superficial and lacking substance. The older brother he enjoyed playing with as a child grew up into a boring man who worshipped capital and the hoarding thereof. "Ah, screw it."

He plunged in.

Jericho walked into the meeting room at the Waldorf, a new suit adorning his much more built frame, and the greeting was cold, to say the least. "Mister Torvalds," Sharon Francis said, ice in her voice, extending her hand.

"Miss Francis," he replied, taking her hand. Eagerly, he tripped his power on and lived years of her life in an instant of real time. It seemed to be days, a clear sign of his improvement. He got to experience her time as a youth on the unforgiving streets of Chicago. She had an uncle who had a 'real job' but lost it when the company downsized. After every legitimate attempt to survive went without success, he turned to selling weed to feed his family, only to be murdered by police. She got to see a family friend arrested and sent to prison for being a lookout for a drug deal, when in fact, he just happened to be waiting at a bus stop less than forty yards from where one took place. She got to see every time her mother drove thirty miles a day to her 'decent job' she got, and how half the time they got pulled over for driving while black. All of these memories and more, years of systemic racism taught to a young girl who would grow up and swear to fight back, he got to experience as she had.

Pulling his hand back, he blinked rapidly and crushed down his emotions, a skill he had developed since the first time with Manfred Voren. A storm brewed in his mind as everything he ever thought about race in America was proven wrong right before his very eyes. The active racism of far-right conservatives and the passive racism of lukewarm centrist liberals alike got shown to him first-hand. There was nothing like experiencing it for oneself, and he had just gotten the biggest lesson of his life on race relations. He'd vaguely heard of things like the bombing of Black Wall Street or redlining, but now he knew about it the way she'd learned about it. She'd learned about it from black leaders and civil rights teachers, and he saw how horribly skewed the education he'd gotten growing up had been. None of these things had been taught by his high school history professors, and now he knew why.

"Let me begin by saying," Sharon began, "I want to address the issue we argued about last time, that is, the fact that you didn't think the civil war and slavery had as much impact on the black community today as some black activists say. You specifically said," she pulled it up on her phone, "that 'we didn't have to go all the way back to slavery to talk about black communities' and that 'personal responsibility takes precedent first and foremost.' What do you say to that?"

He breathed in through his nose, and let it out, slowly, deliberately. "I was simply, utterly, wrong," he admitted.

This statement caught her so off guard her head jerked up from the phone. "Excuse me, what?"

He nodded. "You heard me right," he repeated. "I was wrong. After the civil war, laws were specifically put in place to prevent black people from acquiring wealth. When the first suburbs were built, clauses in the leases prevented them from being sold to blacks. I was so incorrect, it's laughably sad to even look at old interviews of mine. It's an embarrassment."

It took her a few moments to decide whether he was genuine, or, if this was a progressive air he was putting on to save face. "So," she said, realigning, "what's with the dramatic change of tune from just months ago?"

"Let's be brutally honest," he confessed. "I'm a billionaire, I live in a fancy penthouse New York City, I grew up in a nice suburb of

Chicago, I'm sheltered. I'm a textbook example of white privilege. What changed my mind? I spent the past few weeks travelling around to meet real people, and I got to talk to them." That last part hadn't been a lie, he just didn't need to tell her he'd spent only the last few days reliving the memories of dozens of random people.

She gasped a laugh. "Alright," she stated, embers glowing in her voice, "you're messing with me. You know I'm going to post this on YouTube and you want to discredit me. They're going to think you're joking."

He leaned forward and extended his hand. "I can show you how serious I am," he offered.

She looked at the hand and recalled that the FBI had revealed he was going around paying people to let him copy their superpowers. "Why should I trust you?"

"I am many things," he replied. "Many of them are not good. But the one thing I'm not is a liar. I've honored every promise I've made. I'm telling you that you have nothing to fear."

She nervously took his hand. He showed her everything he'd experienced up to that point, making it so it would feel like only a few hours to her. He felt particularly proud of that; it had been his best job so far of compressing the data experienced.

She startled, pulling backward and gasping. "Wow, that's…" She blinked hard a few times. "That's…something else…"

"I've even given you free copies of some of the powers I've got," he told her, "free of charge. You have to live a long life and perform more charitable service, after all."

She had regained her steady breathing. "How," she asked, "how did you come across this?"

He shrugged. "Hey, I didn't think about it at the time," he admitted, "beyond just thinking, 'hey, an empathy power seems useful.' It wasn't until I met Manny that I found just how useful it was."

She reached, shut off the camera, and turned off the audio equipment. "You go out there and make the world a better place, Jericho Torvalds," she told him. "I don't know how much I actually like you, but damn it, you convinced me."

"Believe me," he said, standing up, "I'm going to."

"Keep in touch."

He waved as he left the room. "I will!"

Luther pulled back, after experiencing his brother's and the woman's memory of the event. He didn't know what to think about it. A wave of feelings poured over him. It pissed him off that his brother was such an idiot for so long. He felt overjoyed that the cool older brother might be back. He drove to Subway and got a footlong chicken sandwich with all the toppings. As he ate, he waited for his brother to call. This would be the first conversation that he genuinely looked forward to having with Jericho in literal years.

CHAPTER THIRTEEN

AT A FAMILIAR HOME IN ALTON, a cell phone rang. Manny woke up from his nap to his anime ringtone. "Yeah?" he said. Although he had been doing the superhero thing for a while now, this was the first time Davis had called this early.

"Remember how I said you'll have your opportunity?" The FBI agent said. "Well, you're up."

Manny pulled himself to a seated position. The alarm clock indicated ten in the morning. The previous night, he'd been all over the world, handling minor emergencies. This day, he'd wanted to take the day off and relax. Still, for Agent Wilson to call him this early, indicated something serious was going to happen. "What's going on?" he asked the agent.

"We've been monitoring some QAnon assholes," Davis revealed, "and one of their own just blabbed and said that some guy they know is planning on hitting a campaign stop of a Representative Jan Dunsmith. It's in California."

Manny's eyes went wide. "When?"

"Any time now!"

"Oh shit!" Manny cried, standing up and shifting into his female form. "Why didn't you tell them?"

"I did!" Davis cried. "But you need to be there."

"I'm going!" Jennifer shouted, dropping the phone onto the bed.

She shifted and zoomed out of the house, and up into the atmosphere. Scanning the countryside, she came across the sight of the fairgrounds which held the rally. In a few moments, she stood in back, scanning the crowd for any kind of weapon. Nothing came up. No one except for the federal agents surrounding the congressman had any guns of any kind.

The air erupted with a loud crack.

A second pop sounded as a projectile crashed into Jennifer's outstretched hand, inches from the congressman's face, and vaporized on contact.

"Sir!" she shouted. "Are you alright?"

"You!" Jan Dunsmith cried. "You're that woman!"

A pop sound echoed, and she caught another projectile as it came from a different angle. This time, the assailant had made a mistake. He'd allowed himself to be seen. She hovered over him in a moment, looking down. The crowd instinctively parted, seeing the imposing woman flying overhead. He turned to run, but she reappeared in front of him again. "You're not escaping," she warned him.

He pelted her with pieces of gravel and various screws at orbital velocity. They collided with her hands moving at a blur and she held them up to reveal the dust that his objects left behind, with her skin unmarred. Her arms blurred for just an instant, and then all the small bits of debris on his person lie on the ground around him.

"YOU! ON THE GROUND!"

The shout of several federal agents at once caused the man to kneel.

"Thank you so much!" Jan Dunsmith said, stepping off the stage. He approached; his bodyguards looked nervous as he stepped closer to the powerful heroine. As a handful of large, suited men wrapped handcuffs around the assailant with pistols pointed at his vulnerable bits, the attacker decided to go quietly, as his attack had failed, and he wasn't likely to pull a fast one with this woman here. The congressman watched the would-be assassin carted off and looked just a bit up at her. She stood about two inches taller than him. "What's your name?"

"Jennifer," she replied. "Jennifer Black."

He gave her a confused look. "No codename?" He thought about it further. "I thought they were calling you Capacitor, after the character you look like."

She shook her head. "I'm a real person," she protested. "Besides, if you could fly and were super strong, would you put on a Superman costume and call yourself Superman?"

He pictured it. "No, I think you've got a point there," he replied, a chuckle in his tone.

"Well, do you think you'll be safe now?"

"I hope so," he shot back. "Oh! Wait a minute before you go." He reached in his suit pocket and produced a business card. "I'll be back in Washington in a few days. Get in touch."

"I will," she said, nodding, "because there's something I definitely want to talk to you about." She took to the air, and looked into the distance, seeing the cop car carrying the would-be assassin, and she saw he had no objects on him to use as weapons, and the agents kept their eyes on his hands as they drove him away.

Less than a minute later, she sat in her bedroom once again. She dialed her phone.

"I heard you stopped him," Davis replied.

"Hey, uh," she said, miffed, "how about next time you give me *a bit more warning*? What if I'd shut my phone off before taking a nap?"

"Well, um," Davis countered, "you didn't, and that's very responsible of you!" He sighed. "Look, I figured the gunman might not be a gunman, and it turns out I was right."

"Next time, *please* try to give me more warning," she chastised. "Right now, I'm going to take a break. If there's an emergency, I'll handle it, but as of right now, today's a day off. Got it?"

"Gotcha," Davis said. "You deserve it. Talk to you later."

Manny was back again, getting his equipment ready. He had a purse for Jennifer, but also, he had a burner cell phone, set up just for her, and some plastic bags and waterproof containers with GPS locators. He put on casual clothes and got in his car. He'd avoided anyone seeing him, super speed was truly his most useful power, but still, he wanted some wiggle room. He drove to the Fairview Heights Wal-Mart, some thirty minutes away by highway. In the bathroom, he shut a stall behind him and transformed. From there, she took to super speed again.

The air rushed past her as she zoomed through the atmosphere. The bugs and rain droplets collided with her power and got shoved out of her way. Flight was a real treat; she doubted she'd ever get tired of doing this to unwind. From high above the Pacific Ocean, she saw to the bottom. Impacting the water, she shoved through like a bullet, the cool water flowing past her skin. Her power provided waterproofing to all her clothes and anything in her pockets, so she didn't worry about anything she carried. She activated her vision powers, and the pitch blackness of the depths gave way to sights no human had seen without specialized camera equipment.

She planted her feet at the lowest level of the ocean, the Challenger Deep of the Marianas Trench. The incredible water pressure—eight tons per square inch—produced in her a unique feeling. It felt like walking through pudding to her impossibly durable body. Clothes and hair sat compacted against her skin by the enormous weight of water. She knelt and scooped up some of the soft soil of the bottom. Simple life forms began to float around her, with her body heat making her akin to a torch in the near freezing water. She smiled as she examined the shrimp-like creatures as they floated by. One thing she noticed was how loud the ocean was. She'd read somewhere that sea creatures were dying, killing themselves by beaching, to escape the noise, but now that she heard it herself, it was ridiculous. She heard all kinds of sounds, from whale and dolphin sounds, to a faint tapping sound.

A tapping sound, she heard, over the din. It had the distinct sound of fist on metal.

Three short taps played, followed by three long, then three short. It was the international code for SOS.

She closed her eyes and hovered upward, focusing all her effort into her super hearing. A general sense of where the sound came from began to appear. She turned her body and squinted.

She saw, some nine hundred kilometers away, a research submarine with four scientists stranded in a vessel taking on water, with a crack in its window. It had torn free of the line connecting it to its ship on the surface.

A firm grip allowed her power to hold the vessel together while she floated it back to the surface. Soon, she sat the vessel down on the platform of the ship it had been launched from. The scientists took pictures with her and she decided to sit for questions for a few minutes.

"So," the Korean man said, sitting next to his American fellow scientist, "How is it you can lift heavy objects with your hands? Wouldn't you punch through?" Though accented, she found his English impeccable.

"I'm guessing my power holds things together while I'm touching it," she answered. "There's a lot to this I don't know."

"What brings you out into the ocean?" A man with a Russian accent asked.

She shrugged with her hands. "I'm just out, exploring," she said. "I like traveling."

"How come your clothes aren't wet?" The American asked.

"That's my power again," she confirmed.

"Will we see you about?" The Korean scientist inquired.

"I'm always about," she replied. "Anyway, I'll leave you guys to your work." She took off from the vessel.

After flying away, she soon stood atop the summit of Everest, feeling the frigid, thin air colliding with her skin. It would have been difficult to breathe for a normal person. It honestly struck her as one of the most amazing sights on Earth, staring out into the mountainous terrain, the clouds all around. After having her breath taken away for several minutes, she grabbed some stranded climbers and brought them back to base camp before heading off to her next spot.

Rocketing over the terrain, she felt free. Even stopping to help people here and there didn't bring her down. For the first time in her life, she had a sense of purpose. Years of coasting by, terrified to step out of the comfort zone, and just a few weeks after getting actual powers, the liberation felt total. Sure, the responsibilities were enormous. Every time she ventured out to secure peace or to rescue victims from some horrific catastrophe, her every action, her every decision, determined whether people lived or died. She'd had to stare down guns, and carefully handle people burning from natural explosions or terrorist bombings. Occasionally, the horrors she had to witness brought tears to her eyes. Even so, she finally had something she knew she was good at.

The dry desert wind blew over her as she hovered over the Great Pyramids at Giza. She took in the sights from angles the tourists never got to see. The city nearby bustled, the sounds of vehicles and commerce echoing in her ears. She saw the Sphinx and marveled at the sights she never would have seen on her own. Scanning, she saw down through the layers, to the inner tunnels, and burial chambers. It amazed her how men without modern equipment built such a thing.

A gunshot rang out.

Hastily, she turned in its direction, and saw a man standing on the roof of a building in the city of Giza. She caught the bullet and hovered towards the man. At a football field's distance, she saw the middle age man, police badge on his uniform, and the years of dealing with criminals painted on his bronze skin.

"Sorry!" he shouted, in heavily accented English. "I saw you floating there, did not know how to get your attention!"

"What do you need?" she asked.

He gestured down, and she landed on the roof. "Hostage situation," he said, holding up a tablet with pictures taken by military and police who surrounded a tall office building. "Local political leaders and businessmen. They want prisoners released."

She looked away from him, and a quick scan of the city showed her the building, and the incident currently underway. Then she returned to looking at him. "Okay," she said. "Special instructions?"

He displayed several pictures on screen. "Rescue these men first," he said. "No one gets shot. Okay?"

She nodded. "Got it."

She took a deep breath and steeled her will. From the safe distance of the police building, she could see the floor where the eight VIPs were held. Ten terrorists in all, six carrying machine guns, the rest armed with pistols. A duffel bag of explosives sat next to two in the lobby. *Alright*, she thought. *Here goes.*

She took off. Everything stood frozen as she zoomed in through the front entrance, up to the seventh floor, and snatched the important rich people from gunpoint right away. From the police perspective, they suddenly appeared behind the safety barrier erected around the building, along with a duffel bag full of explosives farther away.

The six patrolling the lobby saw a white woman appear in front of them, and all six converged on her position and fired. Her hands blurred as she caught the rounds in midair. A few seconds later and they ran out of ammo. In the blink of an eye, they found themselves tied up in ethernet cable from the I.T. office. Upstairs, she appeared before the remaining terrorists. She zoomed from one to the next, yanking the pistols from their hands and crushing them. Then she knocked each one to the ground, draped one under each arm like a sack of potatoes, and flew them outside two at a time. In moments, the entire ordeal was over, with ten terrorists safely in police custody, and lots of hostages freed.

One officer went to say something to her, but she remembered her lesson from China and fled at once.

On the way back to the states, she stopped by the Eiffel Tower, Stonehenge, and a few other important spots. Not much for tourism, she didn't feel the need to take any pictures. After each stop, she'd grabbed her waterproof containers and brought them with her and hid them. Her next stop included one of her favorite items: deep-dish pizza. She stopped outside Chicago, set down her waterproof container, and got out her spare change of clothes. While flying across the world, she wore one of her cheap tight t-shirts, double layers of yoga pants, and cheap rain boots. The goal in such cases was to attract attention. While on the ground and in relaxing mode, she wore a different outfit. This way, she had a 'costume' without wearing a *costume* and was less likely to be noticed. The shoes weren't heels, but looked stylish nonetheless, and the pants and top were what Annie had recommended, so she felt secure wearing them. A change at hyper speed later, and she was now just some redhead.

The restaurant had a surprisingly long wait time, considering it wasn't convention season. She took her seat, waited, and surfed the net on the prepaid smartphone. The news reported her deeds in Egypt and how she'd saved Representative Dunsmith. What caught her attention was they had stopped calling her "mysterious woman" and interchangeably called her by her name and sometimes as the hero she resembled. She played the video with low audio and used her hearing powers.

"It turns out to be a busy day for the heroine some call 'Capacitor,'" the black female news anchor said. "Her real name is apparently 'Jennifer Black,' and she first stopped a *superpowered assassin* who tried to take out the Democrat from one of California's less populated districts, Jan Dunsmith. In this fantastic display of power," a quarter of the screen changed to display the footage, "you see her first catch a projectile just inches from the congressman's face, and then, if *that* wasn't insane enough, she then disarmed and helped capture the would-be hitman seconds later. But that wasn't it."

"Right you are, Julie," the male news anchor explained. "Just minutes ago, we got word that a tense terrorist hostage situation in Egypt had been defused handily."

"Excuse me, miss?"

She looked up at the waiter's voice. "Yes, I'll have a Diet Coke," she said.

He nodded and smiled. "I'll be right back," he said.

She stopped the video and sat up straight, feeling giddy. Guns and bullets still unnerved her slightly, but she was getting better, facing her fears. Some elements of spending most of her life as a normal person would do that, she figured. Even so, a positive vibe passed all through her, powered by the knowledge that she was doing something she not only loved, but also made the world better.

"Hey, is this seat taken?" a young man said.

He looked ordinary, slight tan with short black hair, brown eyes, and a vague mix of Italian and Greek facial features, modestly good looking. She gestured forward. "No, I guess not."

"Great!" he exclaimed. "I'm Gary, by the way."

"Okay," she replied, hoping he would take the hint.

He didn't. "You come here often? I like the tutto mare."

"I'm just here for the deep-dish pizza," she countered.

"Meeting someone?"

She sighed nasally, which he either didn't notice or didn't care about. "No," she answered.

"Oh, cool," he said. "So, what do you do?"

"I save lives," she stated.

He tilted his head a bit. "So," he replied, "you're like an EMT? A nurse?"

Good lord, she was used to guys randomly striking up a conversation when she went somewhere alone—something that happened approximately never as Manny—but their fishing for dates was so transparent. No, she figured, she would give him the benefit of the doubt. If he genuinely wanted a real conversation, he would stay after she revealed it. "No," she replied. "I'm a super."

He stared, a look of confusion on his face. As he pieced together the red hair and her face from pictures, his mouth drifted open. "No," he said, incredulous. "Really?"

She held up two fingers, index and middle, and with caused a tiny bolt of electricity to arc between them. "Really," she affirmed.

The waiter arrived and set her drink in front of her. "Sir?" he asked. "Do you need a menu?"

Gary glanced quickly between him and her. "Uh, no," he answered, pushing his chair back and getting up. "I was just leaving."

"What would you like to order?"

She opened the menu to the second page. "I'd like a large pepperoni deep-dish pizza," she replied.

He took the menu with a smile. "Right away!" he said.

"Thanks," she cried.

"Don't worry," a familiar voice said. She looked up and saw another guy sit opposite her. At first, she felt confused, and then she looked with her super vision, and saw underneath the disguise transformation.

"Jericho?" she said, trying to be quiet.

"Just wanted to see you," he said. "You really changed my mind."

A slight chuckle escaped her. "It was all over the news," she replied.

He returned a single laugh. "Yeah," he agreed, "I guess the news people were mad that she decided not to release the video, so they cornered me, and I needed to give them a sound bite." He shook his head. "Anyway, let's not discuss it here. I'll be at your house when you're done. That okay?"

"Sure," she said. "You're serious about this, aren't you?"

"Sure am," he said, getting up. "See you soon."

She sat and waited, and when the pizza came, she dug in.

"You've just been sitting here the whole time?" Manny said, as he opened the front door to his house and walked over to set the pizza box with leftovers in the refrigerator.

"Why not?" Jericho asked. "It gives me time to just sit and think."

"So," Manny began, sitting opposite the billionaire, "how far have you gone?"

Jericho let out a vigorous laugh. "Yeah, you sound just like the CNN business analysts," he remarked. "I'm not sure of where I sit on the political spectrum. All I know is, I'm woefully behind in the 'helping people' category, and I want to fix that."

"That's not the big problem," Manny argued. "The big problem is the sheer amount of wealth being hoarded."

A guilty sigh escaped the man. "I can see that," he replied. "Man, would you believe I actually thought because my mother had been disinherited that I was somehow not rich?" He closed his eyes and opened them wide. "Yeah, that's...that's bad."

"Help me understand," Manny implored.

Jericho gathered his thoughts. "Much of this is public knowledge," he said, "but here goes." He inhaled and exhaled sharply. "My mother was a party animal before I was born, you know. Everyone knows. It was a famous controversy in the nineteen seventies. She was into drugs, alcohol, pills, you name it." He gestured with open palms. "Well, she got disinherited because my grandfather, Johann Torrell, thought she was a disgrace to the family."

The name seemed familiar. "You mean," Manny asked, "Johann Torrell of the Torrell Group?"

"Yup," Jericho replied. "That's the one. 'If it sells, we're involved.' That's right."

"Got it."

"My mother," Jericho continued, "she actually took this lesson to heart, and parlayed her considerable college education into a teaching job at the University of Illinois at Chicago. She met my dad on campus, and in the eighties, yours truly came into the picture."

Manny reclined in his seat. "I'm guessing family history had something to do with that," he noted, "even if she wasn't in the will anymore."

"Hah!" The billionaire laughed. "Old me would've gone to blows with you over that, but yes."

"Gotcha."

Jericho pointed. "So, fast forward," he continued, "I get into Harvard Business School at eighteen. I graduate at twenty-four with an M.B.A. and get this." He leaned forward. "You're *really* going to love this. I get a job straight out of Harvard at a Manhattan investment firm. It's literally waiting for my graduation."

Manny mouthed a 'wow.' He shook his head. "Let me guess," he added, "you thought it was because you were simply that good."

"I did!"

At Jericho's affirmation, they both erupted into fits of laughter. After almost a whole minute, they both had to wipe their eyes. "Oh, that's beautiful," Manny exclaimed.

"Oh," Jericho said, "I happen to be good at picking stocks, sure, but who the fuck am I? It never occurred to me that, wait, why is a major Wall Street investment bank hiring some twenty-four-year-old kid fresh out of college?" He smacked his temple. "Oh! Right! I'm the grandson of Johann Torrell."

Manny pointed. "You started on third base!"

"And thought I hit a triple!" Jericho completed. He wiped his eyes while laughing. "Oh, how much it irks me, knowing what I know now. Literally having other people's perspectives to look at. So, I want to help change the world. Make everything better for everyone. Because maybe that will be something I do that is genuinely *mine*."

"Let me guess," Manny replied, "you figured that just doing what I'm doing isn't enough."

He gestured. "Don't get me wrong," he argued, "what you're doing is great. You've already saved lots of lives. You inspire people just by not being one of the random people who shows off their power in public and then doesn't do crap, or the chuckleheads that pull something and get busted. Decades of comics and here you are, actually doing the whole super thing."

"I thought there were others doing that," Manny shot back.

"They are," Jericho countered, "but you're the most prominent. Anyway, back to my point. The piecemeal approach isn't going to solve systemic problems."

Manny pondered this. "You're absolutely right," he said, "and that's what bugs me." A thought occurred to him. "Super intelligence is the game changer."

"I see what you're getting at," Jericho noted. "I agree, but that can't be the only game changer. I think empathy is a bigger game changer."

"Very true," Manny realized. "The right people, given empathic experiences, like you've done, will change everything. But the question is, who and how?"

"That's something to worry about," Jericho said. "We've got a lot to go over and I'm going to want to have that conversation, but right now, I've got just a few final stops to make."

"Still collecting powers?" Manny asked.

"Just two more," the billionaire said. "After a Reverend Jack Hurst in Oklahoma, and a scientist at Caltech named Raymond Weiss, I'll be done."

Manny rolled his eyes. "Reverend," he noticed. "That sounds fun."

"Yes," Jericho said, his lips a straight line. "So much." He waved. "Anyway, see you."

"You flying solo?"

"People know what I'm doing," the rich man countered, "so I'm flying without the plane for a while. It's more fun."

"True," Manny said. "See you." With those words, the billionaire left.

CHAPTER FOURTEEN

"Yeah," Jericho said, checking into his hotel room in Oklahoma City. "This'll be maybe my last stop. No, Ruth, it's it. I don't need more after this. No problem." He tucked the phone away. The keycard slid into the slot and he plopped onto the bed. It had been one hell of a journey. A billion questions weighed on his mind, and he had a lot of work ahead of him. Saving the world always seemed like a fool's errand before, but now, he saw that real action was within his grasp. They had tools now that never existed before. If nothing else, he would leave his mark upon this Earth to the betterment of all mankind. His polo, jeans, and undergarments hit the bed, and he got into the shower. He wouldn't meet a client if he didn't look the best.

After showering and drying, he put on his boxers and undershirt, and slid on his dress shirt. After buttoning it up, he drew his khakis up to his waist, tucking his shirt in. The vest went on next, then the coat, and finally, his blue stripe pattern tie. The Rolex went on his right wrist and then a spurt of breath spray in his mouth.

He dialed a number on his cell. "Hello?" he asked. "You may not know me..."

"Jericho Torvalds, right?" the aging voice said in a hint of a southern drawl.

A static charge of nervousness went through him. "Y...yes," Jericho replied. "You saw me coming?"

"Didn't have to. The Lord told me you were coming," the man corrected. "Oh! Where are my manners? I'm Jack Hurst. I suppose you knew that."

"Yes, Mister Hurst," Jericho said, rolling his eyes. "And I take it you know why I'm calling?"

"Of course," Jack answered. "You want to give me money if I give you some kind of power. Heh. Sorry; won't work."

That caught the billionaire by surprise. "Why would that be?"

"Simple," the reverend protested. "I don't have a power. I've been visited by the Lord."

Jericho stifled a laugh. "I'm...I'm glad to hear that," he said. "Nevertheless, you do, and I want to give you an offer."

"That's fine," Jack answered, "You can come over in about a half hour. I'm not concerned because I have nothing to fear from you."

"I assure you that you don't," Jericho said.

"Oh," Jack mentioned, "one last thing. Be prepared to meet the Lord."

"I...uh, I will," Jericho said, hanging up. The man struck him as a little too much a zealot, but still, he hadn't gone off the deep end, and he hadn't heard anything about a sudden change in his churchgoers, so he figured whatever power he had, wasn't that big of a deal. Still, just one more, and he would be done. So he wanted to get this over with. He activated his teleportation power, and within three jumps, stood at the end of the street Jack Hurst's house sat on.

Walking down the street of the subdivision, he saw the two-story house standing at the end of a cul-de-sac. There were tire tracks where a car had left. One car sat in the driveway, an impressively maintained antique Cadillac. Jack Hurst would be inside the house. With a scan of his powers, he found the house...

Nothing.

His heart pounded a bit faster. His powers didn't show anything inside the house.

Common sense told him to take off at once. Before he could do anything, however, the door slid open. In front of his eyes stood a well-dressed man, somewhere in his fifties, average height and build, a friendly smile on his face. It unnerved Jericho, though he didn't know why. "Hi there," Jack Hurst said. "Come on in."

"Jericho Torvalds," the billionaire introduced, extending his hand.

"Nice to meet you," Jack replied.

Jericho flexed several of his powers at once. Nothing happened. An inner monologue started yelling at him to leave at once. For some reason, perhaps he didn't want to be rude, he stepped into the house. What did he have to fear? He as Jericho Torvalds, after all.

As he sat in the loveseat opposite the man on the sofa, he found him difficult to read. The Wall Street investor prided himself on being able to spot manipulation and liars a mile away. It had been one of the reasons for his success. Yet, as he looked at this man, he saw neither a willing grift nor mental insanity. He saw a person who genuinely believed what he said. That didn't sit right with Jericho. It meant he didn't quite know what was coming next.

"Need something to drink?" Jack asked.

Jericho waved it off. "No, no thanks," he replied. "I don't want to take up too much of your precious time."

Jack seemed to see something. "Need a rag?"

The billionaire looked puzzled, until something cold dripped on his hand. He raised it. Sweat, he noticed? When had he started sweating? "Uh," he said, "yeah. Thank you."

The man went into his kitchen and produced a towel. Jericho wiped his brow with it and set it on the coffee table. "I'm sorry about that," he apologized. "Anyway, let me get straight to the point, Mister Hurst. My offer is simple: in exchange for copying your ability, I set up a series of investments in your name which will pay out around a hundred thousand a year for the rest of your life."

"Hmm," Jack said, grabbing a quick drink of water. "Interesting."

Jericho pulled out his cell phone and started video recording with audio. "I just have one quick question, though," he added, "one think that concerns me."

"You want to know why you couldn't read my mind or copy my power when you shook my hand," Jack answered.

Jericho almost went limp right there as the man returned from the kitchen. "I...uh..." he stammered, "Yes?" The inner voice shouted at him to leave at once. He wanted to teleport out of there.

A Cheshire grin appeared on Jack Hurst's face. "It's simple," he argued, "I told you. I've been visited by the Lord, and the Truth is right behind you."

Jericho's breathing became harsh. A glow shone from behind him. He closed his eyes. *Don't turn around, idiot*, he thought to himself. After a long second, curiosity got the better of him. The glow faded and he turned around.

He turned around, and the shock of what he saw hit him like a truck. "Oh, OH MY GOD!"

The Lord stood firm. He looked as though he'd stepped out of a romantic-era painting. The light brown hair, the pale skin and the beard all reminded him of every picture everywhere around America of Jesus. At once, the rational part of his mind shouted for attention as the primitive fear centers rattled him to his core. The fact that if Jesus were real, he wouldn't look like a white man didn't change his raging fear. The Lord smiled.

"You have spent your life running from me, child," He spoke to Jericho. "Now is the time for you to make your most important choice: shall you bend the knee and accept that none get to the Father save through me, or shall you be gathered up like dry firewood, cast into the Lake of Fire, and burned?"

No, screw this, Jericho thought, I'm getting out of here. He teleported.

A breath caught in his throat. Oh no.

Nothing happened.

"That is most unfortunate," The Lord spoke. He waved a hand and an invisible force caught the Billionaire and held him up in the air. The cell phone in his hand went flying off to the left. "You could have chosen salvation. Now you shall not escape judgment."

A burning overtook Jericho as a brilliant light surrounded his whole body. An unearthly heat radiated out from his center and his flesh erupted into white-hot flames. He slammed on every durability and regeneration power he had at once, and it still tore through them like butter as they struggled to keep up.

Jack wiped his eyes. It hurt him to see one of God's children refuse the love of their Father through the salvation of the Son. "You should have really accepted salvation," he told the man. "My wife and kids haven't even met the Lord yet. You were the first one besides me."

Jericho screamed at the top of his lungs as he saw his limbs turning to charcoal and falling off. Regeneration caught up briefly, but the fire burned through it and he felt levels of pain no human had previously endured. Thoughts blurred together as he struggled to form coherent ideas for survival. Every escape power he had failed. His torso, all that was left of him, began to crumble as he frantically searched his collection for any power that would help.

He found a power he had almost forgotten he had and smashed it on. Nothing happened. A distorted warble passed through his lips as his voice began to falter. *NO! I DON'T WANT TO DIE!* His frantic mental shout died out.

The light faded and a small pile of ash wafted to the floor of the house. The man was no more.

Jack blinked away tears. "Is…" he stuttered, calming himself with all his will. "Is that it for him?"

"Sadly, yes," The Lord spoke. He shook his head. "It is a tragedy to see any of my Father's children reject his offer of salvation. For his denial, he suffered the ultimate judgment."

Jack went to get a dustpan and broom. "Damn shame," he said. "I wanted to save him." The truth was, he wanted all the world to be saved and receive eternal life and happiness in God's kingdom. However, no one could escape God's truth. And the truth was, if someone like Jericho Torvalds loved money more than God, his punishment was deserved.

"Once we get our message to the masses," The Lord replied, "you will be saving plenty. That is, if you have the strength to see it through."

"I do, oh Lord!" Jack cried.

"aaaaAAAAARRGGHHH!"

Inside a hotel room in Oklahoma City, Jericho Torvalds appeared and collapsed onto the floor. "I did it!" he shouted, half delirious. "I sent myself back a few...OH SHIT!" Halfway through his sentence, a burning sensation erupted inside him. Steam began to pour off of his body as he tore off his clothes. No light emanated, and his regeneration seemed to handle it, but the pain seared through his very being. Still, he was alive. He'd sent himself back a few minutes.

He picked up the phone receiver and hammered the operator button. "Help...me..." he uttered. Then he faceplanted into the carpet.

"Oh! He's waking up!" a female voice cried. "Nurse! NURSE!"

Jericho groggily blinked his eyes. He sat in a hospital bed and every part of him both ached and burned. "What?" he uttered. "Oh, Ruth!" He took a deep breath. He reached up and hugged her. "Oh, thank you!"

"My God," she exclaimed. "What happened to you, sir?"

"You're right," Jericho quipped. He sat up, his head ringing. "I met Jack Hurst, he had a fake Jesus who burned me alive."

"That's..." she replied. "That's rough, sir."

"Yeah, well," Jericho shot back, "I think there's only one person who can fix me."

"I'm glad to see you survived, sir," Ruth answered, "and not just because you sign my paychecks. Where to now?"

"Saint Louis," he replied. "I've got a friend to meet. We're going to have a hell of a conversation." He looked at the table. "Ah shit, my cellphone."

"We didn't find it," she replied. "We'll get you a new one when we get there."

"Right," he said. They stopped by the nearest pharmacy and got a prescription for Vicodin, which he popped along with a bottle of Perrier, and they flew to Lambert airport. From there, he teleported to Manny's house.

"Hey, what's..." Manny's voice trailed off as he saw Jericho standing in front of him. "Jesus Christ, what happened to you?"

"Exactly," Jericho said, smiling. "We have to talk. Now." He pushed past the man.

They sat next to each other, with Jennifer holding his hand. The energy churning inside him perplexed her. It seemed to burn past several defenses and regenerations at once, only for the few remaining to outdo them at the last minute. She flexed her energy manipulation and struggled. The mysterious burning had a potency she hadn't felt before. "So," she said, "tell me what happened."

"I went to see Jack Hurst," Jericho explained, "and none of my powers worked once I got there. I should've left, but I wanted to see. I was curious. Anyway, he summoned a fake Jesus, and I swear, it looked like every painting ever of white Jesus."

A sinking feeling came to Jennifer. "Just fucking great," she lamented.

"Your nose is bleeding," Jericho noticed.

"Gimme a minute," she shot back. A bit further, and, with a final surge, she dissipated the destructive energy.

Relief washed over Jericho like an orgasm. "Oh, oh hell!" he shouted, gasping for breath. "Oh, thank you."

"How did you survive?"

He stuck out his hand. "Here," he offered. "It's best if I show you."

She took his hand, and then recoiled a moment later. "Goddammit!" she shouted.

"Yeah," Jericho said. "Tell me about it."

"You know what pisses me off about this?" she explained. "If it was Bugs Bunny or Superman, everyone would know it's bullshit, but now, he's going to reveal this to the world, and millions are just going to eat it up!"

"We've got to do something," Jericho countered.

"That's what gets me," Jennifer said, a sense of dread washing over her. "Well, we were both worried about something big going wrong." She cracked a sorrowful half-smile. "Here we are."

"We can't just fly out there and kill him," the billionaire replied. "If we do, he'll just be martyred."

She pointed. "But you *know* he's going to pull some horrific shit!" she shouted.

"Yeah, I know," he lamented. "We've got to get allies."

She folded her arms. "You want to bring my friends into this?"

He sighed. "In a word?" he asked. "Yes. Who else knows your secret and trusts you like they do? It's best to start with what and who you know."

A Chevy SUV pulled into the driveway of a familiar four-bedroom house. Three doors opened. "Alright!" Emily Hurst shouted. "You kids bring in the groceries before you bring in your stuff!" She was greeted by a two-man chorus of okays. As they darted from the cargo area to the front door, she grabbed her bags of clothes, which included two new dress shirts for Jack for his sermons.

"Jack?" She set her bags on the couch. She found her husband sitting in the loveseat reading the bible. "Hey, Mister Lotherman across the street said he saw flashing lights and heard screaming from inside the house."

Jack Hurst set the bible down. "Just an action movie," he said. "Here, I'll help with the stuff."

"Thanks," she said, as he got up and headed outside.

A small gray object caught her eye.

She knelt on the soft carpet and picked up a smartphone, which was lying on the ground pointing up at an angle. There was a slight indentation in the wall and a burn mark across the back. The screen had a hairline crack in it matching the indentation. Had this thing flown against the wall? How and why had that happened? She pressed the power button, and the dark screen flashed to life. It had no password locking it. She stuffed it into her pocket as her husband's footsteps approached. Normally, she'd ask him about it but the suspicious circumstances piqued her interest.

"You got some great deals, honey!" Jack announced, setting three bags of clothes down on the couch.

"Thanks, dear," she replied, heading for the stairs.

"I'm going to fold my shirts and dress pants and put them away," Jack replied. "If you need help, just let me know."

She mounted the stairs, heading for the spare bedroom. She locked the door behind her. The phone unlocked with a swipe, and she saw the video was recording. A press and the recording stopped, saving to the memory card. After scrolling for a few seconds, she found the file of the new recording, and played it from the beginning.

Almost at once, she recognized the man standing opposite her husband. He was that investor guy from Fox Business who had been travelling the country paying for superpowers. Her husband and the man had a conversation that struck her as odd. After a few more moments of nervous banter, her husband donned a look that creeped her out; she'd never seen him grin like that before.

Then the camera turned abruptly and caught the Lord in all his glory.

Her teeth clamped together to hold back a scream. At the same time, her mind fired off at least a thousand questions, not the least of which was, why hadn't the Lord's return been heralded by a great shout? All the world was supposed to hear the Lord give a great shout from the sky that would alert them to the second coming. Why hadn't this happened? The question was answered for her when the Lord raised a hand and the phone went flying. It collided with the wall and fell in a position where it kept filming. She'd had the sense to turn the volume way down, and it was good she did.

Because what happened next caught her breath in her throat.

The rich man's body lit up in a brilliant glow and he began to shriek like only a torture victim could. This persisted for about thirty more seconds before he vanished, leaving behind a pile of dust.

She closed the video, collapsing onto the bed and weeping silently. Her sorrow gave way to more terror: her husband had been accessory to murder, but also, he'd been taken in by the devil in disguise. Then, a rational part of her mind asserted itself, and she arrived at the terrible conclusion.

He had a power. That was the only reason Jericho Torvalds would be standing there.

Which meant he'd summoned the creature.

Which meant that *he had committed murder.*

Frantically, she searched through the contacts list. The newest contact was a...Jennifer Black? Where was that name familiar?

Her eyes went wide. She slammed the call button.

Jennifer was in the middle of a conversation with Jericho when her phone rang. She looked at it, at first confused, but then her gaze focused intently on it. "Who is it?" Jericho asked.

"It's...you," Jennifer said. "You're calling me."

She accepted the call. "Hello?" The woman's voice said. "Is this... that woman who's on the news for saving lives?"

"I am," Jennifer replied. "Who's this?"

"Emily Hurst," she answered. "I need to speak to you."

Jericho motioned. "Here," Jennifer said, handing the phone over.

"Missus Hurst?" Jericho said, "Jericho Torvalds. Are you away from your husband right now?"

"Yes," Emily replied. "I'm not safe here, or my kids, am I?"

"No," Jericho said. "I have to get you and your kids out of there."

There was a pause. "How do I know you're going to help me?" she asked. "After all, you just wanted my husband's powers for yourself."

"Ma'am," Jericho protested, "don't be fooled by your husband's tears; he did not hesitate to let his monster murder me. And let me be crystal clear: that was his monster he summoned, nothing more. If he thinks of himself as the right hand of God, your position as his wife won't protect you. Same for your kids."

"I...I guess," she replied. "But how can you be sure of that?"

"Matthew ten verses thirty-four through thirty-six," Jericho answered. "Do not think that I have come to bring peace to the earth. I have not come to bring peace, but a sword. For I have come to set a man against his father, and a daughter against her mother, and a daughter-in-law against her mother-in-law. And a person's enemies will be those of his own household."

She closed her eyes and wiped them. "I...I don't..."

"Anyone who loves their father or mother more than me is not worthy of me," Jericho continued. "Anyone who loves their son or daughter more than me is not worthy of me. Whoever does not take up their cross and follow me is not worthy of me." He paused. "Do *you* want to take that chance?"

She blinked tears away. "I...how can I trust you?"

"I understand your concern," Jericho replied, "but you need to understand. This creature of his is subtly being affected by his thought process. It isn't fully autonomous. That means that as he gets lost deeper in this, he's going to be more dogmatic. If you get in his way of getting to heaven, even by accident, he'll have no problem removing you from the picture."

"I..." She wiped her eyes. "Alright."

"Honey," Jack Hurst cried from downstairs, "are you okay up there?"

She held the phone at arm's length. "Fine! Just a minute!" she yelled. She returned to the call. "Alright, I'll trust you."

"Find a way to get away from him," Jericho advised. "Any excuse. Anything. Call me back."

She hung up and shoved the phone back into her pocket. Descending the stairs, she put on a smile. A quick glance in the refrigerator saw that the meat had finished thawing out, so she set it on the counter on the aluminum foil. Jack walked into the kitchen, caressing her shoulder. "Everything alright, dear?" he asked.

"Just fine," she said. "I'm going to start dinner."

"Great!" he cheered. "I'll get washed up. Kids! Get washed up for dinner!"

The two children followed their dad into the restroom to get washed up. She watched them walk by and had to remember to hide her sorrow. *Why, Jack? Why would you do this*? Her thoughts turned to dark places as she remembered the video. She didn't understand and didn't know if she ever would. One thing she decided, however, was that she didn't want her children around someone who could murder.

CHAPTER FIFTEEN

AFTER THE CONVERSATION THEY HAD with Emily Hurst, Jericho took off to do some last-minute business and get things prepared. The woman had texted them that her husband had plans on Sunday, so normal church services were cancelled. Given that this struck her as an oddity, the best chance everyone decided upon was to intervene during the time he was away. Jennifer turned back into Manny and decided to tell everyone what was going on.

"So," John said, as they all gathered at Ed's house, "you're telling me that the billionaire Jericho Torvalds fought against a fake Jesus brought on by some Southern Baptist preacher, and you're going to help him?"

Manny nodded. "It sounds crazy," he said, "I know, but I want to let you guys know because we need allies, and you're the only people that I absolutely trust."

Annie took a deep breath and let it out. "It's not that I doubt you," she said, "it's just that, none of this sounds real. It sounds fake."

"I thought of that," Manny said, pulling out his cell phone and Bluetooth speaker from his pack. He shifted into Jennifer and dialed the number.

"Yeah," Jericho said, his voice travelling through the room, "I'm almost done here, then I'll be heading your way."

"I just wanted to let you know," Jennifer said, "that I told them."

There was a pause. "Fantastic," Jericho replied. "The first thing I'm going to do is move all three of them to somewhere else because I believe something really bad is going to happen. I think this Jack Hurst situation is going to progress rapidly."

"Uh, no offense," Edward interjected, "but where are we going and for how long?"

"Edward Mitchell, is it?" Jericho said. "Look, I don't want to boss you around, but let me assure you how this is going to go. Jack Hurst is going to likely seek out a large audience. Jennifer and I talked about this for hours, and we both have concluded that none of the people connected to either of us are safe. The first thing I'm doing, right now, is moving my family to safe places. The moment I finish here, I'm heading there. Get packed." He paused. "Jennifer, do you agree?"

She looked at her friends. "I agree," she said. "We're going to get all their family and friends hidden away."

"Uh, can I say something?" John said. "No offense, mister, uh, Torvalds, but why are you helping us? I thought you were almost alt-right."

"Mister Stephenson," Jericho shot back, "You're right, I was. One of my powers is to literally experience other people's experiences. If I'm different, that's why. If you want, I can actually show you my memories. Acceptable?"

"I, uh, okay," John stammered.

"So," Jennifer said, "is there anything you need me to do?"

"Just get them packed," Jericho advised. "Get their friends and family packed. It'll just be a few more hours for me and I'll be there."

"No problem," Jennifer advised. "You heard the man. Let's go."

Each of the friends drove back to their own homes, and Jennifer shifted back into Manny long enough to drive home and pack up. About two hours later, she was back as her female self again, standing in the living room of Ed's house. Ed, Annie, and John's parents sat on the couch, a collection of suitcases and other bags sitting in the corner.

A knock rang out. Jennifer opened the door, and the billionaire walked in. A person would be forgiven for thinking Zeus or Odin had walked in. Everyone found themselves dumbstruck. Then he began taking stock of everyone present. "Alright, I'd like to do something first," Jericho said, "everyone join hands. Form a chain."

"Um," John said, voice cracking, "excuse me, are you really…"

"In a moment there won't need to be any need for explanation," Jericho retorted. "Just everyone form a chain of hands."

The reluctant people present held hands, and the far end had Annie holding Jennifer's hand, and the billionaire took the heroine's right in his left and took the free hand of Ed's mother with his right. He flexed several of his mental powers at once. A moment later, shouts and expletives echoed through the room. "Alright," Ed yelled, "what was that?"

"You know what that is," Jericho said.

"I do," Ed came back, "and that's what bothers me."

"Why give a long, tedious explanation," Jennifer asked, "when you can simply *see* for yourself?" The nervous chatter began to quiet down at her reasonable explanation.

"Also," Jericho added, "this way there's no details lost. You all know who we are, and why you're here. Most importantly, you understand the gravity of the situation. I did my best to filter out the pain I experienced, sorry of some leaked through. I'm getting better at this power."

"I'll take the luggage," Jennifer offered.

"No problem," Jericho answered. He gestured, and they all joined hands again. He flexed his teleportation power, and though it took dozens of jumps, he got there with all the civilians. Jennifer grabbed luggage, extending the long, rolling handles, and hanging them from each arm like grocery bags. Her power flowed through them and she took to the sky. At full speed, she arrived at the site in seconds.

"I'm here," she said. Jericho released a power and opened the door.

"Great," he replied. "I was just getting them all squared away." She set the luggage in the corner. One look at the interior, and her mouth hung open. She'd never set foot in such a luxurious space. From the outside, it resembled a cabin, and it was tucked away in a wooded area dozens of miles from civilization, but on the inside, it looked like an expensive vacation getaway. The living room area was bigger than her house. From the fancy hardwood floor, to the cavernous kitchen just past the far wall, it had everything and then some.

"How did you set this place up?" she asked.

"I kept that part out of the memories," he replied. "I've got other locations I set up after the Lights. With some of the powers I got, it was easy to set up these places off the grid. No paper trail, and they're only detectable to people I choose. All the utilities are provided by a collection of powers."

"Holy crap," Jennifer exclaimed, "you really thought of everything."

"I figured things would get to a point where people were using powers to terrorize," he explained. "These were just a safety precaution."

"So," Jennifer asked, "what do we do now?"

"Oh!" Jericho noticed. "That reminds me. Everyone, I've given you all a teleport power that's enhanced. This way, you can come and go. I'd advise you not to tell anyone where you are." There was a collection of various yeses in agreement. "I've stocked the pantry, the fridge, and the freezer. Everything should be good for a while."

"Uh," John's father asked, "What do we do if we have to move?"

Jennifer and Jericho exchanged a glance. "If worse comes to worst," she explained, "and things get bad, you won't be left hanging. I promise."

"I've got other places to hide you," Jericho explained, "I just can't quite reveal all of them at the moment." He went over his mental list. "There is one I can share with you, though." He touched each of them and showed them the location.

A text message came to him. He glanced at the phone, and nervous concern drew itself on his face. "Is it time?" Jennifer asked. He nodded. "Alright."

Emily Hurst sat in the living room of the house she had enjoyed living in until just days ago. Timothy and Eric sat next to her with their suitcases packed in front of them. She had fought off the urge to break down and cry several times. It occurred to her she'd have plenty of time for that, and she didn't want to freak her children out before she had to. Jack had driven off just a few minutes earlier, and she'd made sure to act natural. She put up just the right amount of nervous housewife behavior, so he didn't suspect anything. It was, after all, strange for them not to go to service on Sunday. If she just let him go without any strife, he'd wonder why she wasn't concerned. So, despite no acting training, she felt she put on a decent act. He'd gotten in the Cadillac and driven away.

The door rang, and she got up and opened it. As the two stood before her, and shut the door behind them, she felt a sense of relief, even as the storm of conflicting emotions raged on in her. "I'm...I'm so glad you're here," Emily Hurst said, blinking away forming tears. "I just didn't..."

"It's going to be alright," Jennifer said, giving her a hug.

The housewife shook her head. "I just don't understand any of this!"

"For what it's worth," Jericho said, "I don't understand it either. The thing is, your husband is probably taken in by the combination of his faith and the appearance of a figure that looks like his Lord."

"But, he's such a good man!" she protested. "How could this happen?"

"I can't know that completely," Jericho replied, "but I can show you." He looked past her. "In fact, get your kids. I can show them too."

"But!"

"Don't worry," he reassured her. "I'll filter out the pain. I've gotten good at it."

She stared at his extended hand. She turned her head. "Kids! Come here!"

He smiled at her call. "We can't make everything right just yet," he stated, "but right now, I can assure you there'll be no secrets."

The two children approached, apprehensively. "Mom," Tim said, "who are these people?"

Eric's face lit up. "You're that hero lady flying around!" he shouted, pointing.

"Eric, Tim, join hands," she said.

They formed a chain. Jericho took her hand. At once, he gave them the rundown on what had happened up to that point, for both himself and Jennifer, and at the same time, he saw their collective memories of Jack Hurst. Years of her marriage to the man appeared in his mind.

They met in high school. His father had built the Full Revival Baptist Church which served three surrounding communities, and his only son had decided to follow in his father's footsteps. Despite playing the guitar in high school, he felt the pull to become a reverend like his father. She saw him constantly working to connect people to religion, and how good he was at it, and his work in the community helping the poor. Once he finished, he'd settled into his role as a figurehead in the communities surrounding his father's church. She'd stood by his side as he helped mend failing marriages, guided young people through the tumult of their youth into adulthood, and had been a pillar of goodness and guiding light in the small corner of Oklahoma they lived in.

His children were born, and the family settled into a happy existence. Their lives moved on virtually unimpeded. Disasters that befell other families just didn't touch them. They never had to worry about their children falling down dangerous paths, and despite the occasional argument, it seemed almost impossible how uncontroversial their lives were. Jericho came back to himself with a view of the man that clashed very much with his current experience. Then again, if this fake Jesus gave him a heightened religious experience, that could very well explain the change. After all, if psychedelics could change a normal person's personality, a magical psychic religious vision could.

"I…I don't," Emily Hurst said, stammering, "I don't see how my husband could have become that person."

"I think he had some kind of religious experience," Jericho thought out loud.

"Time to get going," Jennifer said. "We can discuss this at a safer location."

The kids followed them out the rear entrance to the house, into the fenced back yard. She knelt and wrapped her arms around the kids, making sure to grab their suitcases in each hand. One final shift to make sure she had a firm grip, and she took off. The billionaire draped an arm around Emily, with suitcase in his other hand, and teleported. It took dozens of jumps, but he appeared on the front steps of the cottage just as Jennifer was opening the door to let the two kids in.

"I've got several locations like this I've set up," Jericho told them, as they went about exploring the cabin.

"Jeez," Jennifer exclaimed, "you've been busy."

"You know," Jericho replied, "one succeeds by identifying risks."

"Is this place safe?" Emily asked, choosing a closet in one of the rooms as hers.

"I've gone over it with a fine-tooth comb," he told her. "If someone is specifically looking for me and has a 'finding' superpower, maybe it won't be safe. But no normal person is going to find this place."

Eric and Tim were busy scoping out their new rooms. Jennifer opened the fridge and grabbed a Diet Coke. Emily sat on the couch pondering the experience she'd gotten. Her husband had gone someplace mentally she had never seen him before. He had religious experiences before, but she couldn't see how they would explain this. When he was twenty-four, he had a vision of Jesus that startled him out of bed, but all that led to was intense prayer and a general feeling of joy that lasted for days. Jericho found it easier to piece together, even though it still looked rather murky to him. Jack Hurst seemed to be desperate to save people from hell. To extrapolate that outward to its logical conclusion, if the fake Jesus gave him some kind of vision where he could do just that, then it made at least superficial sense to the billionaire that a man prone to such would fall for it. Furthermore, he'd grown up in an environment where matters of Christ were not allowed to be questioned. Maybe his wife got blinded by her love for the reverend, but Jericho could see how such a person would go all in.

The megachurch in Oklahoma City belonging to one Reverend Hiram Masterfield saw a full capacity crowd pulling in for its Sunday service. Television crews for multiple local and nationwide stations had their camera trucks in the parking lot, ready to cover this week's edition of *The Ultimate Blessed Life Church with The Reverend Masterfield*, which always drew stellar ratings throughout the rural and suburban parts of America. Near the security exit, a vintage Cadillac stood parked in the secure lot. A team of security guards followed Jack Hurst through the VIP entrance and exit, down a specific hallway, towards a specific office.

Jack stepped through the door after knocking and being called in. He sat in a luxurious leather chair, possibly the softest guest chair he'd ever sat in. A series of bookcases off to his right held hundreds of religious texts, some of which even he did not recognize. The tremendous oak desk in front of him held paperwork, some audio and video recordings, and a computer. Behind it, in a chair even more luxurious than his current, sat a man in a suit almost as expensive looking as that Jericho Torvalds had worn. The man, white hair expertly tailored to look professional, with just the right makeup to make him look stately without looking made-up, had a smile Jack at once identified as phony. Paintings on his office walls of the elder Masterfield, who had founded this church before his son made it a multi-million dollar gig, as well as the wife and children, showed a vanity the reverend of the smaller church could not sympathize with. The man regarded Jack with some intrigue, then lay his hands flat on his desk.

"Reverend Hurst," Hiram Masterfield began, his voice a gravel road trained to seem fatherly. "I must say, I'm always pleased to meet a fellow man of God." He breathed out through his nose. "You come with quite the reputation. Some of my churchgoers have told me you are closer to the Lord than even I am."

"I hope they haven't been bragging about me," Jack replied.

The man gave a chuckle. "No no," he answered. "It's just that, I've heard them say that. And I invited you here because, well, let's face it, I want to talk to you about that."

"Before we go any further," Jack said, taking a deep breath, "I have to say, I'm going to be doing more talking to your audience than to you. I don't say this out of spite or arrogance, but you're about to see why in a minute." The feeling of the Holy Spirit came to him, and he closed his eyes briefly.

From behind him, a brilliant glow lit up the room. Hiram held his hands up to shield his eyes. "What's going on?" he cried. After the lights dissipated, a figure stood. Standing just above average height, with flowing brown hair and unmistakable Hebrew garb, stood the Lord. The televangelist found his body move against his will. His eyes like saucers and mouth hung open, he stepped out from behind his desk, and simply stood there, unable to think, even.

Before he even realized what had happened, he was on his knees, hands clasped together in front of his chest, looking up. Blabbering nonsense came out of his mouth as he failed to find words.

"Stand, my child," The Lord said.

Hiram stood. Hands held at his sides, he had to remind himself to breathe. "My...my Lord!" he uttered, forcing his brain to give his mouth words to say. "You've...you've come back! It's your glorious return!"

"You speak the truth," The Lord replied.

"I..." Hiram struggled to collect his thoughts. "Why have so many things in the Bible not happened yet? I thought..."

The Lord put up a hand and the televangelist went quiet. "Do not merely accept the written word as the *only* truth," He said. "My father, in Heaven, is not bound by mere written words."

"Of...course my lord!" Hiram replied. "I...seek forgiveness for questioning you! What is your will, oh Lord?"

"For your services," The Lord answered, "your past indiscretions against my Father's laws will be forgiven. You will provide your audience and your platform to my chosen servant here."

Hiram nodded. "Yes! Whatever you say, my Lord!"

"Your service will be rewarded," The Lord said. With that, he vanished into thin air.

The televangelist turned to Jack, barely coherent. "Uh, do you, um," he uttered.

"It's okay," Jack said, smiling. "Imagine how I felt when he came to me."

Hiram cleared his throat and forced his trembling nerves to somewhat calm. "Do...you want me to introduce you?" he asked.

"That would be kind of you," Jack said.

"Alright." The televangelist affirmed, then straightened his tie and calmly exited his office. It wouldn't be the first time he delivered a sermon with rattled nerves. If anything, he would try to remain professional. A short stroll down the hallway, and through a curtain, and he found himself on a familiar stage. He adjusted the microphone clipped to his lapel. He took a breath and let it out slowly. "Ladies and gentlemen!" The crowd erupted into cheers. "This week, I bring to you a…most unusual service. I only seldom have guest speakers on stage with me, but this time, another shall be giving you a message in my place. I want you to bring him as warm a welcome as you give me and pay close attention. From the Full Revival Baptist Church just a hundred miles away from here, the Reverend Jack Hurst!"

As he left the stage, a noticeable portion of the crowd let out sounds of confusion. Still, enough cheers came up that when Jack Hurst took the stage, he got a decently warm welcome. He waved to the crowd. A microphone had been affixed to his lapel. He cleared his throat. "My fellow children of God," he began. "You may not know me, but my name is Jack Hurst. I come to you from my small town to bring you quite possibly the best news any human has ever put forward." He paused. "Rather than explain it, I figure a demonstration is warranted."

Light shone from the stage, and when it vanished, the figure of the Lord appeared. There were gasps and some shouts, but they went silent when the Lord raised his hand and everyone lifted from their seat and with a lowering, got placed in a standing position. "For those of you who doubt," The Lord spoke, "I shall now remove all doubt whatsoever." With a wave of his hand, a glow overcame each person in the audience. All their illnesses and maladies vanished. Missing limbs were restored. Cancer patients got restored to full health. The paralyzed stood on working legs again. "Now, you shall turn your attention to my chosen servant."

"Let me be clear that I have no idea as to why our Lord chose me as his servant," Jack began. "I am no better than anyone. I am just a man who serves our God on high. Still, a little less than a week ago, Jesus, who stands before you, visited me in my living room. He showed me the glory of his Father's Kingdom of glory and love that shall reign forever and ever. In the coming days He will show it to you, if you are faithful and true to our Father's will."

He walked around the stage. A solemn and serious expression came upon him. "However, I also must bring you the news no person wants to hear. Although His glorious Kingdom is at hand, we have a war to fight. We are locked in the final battle against evil, against Satan's forces on Earth. This is not an enemy who has a capital we can take and force to surrender. This is not an enemy who can be defeated with normal means. The Lights in the sky are not merely a 'scientific event' that 'lacks explanation,' according to the secular minds of science. It is the handing out of weapons for the final battlefield. Those of you who have powers, turn them to the service of the Lord, and take a stand against evil. For this world has gone so far in sinning. We have fallen so far from the love of our Father."

A bottle of water sat on the podium. He took a drink. "This world is full of evil," he continued. "It was not enough that we merely loved the sinner and hated the sin, as our Good Book commands us, we had to go and love the sin. We glorify all manner of wickedness in the name of making ourselves holy. We put ourselves on pedestals and worship our own perceived impressiveness. We deny the existence of our Father in Heaven. We say ways of life known to be the way of sin and evil are things to be proud of." He shook his head. "No more."

The crowd cheered, "No more!"

He took another drink of water. "All ways of sin lead to destruction, and damnation," he explained. "My Lord will be leading me to where I need to go. I will be spreading His word as far as needed.

Once the final hour is at hand, we will fight the final battle against the Deceiver. That is my Lord's plan, and I will obey. Those of you who have powers, turn them against evil, follow us, and we shall conquer those who have chosen the enemy."

The crowd went wild.

He placed both hands on the podium. "Ladies and gentlemen, I leave you with this. The hour for your decision to the ultimate question is at hand. Will you be saved, or will you be cast into the Lake of Fire where those who choose to serve our Enemy will be? This is the single most important choice you make, because if you make the wrong choice, you will have an eternity to regret it." He paused. "Thank you."

He got a standing ovation, and shouts for more. The Lord stayed behind and ministered to those who wished to receive the good word about the Kingdom to come, but Jack had fulfilled the purpose his Lord had chosen him for. Security escorted him back to his car and helped him dodge the crowd. As he drove home, every ounce of joy fired in his brain at once. He felt fulfilled like he'd felt only once before. At last, the time drew near.

The Cadillac pulled into the driveway. As he parked the car next to the Chevy SUV, he thought of all the ways he would tell his wife the good news. Sure, she might have just looked on television and seen it, but he wanted to share with her this information.

The door to the house flew open. "Emily!" he shouted. "Come quick! I have to show you something!"

No sound greeted him, save for the faint hiss of cool air through the vents. The living room and kitchen lights were on, but other than that, it looked abandoned. He looked through the living room and saw nothing. The TV sat untouched, and everything looked undisturbed. No food had been prepared in the kitchen. He looked on the back porch and, in the yard, and nothing looked out of place.

Upstairs, he saw it.

All three suitcases were gone.

He sat on the king bed he shared with his wife. "Dear Lord," he prayed, "I am not worthy to receive you, but I beg for your guidance."

He felt the holy spirit come upon him and the Lord appeared in a flash of light. "My child," he spoke, "what troubles you?"

"My wife and children are gone," Jack answered.

The Lord looked up a moment. Then, Jack saw his facial expression darken. "That man is alive," he told his mortal servant. "He has allies, and they have convinced your wife that you are a dangerous person to be around. They've taken to hiding." He looked at Jack, resolutely. "I will take you to them."

"No," Jack said, holding up a stifling hand. "Let them. We'll get them back after we win the final battle."

"If you ask that of me," the Lord replied, "that is what I shall do, out of respect for your servitude. They shall be left alone until after we prevail."

Jack took a breath. "Thank you." He steeled his will for the coming battle. He couldn't help but clench his teeth to stifle his anger. Now, the battle had become personal.

CHAPTER SIXTEEN

THE NEWS GOT ONTO THE ORDEAL almost immediately.

"Medical records have shown," a news anchor said, "these people experienced a genuine healing event. Mary Withers, for example, had a missing hand from an electrical accident several years ago, and after the sermon yesterday, now has her hand back. Religious leaders..."

Jericho turned off the TV. He turned to Jennifer. "This is going to hell really quickly," he stated.

Jennifer cleared her throat. "It's bullshit," she replied. "They're already riots in several places. I had to deal with a bunch of religious freaks in Arizona going from house to house burning people alive if they seemed non-Christian."

He looked at his phone. "There's a guy in England who's threatening a local Jewish group," Jericho pointed out. "He's got electrical powers. Why don't you go deal with that, and I'll take care of some business of my own?"

"Sounds like a plan," she said, nodding.

I.

JERICHO WATCHED AS SHE STEPPED OUTSIDE the cabin and took off. He changed into a pair of loose jeans and a t-shirt, slipping his cell phone into the pants pocket after placing a barrier around it. Before he stepped out, he turned to the woman preparing food for her children. "I won't be gone for too long," he said.

Her expression told him she had it as together as she could get. "I'm going to feed them and then I'll be off to bed," she said. "I...this isn't right for me to say, but you guys *are* going to have to kill my husband, aren't you?"

A sigh escaped his lips. "I would like not to," he said. "I really would. But it's not looking good. He just made it a life-and-death issue."

She tended the pan. "I know," she replied. "It's just not fair."

"No," Jericho agreed. "It's not. In a fair world, none of this would happen."

He stepped outside and took to the air. It probably wouldn't have taken long to teleport there, but he wanted to feel the wind against him. A wave of calmness passed over him as the air brushed past his body. In a few minutes, he arrived at a small panel house, on the outskirts of a small town, just off a dirt road. He knocked on the door.

A panel slid open and eyes regarded him. "Come in," an older man's voice cried.

"It was a good idea to keep this off the map," Davis Wilson said, sitting in a chair off to the side.

"I kept this place to meet with informants in secret," Sam Louis remarked, shutting the door and locking it twice, "not to meet with people likely to become public enemy number one."

Jericho took a seat at the small wooden table. The house had that late seventies yellowish décor, with faded light blue tiles in the kitchen and ancient linoleum, complete with barred, translucent windows. The outside wore lower class decrepit paneling. All in all, he considered it a perfect fit with the abandoned homes from the 2008 crisis. "So," he asked, "you agree that he's going to target Jennifer and I specifically?"

Sam nodded. "Yup," he said. "And what's worse is, we expect this to happen soon."

"Not that I doubt you," Jericho argued, "but why's that?"

"Logically," Davis cut in, "you're the most powerful ones. And let's face it, we expect that this figure is very powerful. Maybe as powerful as or more powerful than Jennifer." Davis saw the worry building on the man's face. "Let me introduce you to someone." He gestured.

A third man, seated at the table, had been quietly waiting for his turn. Jericho had seen the mid-forties person, red t-shirt with collar, and black jeans, unassuming build, and wondered. Still, he hadn't said anything because he wanted to hear what the FBI agents had to say first. The man had a scholarly look about him, his green eyes and vaguely English features, round chin and close together soft eyes, and a look on his face of intrigue. "You're Jericho Torvalds," he introduced, "Sam and Dave here have told me all about you. My name's Raymond Weiss." A short cut, right parted head of wet soil colored hair adorned his head, with small threads of bangs touching his forehead.

The billionaire open mouth smiled and extended a hand. "I've been wanting to get in touch with you!" he exclaimed. "You're the physics professor from UC Berkley!"

"Believe it or not," the man replied, "I've been wanting to meet you too, because I think this whole thing has gotten out of hand, and you guys are going to need my help." He shook the man's hand. "I think it's best if I show you what's been going on with me."

At the University of California, Berkley, in a physics lab, Doctor Raymond Weiss sat staring at a series of equations on a board. For the better part of two months, he'd been pouring over data sent to him. All of the equations had proven solvable except these. The math had evaded every attempt to figure it out, and his effort was so focused he didn't notice the sound of footsteps approaching.

"Doctor Weiss?" a young voice asked.

"Oh!" Raymond said, startled. "Sorry, I'm just...too focused, I guess." He extended a hand. "You are?"

"Ah, I'm Alan Jordan," he replied, "I was transferred here from Caltech to work with you on this project?"

"Ah, yes, Mister Jordan," Raymond said. "Working on your doctorate. I read your hypothesis, and I must say, it's intriguing."

Alan nodded. "Thank you." He looked at the equations. "Is that the latest results?"

"Yeah," Raymond explained. "They repeated the experiment three times, and these are the equations they came up with to explain the results." He rubbed at the bridge of his nose with his fingers. "I hope we can solve this because otherwise it means they're on the wrong track." He laughed. "Hell, at this point, I hope *anyone* can solve this, but I'd like it to be me."

Alan laughed. "Hey, I thought the money in physics was proving people wrong!"

Raymond returned a chuckle. "Maybe," he agreed, "but on this issue, I want them to be right." His smile soured. "Otherwise, it's five years wasted in the wrong direction."

"I'll, uh, get to work in a minute," Alan replied. "Do you want me to do anything right now?"

Raymond snapped his fingers. "Yes, actually!" he cheered. He reached into his pocket and produced a five-dollar bill. "Go upstairs and get me a Diet Doctor Pepper from the machine and get your-self something."

"Sure thing," Alan said, exiting.

Raymond sat at the computer on the instructor's desk and went over the video of the experiment again. Since the evening sun was setting, and all his classes were over for the day, he wanted to work some more before going home. No students had come during office hours, so he often came back to this lab because it felt like home to him. He'd worked here as a student during his undergraduate days, some years ago, and it brought him back. Color patterns began moving across the screen. He paused the video and the colors continued. It took a moment to register it didn't come from the screen.

He turned his head around to see the cause.

"What in the..."

His words died out mid-sentence. At some point, he found himself having stood up and strolling towards the outside, himself not realizing it at first.

He pushed past the lab door and from the hallway, he saw out through the window to the side corridor, up at the sky. Lights shot through the sky like disco ball refractions strapped to missiles. A frantic hand fumbled in his pocket for his cell phone, and he almost dropped it as he made a mad dash for the courtyard outside the building.

Out the door, he mashed the record button and made it five steps before slipping on a wet patch and meeting the grass face first. An instant later, before pain could register, he slammed a palm down and shoved himself to standing.

With the phone held up, his mouth hung open in disbelief, and his eyes taking in the impossible sight, his mind raced a billion miles per hour. From single white points in the sky, balls of color shot out in various directions and speeds, leaving trails of colored light behind them, and each one varied in motion. A green ball of light moved in a zigzag pattern, while a similar shade of green went in a different direction and a swirling motion. After a few seconds, more than thirty people still on campus stood outside staring up at the event that would later become known as The Lights.

After minutes, a final flash of light shot out and the sky returned to normal.

As Raymond walked back to his lab, he stared at the video he'd just recorded, as it played on his phone. None of it made logical sense. A thousand different possibilities emerged, but his mind didn't feel like settling on any of them. A cursory search of the internet showed every message board and social media feed positively erupting with videos, photos, and every statement ranging from biblical to conspiratorial and all in between. The evidence showed that thousands of places across the globe each experienced the Lights, meaning the whole world had seen these things at roughly the same time.

He slid into the instructor's chair behind the computer.

"Did you see that!"

Alan's shout as he practically threw the door open broke Raymond out of his staring. He looked up. "Yeah," he said. "I did."

"What'd you think that was?" Alan almost yelled.

"I don't have a clue," he said. "Optics aren't really my thing." He glanced between the board and the assistant he'd just acquired. "Well, it's clear we're not getting any of this done tonight. You can go home."

Alan pondered. "Yeah," he concluded, "you're probably right. This isn't my thing, either." He folded his arms. "Are you going to be okay?"

Raymond shrugged. "That depends on what we find out about this…" He stared at the screen, scrolling through the Facebook feeds. "Whatever the hell this turns out to be."

Alan let out a breath. "Oh man, this is going to be huge," he exclaimed.

"It sure as hell will be," Raymond replied, nodding.

"I'm going to go home then," Alan said, a bit of a laugh in his voice, "because I'm going to be useless at figuring this out."

"Don't worry," Raymond advised. "We'll get back on track as soon as possible. I promise."

"Don't leave me hanging," Alan joked. "Bye."

Raymond waved. "Goodbye." He set the phone down and closed the web browser. This ordeal had gone Twilight Zone right away. Whatever this genuinely turned out to be, the scientist in him refused to believe this was a legitimate paranormal event, because that would mean there could be no explanation. He felt there had to be an explanation, even if it didn't come in his lifetime.

Then he noticed it.

He took a breath, closed his eyes, and released.

Unobtrusive, not getting in the way, it was, but it was still there.

There was…something…in the back of his mind. He struggled to describe it to himself. It wasn't *physically* located anywhere in his brain meat. It occupied an incorporeal mental space in the back of his mind, and even that struck him as somehow the wrong explanation. What was it, a twinge, he wondered? Closing his eyes, he focused on it, and the image came to his mind. A glowing ball of light, a dark shade of yellow, sat in what he somehow knew—but couldn't explain *how* he knew—was the "off" position.

He blinked, and let a nervous snort escape his nose. *You're going crazy, Ray*, he thought to himself.

Still, if this was nuts, he wanted to see *how* nuts, so he focused some effort on it and pulled the "trigger." The ball of light popped upward, turned a brighter shade, and latched itself into the "on" position. Nothing felt different. He let out a defeated sigh and rubbed his eyelids. "God, this is just insanity," he uttered. He shook his head.

Then he looked up and saw the familiar whiteboard.

His eyes went speed addict wide.

Within moments of seeing the board, he knew the answer.

"Oh my God," he muttered. "Months of work."

His fingers started scrawling the incomplete parts of the equation in the spots where they should be. Almost before he realized it, his hands wrote the final answer next to the bottom line of the last equation. Standing back and staring at it, he realized he didn't need to re-check his work; his mind had done that several times just by looking at it. He took a picture with his cell phone.

A number got dialed by fingers almost too frantic to type. He held the device to his face. "Yes!" he shouted. "Doctor Weatherford!"

"Do you..."

"No!" he shouted, interrupting the old man. "I don't give a shit what time it is over there! I'm texting you something. Take a look at it." He texted the photo of the whiteboard. Almost at once he had to hold the phone at arm's length because of the volume of the screaming on the other end.

Several hours later, he stood in a lecture hall at Oxford in London, surrounded by dozens of the most brilliant scientists, some of which, he hadn't met. "Gentlemen," he said, "I think it's safe to say I've gotten smarter. The million-dollar question is, why? I think it's related to the Lights, but I don't know anything anyone else doesn't know."

An elderly scientist stepped forward. "Let me tell you something," he began, "I showed these results of yours and some others to a colleague, and he had to be hospitalized after fainting and hitting his head on his sink. This is..." he trailed off into a short chuckle, "this is a fucking magic trick."

Another colleague went over a dozen different photographs of Raymond's recent work. "That's putting it mildly," he added. "Doctor, I hate to sound pessimistic, but most of the people I talked to said they didn't expect these problems to be solved for over a century, and," he fished for the words, "one said it would possibly take sci-fi level artificial intelligence to even figure it out." He looked up. "His words, not mine."

"Your hypothesis," Doctor Weatherford interjected, "is *selective* alterations to the laws of physics."

"Yeah!" Raymond said. "Look, I know it sounds crazy, but hundreds of people have reported seeing impossible things. The guy who could catch fire at will and not be harmed. How is his biochemistry still possible under those kinds of temperatures? What is his fuel source? How does he breathe? The only way this makes sense is if he is altering the laws of physics regarding his body. So, it acts like fire but allows his body to still function as his body. I do not believe this is impossible to explain, and I do not believe this is a religious event."

"You've single-handedly moved at least eight fields of science ahead a century," Doctor Weatherford replied, "otherwise we wouldn't even be talking to you here. Do you realize this could be a mass hallucination?"

"Yes," Raymond admitted. "As a scientist, I must admit the possibility that this is not happening, and everyone has somehow had a mass hallucination." He reached behind the instructor's desk and turned on the television. The news reported several new events. A man in India got run over by a train and had healed by the time it moved past him. A woman in Mexico could turn herself to solid stone, and yet her body still functioned like normal. "But think: if this is a mass hallucination, this is the most complex, most dramatic mass hysteria in history!"

"Seems unlikely," one colleague replied.

"Also," Raymond added, "think about this. That means for most of my life, I've been smart, yes, but not anywhere close to *this* smart, then all of a sudden, in one night, I demonstrate intelligence to easily put me on par with Newton and Einstein?"

"Difficult to imagine," Doctor Weatherford shot back, "but not impossible."

"I'll admit it could be false," Raymond responded. "As a scientist, I must admit the possibility. But you, Charlie!" he pointed to his Canadian colleague. "You're the optics expert. You tell me what the Lights were."

Charlie pondered. "I don't know," he commented, "but you're talking about *magic*."

Raymond gestured. "It could be physics from a different universe or universes," he thought out loud, "but in any case, it behaves like a science. This guy doesn't get a random effect each time, he bursts into flame every time. You go to start your car, and as long as it's working and has gas, it starts. I don't think this is paranormal, because if it were, why is there a pattern at all?"

"Alright," Doctor Weatherford said, "you've made a good point. What do you recommend?"

"Take anything that isn't of the utmost urgency right now," Raymond advised, "and start studying *this*. Powers. The Lights, all of it. This, gentlemen, has to be priority one."

They pondered it. "Yes, I think that's a good idea," Doctor Weatherford said.

Over the next several weeks, he traveled to various corners of the globe, interviewing scores of people who had developed powers, and testing on them equipment he invented. Interviewing particle physicists at CERN and elsewhere revealed that new particles were being discovered, and most of them, to their surprise, had interactions with ordinary particles. This bothered them, because all of the particles relevant to the daily life of people had been discovered; the rest should be either too weak to interact or too short-lived to interact. These displayed bizarre effects not seen before in the Standard Model. So, he had to put his newfound intellect to the test and develop his own equipment.

"So, Doctor Weiss," Alan said, going over the latest report, "anything new?"

"It turns out that there's a dozen or so differences between the same power expressed by two different people," he explained. "The problem is, we can't seem to find a clear answer as to why."

"So, you think there's a hierarchy of powers?" Alan asked.

Raymond nodded. "I think there has to be," he explained, "because we've seen powers express in different ways. A woman in Chicago defended her house against a break-in, a powered individual shot her with a projectile, and the wound healed before she got to the hospital. A guy with regeneration in Ireland got into a bar fight with a pyrokinetic, and his burn didn't heal for a day."

"There could be other variables in play," the assistant suggested.

"Yeah, probably," Raymond said, "but it seems to me that not all of the powers, even the *same* powers, are at the same level."

"Doctor Weiss!" a voice cried.

They turned to see a man rush in. "Something new?" Raymond asked.

"You've studied barrier makers extensively," he explained, "and you said you wanted to study one that could produce more than just a local effect?"

"Yeah?" the professor asked, intrigued.

"We found one for you," the man said. "Lives in a South American rainforest, middle of nowhere, has a little corner of the forest sectioned off by forcefields almost a kilometer in diameter."

"Tell me you got in touch with him," Raymond implored.

"You two have got a flight in three hours to Rio," the man said, "and then you're off to meet him. He trades with locals. He wouldn't tell us his name beyond just 'Ricardo.'" He handed some plane tickets over. "Get all the equipment together."

"Awesome!" Alan cried. "This'll be the best test yet to prove your hierarchy hypothesis."

The next day, they trekked through the jungle. About thirty minutes into their hike, with multiple guides helping clear a trail, they both realized why physicists almost never went into a rainforest. With aching feet and every kind of mosquito chemical smeared on their flesh, they cut and shoved their way through foliage and over fallen brush of every kind.

Until, that is, the terrain cleared out, and they came to an opening. The opening had a transparent wall only visible through slight distortions on light passing through it. Raymond stepped forward and placed a hand against the firm forcefield, pressing against it. It held. "Are you the ones I spoke to?" a Hispanic voice asked with accented English.

"Uh, yeah," Raymond introduced. "Doctor Ray Weiss, University of California, Berkley, I'm studying superpowers and how they interact with the real world."

An inward semi-spherical protrusion stuck inward. They slowly stepped into it, at which point it pinched off the outer wall and let them into the enclosure. They marveled at what they saw. The ground had been levelled by forcefield. A circle of rainforest a kilometer in diameter created the floor of a dome that stretched upward for about a third of a kilometer. Raymond looked up, and even saw the forcefield formed into a fine mesh to keep bugs out and let air circulate in parts. It was the most complex use of the power he'd yet seen. In the center of the area, a house reminiscent of suburban America rather than Amazon jungle. It had a familiar aluminum siding body, complete with windows, a slanted roof, and a front porch. There stood several nearby sheds containing battery arrays connected to huge solar panels arranged around the house for power. What this 'Ricardo' did for water and sewage, he didn't know, but everything else looked modern.

They knocked on the door, and it opened. A mid-fifties man in shorts and a Hawaiian shirt greeted them, beer in hand. "Hey!" he cried. "It is nice to see people every once in a while." He gestured. "Come on in."

Alan and Raymond began setting up equipment in the living room. Everything looked like your average abode in midwestern suburban America. "Don't worry," Alan said, "we brought our own power supply."

"So," Ricardo cut in, "you want to study my forcefields?"

"Yeah," Raymond explained. "We've studied about six different people who can generate forcefields, but none come anywhere close to how complex yours are."

"I guess that makes me special then, huh?" He took a swig of beer. "Man, I ain't never seen stuff like that."

The professor looked at the scanners he pointed at. "Yeah, makes sense," Raymond answered. "I had to invent this whole cloth."

"Neat," Ricardo said.

"I've been studying how these superpowers interact with the local laws of physics," Raymond explained. "And I think we're awash in new interactions we've never seen before in our universe."

Ricardo chuckled. "Dumb person speak, please," he joked.

"Well," Raymond stated, "before the Lights, if you wanted a new particle to do something, like bend a spoon with your mind, you couldn't have it, because we would have seen it already. Sure, there are new particles out there, but they aren't relevant to daily life. These new...things...clearly *are* relevant to daily life."

"Plus," Alan interjected, "these things, whatever they are, are interacting selectively with the laws of reality. That's how someone can regenerate a wound far faster than normal biology should allow."

Raymond pointed. "Oh, if you could," he told Ricardo, "now would be a great time to form a bubble around you. Please create some indentations for these to stick in."

"Gotcha," Ricardo agreed.

A spherical shield formed around him, and the two stuck the

bread loaf-sized scanners into each slot in the bubble and attached them by cable to a large box connected to a laptop. A buzzing sound echoed through the room, and Alan changed some settings on a turn dial while Raymond typed some details into the laptop.

"Look at this," Alan said, pointing to a light on the large box. "There's a slight deviation here."

Raymond looked over. "That's great," he commented. "That's something we want to see." He inserted a few more details into the program. A loud buzzing echoed. "Alright, just a little more."

The box emitted a loud beep and the buzzing stopped. "Did you get it?" Alan asked.

The professor pumped his fist. "Great!" he shouted. "We got it!"

Alan looked at the list of results. "They're all the same..." he scrolled down with his finger, "...except that one!"

Raymond snapped his fingers. "We've got a potential candidate for judging a hierarchy of powers!" he cheered.

"You guys get what you're looking for?" Ricardo asked.

"Definitely," Raymond replied. "It was most definitely worth it."

They disassembled the equipment and packed it away in their cases. Afterward, they backed up the data on several USB drives, and placed it in the computer case. Alan pulled out a cassette recorder. "Didn't you want to record a conversation?" he asked.

"Oh!" the professor realized. "I did. Is that okay with you?"

"No problem," Ricardo said.

They had a chat. After the Lights, the Mexico native discovered he could create forcefields of all shapes and sizes, even ones with sharp edges. So, disgruntled with his job of teaching English at local schools and other odd tasks, he used his newfound powers to extract resources from hard to reach places and used the money to travel into the rainforest and set up a house away from everyone. When he needed resources the jungle couldn't provide, he traded with locals.

"Fascinating," Alan said. "You really don't miss the urban life?"

"Sometimes," Ricardo admitted. "Honestly, it's nice and quiet out here. The forcefields stay up even when I'm asleep, and as long as I keep the air circulating, everything's okay. I'm perfectly safe here, and I have some of the best sights in the world."

"And besides," Raymond noted, "when you go exploring, you can take your power with you."

"Right," Ricardo said, pointing. "I can have as many as I want, and it's great."

Raymond off-handedly looked at his watch. "Oh, geez," he said, "sorry. We've got to go."

"If you want," Ricardo said, "I can give you an easy way out of the jungle." He pointed. "You came in from the northeast, right?"

The two guests looked at each other in confusion. "How'd you know?" Alan asked.

"My shields can pick up sights and sounds," Ricardo explained. "I saw and heard you coming."

Raymond shook his head. "Amazing," he said.

Once they stepped outside, they saw, just outside the dome, a staircase leading up over the forest canopy. "Nice talking to you," their host said as they left.

"Pleasure was all ours," Raymond said.

As they climbed, they saw the walkway had handrails on each side made out of light to keep them from falling off. It was the oddest experience the group had ever had up to that point. They walked over the jungle, with one hell of a sight below them, and without having to trek through brush. On the other end, there was a staircase leading down. As the last person stepped off carrying a huge case, the whole thing vanished.

"Hey, is there a Raymond Weiss here?" a grizzled, old voice cried out.

The whole group turned to see a Jeep pull up, and out of the passenger side, stepped a man in a dress shirt, tie, and khakis, exactly the wrong kind of attire for this climate. The professor approached, apprehension high, arms folded. "That's me," he introduced.

"Sam Louis," Sam introduced, "FBI. I've got a situation and you have a person who really wants to meet you, and I think both our problems have the same solution."

Raymond tilted his head a bit in confusion. "Okay," he replied, "I'm all ears."

"How'd you like to meet Jericho Torvalds?"

The scientist perked up at Sam's question. "I'd love to," he admitted. "Copying powers? That's one hell of an opportunity to study."

"Yeah, well," Sam replied, "you help us, we help you, that sort of thing."

"So, you hit the ground running," Jericho commented, after the vision ended. Going into the man's memories enabled him to get a better grasp on the science. He also copied the man's intelligence power, so he made a mental note to set him up financially in payment. "I have to thank you, you've really done me a huge favor already."

"That's what I thought," Raymond said. He cleared his throat. "I figured we could work better together. Are you working with the Capacitor?"

"So they're just naming her after the character, now?" Jericho mused out loud. He sighed. Copyright law be damned, he figured. "Yes, I am, and she's been great to work with." He coughed. "Regardless, please tell me the mad reverend and his false messiah are as powerful as Jennifer."

The physicist collected his thoughts. "Honestly, I knew both Jennifer and you were heavy hitters because I've built a long-range scanner and a short-range scanner," he explained. "The short-range scanner gives me great results, useful results, but if I just want to find out where the powers are, I can detect a higher concentration of these 'new interactions' with the long range."

"Like a radar for supers?" Davis asked.

Raymond did a seesaw gesture. "Eh, kinda." He paused to gather the right words. "I can't tell the difference in power between Jennifer and Jack Hurst long-range, but I definitely can tell they're at least on par."

"What about me?" Jericho asked, hand on chin, worried.

"You're high-up," Raymond explained, "but I suspect that when you copy a power, you don't upgrade that power in terms of hierarchy."

"Which is why the fake Jesus could turn the powers off." Jericho sighed and leaned forward, clasping his hands together in contemplation.

"And if he is that powerful," Davis reminded, "that means when he says, 'we're at war,' he *means* it."

"So," Raymond asked, "what do we do now?"

Jericho sat in contemplation for a whole minute. They watched him. Davis and his boss looked at each other. "We're going to go back to the office," Sam offered, "and see what we can do before everything goes to hell."

"Good idea," Jericho stated. "I'm going to go get my family and make sure they're safe, and then we're going to meet up with the main group to discuss tactics."

II.

Jennifer took to the sky and, having seen the synagogue under attack, arrived on the scene in moments. The innocents were tied and gagged. The attacker, a man in a brown trench coat, had electricity arc off his hands. One man lay on the ground, twitching but still barely alive. "You made a huge mistake," she warned. She took off running before the sneer could fully form on her face. Reality froze around her, and she drew her fist back for a knockout blow to his chest, just enough to knock the wind out of him.

A man appeared before him and drove vibrating fists into her chest and face. The blows jolted her back and the shockwaves zoomed through her body and disoriented her. She came up for a swing, but her arm sailed through empty air as he delivered a storm of jabs to her gut and dashed behind and got her dozens of times in the back of the head. Her world went spinning and she collapsed to one knee. It took every ounce of effort not to drop out of both super speed powers by reflex. He arrived in front of her and went for a knee to the face.

The knee collided with her temple at impossible velocity, jolting her head backward and sending a sharp needle of pain. Upon its collision, she sent a surge through him. The speedster's entire nervous system went haywire with random jolts of current causing him to collapse to the ground in a seizing agony. As soon as it began, he dropped out of super speed and went frozen along with the background. Now with plenty of time to breathe, she stood there and caught her breath.

A quick scan of the surroundings revealed it had been a trap. A camera hung high above in the rafters, and a position a few miles away revealed where someone could sit and watch. As soon as she arrived, he waited for her to move and then pounced. Damn, she figured, this guy was fast. He outpaced her quite easily.

She grabbed the electrical attacker and zoomed him outside, into the range of police gunmen. As soon as time returned to normal for him, he surrendered once he saw no chance to defeat twenty rifles pointed at him.

Upon returning to where the speedster lay, she had an idea.

The fast man found his body return to normal. The first thing he recognized was that the scenery had suddenly changed. The dark sky hovered above him. The would-be hero woman held him by the waist with her hands. This was absurd, where was he? He went to vibrate out of her grip.

"No," she scolded him. "Look where you are. Look down."

He looked down, and almost went catatonic. Miles of sky and the Earth stood below them. "What...WHAT THE...!" he shrieked.

"We're in the upper stratosphere," Jennifer stated. "At this altitude, you'd freeze to death in less than a second. The reason you don't is me. Up here, you wouldn't be able to breathe. Again, that's me." She grinned. "If I let go of you, you simply die."

He shook his head. "No!" he begged. "Please don't kill me!"

"I won't kill you," she explained, "if you give me all the answers I want."

He began to laugh. "I'll tell you everything," he said. "It won't do you much good."

"Why's that?"

"Because the Lord cannot be beaten," the speedster explained. "Those who will not bend the knee to the Lord are the enemy. We knew a person who uses his powers and does not serve the Lord has loved ones that attend this place of worship. You might have stopped us from finding him out, but no matter. The Lord will prevail against him."

She shook her head. "So, you buy into this 'holy war' crap?"

He shrugged. "It's only 'crap' to you because you are seduced by evil," he stated. "Besides, you know the cops aren't going to be able to keep me."

She rolled her eyes. "Yeah yeah, I get it."

Another zap and he passed out. He woke up in police custody. Sure, she expected him to escape, but right now, she had other work to do. Religious cults in Asia were on the move. She flew down into Russia, where several people were held up in a church.

A scan of the building showed a group of forty Muslims surrounded by supers. Less than a heartbeat later, she exploded through the sealed doors, launching both brutes into the aisle, knocking down cultists like bowling pins. Shouts and shrieks reverberated through the ancient stone and wood structure. Amidst a crowd of Russian, she heard the word "Capacitor," and a ball of lightning streaked past her head and exploded a hole in the front door wall. A huge sphere of ball lightning streaked straight for her. She held up her left forearm, and the electricity danced around her body until she pointed at a cultist standing over a family of Muslims. An enormous bolt streaked across the room and struck him dead on in the chest causing him to ricochet off the stone wall and land in a crumpled heap, moaning. She moved forward.

"Bitch!" the super shouted in Russian as he flung another enormous sphere of lightning at her, this one twice as large as the last.

She caught it in her right hand, and it vanished into her. A smile appeared on the super's face. A pair of huge hands touched her shoulders.

After rocketing backward, she smashed through a series of vehicles and through the wall of an abandoned factory. A critical beam support stopped her ride, and the building collapsed on top of her. She blasted out of the rubble, flying upward, as the two brutes came down, fists extended towards her. An impact like missiles colliding jolted through her as she reached out to catch them and their fists smashed into her. A jerk of her arm released one of them midair, where her foot crashed into his enormous chest, hurtling him into the debris, which erupted like a grenade. She then threw the other slightly above her and clamped both hands on his huge head.

His scream pierced the air as she sent the stored lightning through his head. His body went limp, and careened downward, an eight-foot elephant-sized projectile that crashed through a wrecked car, leaving a sizeable crater. She saw he had a nasty concussion.

The assailants shouted at each other in Russian and one man gave a single command. The gunmen opened fire on the innocents...only there was no gunfire. One second, they had their fingers on the trigger, ready to go, and next, their guns could be seen outside, piled up. The woman stood in the line between the pews. They hadn't seen anything move. The last super they had leapt across the room at her. A left-handed palm strike sent him into the wall. He chose not to get up.

The hired mercenaries decided to flee, leaving six remaining cultists to be led out as a group, tied with rope pilfered from a nearby hardware store.

After this endeavor, she flew over the middle east and dealt with several acts of sectarian violence, stopping rockets and other projectiles from hitting civilian targets.

She found a series of powered women travelling around Iran and freeing victims of trafficking from their hiding places. Wanting to avoid an international incident, she merely identified for them their targets, and then flew away.

As she returned to the hideout, she reflected on the ordeal that played out. A few moments later, Jericho arrived, a dark-haired younger man in a Depeche Mode t-shirt next to him. On the other side, stood a scholarly looking middle aged man.

"Who's this?" she asked.

"The latest addition to our team," he replied, gesturing at the man. "My brother, Luther." He stood aside, pointing to his other compatriot. "This guy is going to help us out with the science of powers."

"Hi," Raymond said, "I'm Ray Weiss."

"I just need to get the stuff," Jericho said, disappearing and reappearing a few moments later. In the room stood a series of black plastic cases of varying sizes, and a huge box. "This all of it?"

"Looks like it," Raymond replied. "You see, what I want to do is help us figure out whether or not we can outperform Jack Hurst, if we have a power that's above his."

Jennifer tilted her head. "What do you mean, 'above his?'" she asked.

"That's a funny story," he explained. "Uh, Jericho? Why don't you do your thing, and that way, she'll understand."

"Oh!" Jericho realized. "Right. Gotcha." He touched her, and she got the memories of the conversation and of Raymond's ordeal.

He spent the next fifteen minutes setting up the equipment. She stripped down to her undergarments, and he stuck small box-like objects to her torso, abdomen, and legs, with one on her forehead. "Pardon the mess," Raymond apologized, "but you can't exactly put these in midair like the last guy could with his forcefield."

"It's alright," she lied.

"This should hopefully only take a few minutes." Raymond tapped away at the computer.

"Didn't you have a lab assistant?"

He looked up from the screen at her question. "Alan Jordan?" he asked. "No, he decided to go into hiding. I don't blame him."

At this point, Edward, Annie, and John came in from the other room. "Is there anything for us to do right now?" Annie asked.

Jericho turned to Jennifer. "What's your idea?"

Jennifer gave his question serious thought. "I suspect my power is going to be crucial to the coming battle," she explained. "You've already demonstrated that a person can have more than one ability, and so I think we should give my friends Ray's enhanced intellect and have them think about characters before you give them my ability." She turned to her friends. "How does that sound?"

"I mean," Edward cut in, "it sounds fine, but how *does* your power work?"

"Honestly," Jennifer stated, "Capacitor was my favorite character. Now, don't get me wrong, I love all sorts of stuff, but, I dunno, something about it just clicked with me." She gestured. "I mean, I've *tried* other characters, but honestly, I think once the power noticed I had a specific choice, it locked that in."

Raymond stepped forward. "I think that's interesting," he mused.

"In what way?" Jennifer asked.

"Um, honestly," he said, "I think what had to have happened is that your power 'chose' your transformed state based on what you emotionally decided was your favorite." He looked at the billionaire. "It's why I think Jericho couldn't use it. He doesn't have a favorite character."

"Yeah," the rich man said, rolling his eyes, "remind me of my personality issues again."

"If it makes you feel any better," John cut in, "you've made a hell of a change."

"No," Raymond added, "I don't mean that. It's that you don't have a strong connection, emotionally speaking, to any fictional character. On the other hand, I think if we give my enhanced intelligence power to these guys, it'll help them make a more informed emotional decision. That could tip the balance."

Jericho motioned, and the three stood up. "Form a line," he advised. "I'm going to give you a series of memories and the power in question, and you'll have a day to think about it. Then, I'll give you Jennifer's power and you'll make your decision. Make sense?"

"Hey, I'm down," Annie said.

"We should probably go for variety," Edward advised.

John looked over at him. "Oh," he said, "It's a bad idea to all have the same powerset? That's what you meant, right?"

Raymond nodded. "I don't know much about comics," he admitted, "but that sounds like a bad idea."

"Right!" John said. "Got it."

"No problem," Annie added.

Jennifer nodded. "Jericho," she said, "I think we should keep track of Jack Hurst."

"You're right," he stated. "We've got to keep a close eye on him."

Just then his phone rang. He picked up. "Dave," he said, "What do you have for me?"

Davis Wilson paused the video playing on his computer screen. "Get to New York," he advised. "Jack Hurst and his monster are in Times Square and there's a lot of people there."

"Shit!" Jericho swore, clicking the conversation off.

Jennifer's eyes lowered into a frustrated expression. "Let me guess," she uttered.

He sighed. "You don't have to."

CHAPTER SEVENTEEN

"So," Jack Hurst said, as he sat in the living room of his house, "what do we do next?" He'd fixed himself a ham and turkey sandwich with tomato and yellow mustard and was taking bites in between sips of ginger ale. His Lord had been gone for the better part of an hour, and he decided to wait rather than act on his own. A few moments ago, the Lord had returned. He went to prostrate himself before his savior, but a waved hand told him to stay.

The Lord looked at him. "We must make the greatest immediate impression," He spoke. "We must get the world's attention. Your speech at the Reverend Masterfield's church got attention, but not the level we need."

Jack swallowed and washed it down. He set the glass down. "Just tell me where, my Lord," he said.

"The heart of New York City," the Lord spoke. "Times Square. You make your sermon clear to them, and the whole world will stand and take notice."

Jack nodded. "A great idea!" He nodded and smiled. "Will you take me there?"

"But of course," was the response. The Lord motioned towards the rear door. "Finish your food and meet me outside."

Jack crammed the remaining third of the sandwich into his mouth, chewed like mad, then swallowed and gulped down the last of the glass of soda. Then he practically sprinted for the door.

The Lord draped an arm around his charge, and then blasted into the sky. Within less than a minute, they were out of the county. Jack felt the wind pass harmlessly around him, like a dog's head out the car window on the highway. However, they flew at over a thousand miles per hour. "This is amazing!" he shouted.

"It is nothing," the Lord spoke. He looked briefly at his servant. "I could go much faster, but I want people on the ground to see us moving, at least briefly."

He saw the ground from up high and felt like a million bucks. A feeling of glory from on high swelled up in his soul, like only being in service to God almighty could make him feel. Inspiration came like the wave crashing against the beach. Words came to him, words that people would doubtlessly find offensive and might even deem hateful, but the will of God the Father required him to say. Duty spoke to him. He had to make clear the stakes in this cosmic battle. The final battle against Satan would arrive in a short while and his words had to rally the faithful and those loyal to the Lord's cause.

In less than a half hour, they touched down in Times Square. At first, many people stopped and either gasped or laughed, assuming it was someone performing a trick using a superpower. Cars continued moving around them. Some recognized the pair from the news and stopped to pay attention. The Lord and his charge looked around, taking in the sight of the enormous crowd.

With a wave of his hands, The Lord made a platform appeared above the concrete of the walkway and hovered about five feet into the air. He turned to his servant. "My children," He spoke, his voice booming. "I bring to you my messenger upon this Earth, bringing my Father's word to you all." He touched Jack, amplifying his voice for all around to hear.

All heard the pronouncement and stopped what they were doing and looked up. Cars slowed to a crawl and traffic began to back up. "Ladies and Gentlemen," Jack announced, putting on his Sunday best voice. "You might recognize my Lord and myself from the broadcast. We have wasted no time because Satan does not rest. The Deceiver does not take breaks. We have decided to act at once."

He saw the crowd gathering. Some looked suspicious and skeptical, while others kept a keen ear on every word. He continued. "People, I wish I could sit here and tell you our task is easy. I know many of you do not believe the Lord is in fact right here. This is unfortunate, as our enemies mobilize while we desperately seek allies. This is how our society has fallen, and why the Lord must come to you at once." He took a breath. "You see, Satan's infiltration of our society has corrupted every level. Where once we sinned, but at least pretended to keep Our Father's commandments on this Earth, now we turn sin into an act of pride. We wear our sins as a badge of honor with a smile on our face. This cannot be allowed to continue."

At these words, anger began to simmer in the people, who encroached from all angles, crowding in to see who dared speak such rhetoric. Jack persisted at his sermon, nonetheless. This was a bandage that needed to be ripped off. "We have fallen in love with Satan's machinations. We praise our children for being 'gay' or 'transgender' when such is evil. It is the corrupt will of the Devil and will only result in separation between a person and their God." Angry cries and loud chatter of rejection rose from the crowd. "I do not wish to see God's children suffer. We have a choice. We have the option to set aside our sin and allow Jesus into our hearts and He will bring His Father's mercy upon you all. He will bring glory into your life, and love into your heart that no amount of sin can fulfill. Only by confessing your sins to your Lord can you gain the eternal kingdom of God."

"Hey!" a voice shouted over the din. "Fuck you, man!"

Everyone went silent as the Lord stepped forward from behind his servant. A single raised finger hovered the man above the crowd and drew him within ten feet. The man had a long dark brown ponytail, skin like coffee with cream, and brown eyes. Also, what most caught the Lord's eye, was the gay pride flag on his shirt. He regarded the man with sad eyes. "My child," the Lord spoke, "this defiance of my father is your daily life. It will bring you nothing except suffering and hellfire. I can bring you absolution. I can bring you into my Father's eternal paradise." He brought the man onto the platform. "Deny Satan's grasp on you, defy your evil ways, and bend the knee to myself and my Father on high, and accept me as your savior." His deadly serious expression stared straight through the man to his core. "For I alone am the savior, and none get to Heaven save through me."

The man quivered in terror. "Christ, man, don't kill me," he pleaded.

"I won't kill you," the Lord clarified. "*You* will be killing you, that is, if you do not accept my Father's will. Don't you want to be saved?"

"I...please..."

The Lord stepped closer, causing the man to fall onto his butt. "That is not an answer," He spoke. "Make your decision, now."

"I...I won't." The man said it as firmly as he could. "I won't be bullied. Not anymore."

The Lord bowed his head. "That is a shame," He stated. His eyes closed and opened. "Because I wanted to save you."

"Wh...what?"

The man's question cut off as a piercing scream escaped his mouth. A great light surrounded him, and an unimaginable flame erupted, with heat beyond compare, that overtook him and reduced him to ash in a second. The smell of burning flesh and fat wafted into the air as the light died down, leaving behind a small pile where a person once sat.

Chaos erupted like a volcano as bodies collided with each other in desperation. People clamored and shoved their way away from the two as fast as their legs could carry them. The Lord lifted a right hand upward, like a strange salute, and walls of translucent light erupted from the ground, sealing off the exits to Times Square. Bodies collided with them and people bashed into the force field with fists and feet. Cars impacted and stopped cold. With a gesture, dozens of cell phones raised into the air and focused their cameras on Jack. A flick of a finger and they started broadcasting to the internet. "You shall not escape the Truth!" Jack said to the crowd present. "Witness the pain of refusing the mercy of Christ, and the glory of God! You have had every chance to repent, to renounce evil and confess your sin! This is your last chance to accept salvation!"

"People of God's Earth," the preacher said into the cameras, "you have one last chance. You have one final decision to make: God's eternal kingdom, or everlasting hellfire. You have until we get to you to make your decision. If you wish to defeat evil, if you wish to serve your God and secure your place in his righteous army against Satan's wickedness, bend your knee to your savior. Accept Christ, your Lord, into your heart and we will give you details on how to do God's work in this world."

A sonic boom rattled the skyscrapers of Manhattan. Hovering over the scene, two figures watched with fiery rage in their eyes. A redhead woman wearing an orange t-shirt and double layers of yoga pants stared at the two with deadly seriousness. Next to her, hovered a man with a weightlifter build in a short-sleeved white shirt and jeans, with chin-length hair the color of desert sand. He didn't know how useful he would be if this Jesus shut off his powers again, but he wasn't going to skip on this one.

"Somehow," Jericho uttered to Jennifer, "this outcome didn't surprise me."

"Jack Hurst!" Jennifer shouted, her voice rattling windows. "You are NOT going to kill one more person!"

"I have not condemned one person!" the Lord shouted. "They condemned themselves by refusing the gift of my Father's love!"

She shifted her gaze to Jack. "This monster of yours just killed someone!" she bellowed. "You shut this thing down at once!"

Jack scoffed. "You accuse me of having a superpower?" he asked. "No! Of course, a servant of Satan like yourself would think that. I am a servant of the Lord! This is the task I've been charged with!"

The Lord stepped past his servant. "My child," he spoke, "you will submit to me now."

Before anyone could see anything, Jennifer flew down, impacting the fake Jesus and shooting up into the sky like a rocket. At a thousand feet over the tops of the buildings, she crashed her fist like a meteor strike into her foe's chest. The sound, like a cannon shot, rattled buildings for miles around. The impact shot the Lord backwards like a railgun, bouncing off the roof of a skyscraper like a stone skimmed across a pond, and sailing for scores of miles. He finally crashed into a wooded area far outside the metropolitan area, smashing into a cliffside and causing the rocks to collapse into the river. Before he could right himself, she smashed into him, plowing rapid fire fists and feet into his body.

"Enough!"

The Lord's shout caused an invisible force to smash into her and shove her back, and then wrap around her, binding her tightly. "You're going to have to kill me," she told him, "because that's the only way you're going to kill anyone else." He hovered close to her.

"My child," the fake Jesus spoke, "why do you serve the Deceiver? You have enormous potential to do my Father's work upon this Earth. I would hate to have to send you to hell."

Jennifer smirked. "I thought you didn't condemn anyone," she replied. "But the way you just worded it, which is it?"

The Lord let out a frustrated sigh and grit his teeth in anger. "It seems you fight against my Father," he spoke. A white-hot fire engulfed her, the light cocooning her. She screeched in agony as her extremities began to burn. "I cannot save you if you will not submit."

As she pulled against impossible bonds, her body became a single solid mass of pain. She fought to manipulate the energy surging through her, destroying her bit by bit, finding it elusive as it slipped past her will. With bubbles appearing on her skin, she fought to keep her mind rational, as the intense suffering caused her to lose calm.

Finally, an option presented itself.

The Lord watched, when suddenly, his nervous system almost completely shut down. Signals went every which way except where they needed to go. Before he even had a chance to react, Jennifer smashed into him after his bindings failed and the fire died down. A storm of blows bashed against him and she drove him into the ground with a two-fisted smash.

Back in Manhattan, Jericho found himself virtually powerless, standing helplessly as an invisible wall separated him from Jack Hurst. He kicked at the barrier, but it did not budge. At a certain point, however, he felt his powers return. Without warning, he teleported inside the barrier and grabbed Jack Hurst. Eyes widened on both men. The billionaire sent a charge of electricity. The preacher's body went limp.

Jericho readied another attack. A sonic boom resounded in the distance.

A battering ram of a blow knocked Jericho into the sky. With effort he flipped over in midair. Jennifer came zooming in a moment later, aiming her body like a kamikaze at the two enemies, only for the Lord to knock her aside without touching her. With a wave of the Lord's hand, the preacher stood restored.

"You cannot defeat the Lord!" Jack shouted.

Jennifer and her ally shared a glance then zoomed downward on a collision course with their foes. The Lord clasped his hands together and stuck them outward.

A great glow and fire overcame the two and they vanished in a flash of unearthly heat.

Screams and cries overcame the crowd as cameras caught the ordeal.

Jack smiled as he saw the servants of Satan destroyed. He turned to the crowd. "This is the fate that befalls all who stand with the Deceiver against God's holy kingdom," he preached. "This is the power of the Lord!" He gestured at the crowd. "Now, kneel before your Lord and accept your savior!"

The crowd's clamor and noise died down. One by one, the entire group knelt.

"Now," The Lord spoke, "rise in holiness."

The crowd rose, silently.

The barriers went down.

"Now!" Jack preached. "Go forth and bring the enemies of God to justice! If they will not accept the Lord as their savior, they must be delivered to judgment!"

Sirens wailed in the distance as the Lord and his charge stepped down, allowing the platform to vanish. "It seems we have attracted attention," The Lord spoke.

A group of police cars and vans approached, and out of them, no fewer than thirty men emerged, wearing body armor and wielding pistols and assault shotguns. They formed a line and took aim. "On the ground!" an older officer shouted.

The Lord regarded the show of force. "No," he simply stated.

A flash of light exited the Lord's eyes and their guns harmlessly turned to dust. Several of them reached for holstered sidearms, only to find them gone. "What the hell have you done?" the group commander shouted.

"You will not be harmed if you swear loyalty to your Lord!" Jack yelled.

"I can't let a murderer go free!" the officer exclaimed.

"This is your last chance," Jack pleaded. "I don't want to see you suffer."

"No!" the officer yelled. "I'm not letting you get away!" With no weapon, only his desire to act, the lead officer leapt for Jack Hurst to restrain him.

The Lord lifted a finger and the man vaporized like water on the desert sand. A collective scream of horror escaped from the officers. Before they had a chance to run, a single glance from the Lord and they stood frozen where they stood. "Pledge yourself to me," He spoke, "and you shall gain my father's eternal paradise. Deny me and you shall be cast into the Lake of Fire."

The officers regarded one another, then slowly, took a knee. "Now, rise!" Jack ordered. One by one, they rose.

"My Lord," one young officer cried, "what do you want us to do?"

"Bring the enemies of my Father to judgment," The Lord spoke. "The forces of Satan hide from the light. You will have to bring them out to be dealt with."

"Please forgive me!" one officer cried.

The Lord placed a hand on the man's forehead. "My child," he spoke, "you shall be saved, for you have sided with goodness against evil."

"How do we serve you?"

Jack looked at the man who asked. "Those with powers can be enlisted by either Satan or by us," he explained. "Find them and if they will not join our cause, they must be destroyed."

"Come with me," one officer said, leading them to a vehicle.

CHAPTER EIGHTEEN

JENNIFER OPENED HER EYES, which was not something she expected to do. A quick once-over saw she was back in the hideaway, and her body had the unholy heat surging through it. Without effort behind it, the hateful power that burned her did not have the potency it had earlier, and with a mental squeeze, she focused on it and dispelled it. The relief that washed over her felt like a cool breeze on a hot summer day. She reached over and touched Jericho on the hand, and focused.

"Oh, fuck," he said, as the destructive power left his body. "That's better." The billionaire pushed himself to a standing position. He popped his back and groaned before walking over to the kitchen and pouring himself a drink.

"I guess I don't have to ask how it went," Edward said, "but how did you get back?"

Jericho took a sip of the strong liquor. He closed his eyes and let it go down, then sighed. "One of the powers I copied was a young man who could go back a few minutes after he died," the investor revealed. "Discovered it by accident."

"I don't think we're going to be able to rely on that to keep working," Jennifer noted.

The billionaire shook his head. "No," he agreed, "If he was able to overwhelm us like that, we're going to have to choose our battles wisely."

"After all," Jennifer added, "the first time he hit me with that attack, it hurt, but it wasn't instantly fatal. His power definitely fluctuates."

"Pardon me," Raymond cut in, "but I have a question. Why doesn't this fake Jesus just destroy us from afar?"

Before anyone had a chance to get nervous, Jericho set down his glass and turned to the group. "Because," Jericho explained, "I got some of his memories before I got knocked away. The man spent years of his life expecting to see the final battle between Jesus and the forces of Satan in one climactic battle."

"So," Edward noted, "since he's influencing this creature without knowing it, he's going to want an audience." He clenched his fists as anger drew itself across his face. "Bastard. He profanes the name of the Lord with his monster!"

As Jennifer made herself a sandwich with the lunch meat in the fridge, she noted the rage on her friend's face. The black man was very much unlike her in one regard. As an atheist, she did not have a point of comparison. To her, Jack Hurst was just another religious fanatic, just one who happened to have a walking nuke. Ed, however, had been raised by parents who went to church. He was a firm believer, and nothing would change that. So, to Ed, it must be galling to see this creature and the horror he unveiled.

She realized something. "Hey, guys," she thought out loud, "did you figure out what you wanted to be yet?"

The three snapped to attention. Annie stood up. "I am," she said, "if you're ready."

Jericho finished his glass and approached. "Okay," he said, extending his hand. "Really focus on it."

Jennifer's friend and Edward's girlfriend took the hand, and immediately felt another power appear in her mental space. She stepped back, closed her eyes, and focused on the mental image of who she wanted to turn into. With effort, the switch flipped.

Her flesh and clothes morphed before their very eyes. In under ten seconds, the five-foot-six woman with vaguely Irish facial features stood a hair under seven feet tall and had at least an extra hundred pounds of muscle. A long, black mane of hair hung down to her middle back, and her dark tan body had tone unlike any she had before. Her face looked Egyptian and her green eyes had turned brown. A desert warrior's outfit with feminine modifications garbed her. The three comic fans recognized her at once.

"Cyroya from *First Breaker*?" Ed almost gasped. "Wow, now *that's* a heavy hitter."

"I figure we need power," Annie said, before pausing at the sound of her voice. "Oh man, I sound so..."

"Intense?" John offered.

Annie pointed. "Intense! Yes," she agreed.

"That's a good choice," Jennifer said, analyzing. "Cyroya is the Goddess of Strength, after all."

Ed sat thinking for a few moments. "I guess I'm up," he said. "I've been thinking about it and I can't come up with a better result." He stepped forward.

"Sure?" Jericho asked, hand extended.

"Sure," Edward replied. He took the hand.

Once he stepped back, he closed his eyes and activated his newfound power. His body morphed into that of a lean but tone man with Japanese features. He wore a multi-layered kimono of black and red and had a katana sheathed at his hip. Dark green hair spread out in a wild pattern on his head, thick and consisting of bunched-together clumps. His eyes were blood red.

"Oh man," Jennifer thought out loud, "the name is on the tip of my tongue, but I can't think of it."

Annie snapped her finger into a point. "Kadosuke from the manga *Spirit Blood*," she noted.

"Kadosuke Otokada!" Jennifer shouted, realizing. "Oh wow, that's a *great* choice."

"I had a number of characters to think about," Edward stated, "but honestly, I didn't think I could do better than the guy who defeated the Dark Spirit Emperor's supernova attack."

John stepped forward. "I have a great idea, you guys," he said. He turned to Jericho, taking his hand. "Ready."

When he stepped back, flipping the switch, the transformation that occurred revealed an unexpected turn. There stood a man chronologically seventy, though not physically a second older than physical prime of twenty-five, toned and athletic, but not in any way superhuman. Long, dark brown hair hung past his shoulders, with safety glasses adorning his face, and a white lab coat over dress shirt and slacks. "How's this?" John asked.

Annie folded her arms, concern on her face. "Doctor Anti from the *Dimension Turner* novels?" she scoffed.

"He, uh," Edward pointed out, "he has no powers."

"No, wait," Jennifer cut in, "that's actually brilliant. Both of you guys went for sheer power, in your own way. This character is super smart."

"Beyond super smart," John pointed out. "Doctor Anderson Antel, a.k.a. Doctor Anti, was the coolest anti-hero in nineteen-eighties science fiction novels. He gave himself eternal youth, for crying out loud, and he built a goddamn anti-reality cannon that destroyed the rogue dimension hopper when the heroes couldn't."

Raymond stepped forward. "You know, I think I read one of those one time," he pointed out. A grin came upon his face. "Imagine what we might make with your help."

John gestured at himself. "That's why I chose this one," he pointed out.

"That's a fantastic idea," Jericho cut in. "We'll get to work setting you up a new lab. I might have some locations ready."

Jericho's phone rang. "Sam, what you got for me?" he answered.

A moment later, his eyes went wide. The phone hit the ground when his arm went limp. Everyone turned to him at once. "What?" Jennifer practically shouted.

He looked at her, his face almost pale. "They..." He slapped himself to get his thoughts straight. "The U.N. just authorized the U.S. government to drop a nuke on him."

A chorus of disbelief echoed throughout the room.

Jack Hurst and his Lord were in the middle of talking to a crowd including dozens of police officers, outlining their plan for proceeding the war against evil, when suddenly, the Lord looked up, concern on his face. "My Lord!" Jack said, a look of shock appearing. "What's wrong?"

"Come with me," The Lord spoke, draping an arm around the waist of his charge and taking to the air. They flew for five minutes or so, until they stood hundreds of miles outside of the city.

"Why did we leave?" Jack asked.

The Lord placed an arm on Jack's shoulder, and the man's eyes suddenly saw with divine clarity. A shape appeared on the horizon about two minutes later, and the preacher's eyes went wide at the sight of the triangular shape. "The kingdoms of man have decided to unleash their might upon us," He spoke to Jack. "They must have been hoping I would see this coming and flee the city."

Jack whirled his head between the plane and his Lord. "But...that's a bomber!" he shouted. A chill passed through him as though a needle of ice touched his heart. "They're...they're going to launch a *nuclear weapon* on us!"

The Lord grinned. "Oh, you of little faith," he spoke, pushing ahead of his servant. The ship passed very nearly overhead. They both saw the bay of the large vessel open, and a huge metallic oval shape drop out. It fell, whistling for a short while.

A light as bright as a thousand morning suns lit up the blue sky. Jack threw his arms up instinctively and turned his head. A scream left his mouth.

And then, nothing seemed to happen.

Jack dropped his guard, opening his eyes and looking up. A gigantic ball of flame hovered high above them, a sphere of translucent light englobing it. A simple squeeze of the Lord's outstretched left hand and the globe shrank, taking its contents with it to harmlessly poof out of existence like a soap bubble on a needle. The Lord saw the vessel flying off into the distance and stuck out his right hand. The entire ship exploded in a brilliant flash, reducing the entire vessel and its occupants to dust in a second.

"Yes!" shouted Jack Hurst. "I'm sorry I doubted you, oh Lord!"

"It is understandable," The Lord spoke, "because you are but a man. I can forgive your fear." He embraced his servant. "Now come."

"Where do we go now, oh Lord?" the preacher asked.

The Lord clenched his teeth for a brief instant. He let out a nasal huff. "The kingdoms of man have demonstrated their intent against my Father's kingdom," he stated. "We must demonstrate to them the foolishness of this act, so they never make such a mistake again." He turned his gaze upon his mouthpiece. "My child, do you have the strength to carry on? This will not be a pleasant experience, and I do not do what comes next lightly."

Jack swallowed. "I...I will persist, my Lord!" he swore.

"Good," the Lord spoke. "For you will have to." They took off.

At the United Nations building in New York City, an armed squadron of men took at once to their positions when two very familiar figures landed twenty feet from them.

"OPEN FIRE!"

After one of the armed men shouted, and what followed was a cacophony of explosions from various assault shotguns, automatic rifles, grenade launchers, and five fifty caliber machine guns mounted on Humvee turrets. A foot from their target, each projectile turned into harmless dust and scattered on the ground in front of the Lord's feet.

After a whole minute of shots going off, the scene became eerily silent after thousands of rounds of ammunition had been expended. Smoke poured from hot barrels as men stared in disbelief.

"Your actions will be forgiven if you surrender," The Lord spoke.

A man drew his sidearm and fired. The Lord closed his eyes and held his head down in sorrow.

Every soldier present went up in an ultra-hot burst of power.

"Depressing," Jack spoke. "All they had to do was accept their savior."

The pair stepped past the military hardware, and into the front entrance to the building.

Inside the building, men and women in suits scrambled at the sight. Guards rushed to take positions behind tables and fixtures, firing pistols. Each one went up in a burst of light and a pile of ash remained. Down a veritable mile of hallways and exotic rooms, they walked past armed resistance, leaving no survivors who acted against them. Finally, they came across a pair of double doors and beyond it, the main auditorium where the nations spoke to one another.

Two armed men with shotguns blocked their way.

"My children," the Lord spoke, "your colleagues came upon us with far greater weaponry. They failed. I give you the offer I gave them. If you accept me as your savior, and bend the knee to my Father's will, you will be spared."

"You're not the Jesus I prayed to in church!" One soldier shouted and pulled the trigger. The gun clicked. "What the…Aaaaa"

His scream cut off as a white ball of light overtook his body, and his ash fell to the floor.

"You?" Jack spoke.

The man dropped his shotgun. "I won't oppose you," he spoke. "But I'm not bending the knee to a monster like you."

The Lord stepped forward, but Jack put a hand on his Lord's shoulder. "My Lord," Jack advised, "we have more pressing matters. His time will come."

"Wise words, my child," The Lord replied. "Alright, young man, you are spared, *for now.*" They stepped past.

The collection of delegates from every nation shrieked and shouted a chorus of horror and anger as the two stepped into the room. Jack Hurst and His Lord took in the sight. An armed bodyguard for the Italian delegation charged, but the Lord simply waved a finger and the man launched into the air. He sailed across the chamber, landing and rolling into the corner in a crumpled heap. More screams could be heard.

The Lord stomped his foot, and a sound of thunder reverberated through the chamber. Every voice went silent. "You all know your Lord," Jack spoke, taking the podium. "Normally, I speak for him, but I think here, it's best if you hear it from him."

He looked at Jack, his servant, and smiled, before taking a walk around the floor, looking at individual people, representing the kingdoms of man. "I have returned," he began, "to bring about the final battle against Satan and his minions. We have all witnessed the world become the battlefield. Men and women of all walks of life saw the Lights in the sky and developed powers." He locked eyes with delegates. "Some have even become paragons of virtue, such as the powered individuals in the middle east fighting trafficking." He took a breath and let it out. "Sadly, the only fight that matters are the one between the Evil One and myself."

He scanned the room once more. "Which brings me," he continued, "to the most important point. Just now, the greatest weapon humanity has developed was wielded against Jack and myself in a desperate attempt." A stern frown of anger painted itself on his face. His brows furrowed. "I have, thus far, only served up judgment against individuals. It seems a demonstration must be given, to remind the foolish kings in their palaces who is *actually* in control of the world. It is not they, nor is it I. It is the Father in Heaven. And as the executor of His will here on *His* Earth, I feel the time has come for me to choose not to spare the rod."

He paused in the center of the room, surrounded on both sides by desks. He blinked a long moment. "Who was the first to raise their hand and authorize this attack?"

The leaders of the world and their delegates looked at each other but said nothing. The Lord waited a good minute, taking in this passive resistance. A decision was made. "Very well," He said, taking in each person as he walked past. "If that is the case, I shall pick one." He made sure everyone saw how serious he was. "And then another. And then another."

"Wait!"

Everyone turned in the direction of the voice.

It was the delegate from India. "Wait, you bastard!" he repeated.

The Lord waded through the collection of stations and came to the station of the delegate from India. "Your leader instructed you to give the United States permission to attempt to destroy us?" he asked the quivering man.

"I did what had to be done!" the delegate swore. "To stop you! Now you cut this out and spare these innocent people!"

The Lord smiled, and placed hands on the man's shoulders. The delegate's middle-aged body was healed. "For your honesty," he spoke, "I will forgive you, and you shall be spared." A solemn look came upon him. "However, your nation has many who are not my Father's followers. An example must be made."

The man began to scream, but the Lord waved him off and stepped away. A dozen men tried to gang up on him, but a simple wave of his hand sent them scattering. The Lord stepped into the center of the room and placed his hands together. A glow overtook him.

Over India, a second sun appeared in the sky. Millions of people couldn't help but glance at it, in a mixture of awe and fear, as a reddish tint appeared from the light. A translucent blue light started on the ground and spread out at impossible speed. It surrounded certain people, rendering them unharmable. It avoided all man-made objects and most people, also surrounding and protecting all plant life, greenery, animals, and waterways. Once it reached the border of the nation, it spread out along the imaginary line. At the Pakistani border, soldiers jumped as a translucent, impenetrable blue wall of light separated the two nations. A plane flying over the nation saw a dome form from one edge of the horizon to the other, completely engulfing the country. People watched with concern as they could not touch the few in a crowd who had been covered in the blue forcefield. The people found they could not touch the grass or the water, and clamor gave way to chaos.

The second, red sun in the sky, began to shrink. As it did, it began to glow more brightly. For about thirty seconds, it dwindled in size until it reached a single white point in the sky.

It exploded with an Earth-shaking kaboom.

Screams of horror and pain echoed out and were silenced instantly. The wave of unnatural heat moved outward at unfathomable speeds, reducing to plasma anything in their path. Roads, buildings, and people vanished in the wave of power. People died with their last breath caught in their throat. Animals ran and panicked at the heat dancing around them, shielded from its effects. Those individuals coated by the protective barrier stood in disbelief, surrounded by a wall of pure heat. It moved outward until it collided with the walls of the barrier and vanished. A light descended from the sky and cooled the air as the dome vanished and took the protective light with it.

A few million people stood surrounded by hundreds of miles of... nothing.

Plants, greenery, waterways, animals, these things were the only sign life had existed at all.

The occasional Christian wandered around what once was a nation.

All sign of man-made anything had been erased from existence. All art, all culture, all of the symbols and the people who made them were gone. A single act, like the breath of an angry child on a birthday cake's candle, had blown it all away.

At the U.N. building, the CIA had been the first to have a satellite over India to see what had transpired. The first sign for those outside the building that something had happened, was that in Pakistan, and China on the other side, had witnessed a horrific event unlike any in human history. Those close to the border had been protected by the barrier, but a select few had taken pictures and video of the event. Crews had ventured into the area, gaping in awe at the sheer expanse of empty land, where much of the land that had not possessed plant life or waterway had been simply leveled by the blast. Every so often, out on the distance, they came across a person, shaking in horror as they wandered around the wasteland that used to be India.

"Goddammit you bastard!" the delegate from Italy shrieked. "What the fuck do you want!"

"I thought that was clear," Jack Hurst said. The Lord turned to him and nodded. "Here is the simple truth. Take heed. First, all opposition to God the Father and his laws upon this Earth—HIS Earth—shall stop at once. Second, any who are not loyal followers of Christ the Son, have one of two choices. They can either agree to serve their Lord or they can be destroyed. Third." He brought out his cell phone and held it up to the secretary. "Our enemies have made themselves known. Satan's premier servants are going to keep attacking us. They and their allies must be brought to judgment."

The secretary put up on screen each person. "The woman the media calls Capacitor after the character she resembles," he explained, "as well as the investor Jericho Torvalds, and all their allies, whoever they are, shall be brought to judgment."

"Take these words to heart," The Lord spoke. "We are in the final stages of battle against Satan's armies. You have until we reach you to make your final decision about whether you want to spend eternity in Heaven or Hell."

Back at the hideout, everyone watched the horror unfold on the TV news. "This just in," the news anchor said, occasionally grabbing a towel to wipe his eyes. "Mere moments ago, the Reverend Jack Hurst and his false messiah had attacked the United Nations building following a failed nuclear attack on the pair. During this ordeal, the false messiah unleashed an attack upon the nation of India..." He paused to weep into his towel. "The nation of India, which was, completely destroyed."

Jericho, leaning against the table, found himself squeezing so hard he broke a corner of the hard wood off.

Edward sat, open mouth crying. Annie had to breathe to stop herself from punching a hole in the nearest wall. Jennifer contemplated genuine murder for the first time in her entire life.

It was Raymond who broke the silence. "What do we do?" he asked.

Jennifer wiped her eyes. "We're going to beat the fuck out of this bastard," she swore. "How and why? I don't know. I'm up for suggestions."

CHAPTER NINETEEN

Everything went fucking haywire.

Jennifer had responded to no less than eight bombings. Across the U.S., eight different holy sites of various non-Christian denominations had been bombed by supers and non-supers alike. The police were overwhelmed. Jericho flew into action, knocking out supers who attacked anyone they perceived as not a follower of Christ. Annie and Edward had taken to the streets as well, aided by teleportation powers they discovered they could stack on top of their existing characters' abilities.

Raymond and John retreated to a new lab to rush whatever they could using Raymond's super intelligence and John's sci-fi impossible genius. At first, it became a clusterfuck of a triage situation, flying blindly to solve one problem after another, but after the first twenty minutes, they got coordinated. Cell phones might not be Star Trek communicators, but they sure as hell made figuring out where to go next easier.

Annie smashed a huge fist into an eight-foot bruiser trying to smash a synagogue. Despite his bigger size and mass, the man crumpled like an accordion. After slamming him into an expanding crater in the concrete, she turned her gaze to the small crowd of non-super men and women with torches. She pounded her fists together and they scattered. She took to the sky, using the goddess's combat sense to locate the next act of terror. Before that, she flew over to where she'd deposited her phone, and called. "Annie here," she said. "This is the nineteenth church bombing I've dealt with, and just a minute ago, I rescued some Jews before a crowd could burn them at the stake."

"I've got good news and bad news," Jericho said, using a combination of the evening news and his sensory powers. "The bad news is, we've still got work to do. The good news is, we're making a huge dent. I believe we've already responded to the vast majority of the situations."

"How big a dent we talking?" she asked.

"Edward just took out a super-powered Klan meeting," the billionaire responded, "and that was the last incident in the state of Kentucky."

"A lot of these guys are too powerful to be kept in police custody when we ain't around!" Annie said. "What about that?"

"Ray and John said they're on that," he said.

"Alright," John said, cutting in on the conversation. "Deal with the last few problems and then meet us at the hideout."

"Gotcha," they both said in unison.

Annie hung up, then flew a hundred miles to deal with the last California incident, a series of mosque fires started by an electrical super.

Jennifer stepped into the hideout. A few moments later, a portal opened, and the others stepped out. Annie and Edward took a seat on the couch. Both had black soot marks on their durable skin and scratches on their clothes from close combat.

"So," Raymond began, "it's a disaster." He took a deep breath and let it out. "But, it's also Christmas."

"Hey, holy shit guys," John said, his safety glasses dangling. "Gotta love nineteen eighties sci-fi. Ray and I have put together a bunch of cool shit already. You saw the portals we can make, but also," he pulled out a nasty looking collar, glowing red at the front. "suppression collars."

"Jesus Christ!" Jennifer swore. "It's been what, four hours?"

Raymond let out a whistle. "Yeah," he acknowledged, "but at the same time, Doctor Anti is one of the most resourceful characters in the history of science fiction literature."

"I'm, uh," Jericho cut in, "interested in these portals."

"Way ahead of ya," John replied. "Ray's right. I've been on a roll here. Turns out, I can portal anywhere in the world with the right amount of power, and Ray figured out the power problem. Not as fast as teleportation, but we've got other dimensional stuff." He gestured behind him. "We've got the perfect hideout: other dimensions!"

"You're shitting me," Edward shouted, looking at the room past them. "Where is that?"

"There, uh," Raymond said, pausing for a moment to collect his thoughts, "there are other Earths out there, and we found one with no intelligent life on it."

Jennifer had to push her jaw upward. "Uh, wait," she uttered. "Wait wait wait. Hold the phone." She let out a mild chuckle of disbelief. "Did you just, um, fucking drop *multiverse* on me as if you were telling me about a meal you ate?"

John smacked his head. "Hello? Excuse me?" he interjected. "You *do* realize I'm the character whose whole schtick was inventing crap that no one could believe he invented, right?"

Annie clapped her hands together. "I don't normally say this," she yelled, "but goddammit John, you are fucking amazing!"

"Uh," John cut in, "and Ray."

"No," Raymond replied, "I'll let the guy who's not normally that smart bask in his glory."

"Anyway," John stated, "some bad news. We're not going to be turning any more villains over to the police."

"Oh, fuck," Jennifer said, as the news washed over everyone. "Let me guess."

"You guessed right," Davis said, stepping out of a portal.

"The United States government has reached a deal," Sam cut in, "the false messiah has agreed to curb his followers' violence in exchange for the government surrendering to him and Jack Hurst."

"How very Christ-like," Edward snarked.

"The good news is," Jericho said, "Jennifer and I didn't turn very many supers over to the government to hand back to Jack and his fake Jesus. We've built a series of complexes on this other Earth and we're storing them there for the time being."

"Isn't that a bit..." Annie began.

Jennifer raised an eyebrow. "Authoritarian?" she asked. "Yeah, but they're in stasis. No time is passing for them right now." She saw the expressions. "And yes, that's another sci-fi thing John and Ray just dropped on us."

"I've got a working theory," Raymond said, "and once this whole shebang is over, I expect to get it published." He saw everyone's looks. "Oh, sorry for changing the subject. The gist is this. There are new types of interactions other than particles and waves in this wavefunction we exist in."

"I thought..." Jennifer said. "I thought the interactions were particles only at our macro scale. I thought everything was waves."

Raymond thought about it. "Here's the way I see it," he explained. "Imagine you had some aliens who couldn't see or detect fire."

Everyone looked at each other. "Okay," Jericho replied.

Raymond grabbed a napkin and a marker out of a drawer and began writing a diagram. "They know," he continued, "that if they have meat, and certain kinds of substances, like wood, and enough oxygen, and a spark, they can cause meat to cook if they hold it over this...thing they can't describe."

"Okay," Annie said.

"They can't see it, they can't feel it, they know if they stick their hand in it, it hurts, but they can't otherwise detect it at all," Raymond said. "How do they go about even describing it, much less detecting it?"

Everyone pondered for a few moments. "That would be a problem," Edward stated.

"We don't know how to describe it," John explained, "other than to say that whatever these things are that streamed into our universe from a hole in space, they cause selective changes to the laws of physics, and we've had to completely upend our way of thinking in order to get half of these ideas."

"It's how," Jennifer stated, "a person can turn to stone and still have their biochemistry work."

"Exactly!" Raymond replied. "It behaves like a science; we just don't know all the details yet."

"That's amazing," Jericho said. "Anyway, I hate to sound rude, but what's our plan, going forward?"

"I suggest," Annie said, "we should keep working on our tech." She gestured. "After all, I'd like something more useful than just...this outfit I'm wearing."

"We're working on that," John said. "Not just that, but everyone is going to get something." He snapped his fingers. "That reminds me! Jericho."

The billionaire turned. "Yes?"

John approached and pulled out a syringe from a small plastic case. "I found out that one of your powers in particular can be enhanced with technology."

"Really?" Jericho said, sticking out his arm. "How does that work?"

"Let's save the world," Raymond cut in, "and then we'll figure out how to explain it. Right now, just accept it."

"So, how'd you figure it out?"

"Well," John said, injecting the contents. "we found out how to tap into the...stuff that all powers come from."

After the nanoscopic device entered his bloodstream, the billionaire immediately felt his mental switch for the teleportation power change color. When he activated it, he saw that his range included the entire Earth. "Holy shit!" he swore.

"How the hell did you have time for all this?" Jennifer asked.

"It was the first thing we did after figuring out how to put people in stasis," Raymond said. "You know, related technology. It gave us ten times as much time. We can only go that far on a lab-size scale."

"I have a hunch," John cut in, "that it works on the same principle as one of your speed powers, Jennifer."

"You know, guys," she said, "I'm not trying to tell anyone what to do, but how about we duck out of here for a while and let them study our powers directly, and that might give them a better idea of what to do."

"But," Edward protested, "what about all the people that will die in the meantime?"

Jennifer took a harsh breath and gave his words serious thought. "I suspect Jack can't end the world without fighting us," she explained, "and his monster seems more interested in gathering allies right now for a fight that comes later."

"So," Annie said, folding her arms, "people are going to die in the meantime and his forces are going to get stronger, but there's not much we can do beyond triaging the situation."

"Ed, you're perfectly right," Jericho cut in, "but honestly, I think if we just keep plugging away like we've done in the past few hours, we lose precious ground." He gestured at the two scientists. "Brains beat brawn, I have to believe."

"Alright," Ed replied. "I'm in. Let's bring our families and friends into this other dimension so we can be sure they're safe."

"Got it," Raymond said. "You guys get them ready and we'll be there waiting."

Inside a sprawling compound on another Earth, a portal opened and over a dozen people stepped out. Everyone had been briefed on what was going on, and none of them liked it. At the front, stood the combatants who would take the fight to Jack Hurst and his summoned monster masquerading as the Lord.

"So," John said, eyeing the new arrival. "Your brother's finally coming into battle?"

Luther stepped forward. "I'm not much of a combat guy," he admitted, "but I'm not taking this lying down." He looked at his brother, confused. "We never shared my memories with everyone, did we?"

"Can't hurt," Jericho said, gesturing for everyone to form a circle. "This way, we're absolutely sure we're ready."

With a bit of effort, they went into Luther's memories.

CHAPTER TWENTY

"Aw!" A TEN−YEAR−OLD CRIED. "Jer! You cheated!"

The two boys looked at the wreckage of their front yard after the game. The younger boy, short black hair thick around the top and thin around the edges, grass stains on his white shirt and black jean shorts, had hands on hips and pouted. The older boy, a teenager with ear-length sandy hair and a black tanktop, folded his arms over his chest and beamed with pride. "No, Lou," the older boy announced, "I'm just better."

"Jericho! Luther!" a woman shouted from the front porch. "Time to get inside and get cleaned up for dinner!"

"Got it, mom," Jericho said, dashing up the short stairs.

"You're five years older than your brother!" Suzanne chastised her eldest son. "You could at least let him win one in a while."

The teen changed the subject. "Are we visiting my cousins this year?"

The mother's lips curled inward at his question. "I don't know, honey," she finally announced, "it depends. They don't come by, and we're not going to up and go there unless they help us pay for the trip."

"No point in flying us all out just to visit rich people," Andrew, the father, said to his son from the entryway.

As Luther came running up the stairs, he'd caught the tail end of that. His brother and he knew of the tension between their mother and their grandfather, who they hadn't met yet. They'd snuck into her room and read her personal musings on the subject. Her father was a company head, they knew, and had cut her out of the family fortune for partying too hard. Despite this, she'd made it as a university professor and had met their father at the same college, and everything appeared to work smoothly. Luther had the same idea as his mother. He saw wealth as something not to be worshipped in and of itself. His brother seemed to have a different idea, but the world their grandfather lived in struck the younger boy as one he didn't want to live in.

After the boys washed up, Suzanne dished out the family dinner. As the family ate, she couldn't help but think of how lucky she was. As a daughter of Johann Torrell, she'd been the public face of the family shame on more than one occasion. As a younger woman, there had been many moments she wasn't proud of, and all that partying had earned her the axe. Of course, it was due to her enormous privilege that she came out of it on even footing and having landed a job as a professor didn't hurt. She couldn't help but feel strangely thankful to her father, the billionaire and corporate executive of the Torrell Group, because it had been his cutting her off that set her on the right path.

"When am I going to see grandpa?" Jericho asked.

She saw his genuine expression of curiosity and tried to avoid looking too dour. The boy gave her a sense of relief on one hand, and dread on the other. First of all, he took to hard work quite well, and didn't complain nearly as much as some other kids his age. He did his chores ahead of time and made sure he did things right. On the other hand, what really concerned her was his lack of empathy. It didn't seem antisocial to her, but he was challenged in regard to the plights of other people.

"When I decide he's ready to see you," she said.

Luther looked up from his plate. "I thought you didn't hate him," he said, repeating what he heard before.

"Your mother doesn't hate him," Andrew cut in. "It's just that he's not the kind of person we want around. I don't think he cares about anything the way he cares about money."

Suzanne decided enough was enough and set down her fork. "I used to hate him for cutting me off," she admitted. "When I was younger, I thought he ruined my chance to live it up. I was a dumb twenty-something. Now I see it was the best thing to ever happen to me. I learned life is more than just having it all."

Luther felt like he understood. His brother seemed more like the kind of guy who'd be into money like his grandfather. He loved Jericho, but the older boy could get selfish at times.

Jericho wanted to protest, but instead, went back to his food. Soon enough, it would be his turn to go out into the world and make his mark. He would prove it was possible to have a lot of money and care about more than wealth. He knew he didn't have a plan for that, but it was his goal, nonetheless.

Three weeks later, an event occurred that threw the wheels into motion, the will of Suzanne and Andrew be damned. Johann Torrell arrived. The Jaguar sat at the end of the driveway, shiny and black, and out of it, stepped a graying man in a suit as expensive as the two-story, four-bedroom Chicago suburb house in front of him. He knocked on the door, and when it opened, Suzanne stood agape, staring. Neighbors peeked out of doorways at the sight. The smile he gave her showed the pearly white teeth and his finely coiffed hair gave off the executive image he worked hard for. "Suzanne," he said, his slight German accent present. "It's good to see you. You sure landed on your feet."

She exhaled a long time. Skeptical eyes analyzed him head to toe. "Father," she uttered. A pregnant pause followed. "I thought we discussed this. I didn't want you to just barge in. Why are you here?"

He sighed. "We've only talked on the telephone," he explained. "I understand why you're reluctant to see me, but I want to see my grandchildren."

"I know you're used to seeing everything go your way," she shot back, "but I would've liked to be in charge of that decision."

"How much longer," he asked, "do we have to just *talk* about it before I can see them?"

"Dad," she replied, "I don't hold a grudge against you cutting me off. In fact, I'm glad you did. This isn't about that."

He gestured outward, hurt. "Then what the hell is this about?"

She huffed. "It's about," she replied, "you being here to recruit my sons. You want to try and hit them with propaganda to sway them into your world. I'm alive today, dad, because I didn't stay in your world. Understand that I don't want you dragging them into yours."

"I wasn't here to do that," he insisted. "And furthermore, that's *their* decision, not yours."

"Grandpa?"

Everyone turned in the direction of the young voice. The older man dropped to a crouching position. "You must be Luther!" Johann Torrell said, meeting the boy at eye level.

Luther recognized the man from the pictures his mother had. "Hi, sir," he uttered, as the man held him in a tight embrace.

Suzanne watched her father hug her youngest son and remained skeptical. This was a man who she'd seen get people's names intentionally wrong to prove a point.

"Grandfather!" Jericho cried.

Johann held his arms wide, and the older boy dashed into the embrace. "I have wanted so much to meet you!" he cried.

"I wanted to meet you too!" Jericho shouted.

Luther remained skeptical as well. This man resembled a comic book supervillain in his eyes. After all, his outfit had a whole bunch of layers. He saw the suit jacket, the vest under that, and the shirt under that. Who wore outfits with that many layers, except the bad guys in comics? Besides, the hair looked like the kind of 'do that he'd heard his dad make fun of in private.

"Where are you guys going?" Johann asked, returning to a standing position.

"We were about to head out for a celebration dinner," Andrew explained, heading outside to see the verbal fracas. "The boys placed first in a regional math and science quiz championship."

"You and mom don't get along?" Jericho asked.

"I...uh, it's not so straightforward," Johann said to the boy. "We have a complex history together."

Suzanne wanted to slap the man. This was his gimmick. He put himself in situations where he seemed like the innocent party despite being forcing his way. "It would be rude of me not to invite you," she said, "but it's not only up to me."

"You can come," Andrew decided, "but you better not make comments about the food."

"I had proper manners as part of my formal education," Johann bragged, ignoring the look shot at him.

"Kids," Suzanne said, "go get ready and try not to take too long."

Jericho and Luther went up stairs to change their clothes and get washed up. The younger boy washed his face and hands and toweled off. "Grandpa seems..." Luther trailed off, looking for the right word.

"Amazing?" Jericho offered.

"No," Luther corrected, "fake. He seems fake."

Jericho washed himself off and dried. "He's rich," the teen argued. "They all have to seem that way."

"I wouldn't wanna be like that," Luther countered.

"Aw, you're just jealous," Jericho countered.

"He's gotta act a certain way?" Luther argued. He shook his head. "No, I wouldn't wanna have to do that."

"I'm gonna be rich like him someday," Jericho stated.

Luther rolled his eyes. "Okay," he said. "Sure. And it'll be because they look at you and know you're his grandson."

"No way!" Jericho shot back. "It'll be because I went out and did it."

"Right," Luther said, sarcasm dripping.

When they came downstairs, Jericho marveled at the older man. Something his mother didn't like about him, just sat perfectly well with the boy. This man, he realized, had real power in the world. Without having to do a thing or say a word, he commanded respect with his mere presence alone. The man had ways of getting what he wanted, regardless of the obstacles in his way. It was a place Jericho wanted to be. It was a position he craved. Luther, by contrast, could not be less impressed. He saw a man who had to put utter concentration and worry on money and status. The younger boy could not want less to be in that situation.

"Let me drive the boys," Johann offered. "I'd like to take the chance to get to know them."

Suzanne found her teeth clenching in frustration, and she had to will it to stop. *Prick has to show off,* she thought. "Why not?" she asked, mock politeness in her voice. "Saves me the trouble."

"We're going to the Denny's across from the Walgreen's," Andrew pointed out.

"It's your family celebration," Johann replied. The boys climbed into the backseat of the huge luxury car. "Are you boys read?"

"Absolutely!" Jericho cheered.

"Yes, sir," Luther said.

As he pulled the car out of the driveway, he saw the neighbors examine the car. He knew the boys saw it as well, and that they would want to ask questions. All he had to do was drive and wait.

"Grandfather?" Jericho asked, sheepishly.

"Hmm?" The businessman replied.

"How did you get so rich?"

The older man smiled at his grandson's question. He looked in the rearview mirror and saw the expression, the curiosity. The boy had a natural hunger and curiosity that anyone could see a mile away. Here, he realized, was someone destined to be *somebody*. This kid would never grow up to be a worthless lay about, like so many, a nobody destined to leech off the hard work of better people like a parasite. This was a kid who was going places. Places, he hoped, that included the world of big business and Wall Street.

"My grandfather came to this country before the turn of the century," Johann explained, "and got a job repairing tractors and other machines. My father and a friend of his turned it into a business, and when I inherited it, I expanded it into a multinational company in a bunch of diverse fields."

"That's amazing!" Jericho exclaimed.

"I guess," Luther added.

"Luther?" Johann asked. "Is there anything *you* want to know about me?"

The younger boy pondered. Finally, he turned his head upward. "What do you do for fun?"

The child's question drew a chuckle out of the man. "When you're as busy as I am," he offered, "there isn't much time for fun." He collected his words. "I mostly like to watch live theater and the opera, I'm a big fan of symphony orchestra, and sometimes, I drive fast cars around the racetrack."

Only the last of those interested Luther in the slightest. "I get it," he said, not wanting to be dismissive.

"What books do you read?" Jericho asked.

Luther shot him a look. Honestly, he figured, he didn't want to read any books that this guy thought of as interesting. They were the kind of books most likely to be dry reads, focusing on money and real life.

Johann Torrell was smiling inside. Jericho had asked the question he sincerely hoped the boy would ask. He loved his daughter and his youngest grandson, but they weren't going anywhere close to the world the chairman and CEO lived in. This boy had the chance to wind up in the correct place. Suzanne had been right about her father's reason for coming, but now he had a perfectly plausible reason to get what he came for. The boy had asked himself, after all.

"I've got a whole list I could give you," Johann said. "But honestly, I learned a lot about how things should be from the works of Ayn Rand."

Jericho then asked the question would shape his future.

"If I read that," the boy asked, "I can be more like you?"

This time the businessman did laugh out loud. "Not so easy, I'm afraid!" he explained. "Honestly, it's just a starting point."

As the luxury car pulled into the Denny's parking lot, Suzanne looked in and saw the bookstore shopping bag in the backseat, next to her oldest son. A feeling of rage suddenly overcame her. "Father?" she asked, fire in her voice. "Can I talk to you?"

He let out a nasal sigh. "Before you say a word," he defended, "the boy asked for it himself. I didn't force it on him. Hell, I didn't even bring it up! He did."

"He's just a child!" she shouted. "You're buying him propaganda to read before he's old enough to know how to counter it!"

"Suzanne," Johann said, trying to calm her down, "he's *fifteen*. Besides, he asked me a question and I gave him an answer. If he doesn't like it, then that's *his* decision. Please don't take it from him."

She fumed. "Alright! Fine!" she exclaimed. "I'll let him read what he wants, but you! You're going to cut this shit out!"

"Alright!" Johann said, putting his hands up in a mock defensive gesture. "I won't tell him anymore!"

"I've seen you pull crap like this before," she told him, "and this isn't one of your business partners to recruit."

"Mom?" Luther asked, stepping out of the car. "Is something wrong?"

She looked at him and saw the genuine concern on his face. "No, honey," she said. "Nothing's wrong."

They went in and ate, and the event proceeded uneventfully from there. Johann, however, sat pleased with himself. He'd gotten exactly what he came for. First, he'd finally met his grandchildren, and his flawless sense of the worth of things and individuals put each person precisely in the category that best suited them. He'd found talent, which was the second thing he'd intended. Jericho would wind up in the world of the Torrell family and their workings in big business, and he didn't have to do anything to foster that desire. The boy wanted to be somebody and would claw and scratch his way up the ladder if need be. Unlike several members of his family, including some of his own children, this boy wouldn't need nepotism to push himself up. He could have cheered at the thought.

He would finally get to see someone pull themselves up by their bootstraps.

He had longed to see such a success story to legitimize his viewpoints and he was going to get it. As someone who'd raised several children and had seen every kind of person come and go in the world of big business, he recognized the look on Jericho's face. The boy had that killer instinct in him to succeed. The world of Wall Street and corporate America required one to be willing to step across a mine field and throw empathy and compassion to the wind in the name of success. It had been his goal to see if either of Suzanne's children had what it took. Jericho had the right first start. Would he succeed? No one knew for sure, but he had faith.

Suzanne shot hateful glances at her father in between bites of food and attempts to be cordial. She knew why he was here. The man had all the narcissistic control freak tendencies a corporate head and Forbes billionaire could be expected to have. He was a notorious pusher who got what he wanted and didn't care who he stepped on to get it. Each of his children had to show their children to him and he made sure to place his influence in their path. He exuded the Virtue of Selfishness and every child of the Torrell family got the bibliography of Ayn Rand to read. He'd come here looking to expand his empire and his sphere of influence, and what's worse, she knew Jericho would eat it up. It pissed her off.

Time progressed without fail. Jericho indeed went in the direction his mother feared and his grandfather desired. As more and more books on investing and business got digested, the boy became a young adult and earned a full scholarship to Harvard Business School. Luther found himself drifting away from his brother, mostly because the elder boy stopped being fun to hang around with. Jericho had always managed to get into adventures with his brother, but after a while, he became the kind of stuffed shirt that the younger boy found so boring. Luther pursued his interests with vigor and passion. He played the guitar and formed a band.

One day, Jericho came back on a break from school, and after they both visited their parents' house, they went back to the house Luther had bought. The eighteen-year-old younger brother sat in his kitchen and poured himself a ginger ale.

Jericho, already independently wealthy by this point off his own investments, looked at the modest house with the yellow seventies' décor and the aging appliances with disdain. The thing that really set him off, however, was the sight of his bandmates sleeping on his floor on air mattresses, and on his couch. They had their things set out in boxes around the living room and in free space in other areas of the house. He gestured for his little brother to step outside, and shut the door.

"Luther," he said, "are you *supporting* these people?"

The younger brother let out a disbelieving chuckle and looked shocked at him. "Are you," he began, anger simmering up from the bottom of his voice, "asking me how I spend my money? I don't have to explain to you how I spend my money. Mister Ayn Rand worship should know better."

A scoff escaped the older brother. "Seriously?" he exclaimed. "We both know you're the only one of them with any talent, and here you are, footing the bill for them to *live at your house.*"

"It's my house and my money," Luther said. "I may not be rich like you, but if I want to support these people, these brothers-in-arms of mine, who've been with me through thick and thin, that's my prerogative."

"They're *using you!*" Jericho shouted. "Besides, how did you make that money, anyway?"

Luther folded his arms. "I don't believe this," he said. "You know how you always brag about your stocks when you talk to mom? I just follow what you do. Besides, I also have a job of my own. Sure, it's only managing a bookstore, but still, I do just fine."

"It's a shame because you have *actual* talent," Jericho countered. "If you had a proper group of musicians you could have made it already. Instead, these losers keep holding you back from succeeding. Worse, you're *funding* their worthlessness!"

"You know," Luther argued, blinking in disbelief, "they were there for me. You know, when I got depressed and our parents were there, but *you* weren't?" He laughed. "You offered to give me money, but you wouldn't come over and talk to me?" A short gasp escaped his lungs. "Money! Fucking money when I could've used actually support!" Before Jericho could retort, a memory came back to him. "Oh, remember when you broke your leg in that accident? Remember how your grandfather, the man you practically worship, wasn't fucking there?"

Jericho rolled his eyes. "Good god," he scoffed. "He wasn't supposed to be there, he had a lot of more important things to do."

"It wasn't necessary?" Luther half-asked, half-gasped. "You mean it wasn't in his...oh what's the term...*rational self-interest*?"

"No!" Jericho shouted without thinking. "No, it wasn't!"

The older brother's shout drew a disbelieving expression of shock from both as soon as the words got out. "Un-fucking-believable," Luther uttered. "You want to take after a person like that?"

"I want to take after a person who took full advantage of his opportunities and capabilities!"

Luther rolled his eyes. "No," he countered, "what you want is to take after a person who takes advantage of people."

Jericho started as if prodded by a taser. "You take that back," he replied, "you're just jealous I'm on the fast track, that I'm doing something with my life."

"I'm doing the things that make life worth living," Luther argued. "Believe it or not, if I never make it big, there's no skin off my ass."

"It's a damn shame you're ok with this," Jericho shot back.

"I just hope you don't wake up one morning and realize you're forty-five with a whole lot of money," the little brother retorted, "and realize you have no actual friends who care about you beyond how much money you're worth."

Jericho huffed. "Well," he said, a half-sneer forming, "I'm at least going to make one of those things come true."

"If you have any other business," Luther stated, "you can say it now, otherwise, please leave."

As Jericho gathered his bag and headed to his rental car, he shook his head. "I'm not bailing you out of this if this venture of yours goes south," he warned.

"I've known that for years," Luther snapped back.

After that, they separated and didn't speak to each other much for years. Jericho made good on his determination and started fresh out of Harvard with his M.B.A. and quickly got started at an investment firm. After two years of taking crap from superiors and investing his and other people's money, Jericho quickly shot up the ladder until he had enough capital to start his own investment firm. After endless grinding and sweating the touring circuit of local bars and small-time music festivals, two and a half years of frustration had led the leftist band *Blood on The Breadline* lead by Luther to get an actual record deal. His mother pitched in to get a decent lawyer so her son could have actual representation, and their socialist lyrics and heavy metal sound managed to hit the big time.

It was at a taping of a tv interview for their debut album, *Dead Fascists Make Good Lawn Gnomes*, on it having reached quintuple platinum in just a month of sales, where he learned his brother had hit a milestone.

Across the hallway, in a different room, he was being interviewed on live television for having become the latest member of the Forbes Billionaires list.

"We're here with the latest member of the Billionaires list," the pundit said, introducing. "He founded his own investment firm, he's got a private worth of one point eight billion, and he's not even thirty yet!" The pundit took a pause to get audience applause. "Is he just that good at picking stocks, or does he possess the wisdom of Solomon?" Laughter emerged from the audience. "With me today, is the talk of the Street, Jericho Torvalds!"

"Nice to be here," Jericho said, making sure his tie sat perfectly straight on his Armani suit.

"So," the pundit began, turning his chair to his interviewee, "twenty-seven years old, worth over a billion dollars, founder of a new but already very successful investment firm, how do you do it?"

Luther sat, unbeknownst to his brother, staring at the spectacle of money worship at this altar of disposable capitalism. Still, he did still love his brother, and it pained him to see the boy he had fun playing with as a child grow up to be among these bloodsucking leeches. His band had finally made it big, and his good contract gotten by a great lawyer gave him more money than he ever anticipated, but it wasn't scant pennies compared to the egregious wealth his brother was hoarding for these parasites.

Jericho gave a chuckle and a cordial smile. "It's actually fascinating how I got here," he explained. "I didn't have my grandfather's money to fall back on, so I had to earn my keep. My parents are both professors, so I grew up in an environment of learning. I had to learn everything and just keep plugging away at it." He paused. "I was taught to learn from every source I could find and that's what I did."

The pundit nodded. "You credit Ayn Rand and the philosophy of laissez-faire capitalism for your success," he pointed out.

"When I met my grandfather, I was fifteen," Jericho explained. "He offered to buy me any book I wanted, and I asked him what book made him successful, so that's what I read." The audience laughed and cheered. "It worked. I learned about the morality of capitalism. The investing skills, though, I had to develop those on my own."

"And *what* investing skills they are!" the pundit cheered. "In four years' time you've turned tens of thousands of dollars into over a billion dollars. Don't keep us in the dark. How?"

Jericho leaned back in the chair. "Where do I begin?" he asked. "You have to realize the market isn't reality. The market is based on investors' perceptions of reality. Once I realized that, it made my job a lot easier. You have to invest based on what people think, rather than what you expect to happen in the world. You react to people reacting to the world." He paused. "If that makes sense."

"You've made billions for others," the interviewer asked, "and over a billion for yourself. Are you worried the gravy train will end?"

"Ha ha," he replied, "not really. I mean, every investor worries about that, but I recession-proof my investments by converting a lot to cash after a huge success. That way, we cover our cash flow problems before they exist."

The pundit cocked his head. "Doesn't that raise your taxes?"

"It does," Jericho said, "but it also means we still have a lot of assets in the event of a disastrous market fluctuation. When we succeed, we succeed big. When we fail, we fail small."

"A bit counterintuitive," the pundit noted. "I like it!"

The interview persisted from there, but Luther got up and left. That had been all the shameless money-worship he could stand. He had just stepped out the front door of the building when he heard running footsteps.

"Luther!" Jericho shouted.

"Jericho," Luther flatly acknowledged.

"I didn't know you were coming to see me!" Jericho shouted. "I thought you didn't care!"

"You're my brother," Luther said, approaching. "I love you. But I wasn't just here for you. My band finally made it big and we were getting interviewed."

"I heard," Jericho said. "That's a hell of an accomplishment." Despite everything, he felt good that his brother had actually made it. What bothered him, though, was that he could have been here a lot sooner.

"Thank you," Luther replied, stifling emotion. "That means a lot to me." What stung him was that his grandfather and a hack writer who'd been dead for two decades had gotten their meat hooks in him. "I just couldn't continue to sit there and watch this worship of wealth and the people who value money more than human life."

"Oh, Christ, not this shit again," Jericho uttered. "Why can't you just see things my way?" He'd grown weary of Ayn Rand and her ideology getting between them.

"I'm sorry, but I can't support this world you live in," Luther explained.

Jericho gestured in disbelief. "You're rich now," he said. "Hell, you're only likely to get richer."

"I've given as much money to charity as you," Luther countered, "and you're about nine hundred times richer than me."

Jericho's arms shot out to his side. "That's because I'm not subscribed to an ideology that makes people into victims!" he shouted. "My god, when are people responsible for themselves? Why are we always expected to prop them up?"

"I hope you never have to suffer like some people," Luther shot back. "Like the ones who are never able to prop themselves up."

"Like your bandmates?"

A painful silence passed over. "You..." Luther began.

"Yeah," Jericho said. "I know I hit a nerve with that one. You've paid their bills, you've bailed a few out of jail, you're practically their sugar daddy, and for what? So they could one day maybe pay you back?" He laughed. "You could've been so much more so much faster if you'd thought of yourself once in a while!"

"You fucking...!" Luther's statement cut off as he punched his brother straight in the face.

"Touch a nerve?" Jericho asked, picking himself up and brushing blood off his lip. "Just goes to show you what I say is true."

"Fuck you!" Luther shouted, crashing into his brother in a whirling mass of fists and feet clumsily slamming into each other.

As quickly as the scuffle began, a crowd pulled each one apart. "Proves my point," Jericho said. "You have no response to that."

"You're a sad piece of shit!" Luther swore. "You're a sad little fucker sitting atop his huge pile of money! Well, fuck you Jericho!"

After that, they swore off speaking to one another. Jericho always felt bothered by the fact that Luther's desire to put others before himself was holding him back. Luther, on the other hand, felt his older brother had sacrificed compassion and empathy in exchange for a giant bank account and the attention of fake friends who wouldn't be there except for the money.

When the Lights happened, Luther had been walking the street in L.A. after a show. He stood and stared, along with dozens of other people outside. Days later, when the news reported that people were starting to show superpowers, he figured his brother would get some, it just seemed like the natural way things would go.

One day, not long after, he was venturing out when he came across a woman sitting on a bench staring at a television in an electronics store window. On screen, the news reported that a man had set fire to a local police station over a possible racial issue. "Crazy world we live in," she said. "Guy walked up and fired something out of his hands. Would you believe that?"

"I would," Luther said. "Strange. They say powers are popping up."

She laughed. "Do you believe that?" she asked.

At that instant, he felt a presence in his mind. A twinge appeared, somewhere in the back of his mindscape. Words didn't seem quite adequate. A thought came to him an instant later. The power called to him, made itself known. He focused his mental sight on it and found it in one of two states. Currently, it was in the off position. He flipped it on, curiosity getting the better of him.

A fire hose of emotions, images, and other thoughts raced through his mind with lightning speed. The man accused of burning the police station had somehow become a wellspring of information. Luther's power gave him every detail about the man, including why he did it, how, and all the other relevant details. In an instant of real time, he knew everything about the action and the man that did it. When the vision ended, he had forgotten he was standing, and he struggled for balance.

"Oh, crap," the woman exclaimed, "are you okay?" She was worried because he started tilting on his feet, but her question died in her mind when he stumbled and placed a hand on her shoulder to stabilize himself. All at once, everything he'd been shown came to her. "What in the hell?" She pulled away, startled.

He pulled away and fled, turning the power off. What was this ability? He could get a complete handle on someone just by thinking about them and activating it? Whatever it meant, he would have to figure it out. At first, he started small, he would listen in and whenever people found themselves unable to understand someone, he would brush up against them very stealthily and give the information to them. With effort and refinement, he could focus on one event or the entire person, and he discovered he didn't have to know much about the target at all. It filled him with glee; he could help the world understand what the 'other' was thinking. Still, he wasn't a naïve moron, he knew some old prejudices wouldn't go away. Either way, any help was help.

His first outings he took slow and safe. Major political groups around city hall were a start. Regardless of party, neither side seemed to understand the motivations of the other. He set out to change that. Each time a tour led him to a city, he would use some of his free time to affect some understanding in the world. One thing he came across was a common theme. Most people who had powers understood they weren't the only one with powers. Most didn't get into fights because they simply didn't feel like the fighting type.

Luther found out Jericho had precisely the power that suited him. The Wall Street billionaire gained the ability to copy powers. It struck the younger brother as a cosmic slap in the face. In any case, he expected his brother to be swift about gathering powers like the greedy miser he was.

What he never expected was to see his brother on the news admitting he was wrong about race after meeting with Sharon Francis of all people.

Luther had left the voicemail. Twenty minutes later, he got a phone call.

"Luther!" Jericho cheered. "I'm so glad to talk to you."

"Tell me you're not fucking with me," Luther replied.

"You were right all along," Jericho said. "Honestly, I'm damn lucky. One of the powers I copied allowed me to relive people's memories, and so I've had my horizons expanded."

Luther paused to take this in. "That's funny," he said. "I've got an empathy power, and I wonder if it's related."

"Let's meet," Jericho replied. "There's a lot to catch up on, and honestly, I think you've got a lot to tell me."

Luther cleared his throat. "I hope you're sincere about this," he said, "because we've got a hell of a lot to discuss."

"I know," Jericho replied, "and there's some people I want you to meet."

CHAPTER TWENTY-ONE

"My sisters and brothers!" Jack Hurst preached from a secure area just outside Washington, D.C. "The hour of the final battle against evil itself draws near!" He took in the crowd. A collection of people, cheering for the downfall of sin, holding up signs that spoke of righteous judgment against sinners, stood crowded around a podium. A wall of armed men created a separation between supporters and detractors. "We shall see our final victory against Satan and his minions!"

Soldiers parted the sea of supporters long enough to allow an armed escort through. Two officers in full riot gear carried a young man under his arms towards the Lord. They brought him up onto the platform, and the preacher stepped aside for the Lord to take his position. He looked down upon the young man, who the officers pushed to stand. Evidence of a struggle painted itself across his face and arms. The Lord placed his hands on the man's shoulders and the wounds healed.

"You, my child," The Lord spoke, "you have worn your sin like a banner. The pride you've taken in your sin stains your very soul."

The quivering, crying man looked at the figure before him. "Please don't kill me," he pleaded. "My...my boyfriend..."

The Lord shook his head. "No," he replied. "You will choose to sin no more. Your alternative is the eternal fires of hell. Make your choice now."

Please forgive me, the man thought, as he thought of his love, whom he would never see again. He dropped to his knees. "I accept you as my savior," he said.

The Lord nodded and smiled, placing a hand on the man's head. "You are forgiven, my child," He spoke, "now stand and join the many who serve the forces of Good." The man stood up and got escorted over to where the supporters stood.

"Hey, wait a minute," one officer protested, "I thought..."

The Lord turned a serious expression towards the man. "You thought you would see a homosexual be exterminated before your very eyes," He spoke.

The officer's eyes shifted guiltily to one side and another. "No, I..."

"Yes," The Lord shot back. "Heed my words carefully, my child. I do not hesitate to condemn those who refuse to accept my Father's grace. But I do not pass out judgment at whim. Any who accept me are saved. Do you understand?"

The man rushed to kneel and place a hand over his heart. "Yes, my Lord!" he swore.

"Good," the Lord spoke, then turned to Jack Hurst. "My servant, tell them to alert the President that we are ready for our next series of locations."

Jack nodded. "I will, oh Lord!" he cried.

"My Lord!"

Everyone turned in the direction of the man's shout. A young man of no older than twenty-two hovered to a standing position on the platform. He immediately took one knee. The Lord turned and analyzed the young man. He wore a white tank top and black shorts, with a short head of dirty blonde hair with a thin wave of bangs sticking out. His deep blue eyes gazed up at his master. The face, although soft in feature, had a hardness of expression that only suffering could bring. The voice that came out sounded youthful but tainted with misery beyond his years.

"What is your name, my child?" the Lord spoke.

"August Dietrich," he said. "I've spent months wondering why my life had gone so rotten, but when I saw you give righteous judgment to the whole of India, I saw the true power of the Lord!" He placed a hand over his heart. "I offer my services to defeat the Evil One that threatens the world!"

The Lord touched the man, and the telekinetic powers he had surged even higher. "My child!" He spoke to August. "Do you have what it takes to fight against the great might of evil?"

"My Lord!" August swore. "I do!"

"Then rise in power!" He spoke.

Just then, a projectile came sailing by at incredible speed, stopping a foot from the Lord's face. The piece of steel fell harmlessly to the podium. August immediately got to work, figuring out where the projectile had come from, and lifted the two supers that attacked from the far back, and bringing them before their Lord.

"This is the sixth time in so many cities where we've been attacked," Jack lamented. "It never works."

The Lord stared at the Asian woman and the Hispanic man hovering before him. "Why do you attack me?" He asked.

The woman scowled at him. "You're not the Lord!" she shouted. "You're just a murdering impostor!"

"We will not serve a false messiah!" the man next to her said.

"You sadden me," the Lord spoke, closing his eyes a moment. "Any time those who stand against God have to be punished, it makes me sorrowful for what could have been." When he opened his eyes, they went up in a brilliant light. The crowd cheered.

"Thank you, August," Jack said, patting his new ally on the shoulder. "You join the ranks of the saved!"

The young man followed Jack past the podium and to a man in a suit. "Mr. Hurst!" the agent replied. "What is your will?"

Jack returned to where the Lord was. "My Lord, where are we going next?" he asked.

"Allow me to speak to your President," the Lord spoke, leaving the podium and approaching the suited agent.

"My Lord!" the agent cried, bowing his head. He led them to a station where a man produced a cell phone.

The Lord took the phone to his ear. "We are headed first to Europe for a series of destinations," He spoke. "First, we go to London, then to Berlin, then Madrid. I will give further instructions from there." The President spoke. "Three days before we leave." He hung up.

"Go and meet with the others, August," Jack advised, joining his Lord. "My Lord! Our army grows by leaps and bounds!"

"We gather the forces of good against evil," the Lord spoke, "and our enemy gathers the forces of darkness. We fight against horrific injustice. The good news is, our adversary's most powerful servants have already made themselves known to us."

"Forgive me, oh Lord," Jack asked, "but I must know. Are you worried about them?"

"My child!" the Lord exclaimed, laughing. "Are you that afraid? I tell you, each time they oppose me they merely demonstrate how glorious the power of the Father is! I tell you, though we will surely see mightier attacks in time, we will not lose. The Father in Heaven does not lose."

"Yes, my Lord!" Jack swore. "I am a faithful servant!"

The large collection of supers in service to the Lord spread out and covered the surrounding city area. Their task had largely been the same everywhere they went. Any who agreed to bend the knee to the Lord would be taken in. Any who denied their Lord and Savior would be judged. The Lord had instructed that any who bent the knee were to be accepted, and any who denied would be judged. A few times, disobedient servants who killed for fun were judged themselves, and after that, no more disobedience took place.

August joined a group of six and ripped the roof off a building where he could sense people inside. The old church's roof peeled off like a sardine can. About sixteen people huddled inside. It had been their guess that no one who thought they were serving the Lord would attack a church. Turns out they were dead wrong.

The psychic and his allies looked down at the screaming group and descended into the church.

Immediately, half the group disappeared.

"Where'd they go?" August yelled.

He focused his telekinesis. His mind over matter allowed him to feel every piece of matter within his sphere of range, extending for miles around him. A figure raced at scarcely fathomable velocities through the area, and he put up a wall around the remaining churchgoers. Before it finished, however, the rest were gone.

August lifted out of the church and gathered some of his allies. "Do we have any speedsters?" he asked.

A young man raised his hand. "Me," he spoke, approaching. "I fought the Capacitor before. Name's Craig." He wore a track uniform that was dark blue and had hair the color of lacquered oak.

The psychic's mood turned around. "Can you get the rest of our extremely fast allies together?" he said. "I've got a plan."

The young man disappeared and returned with three other new arrivals. "We're here," he said.

"Names?" August said.

"Dylan," the young speedster said. His outfit consisted of black running tights and a green tunic-like shirt. His English features and short orange-red hair made him look almost a teenager. He motioned behind him to his new allies. A light-skinned middle easterner with a short, curly goatee and hair, with a collared shirt and loose cargo pants stood firm, decision in his eyes.

"Sahar," the man said, bowing. He stood aside and a man with long blonde hair pulled into a ponytail stepped forward. He wore an elaborate two-piece costume made from leather.

"Malcolm," the tall man announced in an Australian cockney.

"Great!" August announced. "Here's what our team is going to do. It's clear they're monitoring us, and they speed in and rescue whoever we approach. I imagine we're not the only group being attacked. So, we're going to approach a large group and they'll have to act. Then you guys will go after them."

"Great idea!" Craig cheered. "We're on it."

Jennifer pulled the last of the survivors to freedom. The hundreds of people she'd pulled from the clutches of Jack Hurst's loyal fanatics were given comfortable hiding places on the other Earth John's portals gave them access to. Jericho had helped with that. Constructing houses was easy when people had superpowers. The survivors were promised they would be kept safe and were given sci-fi level tech to protect themselves with. Even John didn't know how effective it would be against the more powerful goons the mad reverend could throw at them, but anything was something.

"Jennifer!" Jericho shouted. "They're after a mosque and there's sixty people inside!"

Jennifer sighed. "It's a trap, I bet," she said.

"I'll come with you," he offered.

She nodded. "Okay," she replied. "Great idea."

"Tell me when to open the portal," Raymond said, hands on the device. Jericho pointed a hand in his direction and sent the information to his mind. "Got it." The scientist waited until the two got into a runner's position. "Go!" he shouted, slamming the button, and creating a circular opening in space.

They took off, propelling themselves into the portal. It shut behind them as soon as they stepped through. Almost at once, fists and feet began pummeling them.

Jennifer had taken one step into the mosque when she had to immediately duck beneath a fist and caught a knee in the gut for her trouble. Jericho, who didn't have a speed power quite on par with her got it much worse. The speedsters pummeling him with fists and feet wore gloves and boots that kept him from making skin contact. As Dylan and Craig hit Jennifer, her durability tanked the blows but the sheer speed behind them started to become painful after a few moments. She tried to hit them with electric attacks but they'd been taught, apparently, how to duck out of the way just before the spot they were standing lit up with energy.

Jericho's regeneration and durability started to fail. *Damn it,* he thought, *if I don't do something…!*

The two kicking and punching him suddenly flashed through years of memories, each one getting the whole person's life, no summary. When they returned to themselves, it was only an instant later, but in their disoriented mental state, they didn't react in time and hands grabbed both their necks.

"Bastard!" Sahar swore, vibrating his way out of the grip a moment before a shockwave would have passed through him.

Malcolm wasn't so lucky and got blasted into a far wall. Thankfully for him, his enhanced speed sped up his healing, and he collapsed and recovered a moment later. "Didn't get me!" he shouted.

The grin on the billionaire's face told them everything.

"Shit," Craig shouted, a moment before a fist buried itself in his chest, knocking him off Jennifer.

Jericho brushed a hand against her and showed her everything. She learned about the differences between speed powers; specifically, she learned that there really wasn't one, other than degree of power.

Jennifer focused on her speed powers. She had largely been using them automatically. But focusing on them inside her body, she saw the otherworldly energies that represented her different powers. Although her mind had been doing the heavy lifting for her, taking manual control of her powers gave her pause. The first one represented time; it was how she could stand still at super speed. The second represented actual speed and allowed her to move fast without everything freezing around her. She cranked the first as high as it would go, and everything went perfectly still around her. Now, everything froze, including her. At maximum time-based speed, she found herself locked within her own body. Even her eyes wouldn't be able to move from their current position. The upside was, she figured, that now, she had all the time in the world to think. She focused on the internal map of powers fluctuating within her.

At full time speed, her base speed power vanished into almost nothing. She brought the base speed power up, and the time speed power began to decrease, with reality starting to move again around her. At a certain point, she saw they met at exactly one point. It would be impossible to match them using her powers on automatic and keeping them at the same point required precise manual control, but after a few moments of intense focus, she got it.

Thank you, she thought, sneering at the two speedsters whose memories she'd just gotten. *I couldn't have done it without you.*

Craig recovered and threw a vibrating straight punch at his target's face. Jennifer caught the fist. She seemed to act without moving, even to his speed-enhanced eyes. First, a flat palm strike to the chest knocked the wind out of him, followed by a rapid twist of her left arm, breaking his right in several places. A scream of agony left his mouth. A quick headbutt later and he collapsed in a heap.

Malcolm swung but she ducked beneath his attack and drove an uppercut into his chest, throwing him up into the air. The impact knocked him silly, causing him to lose focus which shut his power off and he froze in midair. Dylan made a run for one of the civilians, but she latched a hand onto the back of his head and zapped him. Sahar made it halfway to her before Jericho intercepted him and delivered two balled-up fists into the back of his head.

As far as any one of the civilians saw, one minute there were hostile supers working for the fake Jesus standing there, and the next, they stood inside a house's living room. Jericho gave them the usual spiel about how they would be protected, and that there were places being set up for additional refugees. Most importantly, they would not be expected to do anything in return for being protected.

"John! Ray!" Jennifer cried, exiting one building and heading into another. "Please tell me you've got something!"

"You're in luck!" Raymond cried. "Everyone gets some toys!"

"Great!" Jennifer shouted. "Me first!"

John pushed his safety glasses up and approached. "I remember how you said you didn't want to wear an elaborate costume," he said, "so I integrated it into your basic outfit." He produced a series of shirts with the Capacitor symbol painted on, and some spandex-looking pants. "They draw upon your existing energies to become more durable without losing flexibility." He produced a series of bands of varying size. "These, though, are my pride and joy."

She regarded the golden bands. "What are they?" she asked.

"Change into one of your new outfits," Raymond recommended, "and then you'll see."

A blur later and she stood in one of the shirts, a bright orange, and pants, a dark grey. "Wow!" she exclaimed. "It feels like..."

"Like you're almost naked?" John explained. "Yeah, it draws upon your powers so it shouldn't feel like ordinary clothes. It's tight without being perverted." She shot him a look and he nudged her. "Anyway, the small bands go on your wrists and also your ankles, just above your shoes. The bigger one goes around your waist as if it were a belt."

She put them on. Immediately, she felt power surge. "My god," she swore, flexing her fingers. "This is unbelievable."

"I don't know how much of a strength multiplier it is," John explained, "but it certainly increases your strength."

"What do you have for me?" Annie asked, entering.

"Only the best battle armor for the Goddess of Strength," John said. He produced a bodysuit for underneath, and a series of ceramic looking plates to go on top. He tapped one with his fist and it clanked like hitting a solid piece of metal. Then he handed them to her. "These may look solid, and to our enemies, they are, but try one out for size."

She skeptically examined a solid arm piece. As soon as it touched her arm, it became as flexible as cloth. She stared in disbelief. "No way!" she exclaimed.

"Way," Raymond replied. "Try this."

After Annie put on the bodysuit, armor pieces and boots, he handed her a pair of shiny silver gloves, thick and looking like solid metal. She slid them onto each hand, and they flexed like ordinary gloves. "They behave like flexible material," John explained, "But otherwise are solid as can be. They draw upon your powers. That's not all." He brought out a helmet that appeared to come straight out of science-fiction. He set it on her head.

"It's like I'm not even wearing a helmet!" she cried.

"The Goddess's lungs filter out all poisons and toxins," Raymond explained, "and the helmet does the same. Also, it becomes transparent when worn by you."

300

"Badass!" Jericho yelled, entering the room.

"Annie," Jennifer said, "why don't we get some training in?"

She tilted her head. "You mean, like," she said, "combat training?"

Jennifer shook her head. "No," she replied. "No one here is a trained combatant, and let's face it, I don't think learning martial arts is going to make a lick of difference. What I mean is, we just beat some of their speedsters. Sure, we're probably going to fight them again, but I learned how to use my power better."

Annie gestured. "Right," she noted. "I get it. Stop using the Goddess's power on autopilot."

"Cool," Jennifer said. "You guys okay here?"

John gave a thumbs-up. "We'll get Edward all set up while you two go out and train," he explained.

Outside, they flew a good distance away from the series of buildings. Having an entire, relatively uninhabited Earth to themselves was a useful trick. They each stood a car's distance apart from each other. Jennifer gathered her thoughts. "I remember Cyroya had super speed," she explained. "Maybe not as good as mine, I don't know, but it should work."

Annie shrugged with her hands. "But how do I activate it?" she said. "I don't sense energy like you do."

Jennifer pondered. She snapped her finger. "She's all about battle," the heroine replied. "Remember, in *First Breaker* she's the bad guy at first. She lives for combat. I imagine you have to think about it in a combat sense." *Let me try something*, the redhead thought.

Annie watched as Jennifer clenched just her right fist. Annie focused, furrowing her eyebrows. In her mind, she saw a series of possibilities as ghost images of the fight to come. After each initial attack, the best possible counter appeared as a ghost image beside it. She saw hundreds of possible fights. As her friend drew her arm back, certain possibilities disappeared, and others took their place. Then the heroine seemed to vanish. Annie's eyes went wide as her vision adjusted. She saw a blur and Jennifer came into view. Instinctively, she went to catch the attacking fist, but it struck her in the chest and launched her backward.

"I saw it," Annie replied, standing up. "I just didn't have the time to react."

"No problem," Jennifer shot back. "I'll go a bit slower and try again."

The redhead drew back and swung. Annie intently focused and time seemed to slow down. She pulled back and her body responded faster this time, and she almost made it. The fist tagged her much later than it otherwise would have, throwing her backward, though she recovered in time to land on her feet.

Annie clenched her fists and lowered into a fighting stance. Her friend threw a straight punch, and this time, she saw the action slow down enough to catch the fist. Jennifer smiled as she pulled back and attempted a kick. This time, Annie's perception became such that she saw the leg start to move in slower and slower motion. Jennifer sped up in response, and a few blocked blows later, they matched speed.

"How's that?" Annie asked.

"You're getting great really fast!" Jennifer complimented. She launched a punch and sped it up at the last minute. Annie jerked her head out of the way as the fist suddenly blurred. She grabbed the wrist and pulled, yanking her friend forward and driving a jab into her abdomen. In response, Jennifer swung an elbow strike upward. Her friend jerked her head back and brought her knee up at the same time, catching the heroine in the chest, launching her back.

"How's that?" Annie asked.

Jennifer shook it off. "Wow," she stated, "just remember to hit the enemy at least that hard!"

Annie laughed. "That's why I chose her," she replied.

"Oh!" Jennifer said, "Gimme a moment!" She dashed back into the lab. "John, if we break the equipment, how hard is it to fix?"

John and Raymond exchanged a look. The younger scientist turned back to her. "We made plenty of spares," he said, eyebrows furrowed, "just try not to break too many of them."

"Great!" she cried, thumbs up.

When she zipped back, Annie took a breath. "Want to go again?"

"How about I get a turn?" Edward said, interrupting the goddess's question.

"What've you been up to, Ed?" Annie inquired.

"Oh, you know," he replied, "the usual. Fake Christians cheering as innocent people are murdered by a false messiah. At least I managed to save a few." He shook his head. "This is fucked up."

"I would say I can only imagine how it bothers you," Jennifer replied, "but then again I've literally experienced your memories."

He sighed. "I'd like to keep my mind off how many people claim to be followers of Christ," he lamented, "and are cheerfully supporting this genocidal prick, thank you very much." He dropped into a fighting stance.

"I thought you didn't know martial arts," Annie noted, standing aside.

"I don't," Edward corrected. "Kadosuke does."

Annie snapped her finger. "Ah, right!" she replied. Then she cocked her head to the side. "Wait."

"Why don't you have memories of the Goddess if what he said is true?" Jennifer pre-emptively said. "It's an instinctive thing."

"Makes sense," she replied. "I guess it's like how I have 'battle sense' when I fight."

"Or how I can just use my powers on autopilot," Jennifer stated.

Edward shot a straight palm strike towards his friend, who barely had time to dodge to the side and throw a left elbow strike at his forehead. He ducked beneath it and propelled forward into a gut punch. Jennifer moved farther aside and pushed him past her. After they passed, they whirled around and faced each other. Jennifer aimed a straight left-hand punch at his face, and he shoved it aside. As her left hand curved to the right, away from him, she went for a hook punch with her other arm. He grabbed it and the other wrist, pulled her close, and delivered a kick to the abdomen that sent her back. While she struggled to regain her footing, he launched forward and went for a straight palm strike to her forehead. She recovered just in time to tilt her whole body to the side and deliver a standing side kick to his chest. He ricocheted off the ground like a pebble skipped across a pond and crashed into and through a tree at least a meter thick.

She gasped and clutched at her mouth. "Oh shit!" she shouted. "Sorry!"

Before the tree finished falling, a blue curve of light travelled through the air, vaporizing the tree. Edward stood, dirt on his kimono, missing a sandal, and clutching his extended katana, which glowed bright as a welder's torch. He caught his breath. "Nice...one..." he huffed.

"You're damn fast," Jennifer complimented. "You've been fighting."

His mind went to his recent fights, and his eyebrows lowered, and a frown appeared. "I fucking hate teleporting fighters," he uttered.

Annie and Jennifer both cringed. "Yeah," Annie chimed in, "I can imagine the feeling."

Just then, the sound of footsteps caught everyone's attention. "Guys!" Davis yelled, running up. "All your families are safe, right?"

The three exchanged glances. "Yeah," Jennifer said. "They're in one of these houses, why?"

"Well," Davis said, "the Illinois State Police just did a raid on all you guys' houses, with intention to turn everything over to Jack Hurst."

A string of cursing and down expressions passed between the trio. "So, what's next?" Annie asked.

"Since the United States government has surrendered to Jack Hurst," he said, "we're enemy number one."

"We're in this," Sam explained, "to victory or death." He shook his head. "There's no going back now. Either we win, or we die."

"Do we have any more allies?" Jennifer asked.

"Some," Davis explained. "Jericho's been helping us find people. We've also been helping people who refuse to accept the government's surrender."

"Holy crap," Jennifer said. "Isn't that risky?"

"Yeah," Sam said, putting hands on hips. "But this is some serious horseshit, and I swear I didn't join the FBI to watch my government surrender to a tyrant."

Annie shook her head. "We've got to act," she said.

"I agree," Jennifer said. She turned to Ed. "Did you get your equipment from John and Ray?"

He nodded. "You were too focused on fighting me to notice," he said, gesturing.

"Ah! Nice kimono!" she replied.

"So," Jericho said, popping in, "what do we do next?"

"We're going to go collect some allies," Jennifer said. "We're going to see who's willing to fight against Jack." She looked to everyone.

"I'm in," Annie said.

"Enough triage," Edward agreed. "We go on the offensive."

"Great idea," Jericho cut in. "Dave? Sam? Let's go get your guys and start fighting back."

"Best news I've heard in a while," Davis replied.

"They're itching to fight," Sam agreed.

As the billionaire led the two agents away to teleport out, he turned to the group. "I'll catch up with you," he said. "Go on without me."

"John," Jennifer said, approaching the building, "make us a portal."

CHAPTER TWENTY-TWO

I.

JACK HURST AND HIS LORD sat opposite each other on Air Force One. They had just finished a multi-day trip across Europe, preaching to the faithful and gathering allies, and their ranks had swollen accordingly. Everywhere they went, the masses fell in line. Even those who did not want to serve their Lord bent the knee when eternal damnation was on the table. Their collection of supers loyal to the cause had grown to over a hundred. *It probably would be more*, Jack thought, *except our enemies are good at interception, the bastards.*

"My Lord," Jack said, looking up from his thoughts. "Where are we headed now?"

"China," the Lord spoke. "It is the largest collection of people in need of my presence in the world."

Jack pondered that. "It'll also be the largest group of supers to join our cause," he noted.

"We'll be landing in a half hour!" the pilot announced over the intercom. "They're refusing to allow us permission to land!"

"That's a shame," the Lord spoke. "I was hoping they would merely accept us. I had thought speaking to them directly would have changed their minds. It turns out, I was wrong." The Lord's eyes glowed.

A few miles away from the plane, three fighter jets sent to intercept vanished in a white ball of light. As the plane streaked onward, a massive display of military force gathered on the runway. Dozens of tanks, hundreds of men armed with heavy machine guns, and thousands more in the waiting outside the runway area, and mobile rocket launchers had taken up residence to stop the plane from landing. As the plane streaked over the Chinese countryside, missile launchers that had been assembled once word of the fake Jesus' arrival had gotten out lobbed their ammo. One by one, the operators went up in inhuman balls of heat, their ash falling gently to the seats. The runway came in sight.

"Sirs!" the pilot nervously shouted. "They're blocking the runway!"

"Land," the Lord commanded. "I will take care of this." He clasped his hands together and stood up.

As the Chinese military stood, prepared to blow the plane out of the sky as it grew ever larger in their sights, the sunny skies turned overcast. A nasty bluish cloud gathered overhead, turning almost violet. Thunder cracked in the sky. Dark blue rain began to fall. It harmlessly rolled off people, but as soon as it touched tanks, guns, or any other weapons of war, they dissolved like sugar cubes in hot tea. Soldiers stood with empty hands and equipment operators sat on the ground with empty air in front of them where tanks and other vehicles had been. Not a moment later, the skies parted, the sun came out, and a strong gust of wind blew the liquid away and pushed the soldiers off the runway.

The plane landed safely. Confused and angry soldiers rushed the staircase that descended from the plane. The door opened, and the Lord extended his hand, an invisible force propelling the men off the stairs. Jack and his Lord exited the craft. A separate jet landed on a nearby strip, carrying their superhuman allies.

A middle-aged gentleman, elaborate uniform on his person, approached. Unlike the fear in the eyes of his men, he stood firm. "You will not destroy our nation" he commanded in Mandarin.

"So, you are the general," the Lord noted, his words translated by magic.

"We will not fall to you the way India fell!" the general shouted.

"Their nation made a choice," the Lord stated. "I responded in kind, with judgment. In spite of what you have seen, I am not here to destroy lives, but to save them. Any who prostrate themselves before me and accept Our Father's love into their heart shall be saved. It is my mere intention to bring about a wondrous kingdom of God, consisting of all mankind under the Father in Heaven, a kingdom of acceptance and love and eternal happiness."

"No," The general rebuked. "Others may see a savior, and the people of the western nations may easily be swayed, but in you, all I see is a false prophet who murders anyone who will not be his slave." He paused to reflect. "After all, I thought the Lord of Christianity was supposed to be a healer and accepting of all?"

"When I return," the Lord explained, "I will return as a conqueror. That is what the Word says. The armies of Satan would marshal together to stop me and I would be tasked in defeating it and bringing the children of God before their Father in love and power."

The general considered. "You have the power to do as you wish," he said, "but understand that there are those who will never accept your racket of 'love-me-or-die' as a gift from a God above."

The Lord's expression darkened. "I am tasked with the judgment of all who refuse His call," He uttered, anger bubbling up. "Should I interpret this as your refusal to accept?"

Helicopters for news agencies hovered nearby. "You will have to be seen killing me," the general said. "I want my nation's people to see the 'love' you bring them firsthand."

The Lord bowed his head. "As you wish," He uttered. When he brought his head up, the man vanished in a brilliant light, his scream cutting off. At this, the soldiers scattered. Superhumans loyal to the Lord gathered around him. One figure hovered down from above.

"My lord!" August Dietrich cried.

"What news do you bring?" the Lord asked.

"They've gone on the offensive," the psychic said. "They're practically begging us to fight them."

Both Jack and his Lord pondered this. "Fantastic!" Jack announced after a moment. "Come on, my Lord, let's go dispatch them now!"

The Lord shook his head. "Not yet," He said. "How many are there?"

August collected his thoughts. "There's about two hundred all over the world saving people," he explained, "but the main group of six or so are hunkered around a base of operations they brought out of a portal into Vietnam."

"They seek to test our forces," Jack noted. "Why don't we throw everything we've got at them?"

"It would be a waste of lives," the Lord spoke. "August, send only our most powerful supers at them. My servant and I will minister to the lost children of this nation."

"A brilliant plan, oh Lord!" Jack cried.

"With their power having grown with my support," the Lord explained, "they will not be able to lose."

"The day of glory is almost here!" Jack exclaimed.

II.

"YOU THINK THEY'LL NOTICE?"

Jennifer looked at Annie after she asked. "They'll notice," she replied. The group stood poised for battle, waiting. Edward had his new kimono on, blade drawn and ready, with Kadosuke's spirit senses stretching out for miles, sensing any oncoming danger. Jennifer hovered twenty feet above the ground, with eyes and ears open for any disturbance. Annie clenched her massive fists and stood firm, using her battle sense to detect any ill intent from afar. John and Raymond stood in the pilot seat of twenty-foot-tall robots. Their immense science-fiction-level intellects had brought the group a smorgasbord of enhancements and ultra-powerful technology, and they looked forward to saving the world with it.

A crack and a bang later, and multiple senses lit up at once. Jennifer and Annie sensed it first. The giant felt pure killing intent emanating from a few hundred miles away, and Jennifer heard the sonic boom. A group of at least thirty supers flew over the terrain, supported by August's telekinesis, and ahead of them a group of no less than twenty speedsters dashed ahead.

"Incoming!" Jennifer thought, and Jericho relayed it to everyone telepathically. Jericho threw up forcefields around the robots.

Shifting into super speed, Edward drew back his blade and swung, a bolt of energy propelling forward at unimaginable velocity. The speedster in front and those to the side dodged, but one unfortunate super got vaporized. The group had been running largely in formation but scattered and attacked, like a swarm of wasps, when the attack began.

Jennifer swung and missed, as a torrent of blows from six different attackers bludgeoned her with fists and feet, vibrating to cause extra hurt. *Fuck,* she thought, *they're faster than ever!* The fake Jesus' ability to enhance people's powers really pissed her off. She tried to zap their nervous systems, but they moved out of her range so quickly she couldn't hit them.

Annie saw her friend get pounded with fists like being sand blasted. Despite the heroine's invulnerable skin, the blows still hurt when they came in at relativistic speeds. Her own durability was tested by the onslaught, and she swung and kicked only to miss each time. Edward had the best luck, as he drove his sword into the ground, and it sent a blast of bright light that knocked people flying.

Jennifer shoved her way through a swarm of fists and feet, absorbing a wasp swarm of blows to get close. A single zap shut them down. Seven corpses hit the ground. A dozen speedsters redoubled their efforts. Speedsters struck for eyes.

Jericho waited until people got close to him and smashed a bubble forcefield on, launching four enemies outward. Annie plowed through her attackers to smash into the airborne enemies before they could regain their footing. A straight kick bent one attacker into an impossible 'C' shape, his spine breaking and blood spurting from his mouth as his internal organs ruptured. Another smashed against her shoulder tackle like the sea crashing against shore. He crumpled to the ground in a heap. The remaining two broke their ankles on landing and were mincemeat a moment later.

Eight remained and they regarded their enemies. They'd done some damage; the redheaded hero and the giant had faces covered in blood from where impossibly fast blows had finally damaged nigh-indestructible skin. The billionaire had his battle suit in shambles, and one of his eyes was swollen shut. Still, they stood firm, and didn't falter. It bothered them. They dashed forward.

Jennifer slammed her eyes shut as she sensed pointed vibrating fingers aiming for them. Relying on her energy sensing, she felt where the attackers were and managed to catch the leg of one. A voice cried out and she remembered it as one of the four she'd fought before. As Craig's leg went limp as his nerves fired in radical ways, she immediately stuck her hand out and smashed a palm into his chest. His torso compacted like an accordion and his body launched backward, splattering across a fifty-meter line. His ally Dylan hesitated for a moment at the sight of his comrade's death. A feeling of horror passed over him. Annie used the moment to plant a fist through his head.

Edward swung, and attackers leapt and dodged to the side. Sahar dodged, but the edge of the curve caught his arm and he bled out a few moments later from the stump. Annie let out a scream as a speedster buried a vibrating hand into her eye socket. He went to pull away, but his hand was stuck in her bleeding skull. A huge hand grasped the speedster's neck, and one swift squeeze ended the man. Another attacker, sensing weakness, went for the other eye, but she stuck out a foot and knocked the man to his knees. Before he could recover, a soccer kick separated his head from his torso.

"You three!" Jennifer shouted. "You see this isn't going the way you wanted! Surrender now!"

They paused.

Edward swung his blade. A curved arc of light shot forward, vaporizing them where they stood.

"Annie, my god," Jericho cried, approaching.

She kneeled. "Do you have a healing power in there?"

Jericho turned it on. "It'll take a bit to regenerate a whole eye," he said.

"It's alright," she said. "Just get it started."

Jericho set a ball of green energy on the space where her eye was. "Just try to keep from getting hit there," he advised. "It'll work, it's just going to be slow."

Annie stepped back. "No prob," she said.

August and the rest of his allies arrived a few minutes later. The pile of corpses and limbs leftover from vaporized bodies gave them pause. Several of the attackers took in the scene and had to compose themselves. The gruesome scene did not, however, impede their desire to see their version of justice done.

A group of barrier supers formed a phalanx and pushed forward while projectiles soared over them. The heroes dodged the enemy fireballs, plasma shots, and relativistic pieces of metal and gravel. Annie dashed and leapt over the barrier, coming down hard on the other side, throwing a leg back and knocking two of them flying, and drove her shoulder into a round barrier. The occupant launched into August, whose forcefield shorted out his ally's, and the man jerked like a fish with the current passing through his body and fell limp to the ground. From the protection of a telekinetic bubble, the psychic grabbed the enormous woman and threw her into the dirt with tremendous force. He then uprooted a stump and shot it at Jennifer.

Edward shoved the end of his katana through August's bubble and shot a bolt of plasma into his enemy. The psychic redirected it at the last moment, burning his shoulder. With a wave of his hand, a battering ram blow launched the hero flying. The katana let out a pulse and the bubble shorted out.

"What the..."

Before August's cry could finish, two robotic fists planted themselves in his face and torso, throwing him into a tree. A healer dashed to save his team leader, only for Jericho to shoot a plasma bolt through his chest. Covered in blood and with several broken bones, the psychic hovered upwards and knocked his foes into the air. A second impact later, and they flew backwards, bouncing off trees and crashing into rocks. He put up a new bubble forcefield.

Annie picked herself up and stood firm. The green glow ended as her eye had finished regenerating. A series of cracks in her armor, and blood coating her from rapidly healing wounds, she spat on the ground and stared at the enemies.

Edward pulled his katana from the ground, adjusted his torn kimono, and took up stance next to his friends. Pieces of gore fell from his blade and his disheveled hair. The angry scowl on his face drew a moment's pause from his enemies.

Jennifer and Jericho both hovered to form the ends of a line. She shook her head. "You're not winning this," she affirmed.

"You can go back to your Lord," Jericho cried, "and tell him we're fighting him, and *that* will be the end of it."

"We're not giving up!" August shouted, holding his broken bones in place. "We'll die for our Lord before we give up!"

"No," a booming voice spoke to everyone present. "You won't."

"You coward!" Jennifer shouted. "You fucking monster! Come out and face us *yourself!*"

"My Lord!" August protested. "We can still win this!"

"They have made it clear that you cannot," the Lord spoke. "Nevertheless, they are right; I will face them myself. Not here, however, and not now. Your service is needed. We have more to do. Return and I shall heal those who are left, and we shall continue our glorious mission."

"Please!" August shouted. "Please! I am willing to die for you!"

"My child!" the Lord commanded. "You will return! The hour is approaching, and I shall finish this work. You will not become a martyr this day."

"You piece of shit!" Jennifer yelled. "Come out here now!"

"No, progeny of Satan," the Lord replied, "you will fight me, in a week's time, at the destined battle. You will face the Armies of the Father in Heaven at the Battle at Armageddon."

"The Valley of Megiddo," Edward whispered, realizing.

"We'll see you there!" Jennifer shouted, clenching her teeth afterward. The psychic gathered his remaining forces and shot off like a bullet.

"He's giving us time to prepare," John said, exiting the robot.

"That doesn't make sense," Annie replied, shaking her head.

"Yes, it does," Jericho thought out loud.

Dark expressions came over their faces. "He knows the story," Raymond added, stepping out of his robot. "He knows the way the story ends. God defeats the sinners, and so he doesn't feel he can lose."

Jack turned to his Lord as they exited a town, followed by a new group of followers. "My Lord!" he cried. "Why did you call them back?"

"I tested their power," the Lord spoke. "And now I know how to defeat the heathens in battle."

"It was a..." Jack trailed off as realization struck. "Wait, you never thought our men could defeat them?"

"No," the Lord said, turning to his faithful servant. "I never once thought anyone besides myself could win against those followers of Satan. The Deceiver gave them too much power. Our faithful are useful for delivering judgment to powered servants of evil. These, however, are special. Only I can defeat them."

"So," Jack asked, "why sacrifice our men against them?"

"I needed to separate the ordinary evil from the special evil," the Lord spoke. "I needed to know which ones only I could face. Besides, those fallen in service to the Father will be seated beside him in the Kingdom of Heaven."

Jack's spirits lifted. "I'm sorry for doubting you, my Lord!" he cheered.

"Go make the announcement," the Lord commanded. "Inform the peoples of the world that, in seven days' time, the Battle at Armageddon, the final battle, shall take place."

CHAPTER TWENTY-THREE

JENNIFER AND HER FRIENDS HAD RETREATED into the other dimension to re-group. Edward swore and paced around the compound. John and Raymond repaired the damaged equipment and worked while the rest pondered the turn of events. "Alright," Jericho said, breaking the tension. "This fake Jesus is limited by the lack of imagination of the person who summoned him."

The group followed this train of thought. "Right," Annie agreed, stretching her arms out of habit. "But we figured that. What's your point?"

"I think I know where you're going with this," Raymond said, chiming in. "Jack probably just thinks of Jesus as the son of God, the creator of the universe in human form, so he can do anything, but he isn't working at maximum efficiency."

"Right," Jericho said, pointing. "Don't you agree?" He turned to Jennifer.

Jennifer nodded. "First time I fought him," she recalled, counting items on her fingers, "he didn't know what I was going to do ahead of time, there were questions he couldn't answer, and when I attacked his nervous system, it worked for a little bit."

Jericho nodded. "And that leads me to believe that He himself might only have a slight grasp of his powers," he added.

"What are you talking about?" Edward said.

"The fake Jesus thinks he's *Jesus*," Raymond replied.

Edward's eyes shot left and right. "Uh, yeah," he stated.

"No," John cut in," think about it. *Think* about it."

"You'd think Jesus would know everything," Jennifer answered. "If he knew everything, we couldn't beat him. If he doesn't, why not?"

"How could he know about modern society," Annie asked, realization drawing itself on her face, "and not know some of the other things?"

"Because he's based on a flawed, mortal, modern man," John answered.

"Wait," Raymond cried, alarm in his voice. "Couldn't he be listening to us right now?"

"Could be," Jericho said, "but I doubt it. Think. He doesn't think he can lose." He stood up and postured. "Think about the way he's carried himself. Jack Hurst thinks of the Second Coming as what?" He pointed for effect. "A *conqueror*. He's supposed to beat evil itself in a final climactic battle. If he thinks of himself that way, he doesn't think he can lose."

"Except," Jennifer interjected, "he's not the perfect Son of God, he's a monster summoned by a man with superpowers."

"Why can't he just kill us from afar?" Annie asked, then immediately cringed, regretting asking it.

"He *could*," Raymond answered. "But he will not, because he has to be seen defeating us. That's the point; he needs an audience."

"So, what do we do next?"

Edward's question brought the somber mood back.

Jennifer stood up, deciding. "I'm going to suggest we spend the last week saving as many lives as possible," she said. "The more lives we save, the more allies we get."

"Also," Annie noticed, "we saw how important speed was. We take out his big-name speedsters and heavy hitters as soon as possible."

"That's a great idea," Jericho said. "We can use this opportunity to do two birds with one stone: we save lives and take out his generals. When the time comes, we want to fight just *him*."

"Just him," Edward agreed.

"We're not going to be much good in the battle," Raymond said, looking at John. "Let's face it, our attack robots weren't much help."

"No, that's a good point," Jennifer said. "Use them to save lives."

"So," a familiar voice cried, stepping into the compound, "you kept me out of that last fight. What do I do?"

Everyone turned to Luther. "You," Jericho said, extending a warm welcome, "are going to play what I believe to be *the* most important part."

He looked at them. "What do you mean?" he asked.

"This may be a shot in the dark," Raymond said, "but I've been looking over your data, and your empathy power, while not a great assault weapon, might be able to do some serious damage to Jack Hurst or the fake Jesus." Before the question could be asked, he pulled up a tablet computer. "Your power is the highest on the hierarchy we've seen yet."

"During the final battle," Jericho said, "we need to get you close to Jack, and you're going to hit him with every person he's killed so far."

Luther looked between the two. "Okay," he agreed, nervously. "How do you want me to do it?"

"Make it *slow*," Jericho uttered, fire in his voice. "Make it *last*. Make him experience every last second of it. Don't give him any shortcuts, don't summarize, don't protect him from the pain and suffering. I want him to get every single drop of misery he's caused in one giant heaping helping."

The rocker's mouth drew itself into an 'O' as he pondered the implications. "That's…" he finally replied, "that's going to be…" Words failed him.

"That's going to be every bit of pain he deserves," Jennifer said. "If fake Jesus is based on his mind, then breaking his mind should affect the summoned monster in some way."

Jericho turned to leave. "I need a portal," he said, steeling himself. "I've got to get back to Davis and Sam and see how they're doing. They got a bunch of American government employees and special agents on their side in safety, but they've been tracking down remnants trapped in all sorts of places."

"Go," Jennifer stated. "We'll take care of things elsewhere."

The billionaire walked through the hole in reality.

I.

Davis Wilson and his boss teleported into the chamber. Several of the powers Jericho had gifted them were active in case they ported right into a trap. Faint candles lit the dark chamber, with the walls of stone echoing with each step. Down a hallway of stone, the faint smell of air freshener and essential oils wafted through the air as a feeble attempt to mask the odor of many people trapped for an extended period. Upon the first step into the chamber, a gun touched itself to the right temple of the younger special agent, and he could sense hundreds of sights trained on him.

"Wait!"

The cry came from a single female voice. A flashlight illuminated the two men. Sam Louis recognized the voice at once. Her gun lowered, revealing in the faint light graying hair with flecks of blonde still present, blue eyes wrapped in dark circles, and wrinkles reflecting long years. She holstered her pistol. "Brenda?" Sam said, arms wide.

320

"Hold it!" she shouted, stepping out of arm's reach to reveal that hundreds of firearms still pointed at her. "You're not with the preacher, are you?"

"Hell no!" Sam bellowed, miffed. "We're the good guys!"

Lights came on, and at least a hundred people stood in squalor, in a cave, and there, off to the side, was a hallway beyond which waste was disposed. Dawning realization came over her and her expression brightened. "Holy shit!" she cried. "Sam?" She propelled forward and hugged him. Tears stained his shirt. "It's been twenty days. We fended off a series of attacks, but we've run out of food and if we leave, they'll find us."

"How's the situation with the false messiah?" one young agent cried.

"Bad," Davis admitted, "but we have hope." He extended his hand toward the woman. "Davis Wilson, FBI."

"Brenda Jeffers, CIA," she introduced. She wiped her face. "Holy shit, this is a fucking disaster."

"You're telling me," Davis shot back. "Our allies just fought against the supers that worship the fake Jesus, and this would-be 'savior' gave a final declaration: a week from now, the final battle, in the Valley of Megiddo."

One could almost feel the wave of horror wash over the group. "So," Brenda uttered, agony in her voice, "this is the end."

"Not if we have any damn thing to say about it," Sam retorted. "How many people do we have here that are willing to fight?"

"Fight?" A man cried. "You fuckin' crazy?"

"No." Davis said, stepping forward. "I mean it. This is it. If we fail, that's the end." He gestured to them all. "All of you, all of us, we're all government agents. We swore an oath to defend the constitution." He scanned the room and saw many different ages and ethnicities. "We all started out, having heard about the evil shit our government did. We all swore we were going to be different. We all decided we weren't going to be the statistic, right? Right?" Some guilty faces greeted him. "All of us had to get our hands dirty, either directly, or by watching our agency partake in imperialism and racism and continuing to support it. This may be our one single chance to actually be the *heroes* for once. This may be our one shot to genuinely make the world a better place. This could be our only shot at making America live up to the idea that America was supposed to have been founded upon." He paused. "I sure as hell am going to take that shot. Aren't you?"

As he looked around, he saw every emotion from despair to horror to hope and back again. Eyes looked bloodshot with fear and stress. Their sense of heroism had been crushed so far down they didn't know if they still had it. "We aren't warriors," Brenda admitted.

"We ain't got to be," Sam cut in. "We just got to be there."

Davis nodded. "That's right," he added. "Sort out the details later. Right now, we have to provide support."

"Imagine what I went through," Sam explained. "I had to organize the looking into of this black magic fuckery right out of children's funny books. We spent eighty-hour weeks turning over every leaf and stone." He let out a huff. "I thought I was going nuts. I don't trust people. And yet, I found myself trusting people I thought were a threat at first." He scanned the group. "The least we can do is help them."

Nervous talk provided a background noise. "I guarantee you won't be going into battle unarmed," Davis said. A din of approval started to form.

"What do we do?" Brenda asked.

"Just a second," Davis said. He teleported. He returned a half a minute later. "Join hands." He turned to the group. "Everybody, form a long chain." After a bit of wrangling, everybody formed one long chain of hands. As soon as the last hands touched, they vanished from the chamber.

A large complex of buildings surrounded by snow and on one side by mountains became the first sight they saw upon reappearing. Some of the agents saw wildlife and recognized it as northern Canada. "Why are we here?" someone asked.

"Because of me," Jericho said, emerging from the group of interconnected cabins.

Brenda stepped forward, greeting the billionaire, and looking him up and down. "What happens now?" she asked.

"Keep your hands joined," he explained. "I don't have time to explain." He grabbed the first hand, and in an instant, everyone was up to speed, and had several new powers. "We've got this place stocked. Get everyone a shower, get everyone fed, and then get going." He vanished.

Relief came over many as their newfound regeneration undid the weeks of tiredness. They piled into the cabins and made their ways towards the shower rooms or the kitchen areas. Davis turned to his elder. "So, boss," he asked, "what's the plan?"

Sam glared at him. "Oh no," he said. "I'm not taking point on this one. You tell me what the plan is."

Davis took in the vote of confidence. "Alright," he said, "We're going to form into teams and take down certain members of the enemy entourage. We target those who committed acts of terror against humanity on behalf of Jack Hurst." He smiled. "But first, let them get relief."

II.

A pile of bodies burned in a pit outside a church in Kentucky. Half the roof was gone, pews in various states of wreckage lay strewn across two acres of land, a wall had a huge hole in it, and inside, a group of supers sat playing cards. They'd arrived, and the church-goers had refused adamantly to accept their Lord, and as such, had received judgment. Some of their ranks had gone super, and the fight had raged for ten minutes. They currently sat waiting for the police to bring them more souls to be judged.

The man standing watch saw a man appear out of thin air. Before he had a chance to act, a white-hot plasma ball burned a six-inch crater where his heart had been. "What the fuck!" some-one inside shouted.

Twenty men appeared on all sides and started firing. One super turned his skin metallic and launched himself at the man in front. A bolt of lightning struck him in the chest and launched him into a group of his men. When four of the agents shot fireballs, a young man in a militia outfit kicked a pew into the path of the projectiles, and it exploded. He turned just in time to get thrown like a javelin into his allies. Three charged the agents as a group. The brutes attempted to smash through like a bowling ball, only to be struck by concentrated plasma fire and collapse in a burning heap.

"Your outmatched!" a female agent shouted. "Surrender!"

The remaining four kneeled with hands up. Two agents placed devices on the men, and they went into stasis.

"Derrick," the female agent said, "take them to storage. We've got to clear the area." The agents holding the attackers called a portal and took them through.

Ten agents teleported to high positions in the trees and got a good view of the area. Local police were patrolling the vicinity and rounding up anyone they found. A chunk of the population had been found already.

"Calling D115," the dispatcher said over the radio on the Crown Victoria police cruiser parked by the edge of a dirt road leading to a farm.

The officer and his partner prepared to answer the call, when strong hands grasped their neck, and glowing hands crackling with raw power sat in their line of sight. "Answer that call," an agent cried, "and I'll burn your skull like a cigarette."

The officers looked and saw their car surrounded. "We're just followin' orders," he offered.

"We know," the agent replied, "and that's the problem."

An older agent sat on the hood. "You're going to tell us everything you and all your buddies have been up to," he commanded.

Five minutes later, the team had found six supers hidden in the woods and several families that had gone into hiding.

"Shh," a younger agent said, consoling the young teen, hiding behind the tree and shivering. "We took care of the police that wanted to hurt you."

"They killed my momma!" the teenage boy cried. "I'm all alone! Those men worship that evil thing!"

A few tense moments of distrust passed, and then they embraced. The now-orphaned boy cried into the man's shirt. "Would you like to help us stop the false messiah?" he asked the boy.

The boy's fear gave way to pure rage. "I sure would," the boy uttered.

With their ranks increasing, and enemies being either killed or paused and put in storage, they cleared an entire county of enemy activity by the end of the day.

A base of enemy supers had formed in an old recreational center in Cincinnati. The former gym had seen better days, but its use had been turned over to no less than fifteen members of a group that had declared loyalty to their Lord. The city had largely descended into chaos, with the police and government officially cracking down on any non-loyal activity. S.W.A.T. teams had gone into homes and extracted loyalty at gunpoint, and where some family had a super unwilling to accept their Jesus as the Lord and Savior, the group of faithful supers had been brought in to bring about judgment. Most of the legitimate businesses had bent the knee, only to quickly find many of their members unwilling to go along with it. Still, a great many people turned loyalist simply to avoid being executed.

"Now that our Lord has declared the date of the final battle," the 'pastor' of the group said, "we will soon be joining..."

A white-hot ball overlapped with his head for just an instant before the smell of cooking flesh and searing fat filled the room. His head popped like a bubble an instant later.

The group turned to see no fewer than fifty agents standing around them. "Surrender and live!" a female agent shouted.

"Fuck you!"

The man who let out the shout launched forward as the circle of agents shot towards the group and bodies collided. The result resembled a shockwave through a pile of straw. Fists met faces in a storm of loud bangs. Screams echoed as plasma scorched limbs. Five minutes later, a pile of writhing, injured bodies sat in the center of the room. "Tag 'em and bag 'em," the female agent shouted, "then get back here and help us."

The rest of the city wasn't as difficult. The base of enemy supers had been the largest collection in one spot. The rest of the city had loners patrolling in search of a quick judgment. In each case, the use of overwhelming numbers had proven the trick.

"We're only getting the small fry," one agent said to his colleague. "Yeah?" he noted. "Well, there's more of them, so we're still doing a service."

"I guess that's good, then."

John stood in the first of many storage buildings they'd set up. Groups of enemies had been coming in since the previous morning. The teams of agents had been scouring the country in groups taking down supers loyal to the enemy and gathering allies. They didn't take risks; they simply found the targets they could overwhelm and did so. The largest group of allies came in the form of suffering young people either orphaned by the enemy or having seen friends killed for refusing to serve a tyrant. Their collective anger had been channeled into taking down the enemy. Each one was given all they needed to get comfortable, and then the option to fight back if they wanted. None of it was mandatory.

These poor bastards have suffered enough, John thought, as he saw the latest group of refugee supers brought in to take a shower and get a good meal. "How's it going?" he asked, as the agents brought in some more paused enemies to be brought to their cages.

"We've been hunting," Brenda said. "I know you guys are the main force, but we want to make it easier."

"Believe me," John said, relief in his voice, "we'll take what we can get." He pointed. "Put the baddies over there."

"Are they frozen?" she asked.

"Just paused," John explained. "Stasis. Once we're done, we can unpause them. Right now, though, we need to make sure they can't act."

"Can we win?"

They both turned to the younger agent behind her. John gave him a serious look. "Honestly, I'm not sure," he admitted. "But I have to believe there are cracks in this fake Jesus' armor. We're going to find it."

A thought came to her. "How can he kill an entire nation," she asked, "and not take you guys out remotely?"

"He probably can," John explained, "but like we said, that's not what he wants. He wants an audience. This monster is based on Jack Hurst's thoughts, and the man's too lost in his faith to see the inconsistencies."

"That's messed up," she stated.

"Guys," Davis said, stepping in. "We just got our best chance yet." They turned. "What?" John asked.

"We might have a chance to get August Dietrich," Davis explained.

John looked over at Raymond. They both shared an expression. "Okay," John said. "Tell me what you need."

"I want to talk to the group and see what they think," Davis said.

A moment later, he vanished inside a portal.

III.

"No, I think it's a trap," Jennifer said, shaking her head.

Edward folded his arms. "I think I can do it," he said.

"But you're not likely to get the element of surprise," Raymond advised.

"Dave, what did you see?"

The agent pondered Edward's question. "They were picking off individual targets," he said. "We saw it from a distance, but it looked like he was finding the 'hard to reach' supers who were good at hiding."

"He didn't have any speedsters?" Edward asked. Davis shook his head. "Then I can take him." He saw the look on his friend's face. "Are you about to tell me I can't do it?"

"No," Jennifer replied, "I just don't want you to get killed."

"This guy is one of Jack's heavy hitters," Edward replied. "We don't want him present at the final battle."

"Then you're sure?" Jericho asked. "You want to do this?"

"You guys have other targets to get," Edward advised. "Leave this one to me."

"Alright," Annie cut in, "but you be safe, okay?"

Edward let out a huff. "Nobody's safe until this is all over," he stated.

A portal opened up and the swordsman and the agent stepped through. They gathered a group of their allies to go with them and stepped through a second portal and stood several miles away from where the telekinetic stood, searching through the hidden cellars and underground bunkers with his powers. Bodies lie along a trail, obviously belonging to those refusing to serve the monster. A dozen or so allies followed him, protected by forcefields. A city lay off in the distance beyond the group of enemies.

"We have to be careful of civilians he might use as hostages," Davis advised.

"I know," Edward agreed, taking soft steps. The agents spread out cautiously.

Edward felt a strange sensation on the back of his neck. His eyes went wide.

The agent standing in front of Davis and him exploded in a burst of gore and dirt as a spherical area combusted under telekinetic pressure. He jumped into the air, grabbing his ally by the belt and hoisting him up, just short of the attack.

"You didn't really believe you were getting the element of surprise," August said, hovering close by. "I knew you were coming."

"You didn't bring any speedsters?" Edward remarked, pulling backward and drawing his katana. "Either you didn't have any or you underestimate me."

"We noticed your group taking our forces off the table," August explained. A half-sneer emerged. "No big deal. The Lord can't be beaten, so killing our men won't matter."

"Then," Brenda asked, calling upon her plasma, "why do this at all?"

"One does what the Lord asks him to do," August said.

With a thought, a group of supers shot out of the ground, protected by force fields. Agents flung plasma bolts that crackled against shields and fizzled out. Edward slashed with his blade, shooting a curved beam of light through the air. The telekinetic hoisted upward and grabbed several of his allies, but an unlucky bunch got caught in the tail end. Their bubbles popped and the agents immediately started raining plasma on them. Bodies got launched into the dirt and rocks. Agents pushed their way past and collided in a whirl of projectiles, fists, and feet as they engaged the other supers. August went to assist his allies, but an arc of power cut through his shield and burnt his leg, forcing him to focus on Edward.

The psychic landed and drew rocks into the air. "Okay," he said, "you're good. But you'll never defeat the Lord!"

"You got healed only to die here!" Edward shouted, slashing forward and cutting a supersonic projectile into dust with his blade, as blue pulses of energy traveled up its edge. He bounced backward just as a foot-wide section of Earth exploded where he'd been standing. After cutting a large rock cut into a point, he dropped into a sword fighting stance.

August lifted over a curve of light that scorched where he'd been standing, and landed, hands up and ready to launch shockwaves. The swordsman shot his head to the left just as a shockwave shot past. He slashed upward towards his foe's exposed arm, but the psychic pulled it back and shot an invisible blast at the lower torso. Edward rolled to the side and brought his blade up just as his foe brought his hand down.

Electricity sparked off the blade as the pulsing power dispersed the telekinetic force ricocheting off it. Edward shot to his feet and threw his blade forward to stab, only for August to pull his torso back and throw a battering ram of an impact into the swordsman's chest. The psychic saw his foe bounce off dirt, throwing a cloud into the air, followed by a crash as a large rock broke the flight. Edward's eyes went wide, and he shot to his right just before the boulder exploded into pebbles. He dashed and ducked, invisible shockwaves shooting right past him. He turned and ran straight for his foe. August smirked and shot kinetic blasts outward, only to see Edward weave between them. The swordsman saw a hand shoot out and he ducked to the side and slashed upward.

August pulled back just as a blade shot up where his torso had been moments before. The light curving off the blade cut through his shield and delivered a nasty slice to his chest and up to his right shoulder. The attack left his foe vulnerable, and he hit the man with the force of a truck crash right in his chest.

Edward shot to his feet, spat blood from his mouth, and drew his katana into a fighting stance. "You're enjoying this," he remarked.

"I *am* enjoying this," August replied. "You're no weakling. That means if I kill you, I'm taking out one of Satan's top generals! This is a great day for me!" With telekinesis, he staunched the blood from the cut on his wound.

Edward blinked and took a deep breath. He shot forward and slashed upward, the curved light shooting through the air from his attack. August shot several kinetic blasts, which dulled the attack slightly, though it still crashed into his forcefield. The bubble crackled as the beam struck it, leaving a wide-open gash. August sneered in delight as he dodged sword strikes. The blue light travelling up and down the blade sparked as it cut through forcefield. Each slash left a gash, until the entire bubble popped. The swordsman became frustrated as he could not cut his foe. A shockwave caught Ed's leg, stumbling him. He then caught a kinetic blast to the chest, throwing him into the dirt, cutting a three-foot-wide gash in the Earth with his body. At the end of his ride, he blinked then shot into the air just before a huge dirt cloud formed when the ground exploded where he'd been.

August shot kinetic blasts upward, but Edward spiraled through the air and landed behind his foe in a heartbeat and spun while slashing. The psychic, not having time to turn, threw up a shield to protect his back, but the sword cut mostly through it, slicing into flesh, and throwing a spurt of blood into the air.

"YAAAHH!" August shrieked, surveying the damage and staunching the bleeding with his powers. "ERrrrgh." He smashed Edward down into the dirt, the knocked him into the air, before holding him there and pelting him with kinetic strikes. A last battering ram then threw the prone man into a tree, cracking it in half. Ed hit the dirt with a sputtering gasp. *It's not a serious blow*, August thought, holding his wound shut. *If he'd gotten any closer, he might have done worse than a flesh wound.*

Edward scrambled to his feet, coughing up blood and fluid. He wiped his mouth. "What's wrong?" he chided.

"I think the fun is over," August remarked, "I've been letting you off too easy. Not anymore."

Edward leapt backward in anticipation of a strike. Instead, a kinetic wave hit him in the back, launching him forward. An invisible force began crushing his neck as he lifted upward. His sword clattered to the ground.

"Don't you...!" Edward croaked, as he struggled to regain some control.

"Are you begging?" August mocked. He shook his head, squeezing. "You're going to die for your service to Satan!"

At Ed's mental command, the sword returned to its sheath. Blue and purple energy began to swirl around the blade and glow around the hilt. He built up the pressure and reached, only for a telekinetic barrier to grasp his arm mid-reach. As he gagged and coughed up blood, he pulled against the bonds. *No!* Edward thought. *I can't die here!*

The blade sent a pulse of light from his hip up through his body, until it reached his right arm. Power pulsed through him, and he mustered every ounce of strength the character had. August gasped as he felt the psychic barrier moving. *You won't win!* He thought, tightening his grip.

Edward's lungs began to burn as he pushed his arm, inches away from the blade hilt. As pressure on his arm increased, he pulled with ever burning anger. His chest ached and his arm screamed pain at him. "Why won't you just accept your judgment like a man!" August shouted, as blood began to trickle from his nose.

The tip of an index finger touched the hilt. A blue pulse traveled from the blade through his arm, and the barrier around his arm shattered. Wrapping his right hand around the blade's hilt, his entire body glowed and pulsed with the near violet light. His hair stood up as electricity arced off him.

August squinted, before marshalling all his telekinetic force, and shooting it outward in one gigantic shockwave. Edward saw space distort in front of him. With one swift motion, he drew his blade and slashed upward and to the right. Air exploded in a mighty clap of thunder from the heat rolling off the boomerang shape of light that shot out.

The distorted kinetic wave impacted the curved attack and rolled off like waves against a ship, impacting the ground to the left and right of Edward. Massive explosions of dirt and gravel launched into the air. The swordsman's attack continued, unabated.

"No!" August shouted. "This can't...!"

The wave struck his forcefield, and like a brick sailing through a window, continued. It struck him a blink later, and his torso above the waist flashed into steam and then plasma in less than a second.

Edward collapsed to the ground, coughing. He saw a pair of legs that used to be a person harmlessly fall to the dirt.

Over a dozen enemy supers turned at the sight of an apparent second sun emerging about fifty feet from them and vanishing a moment later. Forcefields protecting them popped like soap bubbles, and the bedlam proceeded from there. Plasma shots and strong fists and feet crashed into bodies. Five minutes later, they had seven corpses and six surrendering supers locked in stasis.

"Hey," Davis said, spitting blood on the ground, "wanna lock some assholes up?"

"I do," Edward said, wiping his face.

Jack Hurst looked over and saw his Lord close his eyes in prayer. "My Lord, what troubles you?" he asked, rising from his seat on the plane.

"One of our faithful has gone to his final reward," the Lord spoke. He shook his head. "No matter; we will not falter."

Jack knelt by his Lord and closed his eyes a moment, for a silent prayer. "Forgive me, my Lord," he asked, "but shouldn't we stop giving them more time?"

"I understand your concern, my child," the Lord spoke, "however, we want to bring all our enemies to bear at once. We must demonstrate to the world our victory."

"Yes, my Lord," Jack replied. "I will not falter."

"Your fear and uncertainty are normal," the Lord stated. "Just put your faith in me."

He nodded and returned to his seat. His Lord's holiness washed over him like cooling rain on a hot day. The concern and confusion in his heart vanished with a single assurance from his Lord. Soon, he knew, all the children of the world would receive the message as the enemies serving the Devil would be defeated.

CHAPTER TWENTY-FOUR

"We've only got a few days left," Jericho said, going over the events in his mind. Edward had finished being healed, and everyone's equipment had been repaired or replaced. "I feel like I'm going to throw up."

Jennifer took a drink of diet cola. "There's..." Her words trailed off as she tried to put it into perspective. "There's just so many of them. Everywhere we go, we find a few people wanting to oppose the false messiah, but...it's like counting the stars. There's so many who just willingly obey this monster."

Annie ate a sandwich. She washed it down with some soda. "I tell you what," she agreed. "The bigger question is, let's say we win. How do we handle the fact that a good percentage of the human race smiled and cheered when a monster said he wanted them to kill their fellow man?"

"I'll tell you how," Edward chimed in, standing up and approaching the group. "We try those who committed actual crimes, and those who helped, and we never stop reminding those that cheered and hollered and carried signs that they were the bad guys." His fists were clenched. "We never stop reminding them that they were never true Christians."

"Yeah, I guess that's the best option," John cut in.

Luther stepped in, grabbed a drink, and chugged it before plopping into the couch. His brother approached. "Luther!" he cried. "Are you okay?"

The younger brother wiped his brow. "While you guys have been fighting," he said, "I've been using my power on some of the enemies that were captured."

Jennifer perked up. "Really?" she inquired. "What happened?"

He sighed. "We got a few who were willing to go to atone for their crimes," he lamented, "but none were willing to admit the fake Jesus wasn't their savior. Apparently, he'd made a habit of showing everyone who agrees to serve him some vision of his perfect kingdom on Earth."

"And?" Edward chimed in.

Luther scoffed. "Anybody here ever read *The Euphio Question* by Vonnegut?" Jennifer and Jericho raised their hands at his question. "Well, long story short, there's an easy way to make people happy all the time regardless of what is happening around them." He gestured outward. "Basically, that."

"So," Jennifer said, "everyone's just happy all the time and that's his solution."

Luther shrugged. "Yup," he agreed. "There was some emotional fuckery in the vision itself, but if you look at it objectively, he just heals everyone, makes it so no one has to be hungry or thirsty, and then just everyone is happy all the time. There's no goals, no effort, no future."

"Still," Annie chimed in, "I can see why some people would fight for that."

"Oh, I know that," Luther argued, "it's just something I wouldn't want."

"So," Jericho cut in, "we've got just three days left." He turned to Jennifer. "Will we just keep doing more of the same?"

Jennifer pondered. "I want you guys to decide this one," she said.

Annie folded her arms. "We spend the next two days," she offered, "saving as many lives as possible. Then, we rest for the third day, and then go into battle."

"Most of the big boys are either gone or already waiting," Edward added. "I'm with Annie on this one."

John turned to Raymond. "How about we bring out the robots?" he asked. "That way, we're not just hanging around here all the time."

Jennifer nodded. "Sounds like a plan to me," she replied.

Jericho turned to his brother. "Want to go fight on the front lines?" he asked.

Luther grinned. "I've never been more ready," he said.

In Africa, a group of at least fifty men and women screamed in horror as they stared death in the face. A group of cultists loyal to Jack Hurst and his false messiah rounded up anyone who they suspected of being disloyal. Those who refused to join were to be gathered up like firewood and burned, just as the text had said. Six pyrokinetic supers stood on the platform, waiting as the ritual was being performed by the minister. "As the hour of our Lord is at hand," the man said, "the servants of the enemy must be sacrificed." Seven muscled brutes stood watch, waiting for any sign of trouble.

The sound of a sonic boom rattled the area. Wooden buildings jostled and everyone turned to the sound. Before they could see anything, a red streak impacted the ground like a meteor, sending quakes through the ground for hundreds of yards. Men fell to their backs, guns dropped out of hands, and cultists struggled to get to their feet. A figure erupted from the ground, spearing a Jeep like a dart, punching through, and using the two halves to decimate nearby tanks. In the clamor, they saw it was a woman. Standing in futuristic looking armor, the muscled statue of a woman lifted a tank like it was a beach ball and chucked it. It crashed into a group of enemy brutes and smashed one through several trees.

"Bitch!" someone shouted.

The woman started sprinting, her heavy footsteps shaking the ground. As she careened towards the enemies, artillery shots from fifty caliber machine guns pelted her like spitballs, and tank shells bounced off her like a man playing dodgeball with children. Two brutes dashed, driving their shoulders into her. She dug her feet in, tearing a ditch. Her hands grabbed their heads and smashed them together until she heard a crack and a splattering noise. Then their corpses became projectiles that took out nearby Jeeps.

Fireballs began to pelt her. She jumped and crashed into and through the stage, taking several pyrokinetic supers with her on the way down. Mashing sounds were heard followed by bodies sailing in all directions. Two got close and swiped fire across her helmet. She kicked one almost in half, and smashed a fist into the last one, bending him into a tight 'U' shape. His body launched into a truck with enough force to flip the vehicle.

"Anyone else!" she shouted.

She ripped the shackles and ropes off the victims. She pointed them in the direction of the nearest rebel group and took to the sky again. Her battle sense pointed her in the direction of a village a few dozen miles away.

"The Lord has given us a great purpose!" a terrorist leader shouted.

A boot planted itself in his back, throwing him into the dirt. Bullets began hitting her like annoying mosquitos. As he stood up, he saw her, and his face lit up. "You!" he shouted. "You're one of the generals of the Devil! Now you will taste the power the Lord himself has tasked me with!"

He delivered a straight punch to her chest, throwing her backward and crashing through a stone building, collapsing it. She propelled her way out of the rubble and bashed into him, plowing him through a series of vehicles. "I'm the Goddess of Strength," Annie said, playing up her character. "I'm not some *servant*."

He erupted from the wreckage and swung with all his might. She dodged and elbowed him in the head. She saw him reeling back for another mighty blow and planted her feet firmly. He planted his fist in her abdomen with all he could muster. Air burst around her like a hurricane, blowing away loose dirt. This time, though, she'd prepared herself. She didn't budge. "Hey! Not half bad!" she cried. Then she threw a kick upwards, catching him on the chin, mid-stupid look.

At the peak of his flight, she arrived above him and drove an axe-handle smash into his upper back. He hit the dirt and left a thirty-foot-wide crater. She landed.

Men dropped their rifles and ran. She let the feeling of guilt pass over her. Taking lives hurt her, it cut her deep. She wasn't about to give up. Once Jack Hurst and his monster were gone, she could go back to pacifism.

Her battle sense showed her that people were in danger nearby. She grit her teeth and took to the sky.

Jennifer rounded up another group of zealots trying to deliver 'judgment' to the innocent. After agents came through a portal and collected them, she sensed a bigger attack occurring upstate. Landing in north Texas, she found a high school gymnasium that had been turned into a concentration camp. Supers with all manner of powers patrolled the area as innocent people were brought by the truckload and emptied into the building.

She landed in front of the truck. Tires screeched as the vehicle stopped. Ice projectiles shattered against her back. She stuck out her hand in the direction of the attack and ball lightning shot out and exploded the ground in front of the attackers, throwing them backward. The driver and his copilot stepped out and began trading blows with her. She let them hit her a few times for effect. A steel-coated super smashed his fist against her face, to little effect. Grabbing their necks, she smashed their heads against the truck, and they went limp. She dropped the groaning men to the ground, zapping their nervous systems into seizures.

Ten more supers rushed her as a group. She dashed forward and knocked each one out with a single blow. Her electric touch laid them out. A moment later, her allies retrieved the zealots. A quick rip took the door off the gym, and inside, gunmen turned only to see a blur remove them from the building. "It's alright now," she cried. "You're free."

"Oh, thank you!" a woman cried hugging her. "We were so scared!"

"My friends will give you a hand," she said, gesturing outside where agents were waiting.

"It's horrible!" the woman shouted. "That monster is not Jesus!"

"I know," Jennifer agreed. "I have to go; there's more people to save."

She flew high above. From the vantage point, she saw a young man in battle with a crowd of zealot supers. He created light constructs and traded blows with an eight-foot-tall beast of a man pounding away at his energy barrier. Two brutes attempted to rush the young man, when Jennifer plowed into them like a cannon shot. Large construction girders smashed into his barrier, courtesy of magnetic manipulators, and Jennifer threw a brute into each of them, knocking them into piles of debris. A teleporter appeared in front of the young man and hit him with an elbow smash to the face, then teleported out. He appeared in front of Jennifer, who caught him immediately and zapped him.

"Thank...you...for rescuing...me," he said, struggling for his breath. His eyes went wide. "Holy crap! You're the Capacitor!"

"Don't thank me," she said. "I'm just doing what needs to be done."

"Can I help?"

At his question, she stopped, and turned back. "It's your choice," she replied. "I can't guarantee our *survival*, much less our victory."

His expression drew somber. "I don't want to leave this world to nutjobs," he stated.

"What's your name?"

"Andrew Javier," he replied.

"Come with me," she said. She signaled for a portal, and they stepped through.

Luther approached. He regarded the young man. "What do we have here?" he asked.

"Another ally," she told him. She turned to Andrew. "Go with him, he'll get you set up." She returned to the outside and went back to scanning the surroundings for events to respond to. There was no shortage.

John and Raymond communicated with each other from the pilot's seat of their robots. An army of drones followed around each one. Raymond had responded to the incidents in Russia, taking down entire armies of cultists with drones, each equipped with weapons straight out of science fiction. Jericho had assisted with construction where available, using telekinesis and magnetic manipulation powers he'd acquired to construct nanites, and they had used teleportation to scour the asteroid belt for materials. Together, the two scientists had built robots surprisingly resilient against magnetic attacks, and their ability to move quickly even with enormous size had proven enormously beneficial.

John drove his fist into a giant super, whose growing ability had worked against him. A punch assisted by rockets and lots of electricity dropped the big lug. His drones waited for the guy to pass out and shrink down to normal, before picking the man up and carting him off through a portal.

"Ray!" he called, "how's Russia?"

"I think I've just about put an end to concentrated areas of zealot activity," he told John. "There's small activity here and there, but right now, it's just individuals here and there." He paused. "How's South America?"

"A pain in the ass," John replied. "For some reason, a lot of the giant growing supers are down here, and I've had to tango with about ten of them so far. It's a bitch." The ground rumbled. "Gimme a minute."

His visual sensors indicated a thirty-foot-tall man dashed towards him, pushing trees aside like brush. He braced himself, and the man delivered a punch that sent the robot into the air. At the height of his flight, he activated downward thrusters and zoomed ahead of an uppercut, smashing a kick into the giant's face. The giant stumbled as the robot landed, then he delivered to the brute a one-two combo. The gut punch bent the giant over, and then John drove a fierce uppercut into the man's forehead. The brute's head snapped back as he launched into the air and crashed through several trees before falling limp and shrinking down.

"Like I said," John added. "It's a bitch." His drones flew high up and scanned the surroundings. "Yeah, it looks like big groups of zealots are basically gone. The rest are hiding or doing it in secret."

"We've been going at this for nineteen hours," Raymond called. "You want to call it a day?"

John nodded. "Good a time as any," he replied.

Two large portals opened, and each brought their tech back to base.

After leaving their equipment in the large hangar, they strolled across the grass to the main building where they gathered. Dozens of large buildings surrounded the main one, each containing the thousands of people they had rescued and helped. Jennifer sat at the dinner table. Settings had been laid out for each person.

"No one's in the mood to cook," Annie said, gesturing at the buffet table set out behind them, with stations containing each type of food. "So, we went out and got whatever was still open."

Jericho took his dinner plate and travelled to each station. "Nice set," he said, opening the metal lid of one serving station. "It's the best we could hope for, I suppose." He placed two fast food burgers on his plate, then closed the lid, before going to the next station, and grabbing some fried chicken and setting it next to it. At a third station, he grabbed some Waffle House hash browns. He set it on the table and took his drink glass and served himself from a shake machine pilfered from a ruined fast food joint.

He sat down to eat. Jennifer chuckled. "That's not good for you," she quipped.

He shrugged. "Eat like you're going to the chair," he advised. "Why the hell not?"

Despite the macabre humor, everyone laughed to some degree. "Yeah," Edward agreed, tucking into some fried fish. "Help yourself. We've got a little bit of everything. If we live past the battle not fifty hours from now, we can worry about our diets."

"Is that Captain D's or Long John Silver's?" John asked, grabbing his glass and pouring some lemonade from a soda fountain.

"The sign was burnt off," Edward replied. "I didn't get a good look."

The rest filled their plates with a veritable mountain of fast food. Each one took Jericho's dietary advice. After each had put themselves nearly into a food coma, and consumed gallons of fountain soda and milkshake, they sat and pondered the twists and turns that the situation had taken them on.

"God, this is frustrating," Annie lamented. "Time is the worst part."

"No shit," Edward agreed. "I think we've about stopped every major group going around. All that's left are scattered groups of nutjobs. They're too scared to gather together in large groups, or we show up to stop them."

"Pardon me if this sounds messed up," Luther said, picking under his fingernails, "but I need some sleep."

"No," Jericho agreed, "that's not messed up. I think we all need some sleep."

"So," John asked, "why do you think this fake Jesus is so serious about being 'proper' with how he defeats us? Couldn't he just kill us and spin it?"

"It's that bullshit 'decorum,'" Jennifer explained. "If he defeats us with the world watching, that's less work afterward on his part."

"Makes sense," Raymond agreed. "Hey, before any of us goes to sleep, how about we make a statement?"

Edward turned his head. "You mean," he offered, "like our manifesto?"

"No," Raymond advised, "just that we say our side of the story."

"That's a fantastic idea," Jericho cut in. "I nominate Jennifer."

Jennifer looked over, confusion on her face. "Why me, specifically?" she asked.

"Because you were the first to go out and be seen saving lives," Annie replied. "You took initiative when everyone else was too worried to do anything."

Jennifer laughed. "Me?" she argued. "I'm not brave. I'm almost indestructible. Hell, I only felt brave enough to do this because I knew after a while that the threats couldn't hurt me. Anyone who couldn't get hurt would save people from a fire or stop a mass shooting."

"You were willing to die against Jack Hurst and his monster," Annie pointed out. "Jericho, too."

"Die?" Jennifer scoffed. "But I'm still...here..." Her voice trailed off as her eyes went wide with realization. Sure, the power had saved her, but a version of her had perished in New York City against the fake Jesus. "I died against him."

"We both did," Jericho replied. "Neither of us really knew how it worked, so we both went in with no assurances."

"Even if it was the same consciousness that went back," Raymond said, "neither of you will ever be sure. So, I vote to say that yes, you are brave."

Jennifer wiped her face. "Alright," she conceded. "Get it prepared."

John nodded. "Be glad to," he said, getting up and heading over to the lab."

A signal emanated from an undetectable source. It got picked up by every television in the world. Embedded in the signal were subtitles that automatically adjusted for each region. Every news agency on the planet began recording it at once. Jennifer and her immediate allies stood in the frame, in a large room. She stood in front of the rest. She paused for a long moment, took in a deep breath, and let it out.

"Hello, people of the world," she began. She clasped her hands together in front of her abdomen. "I'm not going to go on some long rant about good and evil. I just need to get the basic points across. This will not take long." Closing her eyes, she went over every point with a fine-tooth comb. A moment later, she faced the camera again. "I was like many of you in that when superpowers became real, I thought I was going nuts. This wasn't a comic book, I knew, this is real life. Not long after, evidence started pouring in that made me realize I wasn't losing my mind." She paused to catch her breath. "Then, I immediately thought about the impact of what I'd been given. This was an impossible dream; all my life, I'd fantasized about being able to save lives the way the characters I loved when I was a child did in their stories."

She turned to face her allies and friends for just a moment. "My friends and I have been on an incredible, wonderful, and convoluted adventure. We've done more in these past months than the entire rest of our lives combined. We're never going to be able to get over how amazing this whole thing is." Her expression darkened as she faced forward. "When I first got powers, one thing I feared the most was some nutjob getting incredible powers and bringing about great evil." She sighed. "That fear has come to pass. A horrific evil

347

has come to try and extend his rule to the entire world. I'm speaking, of course, about the false prophet Jack Hurst and his false messiah, this monster masquerading as the Lord and Savior of Christianity."

She paused for effect. "I'm not here to tell you how or what to believe. I am here to tell you that, regardless of your beliefs, this is not the savior of humanity, nor can this monster be the savior of anyone. My parents were religious, and even though I am not a believer, I never forgot what they taught me. They taught me that Jesus was a Lord of compassion, of justice, and of love. This monster commits genocide. This creature uses the threat of death to compel nations to bow to his feet. Most importantly, and I cannot stress this enough, this monster is the creation of a *mortal man wielding a superpower.*"

Jericho approached the camera. "I met the man, Jack Hurst," he explained. "I discovered this fake Jesus appeared not to the world, not to prominent religious figures, but to him. He appeared to one man in his living room." He gestured disapprovingly. "How can you trust this when he blatantly demonstrates the lack of basic characteristics needed to be the savior?"

"If you understand," Jennifer cut in, "that this man and his summoned monster cannot save us, cannot save anyone, then you must not aid him. If you see this abuse of religious faith for what it is—a tool of monstrous control and manipulation—then you must not support this. Now, we aren't going to ask you to follow us to your possible death in combat, but we must ask you to do whatever you can to oppose this creature."

"For the sake of the future of civilization," Jericho said, "we will fight. If need be, we will *die.* Just remember, this monster has promised you an eternal kingdom of happiness. He cannot bring such a thing about. He is not the Son of God, he is not the Son of Man, he is a creature of powers. Jack Hurst may have lied to himself, but we will not."

"Thank you," Jennifer concluded. As the camera cut out, Jennifer wiped her eyes. "Guys, if I die, I…"

"No," Ed cut in, "don't talk like that. I'm not going to hear it."

Jericho put a hand on her shoulder. "We win together," he said.

"We win together," she agreed.

CHAPTER TWENTY-FIVE

Jack Hurst had preached to another crowd in the middle east on their way towards their destination in this holy crusade. It surprised him how receptive the Muslims were. Very few displays of power needed to be made, few resisted, and many stopped and listened without opposition. After his sermon, the Lord stepped forward and began healing the sick and injured. It moved his heart and his spirit. These vulnerable people had been left behind by governments and broken by decades of imperialism on all sides, and to see children who had lost limbs to American bombs get healed gave him pride. Those from young to elderly and all in between stepped up and their maladies vanished as they got blessed.

He noticed the expression on the Lord's face. "My Lord, you look conflicted," he said. "What troubles you?"

The Lord touched a man's hand, fingerless after an IED had exploded, and digits returned. "There is no emergency," the Lord spoke, not turning away from his mission. "It just saddens me when I feel our allies being killed in combat."

"I don't doubt our inevitable victory, my Lord," Jack pleaded, his faith unshakeable.

"Nor do I," the Lord agreed. "There is a limit to how much I can enhance someone's power, and our enemies are crafty and come up with strategies our loyal followers haven't stopped to consider."

"Will it hurt our cause?" Jack asked.

"Not at all," the Lord decided. "Giving our enemies a false sense of security will not hurt us at all."

Those words struck Jack oddly. "Do you think they'll honestly believe they can win?" he asked. "You think they'll fall for it?" He trusted his Lord beyond explicitly. It was the kind of trust a young child gave his mother. Yet, his human wisdom failed him. The faint thought occurred to him that his Lord was making a mistake, and yet, he knew the Lord made no mistakes.

"Once again," the Lord reassured, "I sense and understand your concern. As our allies go to their final reward, our enemies feel their success increase. They might believe at first they aren't letting their victories go to their head, but as time progresses, they will."

"It's human nature, right?" Jack thought out loud.

"Correct," the Lord replied. "The Word of the Father will play out, even if not as written by ancient men."

Jack nodded, content with this answer. The crowd finished receiving their blessings and healings, and they waved farewell to the crowd, and headed towards the aircraft. They walked through a military blockade meant to keep out any except the loyal. A crew of loyal supers got into a nearby jumbo jet while Jack and his Lord took their places aboard Air Force One. Within an hour, the plane took off.

"Sir," a secret service agent said, "in just a few hours we'll be landing in Tel Aviv."

"Fantastic," Jack said.

"Soon, the holy land will receive our final blessing," the Lord said, "and then we will prepare for our final battle."

As the secret service and soldiers took their places, Jack turned to his Lord. "Forgive my wavering," he confessed.

The Lord leaned forward in his seat. "No, my child!" he exclaimed. "You've held firm in the face of nigh-impossible opposition! How many others could have survived the insanity you survived so far?"

Jack wiped his eyes. "Thank you," he said. "I am not worthy."

"Come now," the Lord replied. "Sleep."

Jack leaned his head against the wall, and a soldier placed a pillow under his head. He went into dreams almost immediately. His dream turned to the eternal paradise that God's Kingdom on Earth would provide. No person would ever suffer again. All wounds would be healed, all debts made equal, and no sorrow would exist. All of God's people would enjoy the fruits of the Earth without ever wanting for anything, and no evil would be present to cause misery. None of the servants of Satan would be around to sow discord, as they would all be cast into the Lake of Fire.

"Sir, wake up," a soldier's voice said, cutting through the fog.

Jack slowly returned to awareness. "We've arrived?"

"Yes sir," the soldier agreed. "They've prepared for your arrival well in advance."

"We shall prepare for the final battle," the Lord said, rising from his seat.

As the door opened, and Jack Hurst stepped onto the stairs, they saw the full might of the Israeli army on display. The airspace for hundreds of miles around the airport had been cleared by fighter jets and loyal supers. Military vehicles formed a barricade around the plane after it landed. The airport had been surrounded by tanks and Jeeps with heavy caliber machine guns. A literal wall of soldiers began forming a circle around the craft. No dissenters were allowed anywhere close to the airport. Trucks approached every so often to load the bodies of dissenters shot on sight by the soldiers.

A man in a business suit came up to greet them. "Ah...I..." he said, struggling to regain composure. "I've been assigned to be your official government liaison. What will you be needing?"

"What is the state of the site of the final battle?" Jack asked.

"We've cordoned off a large area of the Valley of Megiddo," the liaison explained, "and all except loyal supers are kept out. We expect your battle to cause many casualties, after all."

"Good decision," the Lord complimented. "Until such time as the final battle is concluded, we don't want to involve those who have not picked a side."

They stepped off the stairs and towards a vehicle. "If, uh, you don't mind my asking," the liaison asked, "what will be happening...after..." The Lord gave him a confused look. "Well, it's just that...well, the text of Revelation hasn't happened as written, so I was wondering."

"I understand," the Lord replied, nodding. "After the forces of Satan are defeated, my Father's eternal Kingdom of glory and happiness shall begin upon this Earth. All who disbelieve shall be cast into the Lake of Fire."

The man swallowed and nodded. "I...see," he uttered. "Let me be the first to say, I am a believer."

He placed a hand on the man's shoulder. "Do not worry," the Lord replied. "I have seen you accept my Father's glory just now, so as long as you remain faithful, nothing bad shall happen to you."

The man wiped his brow. "Thank you, oh Lord," he cried.

An armored troop carrier opened its rear compartment. The Lord and his servant stepped in and sat down. Jack Hurst marveled at the thick metal walls and the armed soldiers seated around them. He took a deep breath and relaxed. This ordeal had been a whirlwind of chaos and confusion. He'd seen the best and worst of humanity. His Lord had performed miracles of healing and judgments decried as murder by mortal men. His faith had been tested to its limit, but he would hold strong. Still, this had been what he'd prayed for since he was a child. *If only the Glory of God happened in my lifetime*, he would pray as a young man. His dream had been to be present when the Lord's Kingdom on Earth returned.

"Sir?"

The question had come from a soldier no older than twenty-three. "Yes?" Jack asked.

"Will I get to see my grandfather again?" the young soldier inquired.

Jack turned to his Lord. "If you believe and have faith," the Lord advised, "then anything is possible for my Father. I will advocate on your behalf."

"Tell me, oh Lord," another young soldier said, "what will we do all day in Heaven?"

The Lord smiled and Jack let out a laugh. "Oh, my child," the Lord spoke. "Your mind wasn't meant to comprehend eternity. Let me assure you that the wondrous experiences that will enter your soul will fulfill you forever and ever. Such is the power of the Father."

The sense of wonder that drew itself upon their faces gave Jack a sense of pride. "To me," Jack preached, "that's what makes this all worth it. Our enemies call us murderers because what they believe is that the physical realm is the extent of pleasures available." He bowed his head solemnly and sighed. "No. The Kingdom of Heaven is beyond any mere Earthly paradise. God in Heaven has no equal and his love and glory will fill us all and guide us to feelings impossible to describe."

"They condemn you as a murderer," a soldier said, "because they only see a forest for the trees."

"Right," Jack replied. "I got into preaching as a young man because I wanted to get across the feeling of love that the Lord instilled in me." He leaned back in his seat. "I don't enjoy the judgments we must dole out. I wish no one had to be judged and everyone could go to Heaven. The problem is that some people are unwilling to accept the Lord. Some are so unwilling to accept their Christ that they fight to defend this broken place."

"Said wonderfully," the Lord exclaimed. "Together we will defeat the armies of the Deceiver and the Kingdom of God shall be restored."

An almost endless crowd stood behind military barriers. Some cheered, some screamed about a false messiah and were immediately shot by soldiers and their bodies dragged away. Loyal supers flew overhead, or travelled nearby, protecting the convoy. A huge barrier got moved out of the way by soldiers, and the vehicle rumbled into the Valley of Megiddo. The preacher marveled at the sight of the land that would become the greatest battlefield in history.

The Lord pointed, and the vehicle rumbled to a stop in the middle of a large clearing. The rear compartment opened, and everyone stepped out. A man in a decorated uniform approached. "Will you be giving a statement to the press?" he asked. He pointed behind him. "There's a number of news outlets who want access to you."

"I imagine that's our purpose here," Jack answered.

"That's the best vantage point," the Lord said, pointing. "Bring them there."

A half hour later, equipment had been set up and everyone took their places. Cameras pointed at Jack Hurst and the Lord, and every kind of equipment had been set up. One newsman gave him the thumbs-up.

Jack took a sharp inhalation. He held it for a moment and let it out. "My fellow servants of Christ," he preached. "In less than forty-eight hours, the final battle will take place here. The Dark One shall marshal his Satanic forces here for the climactic battle against God Almighty." He stared into the camera. "They will be crushed by the holy might of the Lord. After, the Kingdom of God shall reign upon this Earth in an everlasting peace. No longer shall pain endure. Every debt shall be paid, every misery made right. The things that make you less shall be taken away, and your imperfections made perfect, your shortcomings corrected. There will be no want or need; all shall be provided to all."

He paced. "All of this bounty shall be provided by the mighty hand of God in Heaven." His expression darkened. "Our foes are the worst kind of sinner. They blaspheme against their Father in Heaven because they possess righteousness. Satan's influence has convinced them they can prevail against their Lord and their Father, because they believe the lies of the King of All Liars. They have been misled into believing the eternal goodness will be bad somehow." He bowed his head. "Believe it or not, I want my enemies to be saved. Unfortunately, they fight for the Evil One, and their misery shall have to be overcome by holiness and joy."

He approached the cameras. "Should any of you feel like siding against the Lord, your time shall be up, and like our foes, you shall be cast into the eternal Lake of Fire. Your suffering will never end, your pain will be unfathomable. Any who fight against God's Kingdom will be put through agony worse than death. Their suffering shall never end, and no reprieve shall be offered. Any who disbelieve after the final battle will be cast into the Lake of Fire. Only those loyal to the Lord, and to God in Heaven, shall be spared. Fight in glory against evil! All who perish against our enemies in servitude to God in Heaven shall receive their eternal reward in Heaven!"

He cleared his throat. "I leave you with God's mercy."

The camera cut out after the broadcast concluded.

CHAPTER TWENTY-SIX

A CALM AIR PASSED OVER the Valley of Megiddo. Supers loyal to Jack Hurst hovered above the battlefield, watching, and waiting. Outside the enormous barricade that had been erected around the entire area, crowds of people stretching almost to the horizon stood waiting. The morning sun beat down. The crowd stood silent. The Lord hovered several feet off the ground, watching as he turned in every direction. His mere presence awed believer and non-believer alike into submission.

Fifty feet from where Jack and his Lord stood, a portal opened. The Lord immediately threw a protective bubble around his servant. Jennifer touched down, standing firm. Jericho landed behind her, a unique battle outfit tuned to his powers on. Annie planted a foot next to Jericho and behind Jennifer. Her enormous frame stood firm and her head-to-toe battle armament shining in the sun. Edward formed the back of the group. They immediately formed into a straight line.

The tense silence erupted as the enemy supers vanished from their position. Jennifer dodged a stone-coated fist and planted her foot in the man's neck. He sailed backward until a forearm smash from Annie planted his corpse in the ground. Jericho tilted his head and a piece of metal sailed by at relativistic speeds. He stretched out his hand, snatched the telekinetic and pulled. Edward leapt off Jericho's back and slashed, vaporizing the attacker midair.

Two speedsters smashed blows into Jennifer. She pushed her speed to full, and dodged a kick aimed at her head. She nailed the man with a gut punch, and drove her knee into his forehead, snapping his head back at an impossible angle before the momentum launched him skyward. The other's fist sailed past her, and she drove an elbow into his temple, separating his head from his body. Eight projectile supers sailed into the air at Jericho's command. He then clenched his fist and the eight compacted into a sphere the size of a volleyball, before he shot a fireball and incinerated it.

"Enough games!"

The Lord regarded Jennifer's shout with disdain. He turned to his servant. "The time has come," He said to Jack.

"This shall be the beginning of God's glorious Kingdom!" Jack shouted.

The Lord hovered to within fifteen feet of his enemies. Spreading his arms to his side, a brilliant light overtook him, and his robes and sandals disappeared, replaced by golden armor, reminiscent of a hundred paintings of the archangel Michael. "The first time I came," the Lord spoke, "I was the lamb, a sacrifice to rid the world of sin, at our Father's request." He blinked a tear away. "It saddens me to have to return as a conqueror. However, the forces of Satan have arisen, and the final victory is at hand." He clenched his fists. "I shall complete my Father's work upon this Earth, and the result shall be eternal paradise!"

"You talk too much!"

Jennifer shouted, before slamming her speed on as far as it would go. She threw a punch at his face. An invisible force smashed her into the ground, kicking up dirt. Annie rushed up from the left, throwing a punch at full strength. It bent him, but a wave of his hand blasted her through the ground, digging a trench. Jericho stuck his arms out. A black sphere formed around the Lord. He clasped them together, and a dozen explosions went off inside the sphere. A force then threw him upward, and hundreds of handless punches crashed into his body, causing him to jerk like a fish out of water. Then a battering ram blow propelled him through a rock formation. When the sphere vanished, the Lord was unblemished. Ed pulled his sword but saw dirt before he got it all the way out.

The Lord gestured at the fallen warriors. "Is this the extent of Satan's might upon this Earth?" He asked. "Saddening."

In a fraction of a second, all rushed him. Hundreds of fist blows struck his face, chest, and torso. Edward slashed at his back. The Lord simply stuck an arm out and launched the two women like toys. A hand gestured in Edward's direction, throwing him face-first into stone.

"You *fucker!*"

Jericho shouted right as he pelted the fake Jesus with every projectile he had in his arsenal. Everything from lightning, to fire, to gravity bullets, to metal, and beyond, bounced off the golden armor as the Lord strolled towards the billionaire. The Lord simply tilted his hand and the man did a three-sixty flip before faceplanting on stone.

"I honestly expected a battle worthy of the Son of God," the Lord spoke, blasting Jericho through a boulder. "It is really sad how much hope the devil puts in his false messiahs." He flicked his wrist and Annie tumbled through dirt and rock. A finger point caused them to hover upward and be placed safely on their feet. "This is your last chance. You have just one choice: bend the knee to your Lord and receive eternal life. None gets to the Kingdom of Heaven but through me."

"Fuck you!" Ed shouted. Invisible bonds held him in place while a shockwave bashed him in the gut. He spilt his stomach contents onto the ground.

"Say again?" the Lord asked, lifting the man's head up with a gesture.

"You know what?" Ed shouted. "I'm a Christian. Jennifer might not believe, but I do. My mama, you know what she did? She taught me all about Jesus."

The Lord listened with compassion in his eyes. "Do continue," He spoke.

"We read the Bible together," Ed explained. "She always said Jesus was about love and understanding." Red hot fury burned in his eyes. "You, sir, are *not* the Lord!"

Melancholy passed over the Lord's face. "It saddens me, hearing that," He spoke. "Do you know why?" He let out a breath. "It means you will never see your dear mother again. You've chosen, here and now, to suffer the fires of hell."

"I bet!" Ed shouted, slashing upward. The curve of light harmlessly reflected off the armor.

Jennifer threw a kick upward. He ducked his head back and gestured his hand. Her energy detection showed her the blow coming, and she threw a shot of ball lightning that exploded in the Lord's face just as she got launched.

The intense light caused a moment's distraction. Annie leapt forth and buried her fist in his armor as hard as she could. The force pushed him up and shattered his armor. His eyes shot open in surprise, causing a giant shockwave to launch her into the ground. Jennifer appeared and fired a wave of plasma into the Lord's back. He spun around just in time to catch a blade of energy to crash into his armor. He stuck his arms out and a spherical wall blasted all his foes back. The redhaired heroine threw herself headlong into him for a headbutt, but his eyes lit up and she ricocheted off stone like a skipped rock.

Annie threw herself forward and threw a kick, but he hit her with a shockwave right to the forehead, that knocked her for a loop. She landed in a pile of debris.

"You fight for a lost cause," the Lord spoke, as his broken armor fell away, revealing his robes underneath. "That attack did not harm me."

Jericho teleported in front of the Lord, slashing with fire hands and throwing electric bolts at his eyes. The Lord placed a glowing hand on the billionaire's neck, and an intense burning erupted. Jericho screamed in pain. *Now!* The billionaire thought.

The Lord caught that mental command. What did it mean?

His eyes widened. He spun as fast as he could.

A portal opened *inside* Jack's protective bubble. It closed, depositing Luther Torvalds, who then latched both hands onto the preacher's neck. At once, the Lord waved his hand and Luther's head snapped backward as he got launched.

"My Lor....aaaaAAAAAHHH!" Jack's statement turned into a shriek of agony as he clutched his head. The man stood, hands on temples, eyes as wide as possible, a look of utter horror on his face as he screamed bloody murder.

"JACK!" the Lord screamed. He teleported to his servant's side. Jack Hurst had collapsed and was convulsing on the ground uncontrollably. "Jack! Hold on! I will..." He touched a healing hand to his servant's temple.

Breath caught in his lungs, as the Lord felt genuine fear for the first time.

Nothing happened.

He placed a palm on the man's forehead and commanded the agony to cease.

It did not respond to his command.

Horror turned to rage. "YOU!" the Lord shouted, pulling Luther to him. He smacked the young man, healing him. "You shall tell me at once what you have done!"

A grin painted itself on Luther's face. "Why, my *Lord*," he stated, hanging on the last word, "don't you know? I thought you were God the Son."

The Lord's face screwed up in a scowl of pure hatred. A finger extended, lighting up the lower half of Luther with the fire of a thousand suns. He screeched in an agony no human had before felt. A moment later, he was restored. The Lord snatched him up by the neck. "You shall not tempt the Lord!" He shouted. "I will ask you but once more, what have you done to my servant?"

Luther saw the Lord was touching him, and his eyes went wide as possible, and a wide sneer appeared. "Why," Luther yelled, "see for yourself!"

The Lord looked confused. "What? I..."

His statement cut off mid-breath.

Suddenly, the Lord wasn't in his own body anymore.

He was a child playing with a toy truck in a working-class home. The child looked up from his toy, drawn by a strange red glow from outside. The boy stuck his dark brown fingers up in the air, standing up and walking towards the window. "What is that?" he said, in Hindi. The red light in the sky then exploded outward. Stumbling backward onto his butt, the child gasped in terror as a wall of red light rocketed towards him. He had but moments until it overtook him. Every pain receptor lit up at once as his fingers and toes evaporated. The pain arrived at the brain just in time to cause unimaginable suffering. Then the nose melted, the eyeballs exploded, and finally, parts one normally expects not to hurt caused insufferable pain. This lasted an eternity in the few seconds of actual time it took, and then the boy felt nothing at all, ever again.

The Lord experienced a Christian man living in the Punjabi region of India, who saw his entire body light up in a strange blue translucent aura. His friends at his house all watched him with fascination and fear, as they could not touch him. Suddenly, a red light shone into the room, like a heating lamp, only brighter. Suddenly, a cacophony of noise erupted as a wall crashed into and through his house, melting stone like butter in an oven. The wall of light passed him by harmlessly, bouncing effortlessly off the blue barrier. However, his screams died in a mountain of noise as he saw his friends melt and then evaporate before his very eyes. For a brief, horrible instant, he smelled the air thick with cooked fat and muscle, before the wave passed, and he smelled only dead air. A minute later, he stumbled into a surreal sight. There was plant life, and animals, even water ways, but every building, every road, every man-made structure was gone. He saw no people. He could see all the way to the horizon, and only far off in the distance, did he see a few people here and there. He collapsed and cried until he passed out.

This and macabre experiences like it, replicated perfectly down to the slightest detail, with every sense recreated flawlessly, played out hundreds of millions of times over in the minds of the Lord and Jack Hurst. They got to experience firsthand, every single life they'd taken.

The Lord screamed and writhed, trying in vain to banish the experiences wracking his brain. No matter what he did, he saw sights and experienced sensations utterly beyond compare in their horror. He fell to one knee and shouted in agony.

A massive swarm of supers, seeing their Lord in peril, launched into action. The four took positions as hundreds of supers smashed metal fists and spiky feet into them. Every projectile imaginable flew their way. Jennifer crashed punches and kicks into whatever enemy got too close to her and zapped several at a time. Annie threw bone-shattering punches into ribcages as well, but the crazed expressions on the enemy faces told them these were willing martyrs.

A fist headed towards Jennifer, but a hand caught the wrist. The assailant, cross burned into his forehead, looked up to see a muscle-bound woman with Slavic features haul the would-be martyr into the sky and crash an elbow into his forehead. His neck gave way at an impossible angle and he went limp. All the attackers stopped and turned as she tossed the victim aside.

"None of you are real Christians!" she shouted with her Russian accent audible.

"Thanks!" Jennifer cried.

The crowd of enemies turned to see tens of thousands of supers arrive, having turned against the false messiah. "We're here to show this fake what a real Christian is like!" a man shouted. The larger swarm then engulfed the group of zealots like a cloud of gas.

"Go stop the fake Jesus!" the Russian lady shouted. "We got this!"

Jericho slammed on every healing power he had as he regrouped with his three allies. They stood in a circle around their two enemies.

The Lord struggled to his feet. Despite the war raging inside his head, he began to reassert control over his body. He clenched his teeth as he regarded the four, anger bubbling up. He shot forth like a rocket, swinging, She tried to dodge, but his punch clipped a part of her cheek off. As that regenerated, she kneed him in the gut and slammed an elbow into the back of his head. This knocked him for a loop, propelling him into a sword slash across his gut. Annie blasted forward and planted a foot in his abdomen in the same place.

That's when Jennifer saw it.

She only saw it for a moment before it healed, but the wound was there. Instead of a bleeding cut, she saw a crack appear horizontally across his gut. Out of it spilled white light, before it sealed up. In the moment it was there, they all saw it.

All pretense at finesse vanished on the Lord's part. He traded blows with each of them, counting on his durability to hold out. After taking another sword slash, he planted a flat palm into Ed's gut, causing a spray of blood from the man's mouth. He planted a hard kick into Annie's left knee, bending it backwards at an impossible angle. The goddess shouted in agony as she collapsed, before pushing her broken knee back into place to regenerate. He slapped a glowing palm into Jennifer's face, melting a hole in her cheek. She pulled away so it could heal.

Edward pointed his sword like an ice pick and drove it into the Lord's chest. It bounced off skin. Annie drove a punch hard enough to break her fist into the same spot. Jennifer's fingers shot forward, but the crack healed up an instant later.

"You are surprising, servants of Satan," the Lord said, regaining composure, "but ultimately, you..."

Three fists, one glowing, plowed into his face, launching him into soil. A beam of light erupted from the ground, blasting straight through Jericho. "Shit!" he sputtered, before teleporting. The Lord burst forth and smacked a palm into Jennifer. A light shot through her and she felt several organs rupture, causing her to cough up a spurt of blood and a piece of lung. He then extended two fingers and Annie's arm bones exploded into dust at several places. She screamed, but before she could collapse, he stuck out another two fingers and her leg bones pulverized. She hit the ground screaming in agony.

The Lord spat blood from his mouth. "YOU DO! NOT! INTERRUPT THE LORD!" He screamed. Luther appeared and attempted an attack. "AND YOU!" Luther felt invisible hands drag him to the Lord's feet. "YOU DARE HARM MY SERVANT!" Luther looked up to see a look of anger not remotely human painted on the Lord's face.

The Lord stuck out his hand.

Every bone in Luther's body exploded into dust at once. Every organ ruptured. His brain went to seize or pass out from the pain and was not allowed. The sound that came out of Luther should never be heard by human ears. An instant later, the Lord healed him, and repeated the torture. And then, he did it again, and again. His allies watched, their broken bodies regenerating, a sense of dread washing over them as they felt like children.

Jennifer spat blood as her body recovered. "You leave...him alone!" she sputtered.

The Lord turned from Luther, leaving him halfway healed, but unable to move from the torture. He threw him aside like leftover garbage. As he stepped slowly, deliberately towards her, she saw a look she would never be able to forget. The look of anger and hatred that greeted her was one no human face should have been capable of making. It was a look of pure distilled evil. "YOU!" he shrieked, his voice carrying the weight of every feeling of anger ever. "YOUR FATE IS THE WORST OF HELL!"

He tapped her on the forehead.

All at once, her body went limp. Her brain no longer sent commands to her flesh. The entity once known as Manny Voren, or Jennifer Black, no longer inhabited a place that could be described. Without a body, she floated in an endless wave function of pure suffering. It would prove impossible for any merely physical being, regardless of intellect or capacity for description, to put to words what suffering she endured. To say she was dead would be false. She was neither alive nor dead. She was suffering. That was the state she existed in. Her mind hovered in an endless sea of misery, an undefined distance from her body.

Were it possible to describe her pain, the description would not fit within reality.

She existed without sight, sound, or other senses. Only somewhere, an unfathomable distance away, did she remember faintly of sights entering eyes, but those feelings belonged to another reality, and only trickled to her through faint remembrance.

Somewhere, a billion trillion light years away, a million different attacks converged on a single point on the Lord's abdomen. A massive crack shot from one side to the other, bathing the battlefield in a brilliant light.

All at once, as though hit by a defibrillator, Jennifer found herself back in her own body again, in command of her own flesh. Before she would have wasted even an instant getting her bearings, the light called to her like a moth to a flame. Her body shot forward with force she scarcely would have imagined. She wedged both hands into the crack, pulling in opposite directions.

She pushed into the sky like a Saturn rocket, drawing power from other realities into her body and burning it like coal to fuel almost incomprehensible strength. The crack began to seal, causing glass-like edges of the Lord's flesh to cut into her otherwise invulnerable hands. Blood poured onto her face, burning her eyes and focusing her rage.

The Lord smacked glowing palms into her face, burning off her hair and starting to char flesh. She grit her teeth and pulled with everything she had. He stuck out a finger and a javelin of light speared her right hip clean through. Her scream sprayed a bloody mist across his face, but she dared not let go.

Jack Hurst regained his composure just in time to clamor to his feet. "You cannot prevail!" he shouted. "You will not defeat the Lord! No one can!"

Jericho appeared out of a portal. His wound healed; he stuck a right arm through the bubble. The forcefield ate through his clothes and scarred his flesh, but he managed to clasp a palm onto Jack's shoulder. He shot an intense bolt through the preacher, burning him internally. The man screeched in pain and collapsed.

The crack had almost sealed when a loud bang sounded. He looked down to see Jack Hurst collapsed onto the dirt, unconscious. He saw the source of the bang had been the crack widening. Brilliant light shone out like a flood lamp.

The Lord felt genuine horror yet again.

Jennifer's arms screamed at her, her hands were numb, her face was burnt almost black, and her entire upper body was coated in her own blood, but she pulled.

"WHAT?" the Lord shouted.

"rrrrrrRRRRAAAGGH!"

A crack of thunder echoed for miles around as the sky lit up like the flash of a nuclear explosion.

Everyone threw their arms up to shield their face. Four people saw it first.

Jack collapsed onto his butt, his eyes wide and mouth agape.

Annie spat up blood as she healed enough to stand. Ed lie there in agony, but alive, and healing. Luther felt a feeling of joy overtake him as he lay there, unable to even turn his head. Only Jericho stood tall, burnt arm smoking and all.

The Lord had been bisected at the abdomen.

The two halves fell. The light dimmed to normal daylight, except at the open areas where light still emerged. Gobs of glowing white liquid emerged from the open wounds of the Lord, which congealed into crystalline shapes, then cracked into dust, before vanishing entirely. The lower half hit rock and shattered on impact like glass. Fragments lost all texture and color and became white shards of glowing crystal. They congealed into glowing liquid and crystallized, before vanishing.

The upper body hit hard dirt. The Lord's left arm absorbed the brunt force and shattered, leaving a cobweb-like pattern of cracks up the torso. He had landed twenty feet from his servant. He began to pull forward with his remaining right arm, crawling, as chunks of his body began crystallizing and falling away, before turning to dust and vanishing. He dug hands rapidly losing texture and color and becoming pure white into the soil and pulled. "Jack..." he uttered weakly.

Jack regarded this with sheer horror. At first, his body disobeyed him, refusing to acknowledge the reality in front of him by moving. After a moment, he forced himself to react, and he ran at full speed.

The preacher lifted the half body into his arms, cradling it like a wounded child. "M...M..." Words failed Jack Hurst. "I...I..."

"Jack!" the Lord begged, as unknown quantities of fear emerged from places in his mind he didn't know existed. "Jack please! Help me!"

"Uh, I..." Jack tried to think, but his brain fired at a billion miles per hour in a hundred trillion different directions. He could not commit his mind to this reality. "I...the..."

"Jack!" the Lord shouted, his voice warping. "I...I can't! It hurts, Jack!" His face began to lose color. "How...can this be...How...Jack...tell..."

"My Lord!" Jack screamed, his mind latching onto the only words possible. His face ran wet with tears at the sight of the rapidly deteriorating body in his arms.

"The...I..." the Lord turned his gaze skyward. A look of sheer terror painted itself on the Lord's face. "My Father...he doesn't answer me..." A gasp escaped him. "Why doesn't...my Father answer me!"

Finally, his eyes went wide. "Oh, God...!" A realization of horrific implications emerged. "Am I not the...?"

He went silent and still.

An instant later, his body turned to dust in Jack's arms.

The preacher stared at the vanishing dust where the Lord had been. He blinked once, mouth agape.

Then he let loose a scream of pain and loss not even war widow could equal.

With news crews watching via helicopter, everything had been broadcast to the entire world.

Jennifer landed with a thud, her feet kicking up dust. Her blackened flesh dropped away to reveal healed skin, and the hole in her hip healed, but her body bore the remnants of total war. "Water," she cried.

371

A super landed by her. She gestured, and he sprayed her from head to toe, washing blood and grime off as much as possible. Next, he produced a sphere of water, which she drank from. A super stripped one of their beaten enemies of clothes and tossed it to her, and she changed in a flash.

She gave a look to Jack that would cause a bear to cringe.

"How..."

She grabbed his shirt by the collar and hoisted him overhead. "What?" she shrieked.

"How could you defeat the Lord!" he yelled.

She dropped him and barked out a laugh. He stumbled to a steady position.

The strange reaction was like a cup of coffee to a tired man. "What's so funny?" he said, heart still racing.

She guffawed harder.

He clenched his fists. "WHAT'S SO GODDAMN FUNNY!"

"You honestly don't get it!"

"That wasn't the Lord," Annie said, approaching.

That sobered Jack up. "You're lying," he said.

"Nope," Jericho said, his arm healing. "Feel that twinge in the back of your mind? I don't know how you gaslit yourself into forgetting about it, but everyone who has a power has one."

Tears soaked Jack's eyes. "No! You're lying!" he shouted.

"Then you won't be able to summon anything else," Jennifer said. Everyone shot her a look like she was crazy. "Jericho, he does anything funny, explode him."

Jericho stood behind the man and placed both hands on his neck. "Gladly," he said.

Jack shook his head. He would prove these fools wrong. There was no...

His heart sank.

He felt it.

He pictured some harmless cartoon character from his childhood and pulled the trigger. An instant later, the cartoon rabbit popped out of a hole in the ground and stood before them, as real as the ground they stood on. "Hey!" the cartoon rabbit uttered, looking at a wristwatch. "I'm late!"

Jack gasped, hand covering his mouth. "No!" But regardless of what he said, he saw it. He banished it with a flick of the trigger.

He thought of a character his kids watched on those Japanese cartoons and activated his power.

"We're going to have a fight!" the Asiatic character shouted, adopting a fighting pose as his martial arts gi flapped in the wind.

"NO!" Jack's legs gave way, but Jericho hauled him up again. The character vanished when Jack turned it off.

He turned on his power once more and another cartoon character from his childhood appeared.

"You'll never be able to...!"

"OH GOD! NOOOOOO!" Jack screamed, silencing the creature at once by turning it off. The preacher collapsed to his knees again, openly crying into his palms.

Jericho regarded his friends as they waited. The preacher looked up from his hands as pure dawning terror gripped him. "Oh God..." His utterance was barely audible at first. "I killed them." He blinked, then the dam burst. "I killed them!" His eyes slammed shut. "I KILLED THEM! ALL THOSE PEOPLE! OH MY GOOOOOD!"

Annie looked around, and she happened to be the only one who saw it. "Jennifer!" she shouted.

At super speed, she saw the moment extend into eternity. He was going to commit suicide by biting through his tongue.

Jack slammed his teeth together, only for an impossibly hard hand to wedge between them. "NO!" Jennifer screamed. "You're not going to martyr yourself! You're going to face man's justice!"

Annie hauled the man to his feet. Four portals opened, and their remaining teammates walked out. John snapped a nasty, red glowing collar around the preacher's neck. Davis and his superior poked futuristic-looking pistols into the man's back.

"Reverend Jack Hurst," Davis Wilson said, leaning in, "for crimes against humanity, you sir, are under arrest."

CHAPTER TWENTY-SEVEN

THE AIR SCREAMED AS FIGHTER JETS flew overhead. Troops from every first world nation formed a human wall around the pathway. A fleet of tanks and Humvees traveled in a protective formation around an armored semi-truck carrying history's greatest criminal. Jericho and Annie sat in the vehicle, in between the shackled preacher. The collar still glowed red, indicating death could come at any instant. No expense had been spared in securing the prisoner.

Jack sat motionless, his face beet red and soaked from his own tears. He had spent the past few days piecing together the chain of horror that had played out. Ever since he was a child, all he had dreamed about was serving Jesus, and hoping to see, as the song said, the glory of the coming of the Lord. Nothing, he imagined, could be better than that. Yet, he found himself alone with a tropical storm of memories in his mind. They told the cold, hard truth: that he'd become what he feared and hated the most.

I was no better than anyone after all, he thought. As hundreds of millions were ash, all because of a monster he brought into the world, the true horror had come to haunt him. *He* had been in control the whole time, even if he somehow gaslit himself into believing otherwise. Sure, the thing that called itself Jesus had its own will and consciousness, but he could have asserted control over it at any point. The true irony bit him like the nastiest hornet: under a different set of circumstances, he could have been quite the hero. Had he not gotten lost in what he *wanted* to believe was true, he might have been good allies to the people that took him down.

Jericho sat, intently focused on this man. He would not waver, should any problem arise. Still, the mad reverend resembled a deflated balloon emotionally speaking. He placed a hand on the man's shoulder, seeing his guard down, and read his memories in greater detail. This man was a true believer and had a tremendous attachment to Jesus. Jericho had never felt quite as attached to anything as this man to his Lord. What struck him as both sad and scary at the same time was, any number of people could have been Jack Hurst, given the right circumstances.

The semi rumbled to a stop. Soldiers opened the rear door, and an armored inner chamber opened next. Jack and his captors stepped outside the vehicle, snipers from helicopters and nearby buildings training their sights on the reverend. Armed soldiers readied their weapons as the man stalked forward, head down, towards the building. Jennifer hovered overhead, senses trained on any possible interference. Friendly supers kept reconnaissance for miles around. The lack of suicide bombers and martyrs surprised everyone, not the least of which was the media. The news cameras filmed the event in maximum resolution.

As the group led the man into the marble and granite building, delegates from every nation watched intently from the hallways and offices. People couldn't help but stare. It had been more than a week since the final battle, and Jack had been kept in a holding cell in an abandoned mine more than a mile deep. The heroes that defeated him hadn't taken any time off, sleeping in shifts to ensure no one kept the greatest criminal out of their sights.

Jennifer approached, walking lockstep with the group. After a quarter mile of hallway, the armed men stepped ahead and opened the large oak doors to the courtroom. An army of journalists, news crews, and other court officials paused and went silent at the sight. The heroes took a seat in the front audience row. The bailiffs motioned Jack to the defendant's booth. The rest of the audience rows were kept empty on purpose. His attorney stepped up and took a seat next to him.

"All rise!"

The main officer's command brought everyone to their feet. The judge, a silver beard adorning his face, stepped in from a side door and took his position. He regarded the man in shackles and a collar with the same stern expression he gave to countless criminals he'd tried over the years.

The judge cleared his throat. "You may be seated," he commanded. Everyone sat. He took a deep breath and regarded the paperwork in front of him. "Jackson Emile Hurst, you have been charged with crimes against humanity, mass murder, terrorism, acts of sedition, and acts of war." He waited for the official record-keeper to type this information. Journalists filmed or wrote in their notepads. "You have been accused, let me be frank, of more violence against the innocent than any person ever to see a courtroom. How do you plead?"

The reverend took in his surroundings. He saw journalists and their news crews talking. This would doubtlessly become the greatest show in history. The most important trial ever conducted would immortalize him forever in infamy. There would be weeks, maybe months, of witnesses and other major events. At the end, he would give his final statement, and whatever words he spoke would be the greatest sermon of his life. News media could not have asked for a more perfect opportunity. The money made off him would no doubt be in the billions.

A Cheshire smile appeared on his face.

"Guilty."

Everyone started as if tased. The judge looked dumbstruck. One newsman swore in frustration as his colleagues looked on in disbelief. This was the worst possible outcome for them. "Order!" the judge bellowed, slamming his gavel. The room went silent. "Well, sir," he began, "in that case we shall reconvene in five days' time to conduct a sentencing hearing."

"NO!"

Everyone jerked at the shout by Jack, coinciding with his fist hitting the table. "*Excuse me*, Mister Hurst?" the judge replied, danger sounding in his voice.

"Sentence me *now*," Jack demanded. "No more show, no more speeches, no more display. I don't want these vultures making another dime off me." The news media people looked visibly shaken as their opportunities were vanishing before their very eyes. "Condemn me before any more money is made."

The judge let out a low chuckle. "As you wish," he calmly spoke, breathing in and out a moment. "You are hereby sentenced to death, sentence to be carried out in two hours' time." He slammed the gavel down. "Adjourned."

The heroes walked with the officers who led Jack Hurst out of the courtroom and into the rear of the armored truck. After fifteen minutes of securing everything, the vehicle rumbled to life and began rolling. Twenty minutes of driving later, they opened the rear of the vehicle and the heroes took him to his final holding cell, where Jennifer and Jericho sat observing just outside.

She watched intently to make sure nothing went sideways. It bewildered her that Jack had eschewed the opportunity to make some grand speech. Still, there was one spectacle she would not miss: his execution. A few minutes later, a pre-planned event went without a hitch. A portal opened inside the cell and out stepped

Emily, and the two children, Eric and Tim. "You have forty-five minutes," John warned.

Jennifer watched to ensure no shenanigans ensued but couldn't stand to listen to whatever their conversation was. A quick glance told her Jericho was much the same. "So, we won," the billionaire finally said, breaking the silence.

Jennifer let out a sign that was as much mental as physical. "We pulled it off," she uttered. "Holy shit."

"Now," he said, "I swear once this is over I think I'm going to take the longest shower ever."

"Now we deal with the part they don't show in the comics," she replied.

He let out a chuckle. "What's your plan?"

She shot him a look. "For what?" she asked.

He shrugged. "You know," he replied, "for the future?"

She let out a laugh. "You mean," she shot back, "after I take a long nap and play some video games to wind down?" She paused. "I dunno. We'll get together as a team and talk about that."

A thought occurred to him and he smiled while shaking his head. "You know what I just realized?" he asked. "We never once formally sat down and decided we were a team, we just did it." He scratched his neck. "I'd never have imagined as a kid that superpowers would be real, and less than six months later, we'd be getting involved in crazy world saving stuff."

"I'm surprised it took that long," she replied. "In the comics, usually, the villains show up right away." She gestured. "I expected everything to go post-apocalyptic right away. Things stayed reasonably together, all things considered."

"Maybe most people were too afraid of shaking things up," he said. "I mean, there were a few crazy enough to tangle with the cops. Maybe they all thought the villains were coming and didn't want any part of it." He ran a hand through his hair. "Anyway, I have a thing I'm going to do soon."

"What?" she asked. He held out his hand and she took it. Her eyebrows raised. "Oh, that's a good one," she said. "When you said you were going to shake up the status quo, you meant you were going *all in*."

Footsteps approached. They turned and saw officers with riot gear. "Time's up," the first officer said.

"Gotcha," Jennifer said, standing up and knocking on the door.

The knock on the door interrupted the mood. Jack, his face wet, let out a sigh and wiped his face on his shirt. He put a hand on his sons' shoulders. "I love you two more than you can know," he simply stated. His sons were about to protest the intrusion when he simply raised a finger and they went quiet. "No, this is how it has to be." He turned to his wife. "Emily, I should've known better. I should've *been* better. I've put you and the kids through something impossible." He pulled her into a tight embrace. "You deserved better from me."

"Jack!" she cried. "I love you!"

"You'll have to face the future without me," he said. "I may not go where you're going, but even still, I love you."

A portal opened. "Time for you guys to go," John said. "This was all we could get." The wife and sons stepped away from their beloved Jack Hurst.

"Dad," Tim said, wiping his eyes, "I'll miss you."

"Don't worry," Jack assured. "Just make sure you won't make the same mistakes I made. Be accepting and loving. Be wise and strong. Not like me."

"Dad!" Eric protested. "I can't...!"

"You *can*," Jack replied.

With one tearful final goodbye, they stepped through the portal, before it closed.

The cell door opened. He stood up.

As the shackles went on again, and he walked with the heroes following, he felt a strange sense of relief. His faith was in tatters, his beliefs shredded, and he no longer knew what would happen next, but at the very least, he knew his death would bring about the end of the horror he unleashed.

They led him down a hall and into a room with a medical set up. An audience of leaders of various governments, and a few select VIPs, watched as they led him into the chamber. "Jack Hurst," a man in a medical garb said, "take your place on this table." He placed his hands on Jack's shoulders.

Suddenly, light passed through his eyes and Jack Hurst found himself coming awake.

He shot upright. "What the hell!" he shouted. As he spun his head left to right, desperate to see what had happened, he found himself in a large industrial setting surrounded by men in suits. The equipment looked rusted and cobwebs covered everything.

"Before you do or say anything," a man said, "realize that we have ways of finding those you care about, and even now, I know there are those you don't want us to get to." The man had the most elaborate suit of them all, a Rolex on his wrist, and well-styled hair.

"What in the hell is going on?" Jack shouted.

The man let out a huff of a laugh and his grin returned. "You see," he began, "we just knew the heroes were going to insist you be executed after trial." He pulled up a chair and sat down. "Hell, if they didn't, the world governments would have. The big thing was, we expected they wouldn't kill you, because hey, that's not what *heroes* do." He shook his head. "But one thing nobody anticipated was, we can get our own inside anywhere."

The puzzle pieces began to fit together. "Wait," Jack said, "who is 'we' in this case?"

The man flashed a badge. "Joseph Russell, NSA," he said. "Doesn't matter that you know that, this place is surrounded by a faraday cage, so no signals going in or out. It's also an isolated, abandoned factory miles away from civilization since industry left in the seventies."

Jack's mouth fell open. "Wait," he almost gasped, "you mean, my own government falsified my execution?"

"Right," Joseph stated. "You see, Jack, *you* did die. But the executioner has the power to replicate people." He gestured. "Getting supers loyal to the government wasn't difficult, given our resources."

The preacher had to laugh at the horror of it all. "So," he replied, "the world saw 'me' die. Why?" He blinked a long moment. When realization hit him, it felt like being punched in the chest by a bear. "Oh my god."

Joseph grinned and pointed. "You got it."

"Oh my fucking god," Jack repeated.

"You see, Jack," Joseph replied, "we almost lost you. You have this utterly terrible power. You can summon things that can decimate entire nations in an instant. It's the worst possible power." He let out a sigh. "You see, even someone who loves his drone war and doesn't think twice about killing civilians like that prick Obama we have now, probably wouldn't feel right using you." He snapped his finger. "But, next year is an election year! I tell you what, next Republican president we get, that motherfucker is going to rubber-stamp you!" A funny thought came to mind. "Hell, it might even be Trump!"

"Now I *know* that motherfucker would *love* to use this guy," another suited man said.

Jack felt the water spill out of the cup of his spirits. "Oh my sweet god," he uttered, "my government is planning to use me like a W.M.D."

"The world resists our efforts to control them," Joseph shot back. "These suburban cocksuckers like to drive around in their dollar-ninety-nine-a-gallon SUV's and buy their thousand-dollar smartphones and eat their fucking five-dollar fast food pizzas." He got up and stuck his arms out. "Where the fuck do you think all that cheap consumerism comes from?" He pointed. "It comes from poor brown people and poor yellow people being paid fifty cents a week to pump oil and sell it to us for rock-bottom prices and sew our clothes at gunpoint and *fucking put up with it.*" He stalked over. "And every so goddamn often, some poor motherfucker in wing fuck China gets a wild hair up his ass to not put up with fifty cents a week to build our entire fucking economy. Some dumb piece of trash brown motherfucker with a towel on his head wants *his people* to benefit from the oil under his fucking sand instead of us." He coughed out a laugh. "Who the fuck do these people think they are? We're motherfucking Americans!"

The other men cheered. "You tell 'em, Joe!" one cried.

"We're the best motherfucking people on the planet!" he shouted. "No motherfucker gets to have as high a quality of life as us! It's *our goddamn planet!* These fuckers just get to live on it!" He leaned into Jack. "And *you*, my dear friend, are going to put things back in their proper order. Everyone is going to know what to do. Everyone is going to know the right way things should be. The message will be clear. You pump the oil, you build the fucking phone, you don't fucking raise a stink when your kids starve to death. If you don't, you *die.*" He stuck his arms out again. "AMERICA, GODDAMN, FIRST!"

Jack shook his head. "You're an evil piece of shit," he uttered.

"Me?" Joseph looked mildly offended. "Me? Go to any fucking suburban house. Red state? Blue state? Fuck, go to rural goddamn Pennsylvania! Go to rural *Cali-fucking-fornia!* You'll see Confederate Flags! Ask those motherfuckers what they think of this idea!" He squinted. "It would make you *piss yourself* to find out how many Americans think *just like me.*"

"Good thing they just did."

Men shouted and a few stumbled and fell at the sound of the voice. Jack looked up and his eyes went saucer wide. "John?" he almost shouted.

Joseph coughed and sputtered. "What...what the fuck!" he shouted. "How did you find this place?"

Raymond peeked his head out from behind John, still standing in the other side of the portal. "You see," the middle-aged scientist said, "we had plenty of time to think. The first thing we thought of was the fact that some rogue nation or superpower would want Jack for themselves. Hell, did you really think we were so naïve we didn't think some military asshole would salivate at the thought of using Jack as a walking nuke?"

"There were no tracking devices on him," Joseph said. "We made sure. No signals coming off."

John laughed. "Nanomachines!" he shrieked.

Several of the agents looked like they were going to be sick. "Wait," Joseph argued. "We can talk about this."

Raymond pointed up. "Oh, I almost forgot," he explained. "Your faraday cage doesn't take dimensional sci-fi-level tech into consideration." The look on Joseph's face gave both scientists great pleasure. "This whole conversation is going live in full HD video and audio to every news agency on planet Earth, along with plenty of recordings just in case."

They looked up and saw drones streaming the whole thing.

"You gonna take care of it," John asked, "or should we?"

Joseph blinked. "Wait, take care of what?" he asked.

Raymond pressed a button and a forcefield surrounded the portal as they watched. He then pointed to Jack. The agents looked and saw an enormous metal device summoned just behind him.

A moment later, an abandoned factory in Virginia exploded in a giant fireball, throwing concrete and mostly molten steel in all directions.

Days later, after a flurry of international chaos and disorder, Jennifer and her allies sat in chairs behind the Presidential podium set up in front of the White House. Quite possibly the largest crowd in Washington, D.C. history gathered to see the event. Clamor and conversation went quiet as President Obama stepped onto the podium, and immediately, applause filled the air.

"Ladies and gentlemen," the President began, "this morning we gather to celebrate victory in the greatest battle in the history of our planet." Jennifer scanned the audience and found no weapons, no threats of any kind. She relaxed. "We have had our faith shaken, both in our very own institutions, and our fellow man, as a crime worse than any other was perpetrated by an evil wearing the very face of the Lord Jesus Christ." Jericho adjusted his tie as he took in the bewildering turn of events that had led him to being celebrated by the President for using superpowers to help save the world from a supervillain. "In the face of unparalleled wickedness, a team of ordinary people came together to save us all. For that, we gather here to celebrate them. First, the woman who was first to answer the call, Jennifer Black!"

A raucous applause drowned out all other sound. The President stood aside and gestured. She stood up, approached, and placed both hands on the podium to stabilize herself. She'd never dealt with a crowd like this before. "Uh," she began, "I don't know what to say beyond just, well, I couldn't stand by and watch something happen knowing I could do something." The applause signaled the crowd wanted more. "I didn't know what I was supposed to do, so I just started going where people needed help. When the true evil arrived, I knew I had to stop him, because no one else was going to do it for me." She paused to slow her racing heart. "I promise that, from now on, my friends and I are going to do everything in our power to make things not just good, but as good as they can be." She nodded. "That's all."

"That is the best news we've gotten so far," the President said. "And that's something to look forward to. Next, when so many of his kind hid in expensive bunkers, one man stepped away from comfort to risk his life to save us, Jericho Torvalds!"

The billionaire stood up. "Needless to say," he stated, "I must echo the sentiments of my good friend and ally, for she so effectively stated our mission. In the coming days and months, we will begin a process of enriching all of mankind, and I promise this will be some of the biggest opportunities in history. I cannot give specifics at this time, but rest assured, we are preparing as we speak."

"Excellent!" the President agreed. "Annie Wilson, who fought valiantly and brought evil to its knees!" She waved her turn off. "Well then, Edward Mitchell, you had words to say?"

"I did," the young black man replied, taking the podium. "I had something I *needed* to say. My momma raised me with Jesus, so I speak from a different place than some of my friends. When I saw that monster wearing the face of Jesus Christ, doing the evil he was doing, I tried to hide it, swallow my pride and go on, but it ate away at me." He paused to wipe his eyes. "I saw so many of my fellow Christians either standing aside and letting this thing do what it did, or actively taking part in and cheering on the murder, and I knew I had to do something." He coughed. "I think, in the wake of this tragedy, we have to stand up to our fellow Christians, the ones who only use the religion to act superior and to oppress others. Too many are focused on the rules and not enough on loving thy neighbor. We need to stop pretending we're so damn perfect and stop acting all high and mighty and stop treating society as 'us-vs-them' when we're not in any way better!" The audience cheered. "We're supposed to be the ones who are the *most* accepting! How can we be so lazy as to forget that! It's our duty to stand up to those who call themselves Christians but are hateful and exclusionary and care more about laws and regulations than human lives!" He wiped his eyes again. "All I'm saying, is that we have to be the loving, accepting, caring followers of Christ that we're supposed to be. More focused on people and less focused on being 'holier than thou.'" He nodded and stepped away.

"What a magnificent sentiment, I must say!" the President cried. "John Stephenson, along with Raymond Weiss, you two are responsible for making the amazing technological fight against evil possible. Would you like to speak?"

John shrugged. "Can't top what Edward said," he said.

"Nope," Raymond agreed.

"Davis Wilson?" the President asked.

The agent agreed and took the podium. "My boss isn't one for words," he said, "so I figured I'd speak for him and all of us in government who got a rare opportunity to be the good guys." He cleared his throat. "This ordeal shook our very foundations. I work for the FBI, and that means I deal with criminals. But there's far too many examples of the police being a blunt instrument that kills our citizens with little regard for rights. Many of the colleagues who fought with me agree that these institutions designed to protect the haves against the have-nots need to be radically restructured. I think we need to stop letting a system go on treating those who happen to be poor as less than human and treating the rich as untouchable." He shrugged. "But hey, what do I know? I just happened to be one of the good ones." A laugh passed over the crowd.

"A great idea, if I may say so!" the President said. He opened a leather-bound folder. "What I do next, I do with great pride." He pulled out a pen and signed. "By signing this, I hereby grant citizenship to Jennifer Black, as well as authorizing a generous financial reward to all the heroes who assisted her friends and her in their unprecedented struggle against a tyrannical evil."

The crowd gave a standing ovation. The President then handed each of them a document showing their congratulations, with a check attached. Of the group, only Jericho didn't have some kind of freak out at the seven-digit number printed on it. After that, a whirlwind of important people and congresspeople mingling with the heroes happened. Jericho saw the look on Jennifer's face. "Hey," he whispered, "I'll take care of the rest. You go home and rest, you've earned it."

"You sure?" she asked.

"Believe me," he replied, "I'm familiar with situations like this."

"Thank you," she said, hugging him. "I'm still detoxing from the emotional crap I've had to deal with."

"I'm only here because of you," he admitted. "I should be thanking you."

She took off, and landed not far from her house and sped the rest of the way on foot. Hidden by a bush, she shifted back. Manny removed his housekey from his pocket, and stepped in. Although he wasn't physically tired, the emotional toll exhausted him. He set his letter on his counter after locking the door, stripped to his underwear, and collapsed into bed. A dream played through his mind. He saw a scene of humanity taking to the stars. He flew through space with his friends and loved it. His female form would take him places he couldn't go, and that was a gift he wasn't giving up for anything.

After the event, Jericho arrived at the hotel room.

"So," he said, as his brother got up from the bed. "You weren't up for the event?"

Luther hugged his older brother. "Nah," he retorted. "Not really."

Jericho smiled. "I'm so glad you were there to help me," he admitted. "I honestly don't know what I would've done without you."

"Ha!" Luther replied. "Careful, that almost sounds like you need me."

"You're right," Jericho countered, "I do need you. You're going to love what I have in mind."

Luther raised his eyebrows. "That's a scary thought."

CHAPTER TWENTY-EIGHT

THE CAR PULLED UP TO THE MANSION. The Torrell family estate sat in the woods of upstate New York, a giant marble-and-stone building on a wide stretch of land. The mile-long winding driveway led up to the forty-room main building. The young man stepped out of the car. "Oh!" the doorman said, signaling the enormous wood door to creak open. "Christof! I heard you were coming. Your grandfather is waiting for you in the lower dining hall."

Christof Torrell popped the trunk of the Rolls-Royce and hoisted the Styrofoam crate out. He climbed the steps to the front entrance and stepped through the huge doorway into the spacious grand entryway to the old mansion. Inside, he strolled across the enormous front room and past the grand staircase, and through a door into the spacious main dining hall. He set the crate down on the tremendous mahogany table next to his grandfather.

"Sir?"

Johann looked up from his tablet. He smiled at the sight of his grandson and business partner, "Ah, Christof!" he stated. "I've been expecting you."

"And me, you, grandfather," Christof said, pulling a knife and opening the crate. "I brought you some of the champagne from Firestorm Spirits."

The elderly man perked up. "Ah, yes," he said. "I needed to see what the hubbub is all about. Magazines are calling it the best champagne ever devised. I must try it, since all the other important folks are giving it a go." He saw Christof glancing at the screen of the tablet. "Do you believe it?"

Christof tilted his head. "Believe what, sir?" he asked.

The head of the Torrell Group regarded the article with disdain usually warranted of old gym socks. "All the billionaires are funding these massive humanitarian campaigns," he scoffed. "Giving up almost all their wealth. It's almost like the whole world's gone damn socialist!"

Christof laughed. "Oh, believe me sir," he remarked, "it's truly absurd."

"Oh don't worry," Johann assured, "I won't be giving up on the proper order anytime soon." He grabbed a bottle and reached for his corkscrew. "Would you believe I spoke with Stephen Mavil the other day..."

"Oh," Christof noted, "the head of the Mavil family?"

Johann nodded as he pulled. "The one that owns scores of mines across the globe," he replied, "yes that's the one. Would you believe what he did?"

"What, sir?"

The billionaire pulled until the cork popped and he poured some champagne into a drinking flute. He looked up, incredulous. "He said his family and he were giving up most of their mines to their employees!" He shook his head.

Christof gave a startled laugh. "What sheer insanity!" he cried.

"I couldn't fathom living on the twenty or so million they'll have left after what they told me their plan was," Johann stated.

Christof shook his head in dismay. He poured himself a glass and drank it. "Oh, that's good stuff," he uttered. "Anyway, isn't this the spirit-making company that Jericho started?"

"Sure is," Johann replied. "I'm damn proud of that boy." He smelled the alcohol. "I met him first when he was just a teenager, but even then, I knew I could cultivate in him that spirit of competition." He paused, reminiscing. "He made sure of himself. He was no minnow, Jericho, no he was a *shark*. He was destined for the upper echelons of society." He looked at his grandson. "Is it good?"

"All the world's elite are drinking it," Christof noted.

"They know taste when they drink it," Johann said. "Anyway, cheers!" He put the glass to his lips and took a strong sip.

The businessman found himself shot out of his body and into the memories of other people.

A hurricane of scenes, images, and feelings shot by in rapid succession. He experienced the life of a war widow in Africa, watching her children starve while she was powerless to feed them. The scene shifted to a child in southeast Asia dying from a warlord's bullet, bleeding out before his parents' eyes. Next, he found himself a black man forced to sell drugs to feed his poor family, only to be murdered by cops over a bag of weed. This, and a thousand other horrors played out in raw, visceral detail to him.

One instant, Christof saw his grandfather take a sip, and then he almost fell backwards in his seat. The glass slipped from his hand and shattered on the floor. The billionaire's eyes began to well up. "Sir?" Christof asked. "How was it?"

Johann Torrell looked up and saw knowing eyes. "My god..." he said, bewildered. "It's...so horrible." He broke down. "Oh my god! It's all our fault! We could have made a world where these people didn't have to suffer! It's all our fault!"

Christof grabbed another champagne glass and poured some more. "Go ahead," he offered. "Take another drink."

The billionaire grabbed the glass with trembling hands, and forced himself to take another sip.

"I take it you've taken a drink," Jericho said to himself in the mirror. "Using a number of powers, I've put a bit of power into each batch of liquor this startup of mine makes. If, like me, you're a member of the richest and most powerful class of people on the planet, then this will work specifically on you." He paused to gather his words. "When superpowers became real and I found I could copy them, I did what I always did. I identified the new currency—in this case, powers—and sought to collect them the way I collect money." He pulled off his tie and dropped it on the bed.

"At some point, I came across the power to relive memories, not as people remembered them, but as they actually happened. This turned out to be my most important moment, though I didn't know it yet. It caused me to see how utterly wrong I was about everything. I saw the inevitable disaster our wealth hoarding and endless greed would bring. I saw how we would continue ravaging this planet and crippling the common people to our own ends until everything would devolve into chaos. Thankfully, as it turned out, most people seemed too nervous to cause much harm, and the first few weeks after powers became real were unusually calm. Then Jack Hurst happened."

He removed his suit jacket. "So, what have I done? Simple. I've collected many thousands of memories in my journeys and given some to you. These have been hand-picked to clash with your preconceived notions and to challenge your philosophies that have led you to your greed and wealth hoarding. I've chosen ideas that will directly challenge your beliefs in hierarchies and other Ayn Rand horseshit like I used to believe. You might be worried about all this information hindering your mind in some way. Don't. I've taken care of that."

He grinned. "Some of you may wonder if I am a puppet master, controlling you like a marionette. I have not. Nor have I programmed you like a computer. All I've done is shown you the different point of view, and also given you a tremendous boost of compassion and empathy, whether you wanted it or not." He sighed and stepped closer to the mirror. "At this point, I know some of you are cursing my name, wishing they could reach across space-time and strangle me. I don't blame you. In the weeks to come, I know you will make the world a better place. The experiences I've shown you, along with your newfound compassion and empathy won't let you do otherwise. You won't be able to drink yourself away from helping. You won't be able to act as if you aren't a problem. Your conscience, whether you had one to begin with, or just the one I've helped give you, won't let you *not* act."

He paused for effect. "Believe me, I'm not being self-righteous when I say this. I've set aside finances for all the deals I've made, and the taxes and other expenses I'll owe, and other than that, I'll only have a small fraction of what I have now. I'm going to be part of the solution going forward, and now, so are you." He gestured. "You may think what I've done is wrong. You may say I've stepped over a line, that I've committed an unforgivable sin, altering your mind. Just less than a year ago, I'd have believed you. However, the time of man has drawn dangerously short, and the time for half-measures is over. Only drastic steps could save us all. Still, I can give you two pieces of consolation. I believe, in time, you will even come to thank me, and here's why." He lifted one finger. "First, even after you've given away almost every cent, you'll still have more than enough money not to worry. That's how rich you are to begin with."

He lifted a second finger. "And second, I've pulled your neck from the guillotine."

The memory vanished.

Johann wiped his eyes.

A crash echoed through the room. "Father!" a middle-aged man yelled. "I heard screaming! Is everything alright!"

Johann composed himself. "Oh!" he exclaimed. "Reginald, my son! Yes, yes, I'm fine. Don't mind me, I'm just an old codger having a senior moment."

Reginald pat his father on the shoulder. "Well, that's good," he said. "Don't scare me like that again!"

The elder Torrell grabbed a spare glass and poured. "Say, my son," he offered, "why don't you try some?"

ABOUT THE AUTHOR

ALEJANDRO GONZALEZ is an anime and comic book geek who lives and writes in rural southern Illinois. He has been writing for over two decades.

Made in the USA
Middletown, DE
10 February 2021